The
Rebel Wife

TAYLOR M. POLITES

SIMON & SCHUSTER
New York   London   Toronto   Sydney   New Delhi

Simon & Schuster
1230 Avenue of the Americas
New York, NY 10020

First Simon & Schuster hardcover edition February 2012

SIMON & SCHUSTER and colophon are registered trademarks
of Simon & Schuster, Inc.

For information about special discounts for bulk purchases,
please contact Simon & Schuster Special Sales at
1-866-506-1949 or business@simonandschuster.com.

The Simon & Schuster Speakers Bureau can bring authors
to your live event. For more information or to book an event,
contact the Simon & Schuster Speakers Bureau at
1-866-248-3049 or visit our website at www.simonspeakers.com.

Designed by Jill Putorti

Manufactured in the United States of America

10 9 8 7 6 5 4 3 2 1

Library of Congress Cataloging-in-Publication Data
Polites, Taylor M.
The rebel wife / Taylor M. Polites.
        p.   cm.
    1. Alabama—Fiction I. Title.
PS3616.O56756 R43 2011
813.6
                                    2011007100

ISBN 978-1-4516-2951-4
ISBN 978-1-4516-2953-8 (ebook)

To Kaylie Jones, mentor and friend

The
Rebel Wife

One

I KNOW THAT ELI is dying.

Rachel said the rattlesnakes were a bad sign, but that doesn't signify. The Negroes give so much credence to conjuring and signs. But there is something about Eli. He looks so much like Pa before he died. Eli trembles in his bed like Pa did. He has the same fever in his eyes. Losing Pa was terrible, but I don't feel that with Eli. He is not a bad husband, but it will not be like when Pa died.

When Eli came home on horseback, the heat had covered him in sweat. The humidity hung in the air like wet sheets shimmering in the sunlight. Simon had uncovered a nest of snakes beside the carriage house by the apple trees. Rachel and Emma were wild with fear. They closed themselves up in the kitchen. It became so hot the bricks seemed to sweat. John helped Simon kill the snakes with hoes while Rachel called to John from the kitchen window loud enough for the whole town to hear, shouting at him to keep away, to think of their boy, repeating over and over that it was a bad omen. Simon ignored them as if he had no fear at all. His black skin was dotted with tiny beads of sweat from the heat or maybe that was fear. He hacked at them while they shook their rattlers and coiled around each other in a solid writhing mass. Simon warned me to stay back, but I wanted

to see them. And then Eli came riding up the lane almost hanging off
his saddle.

He drank water straight from the pump, lifting the lever and heaving it down as he bent over it, the other hand extended, waiting for the
rattle of the pipe until the water splashed over his palm. The sunlight
glittered in it as he threw it on his face. He drank it in gulps. Simon
left the dead snakes and spoke with him. He helped Eli into the house
and left the horse for John.

Eli is twenty-five years older than I, but he gives the impression
that he could live forever. He has a sureness of youth about him in
spite of how ungainly he is. He is imposing but not handsome. Never
handsome. His waxy scalp shines through his thinning hair. His nose
is bulbous. His jaw sags with awful, long whiskers. He wears odd
Quaker hats to keep the sun off or his skin will splotch red.

He barely said a word through supper last night and picked at the
cold mutton and pickles Emma laid out. He complained of the odor
of her canned tomato relish and the early greens. His wheezing drove
me to distraction. He stared at his plate, red-faced, breathing hard as
if it took all his concentration. I had to scold Henry for shoving his
sopping biscuit into his mouth.

He was dazed when he took to his bed—our bed. He perspired to ex-
cess but would take no water. Dr. Greer's visit was hardly reassuring. He
came late and said it was some fever that would pass. He recommended
cold compresses and tartar emetic to increase the sweating, even though
the bedding was already soaked. And a bleeding tomorrow, he said.

Simon gave him the emetic mixed with molasses. Emma and Rachel kept wet cloths on his forehead. Then I had my turn, sitting with
the lamp low, watching the rise and fall of his chest and the dull rattle
from each exhale. Just once he awoke, but he didn't speak. He searched
the room with his eyes, searching for something, and then he saw me.
His hand reached out and I took it in mine, curling my fingers around
his without touching his palm, resisting him. I hushed him and pressed

the damp cloth against his forehead. I wiped down his chest through the gap in his nightshirt. He closed his eyes and drifted in and out of sleep, disturbed by the spasms brought on by the emetic. I knew then that he would not survive. I know for certain that he is dying.

When Pa died, it was about winter. The trees were already half bare, the lawns brittle and brown. But everything here is so alive. The garden soaks in the sun, thriving in this relentless humidity without the faintest hint of death. The grass is dense and green. The trees are heavy with leaves, drooping with exhaustion. Fat peonies have bloomed, their petals collapsing into so many delicate pieces of torn pink silk on the grass. Tendrils of honeysuckle twine around the thin posts of the back porch, their honey-sweet perfume hanging in the air with no breeze to move it away.

Henry plays on the gravel path. His towhead in the sun is like new hay, a trait he bears from Eli. He is all Eli, with none of the Sedlaw brooding features and dark hair. He squats with a stick in his small hand, poking at an anthill. He has no sense of waiting. He only asked this morning why Papa was still in bed, then shrugged away his concern when Emma came in.

"Come quick, Miss Gus!"

Emma leans from the bedroom window waving a towel. We both look. White turban. Black face. Black dress. White cuffs. And a filthy towel whipping wildly in front of her. No words anymore, just panic on her face. I know what she has to tell me. Thank God she came with me into this house when I married. Mama threw a conniption, but Emma is free to choose as she pleases. Lord knows she was more of a mother to me sometimes than Mama. She chose to come for whatever reason. I didn't force her.

"Wait here for Mama," I call back to Henry. My shoes crunch over the pea-gravel path and click against the steps of the porch.

The shadows of the house are cool. A door closes upstairs, but the latch does not click. I mount the step and my heel catches in my skirts. The hem tears. I pull at my dress and grab the banister.

The odor of sweat and rot slithers around me. It swallows me as I climb. I want to retch. What is all this red? Is it blood? I should go into Eli's room, but this red—red everywhere, smeared on everything. Bowls of pewter and clay are scattered across the hall bench. Blue willow china and cooking pots canter pell-mell over the wood and overflow with wet rags tinted scarlet, dripping red onto the polished hickory, swirling in shimmering iridescent shades of crimson like oil in a puddle. Red smudges the lips of the bowls and pools in their wells. The white door is marked, smeared with red in clumsy finger-prints that are slashes against the gleaming paint. I cannot touch the brass handle of the door. The substance covers it.

I hear Emma's voice. "You've got to keep working at him, Rachel."

I push at the wood with my fingertips. It swings open slowly. Eli lies panting in his bed, prostrated. He is stripped of his clothing, ap-pallingly naked against the white sheets. Emma, Rachel, and Simon all work at his body. The redness drips from his temples like sweat. It seeps from his armpits and the wrinkled folds of his neck. His skin is tinged watery pink. The bed linens are soaked with jagged marks of red saturation around his body like a grisly halo. He wheezes pa-thetically as the servants soak up the fluid with their rags and wring it into bowls. More red seeps through his skin, dripping down his arms and legs as Simon lifts each one, pushing a red-soaked rag across his limbs. The fluid falls from his face, collecting in pools around his eyes and spilling onto the sheets as he trembles. Bowls filled with bloody cloths sit on the bedside tables. The servants cannot wipe it off quickly enough. Their work is frantic.

"I won't," Rachel says. She holds her hands away from herself as if they are not hers.

"Rachel, hush," Emma says, cutting her eyes between us.

"I won't, Emma," she says. "The devil's done bit him on his heel to bleed like that. I won't!"

Rachel rushes around the bed and past me, wiping her hands on her apron. They leave pale pink streaks across the white cloth. Emma and Simon turn to me. "Miss Gus, Mr. Eli needs the doctor," Emma says.

But I am paralyzed. I will my feet to step forward, but they refuse. I can only watch him. I cannot pull myself away. What is happening to him?

His eyes have an unseeing wildness as they search the satin starburst of the bed canopy. They roam in wider circles until finally he stares into my face. He lifts his arm just barely, too weak to move. He groans with a terrifying rattle in his chest. A gurgling sound.

Simon looks at me. "He wants you, ma'am. He wants your hand."

Eli's pupils are dilated to large black spots in pools of red, staring at me as if he wants to say my name. He reaches for me. I lean on the door frame. I think I am going to faint. My heart is thudding in my throat so hard I can't breathe.

"I'll tell John to fetch the doctor," I say. I fall out of the door and hold the banister with both hands, looking down the well of the stairs. My head spins along their curve. All of my insides feel as if they will come out.

Simon is beside me. He has left Emma alone with Eli. He puts a hand on my arm. "Miss Gus," he says. His eyes are hard. "Did you see if Mr. Eli had anything with him when he came home?"

"Simon, take your hand off me."

"I'm sorry, ma'am." He pulls his hand back. "Mr. Eli should have had a package with him yesterday. I think it might have contained some money."

"Don't be ridiculous. Eli needs a doctor right away, and you come asking me for money?" It's a wonder that Eli trusted Simon.

"I think it's important. Mr. Eli would want to know that it was safe." He steps back and his face loses its expression.

"I'm getting the doctor for Eli. I think that's what is important. If you want to help Eli, then you should be with him. Emma's in there all alone."

We both look through the open door. Emma is on the far side of the bed, looking over Eli while he wheezes. Simon's face becomes stern. These servants. Thank God for Emma.

"Yes, ma'am," he says. He nods and goes back to Eli's side.

Rachel had better not have already frightened John with her stories. He'll have to fetch the doctor either way.

The wall clock is ticking by the small hours. Emma and Simon are surely asleep in their beds, although a light from Simon's room over the carriage house glows against the thin curtains. He keeps his lamp lit, a faint flickering glow half hidden by the catalpa tree. Perhaps he is awake and waiting. Perhaps Emma is in her attic room waiting for a word from me. After this horrible afternoon, we are all waiting. His sickness—whatever it is—overwhelmed him so quickly.

Eli's breathing works in a faltering heave and sigh. The lamplight has faded. The oil must be almost gone. At least the bleeding has stopped. Thank God it has stopped. But the scarlet-stained sheets are still under the blankets Greer had us put on Eli to keep off the chill.

How stunned Greer was when he came again, watching the sweat and blood pour off of Eli. His features seemed to fall in on themselves. "I am sorry, Gus," he said. "I have seen terrible things. I have done them, Lord knows. We had to do them. We did what we could to save those boys. Poor innocent boys."

What could I do but nod? Greer is such easy prey to his memories of the war, unable sometimes to speak of anything else. Unable to help himself. We looked down on Eli's suffering face, both of us struck dumb.

"I am sorry, Gus," he said again. "But I do not know this illness, and I do not know how to help him." Then he fell quiet, with only the jagged rhythm of Eli's breathing between us. When Greer looked at me, I didn't turn away. I looked at him more closely than I have in years. His sagging, weary eyes. The heavy cheeks covered with grizzled, rust-colored beard. The scar that cuts from eye to jaw, the slash of a shell wound from Chickamauga, grapeshot that had been blasted into the field where he was working on the dying soldiers. He tells the story so often. The scar is a smooth pink ribbon. It seemed to pulse red, as if inflamed by his memory. He turned away from me.

"We can try to ease his pain," he said. There was shame in his voice. "Put blankets on him and close these windows near twilight. And this. It's a tincture of opium. You know how to apply it."

He held out the small bottle of curiously shaped dark blue glass, but I would not take it. I know how to apply it. I have handled it before. It is a familiar remedy to me. He knew that.

He placed the bottle on the marble-topped table by Eli's bedside and departed. The skin on my arms tingles when I look at it. I cannot help but look at it. The opalescent liquid flared in the glass like a nymph swirling in milky veils. Simon poured it into Eli's mouth, drops dribbling down his chin onto the sheets. I could have kissed him there, just for a taste of it. But Rachel was apoplectic about the blood. She insists we keep from touching it. Simon was relieved when Eli's breathing eased into a shallow wheeze. He slept and seemed less troubled. I was relieved, too.

Emma sat on a chair in the corner, sighing a hymn. The refrain had something soothing to it. What were the words? I think I heard it in the African church west of the square when I was a girl. Mama had taken me there to hear their preacher, who had a reputation. The entire congregation sang, wailing and ecstatic. Their voices were like waves of grief and joy combined.

There is a balm in Gilead
That makes the wounded whole.
There is a balm in Gilead
To heal the sin-sick soul.

Eli coughs and rustles in his bedclothes. Was I sleeping? I want to sleep. I want to cross the hall and lock the door behind me and crawl in between the clean dry sheets and sleep.

Eli's eyes are open. The whites are red-riddled. He stares at me and shakes his head. "No," he says again and again. Is it no? I cannot understand him. His arms wrestle with the blankets. He wants to reach out to me again. He wants some last embrace. I can feel each vertebra of my back against the chair. My hands grip the carved wood arms. His mouth opens and closes. A shudder takes hold of me and my breath will not come. He gasps and the air makes a wet sucking sound as it enters his lungs. He groans. I want to scream but cannot. I want to run from him. The blankets lift with an incredible effort. He is scratching at them, his hands prisoner under their weight. He lets out another shuddering groan. His arms collapse against the bed. He exhales with a click.

And all is quiet. The blankets lie still against the bed. A soft wisp of breath slips from his mouth. His eyes fade. The frenzy and desire in them vanish. They are opaque and bleary. He is dead. My God, he is dead.

I cannot cry. I do not want to cry, though I should weep for him. And for myself. And for these past ten years we spent together. For this thing that was our marriage. Whatever it was. And now my husband has died and left me a widow.

The first pale hints of sunrise creep into the sky to color it a hard gray like gunmetal. Simon's lamp still burns in his bedroom window. He has waited up all night. But I want to linger with Eli. I do not want to move. I do not want to leave this room. Why do I wait? The word widow vibrates in my head. It rolls on my tongue. Widow. My mouth shapes the word silently. I have counted so many days until I could call myself by that name. Widow.

Two

HE SAYS "COME IN" before I knock. He must have heard my steps on the creaking stairs. I push the door open. He is fully dressed, sitting on a chair by his bed. He knows before I say a word. He weeps as I tell him. He slumps in his chair in the inappropriate intimacy of his room and cries into one dark hand as the other rests on his knee. I turn away from him, embarrassed. His tears for Eli come so easily.

His room is simple. Sparsely furnished. A narrow bed. A table with a lamp. Newspapers are neatly folded on it, papers from Mobile and Montgomery and Nashville. There is a bureau with a mirror and a large color engraving in a simple wood frame. The drawing commemorates Robert Elliott's speech in Congress. Elliott the Negro man elected from South Carolina because the Republicans kept white men from voting. Equality and freedom, the picture says: "The Shackles Broken by the Genius of Freedom." Elliott spoke on the floor of Congress in favor of the Civil Rights Act. A Negro man speaking to Congress. Eli talked about it at length, certain it would mean real equality for colored men. Real equality with what? For what? All this talk about freedom and equality never made sense. You take from one and you give to another. That is what has happened. That is what happened to me, and it has nothing to do with equality.

Simon takes his hand from his face and watches me read the engraving. I turn away from it as if I have no interest. He looks at me gravely, his eyes still wet, but with the sadness wiped away. His hands are large, dark-skinned on the back like oak bark, pale on the palm like the raw flesh of wood. Simon the snake killer.

"Did he?" he says, pausing. He glances down at his hand and then looks at me. He sighs through his nose. The nostrils flare. It may be discomfort, as if he doubts what he is about to say. "Did he say anything to you, ma'am, before he died?"

Simon's loyalty to Eli must make him want to believe Eli was thinking of him as he passed. Should I tell him a lie? Something to comfort him? He doesn't turn his eyes away from me. His stare is penetrating.

"No, not a word." The newspapers on his desk are squared one against the other. They will put something in the paper about Eli. Not too much. People cannot know too much about how he died. "He tried to speak. It seemed like he would. But he never said anything." I have to turn away from him.

"Could you make it out—what he was trying to say? Did he indicate anything at all to you?"

His eyes narrow. I want to go back to the house.

"No, nothing, Simon. Nothing at all. He didn't mention any money, either, but I'm sure he has thought of you in his will."

His face is grim. He does not appreciate my response, but that is my answer. There is no more to say. He should be happy I answered at all. Maybe I should have made something up.

"Was there something you wanted to know?"

"No, ma'am," he answers quickly. "I just wondered. If there is anything that occurs to you, please let me know. I'm very sorry for the loss. I'm very sorry."

"I know you were close to him. And loyal. You will always have a place here with us."

He nods and rises abruptly. "May I see him?"

Perhaps I should not have said that. They are free people now. They are not like before, when it was understood we would care for them. When Pa died, Mama assured all the house servants they would stay with us. They could become so excited from fear of being sold or separated from us. But Simon must worry if he will have a place here. Where else could he possibly go?

We walk back to the house, and I leave him alone with Eli's body. He closes the door behind him. He is too familiar, of course, but now is not the time to scold him. As if I have the courage to scold Simon.

And Emma must be told. She cared for Eli, too, I think, although she has been with me from time beyond my remembrance. In my earliest days, she fed me from her own breast.

I knock timidly at her bedroom door. It feels odd to seek her out here at the top of the stairs. She answers already dressed and has a look of understanding on her face. She embraces me. We hold each other for a moment. There is no need for me to explain or for her to condole. She feels some private grief over Eli's passing, but she does not express it to me.

She says she will come with me to tell Henry. She follows me down the stairs and back through the pink bedroom to where the nursery is tucked into a corner of the house. Henry is still sleeping in his short bed. He rubs his eyes in confusion to see Emma and me with him so early. I kneel on the floor beside him, my skirts padded under my knees. He sits up, tugging at his nightshirt and pulling it down toward his feet.

He is my child. Only mine now, although he will grow up to look so much like Eli. And I tried so hard not to have him. Not to have a child at all. Emma's little devices, the cotton cloths coated in sheep fat. Making Eli believe he was inside me while he bore at me between my legs, slick with his sweat. So much vigilance. Some night I was drunk with wine or my medicines, and I stumbled but could not face the horrors of those bottles and pills again. So I bore Eli a son.

"Henry, you must be very strong for Mama." What is my purpose? Those soft blue eyes are Eli's eyes. I do not know what to say to him. How do I put it into words that he will understand? How can I explain that his father's death means marvelous new changes for him and for me, that it is not all a loss but something that has changed our lives in a way that has so much of the better. I was ten when Pa died. Henry is not yet five, old enough to understand. Old enough to be afraid. Emma sits close by in an old rocker, looking out on the garden.

"Your papa has died, honey, and we must say goodbye to him. He has left us and gone to a better place." My words sound silly. How can they provide any comfort to my boy? He shakes his head and rubs his eyes and asks where his papa has gone.

He starts to cry and pull away from me, but he must listen. I grab his hands and hold them. I squeeze them hard. He jerks at them in pain. The more I say to him, the more he struggles to get away. He rushes to Emma, who sits quietly in her chair. She scoops him up and rocks him, rubbing his head and murmuring to him about the angels taking his papa on a long ride up to heaven, where he will watch over Henry and all of us and make sure we are safe like he always has before.

When did I stop believing the things Emma told me? It was late in my youth before I gave them up. Back then I ran to Emma with a hurt or a fear. I preferred her to my own mother. I guess I did not expect that my son would do the same. Perhaps I am too clumsy as a mother, or too harsh, as Mama was. Or perhaps Emma provides a comfort I cannot. All the same, it has happened. The feeling is cold in my heart. I sit here on the floor watching Emma care for my boy. I wish she could comfort me. I am jealous of Henry for his childhood. I wish I could behave much as a child myself.

This is the Emma I have always known. Her life's work has been children, although she never had any of her own. But she did, yes, two small ones who died just before I was born. Mama said once that losing those babies made Emma love us all the more. She has always seemed quiet and sad to me. We never talked about it, but she must still think about them. The pain weakens over time. It fades away. But I am sure she still thinks about them. You turn your head and suddenly the thought is there. A baby that was not. How could she not think about it? I think about that baby every day. What would he have been like? What would have happened to us? I cannot think about it. Not now.

I will leave them together. Henry will fall asleep with his thumb in his mouth as Emma rocks him. That comfort. What a barb, but what a relief, to know that he can find that comfort, even though it is not with me.

Simon and Rachel are in Eli's bedroom, taking up the soiled linens. I can hear them well enough. The door isn't pulled quite to. I'm surprised Simon agreed to help her, even after she insisted. She is afraid, although she won't act like it. Rachel would never let her fear show.

"Stop poking through Mr. Eli's things and listen to me, Simon. I said he didn't die the right way."

What is she saying? Is there a right way to die? Rachel and her superstitions. And they're in there with Eli's body. John and Simon must have already moved him to the cooling board.

"He seems to have accomplished it well enough, however he did it," Simon answers drily.

"You know what I mean, Simon. I told you those rattlesnakes were a bad sign. There's already been death in this house."

They fall silent. The sheets make a soft hush of a sound as they pull them up. I gripped my fists when Rachel asked me what I wanted them to do with the sheets. She should mind her tone. She didn't even nod when I told her to burn them on the fire John is making for the boiling pot. There should be black dye powder from Mama's funeral in the attic. I won't dye very many dresses, just two or three to wear until I can have dresses made from black cloth. After Mama passed, the dyed dresses turned my arms and shoulders and breasts black. The dye ran in gray-tinted rivulets of sweat down my sides. Anything that my corset did not cover was tainted black like deep bruises.

"It's those snakes." Rachel again. "You need to get me those snakes. What did you do with them?"

"They're in the ashpit. Does John know what you're planning?"

"Don't roll your eyes at me, Simon. You know I know my way. You get me those snakes. You keep the skin if you want. All I need are the bones."

"I'll let John know you're looking for them."

Rachel is up to something. More conjuring. I don't like to criticize her, but that tone. And her temper. I don't know how she got along at the Cobb house. Emma said she disappeared after the Yankees came, like so many servants, but found her way back when she realized freedom was not so grand, Yankees or not. Eli hired her on Emma's recommendation. The fights we had over her. Now her tempers have become commonplace. And who wouldn't balk at pulling up those bloody sheets, even without the superstitions her mother gave her.

"You don't need to tell John. And stop being smart. Just get me those bones like I asked you."

I should go. Move up the stairs to the attic.

"Wait," Rachel says. "Shhh."

She knows I'm out here listening to them.

She swings open the door and comes into the hall, but I am already halfway up the stairs. She looks at me hard.

"Rattlesnakes, Rachel?" I ask. I roll my eyes. "Is Little John ready? I'm just getting the ribbon."

Rachel puts her hands on her hips. "Yes, ma'am. He's in Henry's suit. It's a little short on him."

"Does it not look right?" My hand squeezes the railing in front of me.

"No, ma'am. It will do."

"Thank you for letting him do this, Rachel."

"It's all right, ma'am. He'll get paid for it, I guess, won't he?" She looks at me evenly, with impudence.

"Yes, Rachel, I will give him something for his trouble. For both your trouble." I will offer the boy a few pennies and see how her expression changes. My hand relaxes on the railing. Rachel's eyes seem to bore into me so that I have to look away. "Big John doesn't mind, does he?" I ask, looking at her again.

Rachel narrows her eyes at me and smiles. "No, ma'am. He doesn't mind at all. No secrets in this house."

She watches me round the stairs, her hands on her hips. The undertaker will be here soon, and I have to get out Little John with the bell. I don't have time for her tantrums anyway.

Dr. Greer was good to take word to Weems. Greer is so easy about the old times—he does not hold a grudge against Eli or Mr. Weems, Republicans or not. Greer was sad at Eli's bedside. He eyed the blue bottle and looked at me in his funny way. I was almost afraid he would take the bottle away. But he didn't, thank God. I couldn't help but look at the bottle, too. A last look before I closed Eli's bedroom door.

I will be quiet and mournful, like Greer's face. Impassive as a sphinx. They must not know what goes on behind my mask. They will all know soon enough that Eli is dead. After Little John goes through town with the bell, then it will all begin.

The attic room is so hot. The heat is early this year. There are cobwebs everywhere and footprints in the dust. The servants coming and going up here.

The old trunk is still filled with Mama's *memento mori,* the black ribbon and black gloves, a few onyx and mother-of-pearl rings, armbands, black-edged cards and black-bordered handkerchiefs. Black cockades and dyed black feather fans. Mama's funeral was an affair that brought together the society of Albion and the county, family from as far as Huntsville and Tullahoma and even Nashville and Murfreesboro. All of them avoided staying at my home, out of respect, they said. Is it already two years since Mama died? It seems like much longer that she's been gone. Her funeral had been an event. I had made it an event.

Eli's funeral will be a different sight. Who will come—and for whom will they come, him or me? The dusty heat of the attic makes me clumsy, fumbling all these loose mementos. The ribbon and dye are here. The other things can stay in the trunk. New favors can be acquired, if they are even needed. Who will wear a ring to remember Eli? When Mama died, some people in town wore their armbands for weeks, and others wore them through the end of my deep mourning for her.

It was a cool day—autumn—and I opened the house on Allen Street in a way it had not been opened in years. I honored Mama's name in the proper way. To let everyone know that I at least had not forgotten her name, or my own. Judge was proud of it. He is not one to forget our name, either. He did not smile, of course, but I could see the pride in his eyes, in the way he looked at every detail and nodded. He approved. He didn't need to tell me I had done right by Mama. I could tell.

She was embalmed by Mr. Weems and laid out in a mahogany coffin with bright silver handles. Mama was in the south parlor, the largest and the one that faced the river. Pa and Mama had spent their time together in that room. She looked peaceful, resigned, her hands crossed over her waist, a black lace cap framing her tight gray curls, pomaded and dressed by Weems himself. He had given her a touch of color in her cheeks, and I approved while knowing full well Mama would have been scandalized by the thought of wearing rouge, in spite of her vanity. I had practically moved into the house on Allen Street during those last weeks. Mama was confined to her bed, racked with paroxysms of agony from the cancer that ate her. Her passing was a relief to her—to us all.

I wanted Albion to be amazed. Awed. Their tongues should be stilled in their mouths throughout that endless afternoon. They came in a flood of black silk and broadcloth to pay their respects, to collect tokens, and to stare wide-eyed with their mouths pinched at the extravagance of it. I had informed Mr. Weems that there was no limit to the expense, that I wanted the room overwhelmed with flowers. He expressed lilies and white roses on the train from Nashville. Their exquisite scent bled out through the windows onto the porch, suffocating the senses with a putrefying sweetness. The Chinese railings across the front and back porch were dressed in shiny black bunting. The doors and windows were swagged in the same material and thrown open to the autumn air. No detail was too small. Nothing was overlooked.

The mourners thronged the lawns and parlors and the long central hall. They milled around the rooms, looking somber and resigned. Young colored girls circulated among them, dressed entirely in black down to their pantalets, carrying trays of onyx rings and bracelets, satin armbands, and handkerchiefs trimmed in black lace and embroidered with Mama's initials. Mr. Weems had provided cards printed with a lone woman by an urn shaded by a willow tree. On the reverse was a poem by Henry Timrod.

Art thou not glad to close
Thy wearied eyes, O saddest child of Time,
Eyes which have looked on every mortal crime,
And swept the piteous round of mortal woes?

Mrs. Branson, they called me, though I had gone to school with them, played in their parlors and gardens, and cried over the dead with them. That had been before—before I became Mrs. Branson. They treated me with civility. I shrink from calling it coldness, but it was chilling. They nodded to Eli, thin-lipped, extending limp hands and murmuring, "My condolences." Their faces streamed past, puckered, an agony of pantomime that I had not expected. I had thought I would shame them with the house and gardens, the tokens and extravagance.

It was as if they didn't see it. As if they could barely see me. It became their funeral for Mama and I was the intruder. The Yankee officers, those who were left, came, too, and brought their wives, who were unwilling to miss an opportunity to mingle with the old aristocrats. The Yankee women were conspicuous for their stiff and shiny new taffetas and fashionable bonnets trimmed in crape, while the old families wore mended dresses and faded shawls. Those Yankee women took my hands in both of theirs, warm, gushing with sympathy and offering any assistance, begging an opportunity to call on me. Their dress embarrassed me with its newness and quality that was too like my own.

Buck did not come. Judge's son did not even bother to come to my mother's funeral. Judge offered up some excuse, that he was ill or indisposed, but I knew it was a lie. People raised their heads when Judge came in. He came directly to me, without looking at any of them. They moved aside for him. That was respect, what he did for me. By his respect for me, those others, the old families, had to show their respect, too.

Eli did not twitch at Buck's name. He kept his eyes on a small painting of a thoroughbred horse Pa had owned years and years before. And then Mike came up, unsteady on his feet already, his words slurred, and he looked at Eli, so calm and inscrutable, and said, "Sir." It seemed like he raised his voice. "We may tolerate your presence here, but you will never be one of us." What an ass my brother is.

Eli had given Mama an income after we married. He was generous with Mama and with Mike. She was very comfortable. Eli scrubbed the damage of the war years from the house, and it took on the aspect it had when Pa was alive. Eli would send Simon over to the house to report on what needed fixing or painting. The next day Simon would have a crew of men hammering and sawing at the cornices and soffits where rot had invaded, and putting up fresh paint—real paint, not whitewash. I don't think Eli knew I observed these things, but I did. And Mama could not stop carrying on about it. She was shocked to find a gang of Negro men working in her garden or clambering up ladders and peeping through the windows as if she hadn't lived surrounded by them before the war.

The house gleamed, was maintained like a monument—a memorial. As if it were Pa's mausoleum and Mama the last vestal. Or maybe I was the vestal, tending the flame from afar. It was a temple to the past, but without a soul. It was not apparent to a passerby or even to Mama, who lived in the midst of it, scolding her maids about the dusty stairs or how they didn't put enough blue in the wash. But I could feel it with a sadness I carried in my bones like some crippling disease. I honored the house as my obligation, as I honored my mother on the day of her burial. There was no one else to observe the proper rites. It was my duty.

Emma helped me dress the morning of Mama's funeral, and she said that she had had her differences with Mama. Unusual of her to speak so frankly. I barely responded. She knew Mama longer than I did. She grew up with Mama. Would she have spoken like that if she were still a slave? Mama was a strong-willed person. Someone who emphatically knew right from wrong. The mildest scullery maid had her differences with Mama. I did, too, I guess. But her absence left something missing from me. I kept thinking, Who will I read to now? Mama used to sit with me in the evenings, and I would read aloud whatever novels I had while she did her handwork. But now I will read alone, I thought. In fact, I've stopped reading altogether. What a silly question for me to think, but I couldn't get it out of my head.

Three

HENRY CLIMBS ON HIS narrow bed beside me. His solitary games always stop when I appear. He wraps his arms around me and lays his head on my lap. His hair is like corn silks under my fingers. I am petting him. My pet. He breathes out of his nose in short, discontented bursts. He is confused by all this commotion.

The ring of the bell is faint through the open nursery windows. Little John is making his progress through the neighborhood. Soon they will all know Eli is dead. They will see Little John and know he is from my house. The whole town must already know Eli has been ill.

John is a good playmate for Henry. They are so close in age. John was born just six months after Henry and is already the bigger boy. In that way, Rachel has been a help in the house. There are so few boys in the neighborhood for Henry to play with, not for any lack of children. John is a good companion. Rachel brings him with her and Big John when they come in the morning. Just as easy for her or Emma to watch two boys as one. And it eases Henry's loneliness. What must be his loneliness. He is such a quiet child, as content to play alone as he is to play with others. He lives so deep inside himself that he observes more than he partakes. But there is a keenness of mind there. He will grow up to be smart as a whip. He may favor Eli Branson on the outside, but inside he is a Sedlaw. I know it as surely as I know my own name.

"It's too much for you to understand, I know," I whisper. Maybe for myself. "But why don't we go on a trip? Wouldn't you like to go on a trip for a while? Would you like that?"

He rubs his head against me, shy of answering. He is thinking.

"We'll get to ride on the railroad. And on steamboats on a river. We'll go see mountains and the ocean, too. Wouldn't you like to see the ocean?"

Henry nods and says, "Mmm." He looks at me out of the corner of his eye but looks away as soon as I catch him with my glance.

I brush his hair with my fingers. "It's going to be fine, Henry. Don't worry. We're all going to be fine." He sighs softly and closes his eyes.

"Miss Gus," Rachel shouts from my bedroom in the most exasperating way. "Miss Gus, the undertaker's here." She comes to the nursery door and leans her head in. "And Mr. Judge Heppert is here to see you, too. I put Mr. Heppert in the front parlor and the boneman in the music room."

Rachel has finally used her head. She knows well enough to keep Judge and Mr. Weems apart. I suppose I must take that as a sign of progress, although she would know as well as anyone what happened during the war.

I'll bring Weems upstairs quickly. Then I can see Judge. He must have heard Little John's bell. Hopefully, he will not stay long.

Not that Judge and Weems were ever at each other's throats. Everyone behaves so cordially now. You might never know by looking, but those old hatreds are there. I could see them with every one of Judge's frowns or Eli's silences. With so much that we all lost, how could there not be anger?

All of that is past, anyway. Dead and buried with it. I don't have to think about it anymore. It is their burden, not mine.

My hands are so wet from sweating. This relentless heat. The parlor door is closed. Mr. Weems is standing nervously in the music room, rolling his hat over his fingers. He is painfully thin and wears gold-rimmed spectacles perched at the tip of his nose. He looks like a blue heron in a black suit.

"Thank you for coming, Mr. Weems," I say. "Mr. Branson is upstairs."

"Mrs. Branson," he begins. "I want to extend my most sincere condolences." He follows me to the stairs. If only we could get out of the hall. The door to the front parlor is shut tight. My hand is on the banister. Weems looks at me, expectant. He was a friend of Eli's, after all.

"Yes, Mr. Weems." I cast my eyes down. "It is a terrible loss for us all. Let me take you upstairs."

Weems follows me up the stairs to Eli's bedroom door.

"If I may ask, Mrs. Branson," he says. I nod to him and turn the handle, slowly swinging the door wide. "How did Mr. Branson meet his end?" The bed is freshly dressed with white linen. Eli lies on the cooling board in his shirtsleeves and pants. His eyes are closed. A coat and other clothes lie folded neatly on the edge of the bed. His face has lost its ruddiness. It is the wan color of dried putty.

I answer slowly. "Dr. Greer said that it was a sanguinary disorder brought on by the heat. A summer complaint."

"A summer complaint?" He remains at the threshold. The cooling board is laid across two chairs. Simon must have brought up ice to put in the long box under the board. A fine mist rises from its edges.

"Well, that is how Dr. Greer described it," I say, perfectly innocent. It sounds like an excuse.

"Yes, I spoke with the doctor. He seemed, well, baffled, Mrs. Branson." He cranes his head on his long neck, peering into the room. He surveys Eli's body from head to toe.

"I can assure you, Mr. Weems, there is no sickness in the house."

He steps into the room cautiously. "Of course, Mrs. Branson. Of course not. I understood there was a great deal of fluid lost." Eli is almost too large for the board. His feet hang over the edge and rest against the back of one chair.

"Yes, he did lose a great deal of—he perspired a great deal." Eli's face is gray and the skin seems to slide against the bone in sharp edges. His cheeks and eyesockets are hollowed out. A thick knot catches in my throat. He is dead and wasted.

"That will help, then," Mr. Weems says. "There will be less fluid. I have a boy bringing the materials over in a cart. We will begin as soon as he gets here. Do you have a key to the door? We prefer to keep the door locked when we are working, if that's possible."

"Yes." My throat closes. My hand gropes in the pocket of my dress for my handkerchief. The floor seems to move under my feet. "I will give you the key."

"You will see after our work is done. It will be like we have brought him back to life. Just like your mother."

Judge is waiting patiently in the front parlor. He kisses me on the top of my head. His right hand exerts a gentle pressure through the thick, twining braids that Rachel dressed. He should be pleased that I am in heavy mourning, dressed in black from cuffs to hem.

"Poor child, you've been through so much," he murmurs and sits next to me. Judge is always dressed impeccably, almost formally, in dark suits and shoes with a high shine. His hair has turned so white since the war. His beard is neatly trimmed. His pale blue eyes are piercingly clear. Mama always said girls threw their heads at him when he was young. Like Buck, I guess. Like father, like son. Mama almost tittered herself to fits about it. She regretted their close kinship, or she would have married him herself.

"Thank you, Judge," I murmur. "It's kind of you to come so quickly." He pats my hand and sits across from me. "We have seen little of you of late."

"Yes. And I am sorry for that." He nods and exhales, looking at the patterns on the rug, garlands of pink roses and ivy. "My business has preoccupied me. And the party. Politics, you know. I regret it now for your sake, Augusta."

I smile at him, a prudent smile, not too strong, modest and deferential. "I understand, Judge. You shouldn't apologize. You've always been such a support for me. And for Mama." Mama relied on Judge for everything after Pa died. She couldn't make a decision without asking him what to do.

A small smile blooms on his lips, and he reaches for my hand, covering it and giving it a squeeze. "I've tried to do my best by you. I honestly have."

Rachel enters with tall glasses of iced tea. She moves silently and places the tray on the small table in front of me. She nods to me and cuts her eyes at Judge. She turns away abruptly. He barely notices.

The glasses are covered in sweat from the humidity, and the moisture runs down the sides and pools on the black lacquer tray. The tray was a gift to Eli from a Mobile merchant who imported it from China. The tea looks so cold. I am tempted to take my glass in spite of Judge, but I must wait for him. He looks at the drink but doesn't move. His head is cocked, listening to Rachel's soft footfalls as they move down the hall.

"The funeral arrangements," he says. "Can I offer you assistance with them?"

"No, thank you. Mr. Weems is upstairs now." I look at the ceiling as if I can see through it to Eli's room. I cannot look at Judge for fear. "I am leaving all the arrangements to him. I told him I want Eli buried soon. In two days' time."

Judge's eyes follow mine to the ceiling. His face registers no feeling of any kind. "Fine. Fine. Nothing too extravagant, of course. This won't be like Elsie's funeral."

Little beads of water run down the sides of the frosted glasses.

I will take some ice after Judge leaves and wrap it in a towel to rub against my temples. That will help.

"Weems," he repeats. "I thought there was some problem between Weems and Eli. That's what you reap when you try to force nigger voting down men's throats. Weems might have voted Republican once, but he has sense enough to know what an abomination it is to give the darkies the vote. I told Eli he wouldn't be able to keep his party together. We scattered them like buckshot in the last election."

The sunlight is so bright outside, it makes the parlor seem dark. The Corbins' dog trots by, a large piebald hound with his tongue hanging out almost to the ground, panting.

"I wasn't aware of any dispute. Mr. Weems didn't say anything."

"Well, I suppose it will be fine now. Eli is no more. Weems didn't bridle at . . ."

"No, sir. Not at all. He seemed pleased that I wrote to him."

"A dirty scalawag practicing a dirty trade. At least we've taken the state back from them. A disgusting practice. I wasn't happy that you did that to your mother, but I like the old ways anyway. If you choose to do that to Eli, well, I won't interfere."

We sit together quietly. Judge's eyes move back to the ceiling. He looks at me quickly and then at the floor, his hands on his knees. "Augusta, I want you to understand that you will never be in need. I will see to that." He drums his fingers against his knee and then coughs into his hand. He looks at me and raises an eyebrow. "Were you very familiar with Eli's business interests?"

"No," I answer. "But I am very interested to learn." There is a creeping coldness coming over my shoulders. What could he be getting at?

"I have talked with Jim Stephens at the Planters and Merchants Bank, and I will meet with him again soon. He is doing an accounting in detail, an inventory of Eli's assets at the bank as well as his outstanding debts. When I heard how serious Eli's illness was, I went to him immediately."

"His debts?"

"It seems that Eli has been entangled with the bank for some time, and as more than just a holder of capital stock. He took out mortgages on a variety of his properties and against his stock in the bank."

"What does that mean?" I lean forward.

"It means that the economic convulsions of the last few years left no one untouched. Perhaps you were unaware. Your mother was in her last illness. But the panic impacted everyone's interests, Eli included, for all his seeming invulnerability. Eli had interests in railroads and mines, many of which are now worthless. There seems to be more than just losses on investments. He was playing a few rounds of monte with the bank, and it's unclear at this point who the winner will be, if anyone. I am sorry to have to tell you."

"How can that be?" The words stumble out of my mouth. It isn't possible. How could he come here and tell me these things with Eli barely cold?

"Eli and I did not see eye to eye on many things, but we agreed on our concern for you and your interests. It was one of the things we could talk about." He exhales heavily, almost heaving through his nostrils. I nod, too weak even to smile. Judge inhales to begin again.

"We were not allies otherwise. That's true. After the war, I could see the way the wind was blowing. It was no use to fight against it, although I'm proud to say I never took the oath." He pauses and looks at the rug, tracing the curl of the ivy with his eyes. "The wind has changed again, Augusta. I think Eli realized that, too. Maybe he realized it too late. I don't know. But the Republicans were not going to stay in control of the state. They were not going to ram Negro rule down our throats. The people of Alabama—the people of the South—would not let that happen. I could get beyond that for your sake. I know there was a lot of fear in Albion back when you were married, and perhaps your mother, God rest her soul, did what she thought was best. I know you did, too. And I have stood beside you for all that. I stand beside you now. I know that things are not perhaps as you had hoped, but the days we have lived have been full of unexpected—unanticipated—shocks. You will survive this one as you have survived the others."

Shocks? Negro rule? What does any of this have to do with Eli's money? Everyone talked as if the man owned everything in town. And now Judge is telling me there's nothing left? It's all worthless? Because of Negro rule and the Republicans?

"I will come back to you as I know more. I wanted to acquaint you with what I knew at this point."

"Thank you, Judge. I'm sorry, I just can't believe this. I don't know what it all means." He watches me with discomfort. He was never one for sympathy. I tug my handkerchief from my sleeve and grip it.

"It will all work out. I am investigating everything, and I will unravel Eli's affairs. If there is need, I'm sure the bank can extend you something."

"How long will it be, Judge? How long, do you think, before you will know?"

He pauses and scratches his beard. "Give me a week, Augusta. Maybe two. Don't you worry. I am here to protect you. That's why Eli made me trustee of his estate. He wanted me to protect you."

My hand pauses, holding the bright white handkerchief before my eyes. "Is that what he said?" Judge moves his hand over to my knee and squeezes. I put that sadness in my eyes like the woman on Mama's memorial cards.

"Yes, " Judge says, very earnest. "Those were his exact words. It's been several years ago now, but I remember it as if it were this week. He said if anything should ever happen to him, he wanted me to protect you."

"Eli was so thoughtful. I'm surprised he never said it to me." My left hand is clenched on my handkerchief, and I will it to soften.

"He cared for you very much. You must have known that."

"I guess I did."

"He was not one of us, but he could show himself to be a man of honor on occasion. I hope you were able to find some happiness in your marriage."

I cannot meet Judge's eyes. They are on me, probing. Small streams of water pour down the glass. The chips of ice have melted away so quickly, there is only a thin layer left. The chips are glassy, almost invisible except for the way they catch the half-light of the room.

"Yes, I did. Of course I did. And I have Henry."

He nods. "Yes, and there's Henry to think of. You focus your efforts on Henry. He may be Eli's son, but there's Blackwood blood in his veins. And I will see to everything else."

He sighs a satisfied sigh. I reach for my glass, wrapping my handkerchief around it, swabbing the moisture from the base so it does not drop on my dress. I take a long, slow drink. The tea is cool and sweet in my mouth and slides down my throat. I raise the damp handkerchief to my forehead.

"What will you do—exactly—as trustee, Judge?" I ask.

"Nothing for you to worry yourself about. Eli's will is pretty straightforward."

"You have his will?"

"Yes, of course. As soon as I heard he was ill, I pulled it out and reread it. Everything is in order."

"What does it say?" I should keep my voice softer. I look at him and smile.

"Eli has left everything to Henry. You get the income from his investments. And I will oversee the whole. I can bring it to you if you like." His voice is steely, and his mouth curls down.

"No, thank you, Judge. That's very kind." I want to see it.

"It was done with your best interests in mind. And Henry's. Like I said, we have no idea who might come looking for a piece of Eli's estate or where things stand. It protects you from—from all sorts of things."

"Yes, I can see that. It seems very proper."

"I can guarantee you that it is."

"And are there other trustees?"

"Me alone. Are you worried I'm not enough?" Judge relaxes into the divan.

My mouth feels stiff as I smile. He is more than enough. "No, that's perfect. I was worried there would be other people."

Judge rises from his seat, and I rise with him. His mouth is still hard. He does not appreciate me intruding, no matter how gently.

"We will have plenty of time to discuss it, Augusta. Trust me. I will manage it all."

"Thank you, Judge. Thank you so much." The handkerchief in my hand is twisted into knots.

We walk to the door. Judge turns to me. "One more thing. Buck wanted me to send word to you—his condolences. He asks permission to call on you." Judge squints at me. The handkerchief is taut between my hands.

"Oh—so soon, Judge. I don't know."

"He wanted me to ask—not to upset you, of course, but as a good friend. He said, a good friend who has missed you."

I struggle with the handkerchief. "I don't think so, Judge. It's too soon. I cannot. I can't think of it."

Judge frowns and puts his hat on. "I will let him know that you are thinking about it. Take your time. But think about it. It would mean very much to him."

He leaves, walking down the path to the sidewalk, a black cane in his hand that he taps against the bricks.

"Miss Gus, Mr. Weems is asking after you." Emma stands in the door of the bedroom, eyeing me up and down. Her eyes move away when I look at her.

"Is he with Eli?"

"Yes, ma'am."

"I'll go to him." Emma leaves the door open and goes downstairs. She must think I'm losing my mind, pacing back and forth in my room.

I tap softly at Eli's door, and Weems opens it immediately.

"Mrs. Branson, please come in." He smiles with his lips pressed tightly together and pushes his spectacles up his nose.

Eli is still on the cooling board, but his edges are softened. His cheeks are no longer sunken, but puffed and marked with patches of pale pink. His hair is combed and slick across the top of his head. His hands are folded across his swollen belly. How can he have done this to me?

The rear wall is lined with canisters that have coiled tubes coming out of them, some of them streaked the color of rust inside the translucent yellow rubber. One canister has a tall pump attached to the top with a black rubber ball dangling from it. A hand pump. How much did Weems take out? And how much did he put in? The air is acrid with the bitter almond scent of arsenic.

"My boy will remove these shortly," he says, nodding at his equipment. "Mr. Branson looks as if he could be sleeping, doesn't he? Dr. Holmes could not have done any better."

"Yes, indeed, Mr. Weems. Thank you so much for your care." Eli does not look at all as if he is sleeping, though he certainly does not appear dead. He seems waxen and rouged. His whiskers have been smoothed against his jaw in an improbable way.

"Yes, ma'am. It is an art as much as it is a science. Some may sneer at the trade, but it is a valuable comfort we provide to the living. To see once again those they loved as if they still had the breath of life in them. Perhaps it is a deception, but it is a comforting one."

"Yes, I can see that." A comfort for some people, I suppose. After Hill was killed at Nashville, his body never made it home. Must you see someone dead to believe he is dead? I feel my brother next to me so often, like a ghost in the house with me, and I know it is because his body never came home. "Is there anything more? I have so much to prepare."

"I understand." Weems nods and crinkles his eyes behind his glasses. "Did I hear the voice of your kinsman Mr. Heppert downstairs?" Weems's lips stretch thin across his face. "Does he have any objections? I know of his preference for the more traditional practices."

"Not at all, sir. On the contrary, he is very pleased." A lie can't hurt. What does Judge or Weems care either way?

"That is gratifying." Weems's smile is sour. "Although Mr. Heppert often hides his actions behind his words."

"Yes, well. Is that all?"

"We may put people in the ground, Mrs. Branson, but we cannot put the past in the ground. As long as we remember the past, it is not dead and buried. Just like Mr. Branson. I know he will live on in your heart."

"Yes, of course."

"Mr. Branson knew that, too. That we must not forget the past. Mr. Branson did not forget. He was a man very much aware of it, which is why he was so successful—to a point. I would not support him in some things. I do not believe the Negroes are capable or deserving of the vote. Still, I had a great deal of admiration and respect for him."

"Thank you, Mr. Weems. It means a great deal to me to hear that. If you'll excuse me, I'm sure you can find your way out when you are done here."

"It is a pleasure, Mrs. Branson." He nods and almost bows to me. I will not offer him my hand—not after what he's been doing with his.

Four

THERE SHOULD BE HUNDREDS of acres of land. A warehouse by the depot and lots along the square. He talked about railroads. It's so muddled, but I'm sure he did. He owned some sort of railroad. Or a part of it. There were men here who talked about pig iron. At dinner not too long ago. And a cotton mill. He would bring home the yarn for me. He would say he made it himself. He gave one of the first skeins to Mama when she was alive. There must be something left of all that.

The ice is melting through the cloth. It almost burns, it is so cold. The water streams across my wrist, and I want to scratch at it. I can hardly think for this headache. And this heat, dear Lord, it's hot as an oven in here.

How can Eli have done this? It cannot be. Judge must be mistaken. He seemed to hardly know himself what Eli did and didn't have. Eli's debts? He never seemed to worry about money. Wasn't that what Mama wanted from the marriage? Wasn't that what I married him for?

There was more reason than that. Damn Buck. He's to blame for me marrying Eli. That's not right, either. Mama wanted me to marry Eli. She didn't really know about Buck. It wasn't a baby. No, I did not let it become a baby. But for Emma, I don't know what I would have done. I was too far along for Eli to ever think it was his. Damn Buck.

And Judge, too, he wanted me to marry Eli instead of his own son. He pushed me like Mama did. We always did what Judge said—after Pa died. He decided when Hill and Mike would go to school and where. He treated Hill about like another son. Buck was like his brother. He sent them to the university in Tuscaloosa together.

And then the war broke out.

Weems blames Judge for the war. At least men like Judge. So many men ranted on slavery and secession for so long, there was no room for anything but war. And this is what it got us all. I'm sure Judge believes we would have won but for men like Weems. Judge was never one to compromise. Not until after the war. He went in breathing fire and brimstone, and Weems was scorched by him. Judge was such a fire-breather. He signed the Ordinance of Secession in Montgomery with all those other men. He fired his largest hunting rifle fourteen times from the front yard of his house in honor of the Confederacy. And he outfitted a full company of the 26th Alabama.

While Judge was firing off his rifle, the Weems family was shut inside their house with the shutters closed. They refused to take down their United States flag until someone tore it down and nearly burnt their house down around them. After the secession convention, men came and dragged him and one of his brothers into the street and whipped them like slaves. Calling them yellow dogs and cowards. Eli said Weems thought Judge ordered it, or that Judge's speeches had incited the violence. You don't forget something like that.

Eli wasn't a part of all that. Not then. He was locked away in his counting room. He helped the Yankees, though. That's what Mama said before he started asking to call on me. He was head of the local Bureau of Refugees, Freedmen, and Abandoned Lands by then. Hill was dead. Mike was still missing. It was Eli who came out on top. Out of nowhere he appeared, no name and no family. He had been working at Val Heyward's store, and when Val died, Eli took it over. Eli was smart. Who could say that he was wrong? How many men back then envied him for his influence? He was a moneylender, too. Mama would whisper across the fence to her friends that he robbed graves. And he was a Republican, which was even worse. An opportunist. Among the first to be called scalawag. He led the men like Weems and all the newly freed Negro men into some sort of political party while Judge and men like him were fairly banished. That was when Eli and Weems became friends. And now Judge comes to tell me that everything Eli has is gone. I can't believe it.

When Eli asked me to marry him, I refused to see him and sneaked out to see Judge. There were bluecoats on the street corners. They were boys, war-hardened though, and we had heard so many stories of insults to women. Mama said that the commanding officer wanted to make a show of force in Albion to intimidate the Knights of the White Cross. There seemed too few of them to make any difference.

The Knights had appeared over the winter. They dressed in dark red hooded cassocks emblazoned with a white cross and claimed that they were the fallen crusaders of the war come back to take their vengeance on the Yankees and the freedmen. A Negro man had been found dead, shot in the face on the road to Chattanooga with a whitewash cross on his chest. Since then rumors had spread, each day bringing more tales of Union sympathizers harassed, black families burnt alive in their homes, men hanged from trees, white and black, Republican and scalawag and freedmen, subject to some terrifying justice. They would leave notes scribbled with crossed sabers and owls and coffins, telling whole families they had a few days to leave town. Everyone said the war was over, but there was no end to the dead and wounded. They just didn't print them up on casualty lists anymore.

Judge's house stood amid bare trees. Late in the war they used it to quarter Union soldiers. They took out their wrath on the house as if it had belonged to Jeff Davis. They slashed the chairs and sofas, shattered china that had been in the family for generations. They pilfered the silver and broke up the dining room chairs and tables for firewood. They slashed family portraits and tore open the sofas, looking for hidden money or silver. The kitchen became their cesspit. They scrawled profanities over the French wallpaper.

When the war ended, Judge came back from Montgomery to all that. The soldiers vacated the house, leaving the damage for Judge and Sally. He was kept a prisoner in his house for months because he refused to take the oath.

Sally showed me up the stairs to Judge's study. She must have been a young girl when Judge bought her, before Mrs. Heppert died giving birth to Buck. She was a yellow mulatto and pretty—she still is. As Emma remained with me and Mama, Sally had remained at Judge's side.

"Augusta," Judge said as he rose from his chair. He looked surprised to see me. It was warm in his study. His shirtsleeves were rolled up. Legal books lined the shelves and a pair of chairs sat before a fire. The logs snapped and spat sparks up the chimney. "What are you doing here?"

"Please, Judge, I need your help."

"What is it?" He sat down and watched me.

"It's Mama, Judge. She wants me to marry Eli Branson," I burst out.

"Yes, I know," he said. His voice was tender but resigned. He looked at the pages on the small table beside him. "I would find Mr. Branson objectionable, too, if I were you." He sighed and leaned back in his chair.

"You must stop it, Judge! You must talk to Mama!"

"I have spoken with Elsie. I understand what she thinks she's getting. She says she only has your interest at heart. She believes this is best for you. For both of you."

"Do *you* think it's best for us?" I had my hands out to him, pleading. I debased myself in front of him.

He only shook his head and stared at his papers. "Here," he said, picking up one of the sheets. "This is what *I* am being forced to do."

The page was covered in Judge's clean, even hand. A letter to General Swayne and President Johnson, seeking a pardon.

"There is no possible way they will give it to me unless some sort of miracle occurs. We gambled and lost, and this is what we are compelled to do. Beg forgiveness when we have done nothing to be forgiven. That is the cost of being vanquished." His eyes hardened, and he shook his head again. "I understand your antipathy, Augusta, but I am lucky to have my own freedom. You should consider yourself lucky not to face much worse. It is a stroke of fortune that Eli Branson is courting you. What if you were a plain girl? Where would you and your mother find yourselves? Starving, most likely, like half the families we know. The earth has shifted under our feet."

"That can't be, Judge," I said, thinking of Buck and his betrayal. He had left me alone, and even when I looked for him, I could not find him. Not at his father's house. Not anywhere. I needed desperately to speak to him. He had to know. I had to tell him. I knew if I could speak to him, I could make him marry me. "There must be another way."

"I'm tired, Augusta. And you are trying my patience. I have spoken reason to you, and you won't hear me. There is no other way." He shuffled the papers and picked up his pen, dismissing me without a glance.

"Is—is Buck here?" I asked haltingly.

Judge's eyes held pity or maybe contempt. I could see it. He remained unmoved. "You must put Buck out of your head. It is an unsuitable match."

What an effect those words had on me. I abandoned everything I had thought to say to him. Poor broken Buck. Who knows what was in his heart? He was never the same after the war. No one was. A week later, I was married to Eli. February 10, 1866.

And now Eli is dead. Someone must know about his money. It can't be as simple as Judge says. Judge can't be the only one to know.

Simon is in the far back of the garden. I shouldn't bother him, but I have to ask. No one else knew Eli as Simon did. Simon may not have known Eli that well after all. Who knows? I lived with him for those years, but what did I learn from him? Nothing. I didn't want to learn from him. I assumed the things I knew made me superior to him. Maybe they were. What did that pride gain me? Were they right to make me marry Eli? I don't know. Maybe Simon will.

He is working at one end of the grape arbor. Though the catalpa tree shades him, it is still so hot. He wears leather gloves and rips at a large weed, pulling it up and tossing it aside. The weeds grow in clusters with hairy stems and spiked leaves. He uproots them and then digs into the soil with a trowel, searching for the pale roots that look like undergrown white radishes. He wipes his arm across his forehead. This heat goes on. It's too early for this kind of heat. So heavy and damp. The air feels thick, as if you have to drag it in to breathe.

He stands and grasps a bundle of the weeds and heaves back. They snap and leave their roots behind. He tosses the weeds on the pile. They seem to wilt right away. Some of them have small purple flowers just starting to bloom. The grape vines are a tender green.

"These weeds will spoil the grapes if I let them go," he says. He nods at the pile, his hands on his waist and his face streaked with sweat.

"Simon, you shouldn't be doing any work today."

He nods, looking at the weeds. "I'd rather keep my hands busy, ma'am. And this vetch won't wait for me."

"Is that what it is?"

"Yes, ma'am. It must have blown in here this spring from across the way." He nods at the Sheffield garden. Their carriage house is weathered with split boards. Masses of the purple flowers and spiky leaves climb its sides. He lets out a sigh. He is waiting for me, but I can't speak.

"Is there anything wrong, ma'am?"

"No, Simon." How on earth can I ask him? It's so inappropriate. I was Eli's wife. I should know these things.

"Can I help you with something?" He frowns at me.

I must look a fool, sweating like mad in this black dress. "Yes, I . . ."

"Ma'am?"

"Simon, were you familiar with Mr. Branson's business affairs?" This is ridiculous. Asking a Negro man about my husband's business.

Simon's face doesn't change. He kneels at the vines and picks up the trowel, digging into the earth with a sharp stroke. "To some extent. Did you have some questions about Mr. Branson's business?" He doesn't look at me. He levers up the trowel, and the dirt spills over his hand. The earth falls away and leaves a bundle of the white radish-like roots. Simon handles them loosely. He brushes off the dirt and throws the waste on the pile of dead weeds. It's so hot out here. He shouldn't be working at midday.

"Well, I guess I do. I don't know."

He sticks the trowel deep into the earth and lets it go. He looks up at me. "Did you speak with Mr. Heppert about it?" His expression is bland, and his eyes are calm. But his voice. There is something knowing in his voice.

"Yes, I did."

"He came to you very quickly. Did he have anything to say about Mr. Eli's business affairs?" He goes back to his work, feeling deep in the earth with the trowel and levering it up, searching for more roots.

"Yes, he did. Some things that I find confusing."

"What was confusing?"

"He said that—Well, he said that Eli has gone bust."

Simon separates the dirt from the roots and throws them back on the pile. He puts a hand on the grass to push himself up and stands in front of me. "It's very warm out here. Maybe you'd like to sit under the arbor?"

"Is Eli—is he in so much debt?"

"He had some difficulties in recent years. What did Mr. Heppert tell you?" Simon wipes his hands on his pants, leaving behind traces of earth. He watches me as if he can see the answer in my features, in the number of times I blink or the pace of my breath.

"He said that Eli's estate is tied up with debts. That Eli nearly made the bank go bust. Is it true?"

There is no one around. We are alone.

"I don't know. If it is, I am sure Eli had a good reason for it." Simon looks down at the holes around the grapevines, looking from one to the other as if he is asking them my question. He doesn't even say "Mr. Eli." He is too familiar with everyone. The sticky black earth clings to his gloves.

"I don't see how Eli could be in trouble like that."

"Well, ma'am, I guess politics is an expensive business. People spend a lot of money to keep things running."

"Politics? Judge said it was the panic."

He looks up at me. "Is that what Mr. Heppert said?" He considers for a moment. "I guess he's right, too. He knows as well as anyone the cost of politics."

He goes too far. Is he insulting Judge?

"Judge doesn't need to spend money in politics. He's very respected. He always has been."

Simon almost smiles at me. "Yes, ma'am." He shows a corner of white teeth where his mouth curls on one side. "I am sure he can answer all your questions now that he has taken charge of things."

"Judge is a very accomplished man, Simon."

"Yes, ma'am. You could not find yourself a better adviser."

Simon is full of sarcasms. His tone is flat, but he means to be snide.

"Eli himself respected Judge. Why else would he name him trustee?" The sun is so hot. The sweat streams down my temples so I can't wipe it away fast enough.

Simon raises his eyebrows. "Eli made Mr. Heppert the trustee?"

"Of course. It's in his will."

"Have you seen his will?"

"No, Judge told me. He said he would bring the will to show me."

Simon looks back at the earth. He kneels down and picks up the trowel, poking it at the dirt. "Oh," he says, "that is interesting."

"What do you mean?" My Lord, I sound like my mother. But Simon will answer my question. I won't stand for this impudence. He has told me nothing.

"Nothing at all. I did not realize Eli had so much trust in Mr. Heppert."

"Why wouldn't he?"

Simon looks up at me again, his mouth stretched as if he is repressing a smile. "Miss Gus, it cannot have escaped your understanding that Mr. Heppert and Eli were on opposite sides of a very wide political chasm."

"Yes, I know that, Simon, but they managed to be civil and respect each other. Which is more than you are being to me right now."

His face changes, and he rises to his feet quickly. He is no longer laughing at me. He seems surprised. "I am sorry. I did not mean any disrespect to you, ma'am. Please forgive me if I have offended you."

At least he knows enough to apologize.

"You mentioned that Eli had some money before. When he was sick."

Simon's eyes indicate no recognition or surprise. He is watching me.

"Did you find the money?" I ask. My stomach churns, and I cover it with a hand.

"No, ma'am," Simon answers with no inflection. "I think I must have been mistaken."

"There was a package, wasn't there? Did you find it?"

"No, ma'am, I did not."

"But you have looked for it?"

"Yes, ma'am, I did some looking. As I said, I think I was mistaken."

He looks at the pile of weeds, his hands at his sides. He must be hiding something. There must be more that he knows.

"Excuse me," Simon says, "I'll be getting back to my work." He turns his back to me and grasps a thick clump of vetch. He pulls at it, tearing again at the soil and tossing the plants aside.

The laudanum is working. I should have kept it with me. Why did I put it back in Eli's room? I can barely breathe in there, but thank God

Weems got the work done. Eli's face is like a wax mask. Poor Eli. Ten years with him, and what did he get? What did I get? No one seems to know.

I should stay away from the laudanum. Eli did not like it. Mama never did, either. But I need something for this headache. And no one saw me cross the hall. It was a small dose. It is because of this tremendous heat. What is left for me after almost ten years? And what will Henry get?

Unanticipated shocks? I could almost laugh at Judge, although he would never abide laughter. And he is the only one to know. I should not have asked Simon. Foolish of me. What could Simon tell me anyway? Yes, Judge knows the shocks. He knows that I know them. Since Pa died, it has been nothing but shocks. The war. Hill going to battle with Buck. The deaths and the loss.

When North Alabama fell, we could hardly believe it. That was all after the battle at Shiloh. I was still at school in Huntsville. Our soldiers seemed to give up without a whisper of a fight. The whole Tennessee River and the Oosanatee along with it abandoned to them.

I was fourteen. Albert Sidney Johnston rode through Huntsville on his way to join Beauregard and the western army at Corinth before the battle. My girlfriends and I lined up along Eustis Street, waiting for him to pass. He was dashing, with a large feather waving from his hat and his long mustaches hanging to his chin. A few weeks later, he was dead. The horrible numbers of dead and wounded flooded into town on the railroad. And then nothing. The trains stopped. There were rumors everywhere, and as if on the breeze suddenly the Yankees were around us. Soldiers on leave and politicians still in their nightshirts ran from their homes before dawn. We weren't even surrounded, we were simply overwhelmed.

Jennie Heyney's father took us both back to Albion in a great barouche with a safe passage from the Yankee general. Mr. Heyney died in the sickness that came after the war. Cholera or dysentery or something. Mama squeezed me so hard when she saw me, and Emma was crying, too. Mike kept asking if I'd seen any dead bodies, and we had, though I didn't tell him. Two men in blue jackets and homespun trousers dead in the woods off the turnpike. Stragglers or sharpshooters or bandits. Mr. Heyney told his coachman Old George to drive on fast. But we saw them, Jennie and I. Faces upturned, bloated and black in the sun, swarming with flies and God knows what else, left there to rot among the pines.

That was the war. Albert Sidney Johnston killed, along with thirty thousand dead and wounded. Six times the number of people in Albion. Inconceivable. Horrible beyond comprehension. Who were they all? Where were their families? Didn't it mean anything? But it was the war. We had to defend ourselves. Jennie had a brother in the 26th Alabama, like me. Even Mr. Heyney looked gray.

Who was I then? Am I still that girl?

I am Gus Sedlaw. I cannot forget my name. Augusta Belier Blackwood Sedlaw. And then Branson, a name I will bear like the mark of Cain until I die. Eli's name that was put upon me. Ten years ago, I was not married. But wanted to be, I think. Who knows what I wanted or what I was thinking. That day did not seem possible until it happened. Like Eli dying. When I talk about my marriage, it will be about a thing that no longer exists. Ten years gone in a moment. None of that matters now, anyway.

Mama wanted it so. She knew Eli was not a good match. Not by the old standards. The war wiped away all that. Our name meant something before. And I suppose Eli thought it meant something, too. For Mama, our name meant nothing if we didn't know how we would eat or if we would keep our home. The blood of the Blackwoods and the Sedlaws to be united with the scalawag Branson, and in the front parlor of the house my father had built.

Sedlaw is a fine old name. Pa told me he came to Albion from Nashville when he was a young man, just as his father and mother had come to Nashville from the Virginia Tidewater with their old names. They bought virgin lands, leading gangs of slaves who burned the forests and tore up the charred tree stumps. They planted cotton, tobacco, and corn, and they speculated in tracts along the Cumberland and Harpeth rivers, the Duck and the Elk, along the Tennessee and the Oosanatee. Pa said he inherited five hundred acres in Riverbend County and fifty slaves. When he died, he owned 234 slaves and 2,500 acres. He was a planter and a politician. A gentleman.

There was no difference between Pa's family and Mama's, even if Mama and Judge shared the Blackwood name. Mama's parents came with Judge's, their mothers Blackwood sisters. They must have been rugged women. Tough and tireless, traveling overland in a long wagon train to the Oosanatee valley from up-country South Carolina. They cleared out the Indians with a gentle push from President Jackson. "When I was a boy," Judge always says, "there was nothing here but Indians and rattlesnakes." The rattlesnakes are still here.

Sedlaw. Blackwood. And Belier, from my mother's grandmother, who is buried somewhere in the swampy rice lands of South Carolina. Wardwell, from my mother's father, like Judge is a Heppert from his father. They are names of quality of which I am proud. I was taught to be proud. This town that they built, Albion, was a place of which they were proud. My grandfather Wardwell and great-uncle Heppert and our Blackwood kin. They came here with their families, white and black, to carve civilization out of the raw wilderness. And they did make a civilization here. If anything, they were too proud of what they had made.

But the names go on in spite of anything we do. Adams, Hilliard, Belier, Blackwood, Wardwell, Sedlaw. And now Branson. From father to son and mother to daughter. Like in the Bible. I am connected to the past by these names, as if all the actions of my father and his father and his father's father are contained in my veins, are pulsing in the blood pushed by my heart. The names go on forever if you look deep enough. An honored name is a tradition of greatness. Of achievement, like the Blackwoods, who have been governors and senators and held positions of power even before there was a United States. But all that's past now. Pa is gone and Mama is gone. Hill is gone and the house on Allen Street. My name is different.

That first night with Eli, he brought me to this house. It was the Chapmans' house before. They moved to Nashville so Hugh could find work in spite of his one leg. I had sung a duet with Carrie in the parlor downstairs at the war's start. Carrie sang so sharp.

"Better for them to go than stay here and starve," Eli said. He put a hand on my shoulder and walked me inside. Emma was right behind us. It was dark and dusty in the house but still the same. The paintings were mostly gone, but the tables and chairs, lamps and ornaments were all there as they had been four years before. The pianoforte was still in the music room. It was like a ghost house, filled with the past.

Emma took my arm. "Let me help her out of these clothes, Mr. Branson," she said. We knew the house better than he did. She took me up the stairs, holding my hand and almost pulling me along. She closed the door and came to me, wrapping her arms around me.

"Shh, now, honey," she said over and over. "Don't worry, Emma is here. Emma will take care of you."

I cried into her breast like a baby. "Emma, what will I do? I can't do it. I can't."

"Shh," she said. "Don't worry, honey. It doesn't take long."

"Emma, I don't know what to do."

Emma wiped at my face with the edge of the cloak. She removed Mama's garland of wax orange blossoms that I had half crushed. "You don't have to do anything, Miss Gus. And if you don't want his baby, you don't have to do that, either," she said softly. "There are ways to keep from it. I know some ways."

Emma pulled a piece of cotton wadding from her pocket. It was smeared with sheep fat, and she told me how to use it. She knew medicines, too, bottled medicines that could bring on my flow. That was the answer I needed. I was sick from the medicine for a week after I took it. I thought it might kill me, but I would not have minded then.

"Do you have them with you?" I asked her, and she nodded. She looked at the small carpetbag packed with her things.

Eli knocked at the door and Emma opened it. She curtsied to him and left us. I was silent. I knew what he came for. My God, of course that was what he came for.

And that first night, how awful it was. Awful and groping and wet. That first night, I felt like I had died in that bed.

Five

THE SEAMSTRESS STABS ME with her needle. The pain is sharp, like a bee sting. We look at each other until she turns her eyes away, the needle suspended in her fingers between us.

"I'm sorry, Mrs. Branson," she says. She has a mountain accent, was probably a refugee during the war who came to town and never left. "Please stay as still as you can."

Eli will be buried soon. In an hour or two. Mourners are arriving, waiting for me downstairs, but I won't hurry the women. I shift a little on my feet, slowing their hands, risking another barb from the needle.

Another woman on her knees works at my hem. They have been sewing for two days, virtually since Eli died, to make the dress. The pattern came with an engraving from *Godey's* where a young widow with drooping eyes holds a bunch of lilies in her hand. *Godey's* painted it in shades of gray and lilac, but for me it must be all black. The perfect picture of mourning. There is an art to mourning. We have all learned it well. There is a cost, too. Judge will have to settle the bills.

We are in the room with the pink-ribboned wallpaper, across the hall from Eli's room, closer to Henry. The wallpaper has garlands of climbing flowers entwined with the ribbons. A white girl has brought boxes of veils and lays them across the bed and on the backs of chairs, reminding me of the house on Allen Street during Mama's funeral. Black veils of the gauziest tulle and sheerest English net shimmer in the sunlight. The room is so beautiful swagged in black. I want them all.

Judge was in such a rush to see me after Eli died. Not a word from him since then. How can any of it be true? He says he will take care of everything. He will find out what Eli has left. For Henry and for me. Judge can say what he likes, but I know it is not really for Henry, not while Judge is the trustee. Judge is the owner. The real owner. I want to see the will. To see the words written in Eli's hand. To see his signature. And to see who the witnesses were.

"There you are, ma'am. All done." The women get up from their knees and look at me. They have finished, and it is a lovely thing. My reflection eyes me from the mirror, turning from side to side, assessing me, appreciating me. A fragile figure in black grenadine with a polonaise trimmed in low flounces over a black satin underskirt. Dozens of silk-covered buttons line the sleeves and the front of the basque up to my throat.

"You look like a real queen, Miss," the woman with the accent says. She takes pins from her mouth and sticks them into her white apron near her breast.

"Thank you," I say, and step down from the stool. They gather their cases and small, delicate scissors. They nod as they depart, taking the back stairs, leaving me alone with the girl. An awkward thing, a country girl with crooked teeth that make her "shh" through her sentences. I believe her name is Mary.

She approaches me with a veil, spreading it out across her arms to avoid catching the smooth, sheer cloth. I drape it over my small hat of shell-shaped black chip. The veil is exquisitely black, trimmed with a fringe of tiny jet beads that descend in shameless luxury almost to the hem of my skirt. The beads click against each other, a soft, comforting sound.

"I will keep all these for now, Mary. I'll send the ones I don't want back to Miss Graves tomorrow." Mary makes a graceless curtsey and takes the back stairs, too. I am alone.

The voices in the hall and the noise of shuffling feet travel up the stairwell along with the thud of horses' hooves in the dry, dusty street. There is a breath of air through the door to the sitting room that faces Greene Street. The windows are wide open. A chair sits near the window with a view onto the street and the lawn, and I move it back so as not to be seen. An old oak creates a shade for me, and I watch through its tortured branches as if they are a Spanish screen.

Carriages line Greene Street. Mr. Weems has Negro grooms-men taking horses and holding reins as the mourners arrive, flock-ing the sidewalk in blacks and grays and lavenders. The men gather on the lawn, old men whom I have known since childhood. They idle with their sons, now adults, all on their way to infirmity. The women pluck at their black skirts and wield black parasols against the sun. They do not bide their time outdoors but rush inside, hoping to escape the heat. The men kick at the turf and spit to-bacco juice on the roots of the oak. They talk and laugh as if they are on the square at court day. They talk about cotton and the heat and the lack of rain. They talk about John Breckinridge, who died two weeks ago, but the news still seems fresh. He ran for presi-dent in 1860, one of the candidates who fractured the Democrats. He lost like the others and fought for the Confederacy, always in-sisting Kentucky would follow him. It didn't, but they talk about him like he was a hero. They talk about Reverend Henry Ward Beecher and the adultery trial in Brooklyn, laughing at the Yankee scandal. They talk about Senator Spencer—Eli's friend, an impor-tant friend—and the investigation into how he bought his Senate seat with bribes and threats and even begged President Grant for more troops in Alabama to help the Republicans win. They talk about a Negro man who was hanged from a bridge in Nashville after he was beaten. They say he attacked a white woman. They say his body is still hanging off that bridge God knows how many days later. Let that be a lesson to them, they say.

And always before the war. They say it again and again. Before the war. Before the war. It is our common currency. The only way we understand things. What do I know of before the war? I was barely more than a child. It seems that nothing really existed before the war, certainly nothing that I was aware of. I remember the house full of servants and Pa always writing something, scratching his pen against paper. Hill laughed all the time, pulling pranks. I remember going with Mama on her calls and Cicero, our old coachman who drove us. He ran off with the Yankees in '64 and died of typhus at their camp in Nashville.

All those things remembered are nothing next to what I felt before the war. Back then everything was certain. Like the rising and setting of the sun each day. Like the seasons and the rains that come and go. I guess I remember most the garden on Allen Street, spread out around our home with groves of trees and trimmed boxwoods and wide lawns that went to the bluffs over the river. You could look across the valley to the hills in the distance and almost see forever.

That feeling of before the war, that sense of being in this quiet town on the banks of the Oosanatee, a name like so many Indian names that blanket this place, a name that seemed to dictate the languid cadence of the days. Oosanatee. I remember late summer, when the air moved so gently it was like a caress. I remember lying on the shade-dappled lawn, somnolent in the thick clover, feeling my body vibrate with the buzz of the earth, the beautiful, almost fluid warmth of the sun soaking through me. The river, flat and winding through the trees below, glittering with sunlight. The little Oosanatee set deep in a forested valley with the scent of clover and jasmine in the air like the land of the lotus-eaters.

The memory is so real to me. It brings tears to my eyes. And then I married Eli, and we all became afraid of each other. My family. My friends. The people I had known my whole life. Our world had changed so much, I guess none of us knew whom to hate and whom to love anymore. We became afraid of our neighbors. Afraid of our freed slaves, people we used to say were our family. But we have learned to live with fear. We have become accustomed to it. We gladly traded the chaos of the war for it. Better to know what to fear than to fear all the things that you don't know.

"Miss Gus."

Emma's voice. She is watching me from the door.

"Miss Gus," she repeats. Her skin is dark—not coal black, but dark brown, like a chestnut. She has grown thick as she has aged, and she was never tall to begin with. I guess I didn't realize how much older she is than I. Probably by twenty years. Maybe a little less. She doesn't know her age herself, since she was purchased as a young girl to help in the kitchen when my parents were first married.

When I was born, she must have been young. A young woman. Maybe my age when I was first married. But now the gray has grizzled her hair, which she keeps pulled back in a tight chignon. There are deep lines that crease from her eyes to the corners of her mouth. And her hands are thick and calloused. Tough hands that have seen years of work. She stands at the door wearing the same simple black dress she always wears, as if she is in some perpetual mourning. She looks at me as if I were twelve again. Just like the days before the war. I wonder if she would go back there as easily as I would. I can't imagine what her answer would be if I asked her, and I would never ask her.

She has been with me my whole life. I have never been afraid of Emma. Never. She is devoted. Quiet. Sad. She smiles at me, a faint smile. It is because of the new dress. Or this veil. "There are ladies downstairs asking for you. I've been putting them in the music room."

An irrepressible smile spreads across my face and I pull down my veil. I must look like some sort of haunt. Emma shakes her head, still smiling, and I follow her down the stairs.

The hall is filled with voices from the front parlor, masculine voices that make little effort at being subdued, although the coffin must be there by now. Mike is there. His voice is higher than the rest, loud and slurred. Buck is not among the men I can hear. Perhaps he will not come. If he were here, surely I would feel it.

The music room is across the hall from the front parlor. Emma weaves through the crowd. They fall silent as I pass, and soon there is a hush. Emma opens the door to the music room.

It is dark. The shadows and black cloth seem to blend. Great swells of bombazine and barege fill the room, along with flurrying ribbons of crape and velvet and great veils pinned against black bonnets. They are like so many crows picking their way under the trees. Black-gloved hands reach out for me, resting on my arms and head. Soft black kid falls on my cheeks and against my hair. They lift my veil from my face as the door closes behind me.

"Poor dear," they murmur, and "Poor darling." "Come sit." "How are you, dear?" and "It's been too long, Gus." They speak in soft whispers of consolation. Jennie Heyney puts her arm through mine and walks me into the room. They surround me. We are all in black and time has stopped. The dark shadows of the shuttered music room and the blackness of the cloth hide whatever might be threadbare between us. They pet and coo at me like a foundling child. And all I can think is that Eli left no money. How can it be?

"Gus, what a beautiful veil."

"Gus, what a lovely dress."

"Augusta, you look so young. Why, you could be sixteen."

"Gus, with those eyes, you won't wait long."

"Great blazes, let her sit, won't you? Bring her here to me." The women part like the Red Sea to reveal Alabama Buchanan. She sits perched on the edge of a high-backed side chair and pats a gloved hand on the seat next to her. "Here, Gus. Come and sit."

How many years since Bama spoke to me so familiarly? And that name. Her overenthusiastic father was a delegate from Albion to the state convention in 1819, when she was born. The Buchanans have always been an important family in Albion, but childless Bama lost Colonel Buchanan at Gettysburg and never remarried. She recovered his body—some unwitting Yankee farmer plowed him up, and a note was found pinned to his coat with his name and company written on it, legible after six years. The colonel is buried in the New Cemetery along with the other recovered sons. After all that, Bama found herself fairly destitute, like the rest of us. Like I may be again. At least she held on to her plantations. Virtually everyone around me, these ladies, is supported by the meager cotton crops that have been pulled by tenant farmers from what remains of their families' lands. Cotton is not what it used to be.

Bama grabs my hand, glove to glove, and pulls me onto the chair next to her. "It is hot, isn't it?" she says. Her smile shows a gap on the side where the barber pulled three teeth. She squeezes my hand. "The fever will be coming up early from the river this year." The room rustles with fabric and fans.

"Mr. Branson didn't die of the yellow fever, did he, Gus?" Sally Mabry asks.

"No, Sally," I answer. "It was a blood disorder."

"Oh, Gus," she gushes suddenly. "It's just so good to see you." She behaves as if we were still at school in Huntsville. She rushes to me and hugs me impulsively. The women nod as if they agree.

"That's right, Gus," Bama intones in her gruff voice. She grabs Sally's arm and pushes her away without ceremony. "And rather than smother you with mourning, we want you to know that you are welcome back. Welcome home, Gus."

The pale, black-framed faces look down on me with sympathy, but they are reserved. That coldness, the bitterness of loss and deprivation, is in their eyes.

"It came on so sudden, didn't it?" Mattie Hearns shakes her yellow curls from the edges of her bonnet as she speaks, her blue eyes wide with excitement. "I mean his illness. I heard it happened so fast?"

"It did," I answer, looking around the room at their faces. "I—"

Bama interrupts me. "Yes, and so it should be proper to bury him quickly. I quite think you are right to put an end to this sooner rather than dwell on it."

"Of course."

"Was it very gruesome?" Caroline Lensch speaks with her handkerchief to her mouth. "Was there a terrible lot of blood?"

"Carrie, enough," Bama interjects as I sit mute. "Let's leave Augusta alone. It's enough that she is burying her husband today."

Mrs. Mastin steps from the shadows. "But what was it, Gus? Was it cholera? My daughter is ready to pack up her boys and get on the train to Chattanooga. Lord help us, it'll be just like after the war, when smallpox and typhoid was everywhere." She trembles as Beth comes forward.

"Mama, please," her daughter says. "I didn't say that!"

"It's from those shanties across from the railroad," the old woman goes on. "Those coloreds and poor whites. Remember, Bama, after the war? It was like a plague over the whole town. The niggers and the soldiers brought it with them. And things are worse than ever over there. People living in squalor. Your husband mixed with that lot—out at that mill. We'll all be sick from it soon!"

"It wasn't typhoid," I say uneasily. "It was—it was a blood disorder—the heat—it affected Mr. Branson."

Bama casts a hard glance at the women around us. Their fear surprises me. The things they know surprise me. Bama coughs without covering her mouth, a loud hacking sound, and then speaks. "Ladies, if it was something for us to worry about, you know old Greer would have told us. None of us would be here otherwise."

"Well, Dr. Greer is talking." Sally Mabry again.

"He is talking some nonsense that we'd all best ignore. He's not talking about typhoid or malaria or smallpox, God forbid, and we will leave it at that. We all know how Greer is now."

An uneasy quiet settles over the room. Their faces are half shrouded in shadow. Who are they? These are not the women I knew during the war. They are changed women—changed faces that I cannot recognize. The hard bite of circumstance has changed us all, and they look at me, too, as a stranger.

"It is a shame, Gus," Bama says with a long sigh. "If Mr. Branson had died two weeks ago, you could have come down to the cemetery with us for Decoration Day." Someone gasps while someone else titters behind her fan. "Hilliard is down there, isn't he?"

I have to wait a moment before I answer. "No," I say. "No, his body was never found."

It is quiet again. Bama reaches out for my hand and squeezes. "Yes," she says. "I am sorry. I am forgetful."

"Miss Gus," Emma says anxiously. "You should come." She slipped into the room as silent as a ghost. The women step back from her and turn their heads.

She leads me into the hall. Sunlight floods in from the open front door. The brightness is painful after the shadows of the music room. There are more visitors, men and women. I don't know half of them. There are the Yankee officers, although most of them no longer serve in the army and have put away their blue uniforms. They have businesses here, or land in the county that they call farms. The bankers and newspapermen are here with their wives. They crowd the hall with their beaver hats and fans trimmed in ivory and feathers. They jostle me and excuse themselves. But for my dress, many would not even know who I am.

Outside, the men are still on the lawn. Eli's coffin is visible through the open front windows, sitting in the middle of the parlor crowded with mourners. The men have stopped talking and face the street, cigars poised in their hands. Some stand on their toes. Just beyond them, Judge's voice is booming. He is on the sidewalk, practically in the street, shouting and waving his hat at a group of Negroes from town. Some of them used to hang around the kitchen door, asking to see Eli or idling with Rachel and Emma.

"Now, get on with you all," he says, and he sounds angry. "Only friends and relations here. Get on with you!"

Emma pushes forward through the last line of mourners, and one of them calls back at her, "Mind yourself, nigger." His voice has a Northern twang. The hometown men have their eyes trained on Judge, some with hands on their hips, as if reaching for pistols. My God, bringing guns to a funeral? It's indecent. But they would line up in military formation, like in their army days, with a single gesture from Judge. They must be here for him. They are certainly not here for Eli.

We reach the black fence that runs along Greene Street. I grab hold of the pointed finials and lean against the cast-iron palings. "Judge," I call. "What's the matter?"

"See here, Augusta," he says, approaching the fence. "You don't need to be out here exposing yourself like this. You go on back into the house."

"What do they want?" I ask.

"They say they want to pay their respects to Eli." There are two dozen Negroes in the street. Some of the men wear suits, and some are dressed no better than field hands. Some wear black armbands and hold their derby hats in their hands. There are women, too, in black dresses and others in somber calicos and osnaburgs, dark colors like their dusky skin. They watch with stony faces, stubborn and resistant. "Augusta, you get on inside," Judge repeats. "You don't need to be bothered with this nonsense." His face is red, and it makes his whiskers turn pink, like the skin of a white rabbit. He turns back to the gathering group. "If you don't want any trouble," he says to the crowd, "you'd better get going."

Emma eases closer to me. "Miss Gus," she whispers low, so no one else can hear. "Ain't they got a right to mourn Mr. Eli like anybody else?" She meets my eyes evenly. "Don't you remember when Old Master died, didn't we all—all his people—get to walk with him to his grave?"

Mama and I rode in the carriage while Hill and Mike walked behind the hearse. Behind us, the whole town and virtually every servant in the neighborhood walked in silent mourning, such was the great love my father's people felt for him. They came all the way from the farthest plantations in the county simply to walk him to his burial place.

Emma watches the men and women in the street. "It ain't no different here, Miss Gus," she presses. "They just want to give him their respects for all the things he did for them."

"Judge, please," I call. "Let them pay their respects." My face is hot and everyone's eyes are on me. "When Pa died, his people gave him his due. They want to do the same for Mr. Branson."

Judge looks hard at me, his nostrils flared. He is caught, though it is not my intention to trap him. He can hardly defy a widow's request in front of the whole town. He knows too well how petty such behavior would seem.

"Fine, then," he mutters and turns back to the Negroes in the street. "You stay behind this fence and you keep your distance. You show your respect. You hear?" He sneers at them. The Negroes stand stonily silent. Everyone is silent. The men on the lawn have stopped their nattering and part for Emma and me. Simon is at the back of the hall, tall and somber. He nods to me, just as stony as the Negroes on the street.

Pastor Peekum stands in the front parlor near the casket, rubbing his thin bony hands around a worn leather Bible.

"We're ready for the service, sir," I whisper in his ear, and he nods coldly. Bama comes and sits beside me. Rachel has brought Henry from the nursery, and I squeeze him against me. He is mystified, awed by the people in the house and how they handle him. They squeeze his cheeks and his plump arms, declaring they see the Sedlaws or the Blackwoods in him yet.

There is no eulogy. The idea is vulgar. The mourners will in no way appreciate a litany of Eli's merits. There are no pallbearers, either. Mr. Weems has hired four men to serve in their place. Weems agreed with me that it was ill advised to ask a group of citizens to so distinguish themselves.

Peekum gives a hellfire-and-brimstone service. He is from the Holy Blood of the Redeemer Baptist Church on the west side of town. It was Eli's church before our marriage, and Peekum was Eli's pastor. I never went there. Mama and Henry and I always went to the Presbyterian church. Eli hardly went to church anyway.

Peekum is ascetic, with rough stubble on his chin and cheeks. He says that we all face a final accounting before God that will make the experiences of the late war a trivial dance. He says we must beg forgiveness for our sins and that even contrition may not be enough to save us. He agreed to give a short sermon, but he keeps talking. He shouts about Jesus in the garden at Gethsemane, alone, kneeling in prayer and knowing he would be crucified. He sweat great drops like blood as he prayed.

The heat rises in the parlor and chairs creak. Fans make a rush of sound without seeming to stir the air. The murmur of voices comes in from the street. We sit with our backs to the windows.

Pastor Peekum says that we sin, and the ineffable stains like blood are on our hands. That we are like beasts that ravage through God's garden. We walk the winding path of salvation and stray from it, indulging our avarice, our lust, with gluttonous indulgence. "Turn back," he cries, "turn back and follow the Lord before you are washed away in a flood of holy blood poured down on us from heaven. Repent."

Is he condemning Eli or praising him? I grab Henry's hand, and he looks up at me, frightened. I shake my head at him. What sins might I have committed to warrant such a sermon? These backwoods preachers will take any opportunity to shout the devil at you.

Henry is beside me on the gravel drive. A horse stands harnessed to a black hearse. The animal is dressed in black leather bridles and black silk bunting. Black ostrich plumes spring from his black blinders. The hearse has clear glass windows on all sides, and the coffin sits displayed inside it, piled with greenery and lilies of the valley. Henry's hand is fast in mine, and we watch the crowd milling on the lawn and Greene Street. The hearse rolls forward and then back with the anxious movement of the horse.

The group of Negroes on the street has grown. I cannot count them all, but they stand watching and waiting, maybe one hundred of them, maybe more. They fill the street up to the corner, fanning themselves in the sun with palmettos and newspapers and hats. They are waiting for a sign, for a movement—and I have to give it. I lead Henry away from the group of ladies gathered at the corner of the house. Judge watches as we approach.

Buck is a few steps behind Judge. He is with Mike, who weaves on his feet, obviously drunk. Buck holds Mike's arm. He looks at me and gives a subtle bow. His face is sad but so handsome. I am glad he cannot see me through my veil. Heat burns my cheeks. Still so handsome. It has been two years since I last saw him. His hair is black with a hint of gray coming in at the temples. He has a long mustache like a cavalryman. Like General Custer. A dashing look. I squeeze Henry's hand and walk past without a sign. I can feel that hunger, like an itch deep in my belly, dead so long I didn't think I could feel it again.

Judge meets me as we near the hearse and scowls at me. "What's all this about?" he demands.

"I am going to walk behind the hearse, Judge. It's my place and my son's place." I say it breathlessly. He stands silent. He believes women and children should be hidden in the carriage. He can tell me no. Surely he would not insist with the whole town watching. I have pushed him too much already today.

"Fine, then. Let's get on with it." He walks back and speaks to Buck and Mike. They are all waiting, black and white, men and women, watching me. The breeze presses the veil against my face and shoulders. It flutters against Henry's arm. I nod at Simon to begin, and he tugs on the horse's bridle. The horse jerks forward, but Simon's hand steadies him into a slow, even pace.

There is a rumble of steps behind us as we enter the street. All of those people like some solemn army marching along, men and women, friends and family, and the hundred Negroes who have come to bury Eli. We move in a strange and grand procession to put this body in the ground, to bury with it all that he means to each of us. To forget him and the past. Not like Weems said. We all want to forget. We want to bury this body and forget him.

The procession moves slowly down Greene Street under the oaks and elms. The air is so still, nothing moves except the shuffling feet. The old brick homes watch us as we pass. They were all so fine once. Now many seem like ghost houses with gaping mouths and blank eyes. Their wrought-iron gates are rusted, and weeds climb their walls as if to swallow them whole. The boxwoods grow unkempt and wild. The lawns are more thistle and dandelion than grass. They grow tall in front of the houses as if to hide them for shame.

The New Cemetery spreads out behind a low stone wall, mostly wide lawns and young trees. Graves are scattered sparsely, except for the small field of white-painted crosses commemorating the men of Albion dead from the war. Eli will lie in a spot of green lawn shaded by young oaks where a red-earth hole has been opened. There is a plot for me next to him. From the brick-walled entrance, I can clearly see it. The black box in front of me will be lowered into it, and he will become one among the legion of dead who haunt this town.

Behind us, at first as a low hum, there is singing. The harmony begins to rise into a full song. The Negroes are singing. The men behind me pause in their steps, twisting their feet in the dirt, turning to look. I can tell which footsteps are Buck's. He is a few feet behind me. I can hear the crunch of Judge's shoes, too, just behind me. And Mike's stumbling tread. He hangs against Buck as they walk. All of those feet pressing me. Henry's hand is damp from the heat. This relentless heat and those footsteps. Purposeful steps like marching soldiers. The singing grows louder. Murmurs wash over the crowd of mourners, but I look ahead, my eyes on the hearse and coffin, on Simon's black hand holding the reins of the black horse. The voices rise as more of the Negroes begin to sing to the rhythm of this funeral march. The strangeness of it. The disturbing strangeness of it.

> *Lord, I can't stay here by myself*
> *By myself*
> *My mother has gone and left me here*
> *My father has gone and left me here*
> *I'm going to weep like a willow*
> *And mourn like a dove*
> *O Lord, I cannot stay here by myself*

Six

THE MORNINGS HAVE BECOME strands of quiet moments that grow into afternoons and afternoons into days. It feels like Judge will never come. This heat won't relent. Perspiration beads Henry's forehead and makes his blond hair stick to his temples. The servants move slowly. No work can be done at midday. The town seems asleep from noon to four, and even outside of those hours, few riders pass under the windows.

Late each afternoon, a bank of clouds rolls in, dark and ominous, and yet the rain does not come. The nights are sweltering and restless.

The street is empty. I half expect a caller. Someone must come eventually. I am more a prisoner of this house than I was before Eli died. I could at least go out before, but now mourning keeps me here alone. Where can I go anyway?

Away, but for the money. I could leave Albion and this prison and these ghosts and go away. When will I hear from Judge? How can Eli have done this?

Simon is working in the front yard. He is always toiling in the garden. He seems so calm. He pushes the lawn mower, a whirring contraption that has a canister filled with spiraling blades that move inside each other in a dizzying whirl. Back and forth, it whines with each push, back and forth across the grass from the fence to the boxwoods. The grass is lush. Simon will hand-carry water each day from the pump, little by little, until it rains.

The garden used to be mine, but Simon took it from me. He was right to take it from me. After that first year with Eli, all I could manage was the garden, even if I did become distracted. Sometimes the honeysuckle grew wild up the back porch posts. And in the fall, those dead gray tendrils stubbornly clung to the peeling paint. There were summers when the garden looked as untended as our neighbors'.

Then Simon stepped in. He asked permission of me to maintain the hedges, then subtly suggested planting climbing roses by the front door. He remembered, he said, delivering messages by the Chapman house before Eli bought it and always admiring the tender pink roses there. By summer's end, he had taken over. I assume it was with my consent. Perhaps I agreed to it all at a time when I was—not myself.

But the lawns are clean and clipped. The trees are pruned and heavy with budding fruit. Irises line the walks, rioting with flowers. All the climbing vines by the front door bear soft pink roses that give a sweet smell that comes to me in my upstairs sitting room. The faintest scent of roses when the perfume is carried on the breeze, like a tiny, unexpected gift. I love to look out upon the flower beds, to smell the roses, and to watch them change from season to season. To see the work and care that Simon takes with them, as if it is all done especially for me.

The servants are quiet when I enter the room. Their conversations stop midsentence. They will resume as soon as I leave. I hear them talking as they do chores, gathering the laundry off the line from the end of the garden or in the kitchen. They've started whispering because they think I'm listening. I surprise them too often. I walk in on Simon standing in the rear parlor or in Eli's office, staring at the walls. Then he nods and leaves without a word. It would be different if I had something to do. But Judge keeps me waiting. He tells me Eli's money is gone and then forgets about me. And there is something going on with the servants. I know it. They look at me sidelong when I walk by. They watch me from the windows when I am in the garden.

Rachel is with John in the carriage house. Henry's feet scrape on the gravel, and his prattle keeps me from hearing. If we were closer, I might hear more. Rachel says she is unhappy.

"Henry, shush," I whisper.

She tells John he should be worried.

Just one step closer, holding Henry's hand as we step onto the quiet grass.

She tells him that he should be a man for their family. That he should lead. If she were in charge, they'd already be gone. John tells her he is the head of the family and he will make the decisions. Not likely, with Rachel as a wife. John should have thought of that before they married. He says that he has been watching her and Simon. He wants her to tell him what is going on. She is laughing at him.

The air is so hot and still, and the only sound is the heavy drone of the cicadas. On and on the cicadas chirp. The background to a domestic squabble. I never had a domestic squabble with Eli. There was no need. There was nothing for us to squabble about. When Eli was angry with me, I couldn't respond. He would chide me for coldness to our guests and then say I was too warm with the Yankee officers. When he hired Rachel, I told him she had a bad reputation and I would not welcome her into the house. His face turned bright red, and he blustered on about the Negroes and second chances and Christian charity. He flapped his arms up and down like a pelican. I couldn't answer. I could only laugh hysterically into my hand until I was almost in tears. Absolute tears. I was almost out of my senses. He left the room, confounded, I guess. The next day he brought Rachel to me so that I could welcome her to the house. My protests were always for nothing.

After Henry was born, all Eli really expected from me was that I listen. He would talk at dinner and in the evening if we did not have guests. I knew by then to nod and smile or make some encouraging noise. He would talk on and on about the Republicans and Negroes and trying to keep the party together and cotton and railroads and progress. He always left money in a box in his office that I was free to take, although I barely touched it. All my accounts at the stores in Albion or Nashville or New Orleans were paid without question, regardless of the extravagance. Maybe it was wrong to spend so much, but I felt pushed almost to see if there was an item that he would find unacceptable or ostentatiously expensive. Ruby earrings. Gilded cameos. Brooches of gold filigree studded with tourmaline. Nothing seemed to ruffle him or even make him raise an eyebrow. Now the bills are stacked on my dressing table. Emma brings them to me one by one as they arrive. What am I to do with them?

"Do you think he'll come today?" Emma asks me as she buttons the loose black sleeves of my dress. A fine new one just arrived from the dressmaker. I don't know if I have the money to pay for it, but Judge is managing the estate. Surely he can find the money somewhere. The handwritten note it came with is on the bed. Graves is requesting payment for the dress and all those veils. The servants' wages are due as well. How long will they endure my pretending to be unaware? If only Judge would come.

"I don't know," I answer, extending an arm for her. "I hope he does."

Her face is impassive. We both jump from the crash of Henry's toy train against the floor. He sits near the wall where there is no rug, rolling the train back and forth.

"Henry, shush," I say. He looks at me and then at Emma, who smiles at him.

She must have respected Eli. Cared for him, too? Like all those colored people who came to Eli's funeral. There were so many. "The Negroes loved Eli, didn't they, Emma?"

She does not look at me as she slips each button through its eye. "Yes, ma'am, they certainly did." She nods when she says it.

"Were you very fond of him?"

"I was, ma'am, in my way." She will not look at me. Emma is always shy of people's eye. "He did more for us than many people have. Other than Mr. Lincoln."

"Did he?"

"He tried to help us get along. Mr. Eli, he always tried to help us get along."

I look away. I don't know why it irritates me to hear her praise of Eli. "Well, maybe now he'll help me get along, too."

Emma represses a smile. She keeps her attention on the buttons. "You want to move on so bad, Miss Gus? Where are you going to?"

"Emma," I exclaim, "you're coming with me!"

"Well, Miss Gus—"

"Emma, you must. I can't possibly travel alone with Henry. And you know Rachel won't go. How could I get on without you?"

She finishes the sleeve, and I raise the other arm.

"When are you going?" She focuses her eyes on delicately pushing the black silk buttons through each of the velvet bands that ring my sleeve.

"Soon, maybe. I have to talk to Judge first." I look at her, but she does not meet my eyes. "Rachel can see to the house. Is she helpful to you?"

"Oh, yes, she gives me good work, and she's good with the boys." Henry has moved the train from the straw rug back to the bare floor. The wheels make a clatter as the train crashes into the wall.

"Yes, she is good with them. What did she do with the rattlesnake bones after all?"

"Some potion or something, I guess. She's always working on something."

"The idea. I can't believe she'd touch them. Henry, don't make so much noise." Henry looks at me and makes the sound of the engine as he rolls the train back onto the rug.

"Rachel sets a store by all that. She says the snakes being under an apple tree means something. It gives them more power."

"Does Rachel think she's Eve now?"

"No, ma'am, Rachel ain't Eve, that's for sure."

"Mary Magdalene, then?" I smile at her from the corner of my eye. Emma told me before Rachel was hired how she followed the Union army, doing their laundry and I can guess at what else.

She shakes her head, but she is trying not to laugh. "No, ma'am, just Rachel."

"She shouldn't waste too much time on all that. When she's here, she should do her housework."

Emma pauses her hand on my sleeve and looks serious. "People go to her. Lots of people. They think they see her ma in her eyes."

"What do they go to her for?"

"Potions and charms. Things to keep off spirits or for love or good luck or to protect them from sickness."

"Is that what she did with the snake bones?"

"I don't know, ma'am. She's been talking a lot about sickness. Mr. Eli's death struck her mighty hard. And she's been asking around about sick people."

"Are there people sick?"

She finishes the buttons and pulls out my skirts. She sweeps them with her hands so they lie out clean and full behind me. Henry plays near the wall again where there is no rug. The metal train clacking against the floor jangles my nerves.

Emma looks at me curiously, sympathy mixed with pity. "She heard there's some sickness, is all, ma'am. She said they found a family all dead out in the county. Upriver."

"A family? All of them? From what?"

"She can't say. I guess she doesn't know. Some poor whites out in the hills. It's as likely as not they died from hunger as anything else." Emma moves around me. "Come on, Henry," she says, bending down

to pick up his toy train and taking his hand. "Let's go downstairs."
Henry looks at me but walks with Emma to the door.

"That's all she's heard?" I ask, following her.

"Yes, ma'am, that's about all any of us have heard." She opens the
door and moves to the stairs.

"You'll tell me, won't you, Emma, if you do hear anything else?
Anything at all?" I stay close behind her as we step down the stairs at
Henry's pace. There is a rustling coming from the hall and then Bama
Buchanan's voice.

"Hello, the house," she calls. "Is anyone here?"

Bama stands in the middle of the hall, her umbrella gripped in her
hand. Emma takes Henry's hand and rushes him toward the kitchen.

"Hello, Bama. How kind of you to stop in," I say.

"Gus, you should take a firmer hand with your servants. I walked
right in the door with nary a soul to stop me." She shakes her umbrella
at me.

"I'm so sorry, Bama. But they run the house, not me."

Bama sits in the parlor, dressed in pongee silk and black drap d'été
with an old round bonnet on her head. We both fan ourselves in the
heat.

"The estate is that extensive, then?" Her question is indelicate, but
she does not seem to care. Rather, she looks directly at me.

"I have no idea," I say. "I was never privy to Mr. Branson's business
affairs." Perhaps she has already heard something. Word travels fast.
What grim pleasure those women would take in the truth. The black
embroidered handkerchief in my hand is already damp.

"I imagine you'll be making arrangements to be off. As you should.
Some time away will do you good. You have no one traveling with
you?" She speaks pointedly.

"No, just myself and Henry. And Emma, of course."

"Yes, of course. My niece and I—you remember Emily Whitcomb? She was a Banner before she was married. She and I are traveling up to Viduta on Monte Sano in a few weeks' time. You are welcome to join us there, if your travel plans allow it."

"Thank you very much, Bama. I'm much obliged." Viduta. There will be so many Albion people there. They only go there because they can't afford to go further. "I have to wait, of course, until I've spoken with my cousin."

"Your cousin? He is traveling with you then?"

"No, he is overseeing the estate," I answer, confused. She meets me with her own confusion, and the black ribbons of her bonnet shake.

"Oh, you mean Judge. I thought you meant young Mr. Heppert." I feel myself color and Bama remarks upon it. "You know, there was talk of a union there at one time. I have no doubt you made the wiser choice. Time has certainly proven it."

I look away. "Yes," I say. "I suppose it has." Buck did not even speak to me at the funeral.

"Women have their ways, don't they, Gus?" She smiles at me, showing the missing teeth in her upper jaw. "And there's time yet for you. You're still young. And now very, very marriageable. Don't you think so?" She laughs out loud.

We sit quietly for a moment. Bama seems to wait for an answer I will not give. I shift in my chair.

"Have you had many callers?" Bama asks.

"No, none to speak of. Some of the Yankee women have left their cards, but I don't feel obliged to return the call."

"No," Bama says with her nose pinched tightly as she shakes her head. "No, no reason to do that. No reason not to, of course, but no reason to do it, either." She picks at her skirt with fussy hands. "How is Henry?"

"He's well. Thank you. He's so young. He doesn't understand. He spends much of his time with John, Rachel's boy. They're very close in age."

"Don't let him get too used to that. You don't want him to grow up niggery. Time for him to go to school soon, isn't it?" The bones in her hands stand up against her skin. She keeps plucking at her skirt, gently lifting it between a gnarled thumb and finger, then letting it drop.

"Yes, I was hoping that after we had gone away for a while, I might start him in school."

"Here in Albion?"

"I suppose. Where else?"

"Nowhere else. Just wondering. None of your old friends have been by?"

"No, I don't expect them. It's been so long. I'm not sure what we'd have to speak about."

She nods with thinly pressed lips. "It will take some time for them. That's all. But you are one of us again. Don't ever doubt it."

One of us. I don't feel like them, but I don't feel like an *other*. I don't know what I am in Albion anymore. "Was it so bad that I married Eli?" My voice catches on the words.

Bama looks at me hard from under her bonnet. "Bad?" she hacks out, gruff and contemptuous. "Bah. Bad is nothing. It wasn't marrying Eli so much as what he was up to. Helping the Yankees. Taking our money and our land and handing it out to the Negroes and the bluecoats. And then the voting. My God, the day they let a colored man vote. I know Colonel Buchanan was turning in his grave. If he were alive, he'd have dug his own grave, he would, rather than see that. Somebody's grave, at least, wouldn't he?" Bama laughs through the gap in her smile. "But that's all in the past, isn't it? Dead and buried with Eli. And you're back with us. You can't blame them for finding it difficult—you understand. Your mother understood."

"Mama did? She's why I married him."

"Of course, of course," she says, and reaches out her hand and takes mine. She leans forward to place a kiss on my cheek. She is so close, I can smell the snuff and whiskey on her breath. She smells like Eli.

"No need to dwell on the past. We've all suffered in so many ways. No need to think about it at all. Besides, you're in an enviable position." She looks toward the door at the sound of footsteps on the brick walk outside, then trains an eye back upon me. "Don't think it hasn't been noticed. And discussed."

She lets out a laugh and throws her head back, showing her missing teeth again.

"Is that what people are saying?" I ask.

"You know how the ladies are here in Albion, always have to be in everyone's business."

We turn at the open door. Judge is there, his hat and cane in his hand.

"Why, Judge Heppert, you old dog," Bama exclaims. "I'm glad I imposed on Gus long enough to catch sight of you."

Judge blushes up to his ears. He presses his lips together in something that is not quite a frown but is still disdainful. "Gus. Bama," he says, giving a slight bow to each of us.

Bama rises from her chair and holds her hand out to Judge. She smiles, almost winking at him. She must have been a coy flirt in her youth. Judge is discomfited and takes unwilling steps toward her. He takes her hand and leans over it, placing cold lips against her papery skin.

"There, now," she says with almost a sigh. "That wasn't so bad, was it?" She laughs out loud again. "The Heppert men are always so courtly."

"And the Tunstall women are rightly known for keeping their beauty." Though Judge does not smile, Bama is undeterred.

"You must call on me, Judge. Imagine the compliments we could exchange!"

Judge blushes again and looks at his shoes. Bama knows how to render a man speechless. She gives Judge a wide smile as if trying to expose the gap in her teeth and the ashen color of her gumline.

"Well, Gus," she says, turning to me, "I'm sure you and your cousin have much to discuss. I'll leave you. And remember," she goes on, taking my hand and looking into my eyes, "you're very beautiful. You'll have whatever you want. But take a trip. Come to Monte Sano. I hear the fever has already started—as I thought it would. This infernal heat."

"The fever?"

Bama smiles and narrows her eyes. "The yellow fever. Nothing to worry about just yet as long as old Greer is doing his job!" She stomps her umbrella twice on the floor. "I'll come again soon. And I'll bring reinforcements with me next time!" She waves the umbrella like a standard-bearer on a charge. She gives a quick nod to Judge and a coquette's wistful laugh. "I hope to see you again very soon, Judge."

Her coachman, sitting in the sweltering heat, hops down to take her to the next call.

Judge grimaces and shakes his head. He turns his eyes to me and scans me up and down as if under instructions from Bama.

"You're looking well. Is that a new dress?" His mouth curls down to pinch his white beard at the corners. "Gather the servants together. On the back porch. I need to speak to them."

Seven

THEY ARE TAKING THEIR time in coming. Even the shade is hot. A frayed palmetto fan lies on the glossy white planks of the porch. Henry climbs into my lap, and I wrap an arm around his stomach. I pick up the fan. It moves the air but does little to cool.

Judge stands on the gravel path, pacing. The servants arrive slowly. First Emma. Now Rachel comes out through the dining room with Little John. They sit on weather-beaten chairs arranged in a row.

Big John takes a seat next to Rachel. He is not tall but is solidly built, with broad shoulders and big hands. He is a handsome Negro, square-jawed, with close-cropped hair that curls tightly against his scalp. He is darker than Rachel. His skin is close to Emma's in shading, dark brown and even, like a chestnut. His eyes are pale gray, almost blue. Ghost eyes that suggest white blood in his veins, though we all pretend we don't see it, like Rachel's yellow skin.

Simon ambles from the carriage house to the porch. Judge is impatient, walking up and down the path, watching the servants line up before him. He steps up to the porch and stands next to my chair, facing them. Henry squirms against me and I shush him.

They sit in front of me, in front of both me and Judge. Simon. John. Rachel. Emma. They are my household now. The things that I once called Eli's, I may now call mine. What a strange reversal. I look at their black faces, shaded so differently but all black. These are not slavery days, not anymore. Life has not changed so much as all that, I guess. They are free, but they work for me, don't they? The work they do is for me. There is something satisfying in that. Judge can have his few minutes to lord it over them. To lord over me, too. With Eli gone, he is the *paterfamilias*. He is so old-fashioned, but he will do right by me. He is my kin. I just have to learn how to handle him. I can't help a smile as he steps up to the porch. He rests a hand on the back of my chair. Of course he makes me wait until he has talked to the servants. He must know I am wild about the money.

"You all were loyal servants to Mr. Branson," Judge says. "And he recognized that in his will, leaving each of you with a small bequest. A token." He turns his head to clear his throat, then looks at each of them. Only Emma looks down at her hands, nodding to herself. The others look Judge right in the eye. His voice grows louder as he speaks, and he stares them down until John looks away, too, averting his gray eyes to the floor. Little John has the same pale gray eyes. He shifts in Rachel's lap, curling up, although he is getting too big for her.

Henry squirms and says, "Emma," in a whisper. His restlessness is so distracting that I must let him down. Judge watches, his cheeks suffused with red, as Henry clip-clops in his little shoes to Emma and climbs into her lap. He is next to Little John and seems happy because of it. Judge looks at me and grimaces, disapproving.

"They are not important sums," he continues. "Simply tokens. But you should know that Eli was concerned for your welfare and left the disbursement of funds in my charge."

Simon shoots Rachel a look, something critical, maybe disbelief, but Judge does not catch it—or pretends not to.

Emma nods. Her arm is wrapped around Henry. He dangles his legs and reaches an arm out to pinch Little John. Emma grabs his hand and holds it in his lap, making him giggle.

"The estate is very complicated, and it will take some time to un-wind, so until then I will keep a record of the funds allocated to each of you. They will be payable after the settlement of the estate's debts." Judge looks at each of them evenly, challenging them.

Rachel knocks her knee against Big John, but he won't look at her. She does it again and then puts her hand on his arm. She jerks her head toward Judge, but John won't do what she wants. She is becom-ing agitated, and her boy starts to struggle in her lap, arching his back against her.

"That is all. You may go," Judge says, and he waits for them to get up, but no one moves. Rachel turns to John and whispers something to him. Judge glares at them. Emma's eyes, too, nervously dart to them.

"I have a question, sir," Rachel says. Judge looks at her and doesn't say a word. "How long before we get our money?"

Judge's mouth curls down again. His nostrils flare. He turns to-ward the garden, scanning the lawns and flower beds, taking his time, then turns back to Rachel. "I can't give you a time. It may take several months to go through your former master's estate. There is a lot of work to be done. When it is done, you will be paid."

"He was never my master, sir," Rachel says with the thinnest ve-neer of respect in her tone. "And if the money is ours, why can't we get it right now?"

"Because I said, that's why," Judge answers sharply. "Now go."

"Thank you, sir," Emma says, and she gets up, taking Henry by the hand and leading him into the house.

John gets up, too. "Come on, Rachel, enough now," he says in a low voice. Simon shoots Rachel another look, and she nods back to him.

"I said enough, woman," John says more forcefully. He takes her arm and pulls her up out of her chair. They go inside the house bicker-ing, Rachel holding Little John like a sack of flour.

Simon gets up and turns away from Judge. He ambles back to the carriage house, his head high and his steps easy.

"Now, Augusta." Judge turns to me. "We should talk." He looks over at the office at the end of the gallery. He walks toward it, not waiting for me. He is in no mood for anything contrary. "Eli acted like he was a Chinese king," he says, shaking his head and looking back at me. "I always thought he built that office so he could see whatever was coming at him."

He must mean the windows. They make the small office seem so much bigger. Just after he bought the house, Eli added the extension "to modernize the old place," he said. In his optimism, he added a nursery above the office, both connected to the house by an interior staircase. With Eli's changes, the back of the house appears as a jumble of interconnected and interrupting blocks—kitchen, extension, a stretch of porch cut short by the office. I never liked the changes that altered it from what I knew before the war, though I never protested them. Rather, I gave Eli a cold consent and cursed him secretly for desecrating the Chapmans' home.

On Eli's days at home, I would stay upstairs with Henry in the nursery or the front sitting room. The colored men would line up in the garden outside the office or along the porch. They would sit on the back steps or skulk around the kitchen door. On days of bad weather, they would line the hall and the back parlor, waiting for their opportunity to see Eli to ask him for a favor or help. As the head of the Freedmen's Bureau after the war, Eli was seen as some sort of benevolent protector. He gave out the food rations provided by the federal government—and not just to the freedmen but to the poor whites who came into Albion after the spring of '65, starving and desperate. Eli negotiated contracts for the freedmen, too. He decided who would work and where. All with the backing of the United States Army. The motherless young colored girls, he indentured to the homes where they had been slaves a year or two before. He set the terms of the contracts for the Negro families who took twenty acres from their old masters so they could grow cotton and corn and then give away half of it as their rent. Eli would intervene on behalf of the Negro tradesmen in town who insisted the white men weren't paying them fairly. He saw them all and profited mightily by it, skimming off the top, taking money to push through a contract here or to place the best laborers on his friends' farms. After the bureau was shut down, he remained a man revered by the Negroes, and they kept coming, wandering about the lane and the carriage house and sitting on the benches—those, at least, who were not so impudent as to ring the front bell.

Judge takes Eli's chair behind the desk without hesitation, his back to the door into the house. What a curious thing for him to say about the windows, but he's right. When Eli sat at his desk, he looked at windows on three sides of him and could see the whole garden and anyone who might be lurking outside.

Judge opens the leather portfolio. There are dark wine-colored stains on the leather. "Augusta, I'm afraid I don't have very good news for you today. I will work things out. You will never have to worry, but a prudent economy is what is required. No more of these spendthrift ways. Eli is not alive anymore."

His tone is harsh. I study my hands. They are small and delicate and white. I have been lectured by Judge before. Does he resent me for asking his clemency the day of Eli's funeral?

He turns the pages in the portfolio one after another. He scans them from top to bottom. I lean against the wooden slats of the chair, my hands folded over the stiff black material of my dress. Judge grimaces at me. He presses his lips together, and it ruffles his beard like a chicken's feathers. "I'm sorry to say it. There's a selfishness in the Sedlaws, a greed that rises up now and again. I encourage you to banish it from yourself. I saw it in your father, in his desperation to pull off any kind of trickery to win, and it is a most unbecoming trait. I don't say you have that quality, I know you have a fine character, but I see hints of it, and I wish your Blackwood blood would overcome it."

His chiding galls me, but what can I say? He always has to sermonize. He carries so many resentments. He has carried them a long time. I have nothing at my disposal to counteract them, least of all the pride of my father's name.

Judge rests his hand on the papers. His eyes are ice blue and seem to bore through me. He drums the papers with his fingers. "These papers," he continues, "contain the various investments Eli has—or had. Some of the bonds are still worth something. The Alabama and Chattanooga Railroad notes were never exchanged for the new road, and I think we can pursue that. But there are heavy mortgages on his county lands, and it will be years before they are unencumbered. Eli's pressure on Mr. Stephens almost caused the bank itself to suspend payment. It's unclear what happened to the capital of the Freedman's Bank. Whatever was left in specie was meant to be distributed to the account holders. He may have taken some of it to shore up his debts and deposited it at the Planters and Merchants Bank. It's going to take a while to untangle.

"What is reassuring—what should reassure you—is that the mill remains profitable, although burdened with some debts. It will take time to recover, but I am certain it is possible at this point. Any thoughts of travel and extravagance, however, should be put aside. A prudent economy is the course you should set for yourself. I am certain you will remain comfortable, if temporarily . . . constrained."

"Eli stole from the Freedman's Bank?"

"Well, perhaps I spoke too soon. You know Eli headed up the Freedmen's Bureau, and he was the president of the branch bank that was chartered here. When the Freedman's Bank collapsed last year, the assets and specie were suspended. Mr. Stephens suggested that Eli was able at critical moments to come up with payments to him in specie. We assume they came from the Freedman's Bank. It is unpleasant."

A shiver runs over me. "The mill at Three Forks?"

"The mill at Three Forks. A cotton mill."

I know the area, hidden out in the woods, almost. I used to ride there with Buck.

Judge shifts in his chair, irritated. "It was a venture started a few years ago. He had partners in the mill, which is why he could not use it as a pledge at the bank. He did inquire with Stephens about that. It's been running profitably, and I'm confident it will produce dividends for you."

"That's all that's left? A cotton mill?"

"Not all. We have to figure this out, and then we will know where things stand for you. I feel obliged to say, if we find more, there is a chance you and Henry could have much less."

"I can't go away, then. I can't go anywhere." Judge looks away from me. "There are so many bills already, Judge. Is there enough to go to Monte Sano, at least?" It seems pathetic that I should find myself begging Judge for money. It can't all have vanished. There must be money somewhere.

He smiles at me as warmth creeps back into his face. "I am sure we can find a way to get you up to Monte Sano." He takes his hand from the papers and reaches out to me, patting my hand on the desk. The papers are ragged at the edges from clipped coupons, others scrawled spidery with black ink like hieroglyphs.

He rises from his chair and places the papers back in the leather case. "I will come back to you as I know more. I wanted to acquaint you with what I knew at this point."

"Thank you, Judge. I'm sorry, I just can't believe this."

He watches me with discomfort. "It will all work out. I will see what we can do to get you up to Monte Sano."

"How soon can I get the money? And the will. Did you remember the will?"

He frowns as if he's drunk sour milk. "I'll let you know about the money as soon as I can. And the will. Does that satisfy you for now, Augusta?"

"Thank you." He is leaving. There are too many questions for him to leave. "It's just that Bama Buchanan said the yellow fever has started."

He looks back and shakes his head. "It won't be too long."

He leaves me with a curt nod. Through Eli's three walls of windows, I watch him stalk down the garden path and up the lane.

Even with the windows and doors open, the office is as hot as the kitchen. The heat is thick and wet. The sun streams through the glass panes, searing the floor. I don't want it to touch the black of my dress. I feel like I will combust. Judge is unfair. I can't believe what he says. He didn't like Eli, Simon is right about that. With Eli gone, Judge says what he wants with no one to stop him.

Pa never liked Judge. Seventeen years after Pa is dead, Judge still hates Pa. What a fantasy about Pa using trickery. I don't know where the enmity started, long before I was born. Mama talked like Judge had courted her at one time. She hinted that Judge's father disapproved of a match between them, they were so close in blood. Mama seemed to have considered it a possibility—even after Pa's death, she hinted that she would be open to a proposal of marriage. Maybe that's why Mama didn't want me to marry Buck.

Pa was a peaceful man. A man of thought and word. Judge was always a man of action. I imagine he was like Buck when he was young. That confidence, a certain dash. A hotheaded cavalier. Pa was never hotheaded. He was a gentle man. Firm when he needed to be, tough when he was in his cups. But when he was not drinking, he was a just and honorable man. If nothing else, they are both men of honor.

I was young, but I remember the election of 1856, when Pa and Judge ran against each other. Just one seat from Albion in the Alabama statehouse, and they both wanted it. And then to have them lose the election to an old tinkerer. He came from the mountains and spoke in silly parables that made the farmers laugh. Mama would take me to listen to Pa's speeches. Cicero drove the open-topped Victoria, and we followed Pa around the county. We would sit at a distance, watching young men chase after a greased pig or grasp for the slippery neck of a goose hung by its feet high in a tree. Pa would pay for a whole ox to be roasted on a spit and great black kettles of stew. And, of course, whiskey. The crowds could get wild from whiskey and opinion.

Fights were common. The feel of the frontier was never really lost in the county, until the war finally killed its spirit. Pa would mount a block, sometimes half tipsy from the slugs of whiskey forced on him by the county men—the small farmers, the blacksmiths and other mechanics on whom he depended for his election. With the raucous crowd around him, sometimes so noisy that we could barely hear a word, he would talk about the value of the Union and our place in it.

Once a ruffian booed and called Pa a Yankee lover. Hecklers were frequent, and Pa always swore that Judge paid them. A knife fight broke out near our carriage once. The men, both drunk, began to scuffle, and a crowd opened into a circle for them, cheering them on with whistles and obscenities. The two men nearly cut each other to ribbons. One had an eye gouged out. Pa was furious at Cicero for bringing us too close to the crowd. He beat him horribly that night, his voice slurred from the whiskey. Mama was terror-stricken when he came back to the house. He smashed a mirror in the parlor. He threw a porcelain vase of cherubs and rosebuds straight at it. We all hid in our beds, terrified he would come up the stairs. The whiskey always made him rage. He could have a terrible temper. But he was a good man.

Pa and Judge never spoke after all that. They were barely civil before then, and the election put the final nail in that coffin. Judge won the seat in 1858. The mood had shifted. Perhaps he had found better ways to win, too. Defeat is unacceptable to someone who believes the world will end if he doesn't win. Judge's worst fears must have come true by war's end. His world really had ended.

A shadow moves across me. Simon is standing at the door. His face is expressionless. How does he find it so easy to conceal his emotions? That is the face I should wear.

"Hello, Simon."

"Ma'am." He stands immobile, watching me.

"What do you need?"

"I saw Mr. Heppert leave. I was wondering how the interview went."

"It was very informative. Judge said Eli stole from the Freedman's Bank."

Simon steps into the room without a word. He is unimpressed by this latest revelation. He walks behind me to the far side of Eli's desk.

"If I were to need money, Simon, where might I get it?"

His mouth is slack. He looks puzzled. "Can Mr. Heppert help you?"

"Yes, of course, he will. Can you help me, too?"

"I don't know, ma'am."

"You are looking for the package, aren't you? The package you say contains money."

He looks at the floor and doesn't answer.

"You are looking for it. Why won't you tell me the truth?"

Simon's frown deepens. The sun floods in around us, casting bright shafts against his legs.

"I want to trust you," he says. "I know Eli wanted to trust you, too. But by telling you, I am putting myself at risk."

His eyes question me. His voice is grave, as it always is. He has never been one to grovel or to speak with his hat in his hands.

"What are you saying to me, Simon? What kind of risk?"

He sighs and offers Eli's chair to me with his hand. I push myself up from my seat and move behind the desk. Judge was sitting here only minutes ago. Simon takes the chair I have abandoned. He rubs his chin, looking at the floor. He eyes me, then looks at the floor again and begins to speak. "I worked for Mr. Eli for many years. From the time I was fourteen. Mr. Eli had a great deal of trust in me. He would often have me go on trips to Montgomery. He trusted me to deliver certain things for him. He had many friends there, and he enjoyed doing favors for them." He pauses, his eyes looking steadily into mine.

"Favors," I say, raising my eyebrows.

"Monetary favors, ma'am," he says, and his eyes do not waver. He is so cryptic. "Before Mr. Eli's passing, I was intended to make a trip to Montgomery for him. I was meant to leave the day he fell sick. He never had the time to give me the package I was to deliver or my instructions."

"Yes?" My arms feel weak and my stomach turns.

"I believe—I am certain, ma'am—that Mr. Eli had prepared the package for me but he was not able to give it to me."

I lower my voice to a whisper. "How much money was there in the package?"

"I think about five thousand dollars," he whispers.

He has lost his mind. It can't be possible.

"Depending," he adds, nodding.

"My God, Simon," I say, trying to keep my voice low. "He would send that much money with you?"

"Yes, ma'am. It is a great deal of money."

"In greenbacks? Or gold?"

"Sometimes one or the other. Sometimes in notes of exchange."

"You have not found it."

We are both of us perfectly still, watching each other. The cicadas chant outside. The air is hot.

"I have searched everywhere I can. The rooms down here, the office, the saddlebags he usually used, but I have not found it. There's a compartment behind a drawer in that desk. There are several false books on the shelves behind you. There is a loose floorboard against the wall behind me. They're all empty. All the drawers in that desk. All the books. The cabinets. Every inch of this room has been searched. I would have searched Mr. Eli's room, but you have kept the key and locked the door."

The walls are painted bright white. The shelves are lined with books end to end. Everything is neat and orderly. What would Judge say about all of this?

"Why are you telling me this?"

Eli's wide desk sits between the two of us. The corners of Simon's mouth curve in a vague smile. "I wondered, to be honest, if you were aware of it already. I can see by your face that is not the case."

It is not funny. Simon should have nothing to smile about.

His mouth twists into a frown. His shoulders make a light shrug.

"I believe you have a need," he continues. "I know the bills are not being paid, and perhaps you would prefer to have the money yourself rather than rely on Mr. Heppert. It is Mr. Branson's money, after all."

"I should go directly to Mr. Heppert and tell him."

Simon nods again, and that curl of pale smile returns. "That is the risk I am running, ma'am. How much of the money do you think you'll see if you do that?"

"Why would you say that?" What gall he has to speak of my blood kin that way.

"Because I have been in Albion many years, and I know Mr. Heppert."

"Does he know you?"

"Most certainly."

"How?"

"Albion is a small town."

His evasions are insulting. How can I trust him, in any case?

"It is a week since Eli died," I say. "How can you be sure this money exists—or ever existed at all?"

"I am sure it exists. Where is a very different question." He comes around behind the desk toward me. I shrink back. It is a reaction, instinctive. I am embarrassed by my fear. That I should shrink before someone I have known for ten years. And a servant.

Simon ignores me and opens a desk drawer. He pushes a trigger at the back of the drawer, and the bottom springs up. From underneath the false bottom, he pulls out a long, thin ledger and drops it on the desk in front of me. It falls with the sound of a slap.

"Mr. Eli kept this ledger here," Simon says. "I hid it the day he fell sick. He was not yet dead, but I knew that he would want this hidden. Disposed of."

The ledger is worn at the edges and turned toward me. Simon opens it, flipping through pages filled with numbers, long rows of numbers with cryptic figures that look like Greek characters heading each row. Simon stops at the last page that bears writing. He points at different numbers on the page as he explains. His finger is dark like ebony but white underneath the nail. The pale skin turns pink from the pressure he applies to the page.

"This is the day before Mr. Eli became ill," he says. His finger travels across the page to other numbers and the Greek headings beside them. "This is the cotton he bought for the mill. This is the price he paid and this is the price he recorded in the books at the mill for Mr. Hunslow to see. The difference he took and kept hidden."

"What is this?"

"It is a record book. Mr. Eli was very careful. He kept track of everything in his ledger." Simon's finger moves along a row. "These are debits to the cash he took from the mill. They are the payments he made to his friends in Montgomery and in Washington. Among them Senator Spencer. He even had friends here in Albion to whom he made these . . . loans. To make sure things ran smoothly for him."

Simon's finger rests on the page. His eyes are on me.

"Payments to his friends? Why on earth would Eli need to bribe people?"

Simon takes a deep breath, resting his hand flat on the desk. Perhaps I am boring him with my questions.

"Eli had many business interests. And state politics have been turbulent. More recently than before. He was an influential man in the Republican Party, but he needed friends who were Democrats and Conservatives to protect his interests. To help pass laws that would help his interests.

"And since the panic, he was struggling. It wasn't just the money, although that was a worry for him. He saw the Republicans failing— because of the violence that kept the colored people away from the polling stations. The men up in Washington didn't care anymore about colored men being strung up or harassed. In the last election, many Republicans were voted out of office. He had to make many friends. With the new state constitution men are talking about, he needed the men in Montgomery, whoever they were, to help him. When the Union League burned, everything became harder. He couldn't start over again. Not like he had before. He had you and Henry, and he couldn't walk away from you. He knew you couldn't start over like he could."

I slump against the chair. Eli's chair. He was tall and ungainly. Quiet. Taciturn. Sometimes jovial. He used to play with Henry, sitting on the floor with his blocks or his toy soldiers. Simon says one thing and Judge another, but they sound the same to me. Who was Eli? What was he doing all these years?

"Has Eli really lost everything?"

"I don't know, ma'am. But if your cousin Heppert tells you he has, I would think twice before you believe it." His face is calm. He nods at the page. His finger travels down a column of entries and reaches a final one. It shows a debit of five thousand dollars.

"This is the money. The last entry. It could be more than this. I don't know if it's greenbacks, bonds, or coin, but I know it is somewhere. There are elections coming, ma'am, to draft a new state constitution. Eli would need a lot of friends in that convention. He would never put down the names of the recipients. Not in here. But he would include the list of recipients with the money. Before my trip, he would give me the bundle wrapped in brown paper. If I was to set out before dawn the next day—and that is what I was to have done the day he passed—he would give it to me the night before. I would have to memorize that list and recite it back to him before I left. Then he would destroy it. That is why I am convinced the letter and the money are in the house. He was going to give them to me that evening. But he fell sick. I could see in his eyes he wanted to tell me something. I stayed by him as long as I could. He never regained control of himself to say it. Did he not say anything to you, ma'am?"

"No. He tried. I thought he was trying to say something." I look up at Simon again. He comes here, telling me a fantastical story about money and that my kinsman, my protector, is not to be trusted. "So the money and the list of men Eli was going to bribe is somewhere in this house?"

"Very likely, ma'am." Simon folds the ledger and puts it back in the drawer. "And if Mr. Heppert is aware of it, and Mr. Heppert is a very knowledgeable man, then you can believe he will do everything he can to find it. That list of names would be worth even more to him than the money. You understand how important it is that no one finds this ledger?" He locks the drawer, lays the key in front of me, and walks back to his chair.

"Yes, I do." I take the key, a tiny piece of metal, and put it in my pocket.

"I hope I can trust you," Simon says. Why is he such a sphinx?

"What do you want in return for your trust? Do you expect me to dig up the garden looking for this package?"

Simon smiles. "No, ma'am. I would appreciate your discretion. The door to Eli's room is locked, and you have the only key. Besides, I wouldn't look in the rooms upstairs without your permission."

"I will unlock the door, and you have my permission. What else do you want? You are not looking for the money out of Christian charity, are you?"

His face is blank. Completely inscrutable. "I would appreciate whatever you think is appropriate, ma'am. And the bequests that Eli promised to all of us." He speaks formally, like a servant.

"How much, Simon?"

"Half," he says coolly.

Half. A lot of money. A lot of my money. If it even exists. "And you give up Eli's bequest. That's still a small fortune for you."

"Very good, ma'am," he says with a knowing smile. "If Emma or Rachel questions you about why I have invaded their territory, I would appreciate you telling them it is simply to clean up Mr. Eli's things. Whatever can be done to avoid suspicion would be best. I would hate for them to talk to the neighbors and find that stories about a search of the house are circulating through town. It would be unfortunate if that made it to anyone else's ears."

I nod. So that is his fear. He is right, if this money story is true. The kitchens of all our neighbors will be buzzing with rumors, and Judge or Greer or someone will hear about it.

"There is another place," he continues, "that I have not looked. That I cannot look. The mill."

The mill at Three Forks. Eli was there almost every day, overseeing the operations. Perhaps the package is there. Neither of us can go there. How could we explain why we were searching the office? Impossible.

"You might send me out to the mill to collect Mr. Eli's things?"

"You are asking too much already, Simon. I'll think about it. Neither of us can go skylarking out to the mill."

He frowns, looking out the windows.

"Maybe I will send a letter to Mr. Hunslow," I offer.

"Shhh, ma'am," he says. He nods in the direction of the garden. Rachel is coming. She sees us and has a curious expression on her face, twisted in confusion. Even disapproval. How like Rachel.

"Ma'am," she says as she steps into the doorway. "Henry is asking after Little John, and Emma needs me in the kitchen. I wanted to see if he could play with him where I can watch them both." She frowns at me.

"Thank you, Rachel. Bring Henry to the garden. I'll watch the boys." She turns away, leaving the door open and throwing back a glance at the two of us with her eyebrows raised.

"Does Rachel know any of this?" I ask.

Simon looks at me, surprised. "No, ma'am. Not a word."

"Is there something between you two?"

Simon almost laughs out loud. "Not a thing, ma'am." He is smiling, but I am not.

"I will unlock Eli's room for you." I hold the small ring of keys. They click against each other. "I trust you will tell me what you find."

"I want to be careful. I will have to wait until Rachel and John have gone. It may be best to do it early in the morning, before Emma is up. And if there's any way to go out to the mill . . ."

"I don't know, Simon. What if Eli never made the package? He was ill. He could not have been in his right mind."

He stands and opens the door into the house, waiting for me to pass through. "We won't know until we look," he says.

I walk by him. Who is he, after all, and how much of what he says is true? I will have to watch him, as I am sure he is watching me.

Eight

I CAN HEAR THAT bottle in Eli's room as if it is calling me. It has a sweet song. Different from the Vinegar Bitters or Dr. Scopes Elixir or the pills of mercury tartrate that give sweats and spasms. The song started low and whispering but grows louder as the days pass. Maybe I can have a little—just to calm me.

The money and the will worry me. Simon worries me. This story of a package. It seems so far-fetched. He said he searched the bedroom but found nothing. How can I believe him? How did Eli trust him? Eli's absence, too, has a strange effect. After so many years of resentment, how strange when those feelings begin to fall away one by one, like a flower losing its petals until only the stem is left. He was the axis of my day for almost ten years. Now, in the time between sunset and sunrise, everything has changed. The questions are still here, though, and the problems pile up on each other like those bills that Eli is not here to pay. Do I resent him more now that he is gone? He can't answer the accusations that Judge finds it so easy to make. Or Simon's stories of bribing and politics.

No, Eli is not wholly gone. He is strong even in his absence. He is in the room with me. I can feel him like I do Hill. Perhaps Weems was right. He will stay alive in spite of everything.

He haunts my steps. He chases me down the hall, into the corners. His bloody face with gaping eyes is before me. My dreams are filled with images of him wet with his own blood, embracing me. He seems to reach his hands out and I quail, terrified but powerless to move. I choke, smothered in winding sheets, and awake, unsure if I have cried out. I dream of that family in the county soaked through their clothes with blood. It rushes from the rude door frame of their cabin.

Emma shakes her head when I ask her about any sickness, saying she hasn't heard any more. I cannot convince myself that she is telling the truth.

I am fretting these days away, snapping at the servants. We are trapped here together. Simon and John have wisely forsaken the house for the out-of-doors. It is quiet out there, but so hot. Simon keeps to the garden, digging up bulbs and clipping boxwoods. How can he be so calm?

My jewelry is spread across my dressing table. The bills are in a neat pile. The butcher. The milliner. The man who delivers the milk. And, of course, the servants. They will all want to be paid. I can hardly rely on some mysterious package that Simon believes exists. Perhaps he is a fool. Judge would say so if I told him.

The gold is separated from the silver, the earrings from the necklaces, bracelets, and lockets. The onyx is worth keeping. It would not bring much, and it is wearable for mourning. A gold necklace studded with garnets, I can part with that. It was a gift from Eli. How much is it worth?

The back stairs creak from someone's weight. They are sneaking around the house, trying to avoid me. But there's Henry's voice. And Little John's. Rachel must be taking them into the nursery. I've never been good with the servants. Mama was better with them, although I don't think there was one among them who had much affection for her. She was hard on them. Perhaps I should be harder.

"Miss Gus, ma'am," Rachel says. She is almost beside me and I didn't even hear her. She must have crept in through the door from the back stairs.

"Yes, Rachel."

"That Mike is outside to see you." She makes a sneering frown. She doesn't like Mike coming around. That must be why she took the boys to the nursery.

"My brother?"

"Yes, ma'am, that's him."

"He asked for me?"

She tightens her nose and exhales sharply through it. "No, ma'am, he's sitting on the back porch waiting, and I figure it's for you. I've got the boys in the nursery to keep them away from him."

Rachel pushes too much. They are all pushing me. What Bama said. Maybe I shouldn't let Rachel keep the boys together so much.

"Tell him I'll come down." I open the drawer and push all the jewelry into it, locking it closed with a small key.

"I'd like to have a word with you, too, ma'am." She takes a step closer. She smirks at the key in my hand as I slip it into my pocket. Her arms are bare almost to the shoulder. Rachel has strong arms. She has spent the morning beating the winter rugs before they are rolled up and put away. That should have been done weeks ago.

"I wanted you to know, ma'am, that before long, John and I are going to be going." She looks me in the eye and frowns. She is relentlessly blunt.

"I don't understand. Has someone offered you more wages? Where are you going to?"

"We're going on to Kansas. There is a group of colored folks getting together. John has a brother Garson in Tuscumbia, his only brother left after Wendell was killed. He's going with a whole group to settle on government land up in Kansas so we can farm for ourselves."

"Are you unhappy here, Rachel? Eli has so much land, surely you could farm on that if you want to farm." Kansas? She must have lost her mind. Next she'll tell me they're going to California to prospect for gold.

"We want our own farm," she says firmly.

"I could sell it to you over time. You could buy it for yourself if you like. Then you could continue on here."

Rachel shakes her head, her eyes never wavering. "No, ma'am," she says, and I bristle at the sound of it. "Mr. Heppert would never allow us to buy that farm. You know that as well as I."

"Mr. Heppert doesn't have anything to say about it, Rachel, if I insist on it."

Rachel narrows her eyes in disbelief. "I mean no disrespect, but Mr. Heppert and those others are not interested in helping out colored folks. They want us under their heel, and they've got us there no matter what Mr. Lincoln said. Nobody I know ever got forty acres and a mule. I had to watch my father killed by slavery before the war, and I thought things were going to be different. But they are back to the same. There isn't any future for colored folks down here. There isn't any future for my boy here. Mr. Eli tried. He was a good man. He helped a lot of us, helped us try to make something out of the nothing we had. And I was willing to stay for John as long as Mr. Eli was here. But now with him gone, I don't see any way around it. I've watched what those Knights have done, what they did to Wendell. They beat him and strung him up on a tree for running a farm the way it should be run. There's no place for us here. There never was except as slaves to somebody else. So we're going. That's all there is to it. I just wanted to let you know. We're not going today, but we're going. If you want to send me packing, that's fine. That's your choice. But I'll expect my wages."

Rachel exhales again and stands looking at me for a moment. She turns and walks to the bedroom door.

"When did you decide all this?" I shoot the question at her, and she stops in midstep. She turns back to me gravely.

"John and I have been talking about this for a long time. You know John sat down with Mr. Eli all through this past winter and talked about it. The only thing stopping us was the money. When the Freedman's Bank went bust, we lost just about everything. We were going to stay longer and try to save up some, but with Mr. Eli gone, it's safer to go with no money than to stay here. The longer we stay, the less chance we'll ever get out of here." She fixes her eye on me and nods.

"Rachel, I don't like the boys spending so much time together. After Mike leaves, make sure you get Little John from the nursery."

She shoots me a dark look, then leaves the room, closing the door to the back stairs behind her.

My stomach tightens at the sight of him. "What are you doing?"

"Oh, hey there, sister," Mike says. He slams Eli's desk drawer shut. "Just looking to see if old Eli has any leave-behinds. You never know what you'll find around old Eli's office." He smiles and swaggers past me to the porch. The desktop is littered with papers, and books lie open on their spines across the floor. Half of Albion has searched this office. Would Eli leave money lying around here? Why didn't I look?

On the porch, Mike pulls a weathered canebrake chair toward him and sits, tilting it back on two legs. He pushes his muddy boots against a porch post. He has a tattered Union cavalry officer's slouch hat in his hand. The insignia has been removed, but it is trimmed in worn gold braid and has one side of the brim pinned up to the crown. Mike was wearing it when he showed up at the house on Allen Street long after the war was over, and he always gives a wry smile whenever he is asked how he acquired it. He spins the hat by the brim with one hand and whistles as I approach him.

"Where's that boy of yours?" he says with a smile on his face. He has a thin growth of silky hair for a beard. Hard to believe he is only twenty-six, barely a man. The things he must have seen and done.

When he came back in the fall of 1866, Mama acted like Jesus Christ had been resurrected again. She sent a runner to me and demanded I go to them immediately. She had been given a reprieve of some kind. But Mike is hardly a blessing. She left him everything she had when she died. He sold it all and went through the money like it was water. The house. The gardens. The books and furnishings. All gone but for my father's bench upstairs.

"Henry is off playing. What do you want, Mike?" I stand before him, keeping my distance, clasping my hands in front of me.

"Now, is that any way to welcome your brother? Have a seat, Gus. I'm just here to check up on you. I am the head of our little family now, aren't I? At least until Henry gets big enough to whoop me." He laughs and leans back further. An empty chair sits near him. I pull it a distance away before sitting down.

"What do you want, Mike?"

"Just checking on your health is all." He takes his feet from the post and lets the chair fall onto its four feet. He squares his feet with the chair and rests his arms on his knees.

"My health is fine, Mike. We're all fine. What have you heard?"

He raises his eyebrows. "Why, nothing, Gus. Nothing at all." He half grins at me as if he knows something I don't. "And have you got everything all figured out with Eli's money? You're set up now, ain't you?"

This is what he's after. He did not take long to get to the point.

"Everything Eli had is entailed to Henry, and Judge is the trustee. He's reviewing things now."

"Is that so?" He raises his eyebrows and leans back in the chair, lifting its legs again.

"Yes, Mike. That is so."

"From what I hear, you're going to have a lot to spread around here, though. Ain't that right?"

"And you're looking for a share of it." He won't get anything from me.

"Maybe I am." He smiles again, looking at the whitewashed boards of the porch ceiling.

"That's not something I can give you, Mike. Judge is the trustee. He'd have to approve anything I do with the money."

"Oh, come on, sister. Don't be so stingy." He sounds almost like he is making a joke, though he is not laughing.

"I doubt he could see his way to giving you an allowance, given how we both know you'll spend it." I am not laughing, either.

Mike lets the chair feet crack against the floor and looks at me. His face is hard. The years he spent at the war, the youth he gave up to it, are plain in his eyes and the snarl of his mouth. He stands and points a rigid finger at me.

"I ain't looking for an allowance," he says, fairly spitting at me. "I'm looking for what's mine. What should have been mine if that filthy scalawag hadn't stolen it all out from under us—from *me*."

"What are you talking about, Mike? About Eli? Stealing from us?" His reasoning amazes me. If anything, Eli did nothing but give Mike handouts since he came back.

"Don't play dumb with me. All that land Eli got was Pa's land—it would have been my land by rights. And that's who it should come back to." He sits again and pounds his fist on his knee. He whines like a saw.

"I don't know what you mean, Mike. It's out of my control, anyhow. The estate is in Judge's hands."

"Goddamn Judge and goddamn you," he shouts, standing suddenly. "You're all a bunch of liars. I'm going to get what's mine."

I won't be bullied by him. Not in my own house. "You had your share, Mike. What happened to the money you got from selling Mama's house?"

His face is terrible. "That's none of your goddamn business, you hear?" he shouts at me. His hand is clenched in a fist. The wild look in his eye.

"Mike, please." Where are the servants? The windows are open, but there are no shadows observing us. Where are they?

"You know all Judge ever cared about is himself. He always hated Pa." Mike lowers his voice and leans in to me. "He's lying to you if he says you can't get that money. Buck told me you've got all the money in the world. All the money in Riverbend County for sure."

"Mike," I say, looking around again. "You talk like Eli had the Confederate gold. He's lost everything."

"Bull, Gus," he spits back at me. "Bull and crap. That's what you're talking. That mill at Three Forks practically prints money. You think I'm so dumb I don't know that?" He takes a step closer, and I shrink back into the chair, trying to get away from him. He grabs my arm and pulls me to him, whispering fiercely. "Is that how dumb you think I am?" I pull back, barely breathing. "Answer me," he says.

"No, Mike." My voice wavers. I do not want him to see my fear. "I don't think you're dumb."

"I talked to people, Gus. Buck and other people. I know that mill's got money in it. Your money, you hear? All you've got to do is go down and ask for it. It's yours, ain't it? And that goddamn Judge can't say nothing about it, can he?"

"I don't know," I say, trying to pull my arm away. His grip tightens until I cry out in pain. "I don't know," I insist, resisting the urge to scream. "Let go of me!"

Simon walks from the carriage house, carrying a crate of seedling plants. He has a long, sharp hoe thrown over his shoulder. The same hoe he used to kill those rattlesnakes. Mike turns me loose and I step back. Simon looks at me and nods. I rub my forearm where Mike's fingers have been and watch Simon move across the path to a freshly turned bed waiting for planting. He looks at Mike evenly and nods at him, then kneels down, focusing on his task.

Mike relaxes back into his chair, and a thin smile curls his lips. He must be crazy. Or drunk.

Simon keeps his back to us and sets the seedlings one by one on the grass. Mike watches him and then looks at me.

"I'm just giving you a little advice here, Gus," he says. "That's all, just a little brotherly advice. You go down to that mill and see for yourself, why don't you? I'll expect a share of it. Don't forget that, either."

Mike leans back in his chair, then lets it fall with a final crack against the wood floor. He gets up without looking at me and saunters down the steps. Simon stands up and brushes the dirt off his knees. He holds the hoe, blade up, and leans on it as Mike walks down the path near him.

"Mr. Sedlaw," Simon says, looking Mike in the eye as he passes. Mike makes a grunting noise, jerking his chin at Simon and slapping the slouch hat against his leg. He keeps on through the garden past Simon, looking back with narrowed eyes at both of us. We stand still, Simon and I, and watch him go.

Nine

HENRY AND JOHN ARE playing marbles in the shade of the arbor. The boys share them, taking turns aiming them and flicking them with their fingers into a ring drawn in the dirt. The faint click of glass is just audible, except when the servants have raised their voices. They are in the kitchen with the window open. John and Rachel are arguing. Emma is there, too, but she doesn't speak.

They are arguing about Eli's will. He was generous with the servants. Their wages were more than generous. He gave them gifts at Christmas and on Emancipation Day. He even asked Rachel and John to live with us in two rooms next to Simon's in the carriage house. They declined. Because of Rachel, I always thought. She holds the reins in that marriage. They prefer to live in that awful back slum north of the depot. Lord knows why. I guess Kansas would be better than living over there.

"It ain't his money to hold on to. It's ours. What's he doing with it, anyway?" Rachel asks. Her voice is sharp. Maybe they won't be leaving for Kansas so soon after all. A dull pounding comes after her words. The thud is repeated again and again. Emma must be making biscuits, pounding the dough with her wooden rolling pin.

"That ain't none of your business, woman," John says in a high voice. "That's Mr. Heppert's business, and the more you argue back at him, the more time he's going to take."

"He ain't my master. He sure acts like it, though, doesn't he, Emma? Telling lies about Mr. Eli like that. He didn't steal from the Freedman's Bank. More likely Judge Heppert did."

"How do you know that? How do you know what Mr. Eli did or didn't do? Is that what Simon told you?" Emma keeps pounding at the dough like the beats on a metronome. Thud. Thud. Thud. A slow waltz.

"I don't have to listen to Simon to know what Mr. Eli did. Though he's got more sense than you when it comes to Mr. Eli. You talk like that old billy goat."

"I saw the way he looked at you, Rachel. Don't try to fool me. There's something going on. You tell me what's going on." Their voices are higher. Almost shouting. Emma pounds the dough faster, and the strikes sound like the smack of a hand.

"There ain't nothing going on, fool. You just sit around here all day making things up. I think you need more work to do. I've had enough of your fooling around."

"Don't you walk away from me, woman! You answer me."

"John, if you were a husband to me, you would have gone and got that money from Judge Heppert, and we'd be long gone from here. Mr. Eli would have gone and got the money. He would have gone straight down to that office and looked that old man in the eye and said, 'Give me my money.' All you do is sit here talking like a fool."

"If you're so worried about money, why don't you go after Miss Gus for our wages? We haven't seen a penny since Mr. Eli died."

The door creaks on its hinges and slams shut. It creaks again. They must be coming outside.

"That's what I thought," John shouts. "This ain't over, woman."

I walk to the other end of the porch, watching Henry and Little John.

Rachel comes out from behind the kitchen, headed toward the boys. Big John follows just behind her but walks down the gravel drive past the apple trees to the carriage house. His shoulders are hunched forward, fists clenched. He hurries, almost running.

"Little John, what are you doing over there?" Rachel calls out to her son. Henry looks at me, and she follows his gaze. I do not look at her. Her eyes narrow, and she watches me as she walks. I have to get away. I can't take her stare. I turn my back on her and rush into the house. Emma is still in the kitchen, beating the biscuits.

The grip Mike held on my arm has made a bruise. The pressure of his fingers is marked in four short, pale lines. I've looked in every book and ledger in Eli's office, but no money. I don't know why I thought I would find anything in the first place. Only entries in long columns and manuals on agriculture and mechanics. Why even bother opening the drawers. Mike has already pilfered what he can.

I understood his meaning, as twisted as it is. The war destroyed everything. It is not Eli's fault. The land would have been gone if Eli hadn't saved it. And still Mike comes around, scavenging for money.

When Mike left home, it was after Atlanta fell and the Confederate army under Hood was limping its way to Nashville for a last desperate stand. He left a note for Mama that he was gone to join Buck and Hill—that he was old enough to fight. He was only fifteen, but he had always been spirited, almost wild. He would pick fights with boys bigger than him or whip the servants as if he were master of the house. Mama couldn't control him.

Mike never made it to Hood's army. He said that he found General Roddy down south in Coosa County. He bragged about how they harassed the Union rear guard, disrupting supply lines that stretched back to Nashville. His stories overlap and contradict each other. By the time he staggered back home late in '66, he said he had been to Texas and back. Fighting Indians and keeping civil order. He found Mama alone, living off of Eli. The land was gone, confiscated for taxes and debts. The Confederate bonds Mama had bought at Judge's insistence were worthless, no good even for lining your shoes. All of it was gone. But I had married Eli by then.

That was about the time Eli started to buy land. He had already taken land for the unpaid loans of my family's friends. He began to broker deals for cheap land with newly arrived Yankee officers or their carpetbagger friends—Eli's friends. He bought land through the Freedmen's Bureau. As its head in Riverbend County, he was responsible for what they called "abandoned" lands. He said he bought the Sedlaw and Wardwell lands for me. For the children we would have. So they are Henry's now. As they should be. Henry is the only living heir of our next generation. Henry Blackwood Sedlaw Branson. Henry's name was one thing Eli and I agreed on. All the lands will be his if Eli hasn't lost them for him.

Simon wants to go to the mill, and Mike says there is money there that is mine for the asking. Buck told him so. Maybe that's true. Can I go to the mill and ask for it? It is my money, isn't it? Whatever Mike and Buck talked about, Buck had some idea from his father about the mill's profits. Mike knows more from Judge than I do. I am left alone in the house, ignored as if I am irrelevant, disregarded. Even the servants seem to have no respect for me.

Emma and Rachel avoid me. Emma stays in the kitchen and Rachel has suddenly become emphatic about the laundry. She stays behind the carriage house with John and the boys, mixing soap and pearlash in pots of boiling water. I catch her and Emma together, the two of them whispering, Rachel's arms bundled with our family linen. Am I a wraith to them, a haunt who shadows them and whom they evade? Am I like the shade of Eli who stalks my steps through the rooms of the house?

This heat increases every day. I wake up sweating and go to sleep sweating. Henry is cranky. He cannot sleep well. He cries and asks for his papa so that I can barely keep myself from slapping him. If only I had the money, I could be gone from here. There is money at the mill. And it is my money. How dare Eli have entailed everything on Henry? What does that leave for me? I will go to the mill. It is very simple. I will go to the mill and demand my money from them. Judge be damned.

Emma and Rachel's muffled voices carry through the door of the china closet that makes a passage from the dining room to the kitchen. Rachel is whispering furiously about something. I open the kitchen door and step onto the brick pavers. Emma stands at the sink, and Rachel is beside her. Emma has been pumping water, and it scatters in fitful sprays from the red mouth of the pump. Her back is to me, and she extends her hand as if she is pushing Rachel away. They look at me in surprise, their mouths open. Emma clenches her fist quickly and puts it in the pocket of her apron. Rachel rushes to the open door to the yard. Emma and I are left alone.

"Emma, what did I interrupt?" I ask. The kitchen is hotter than anywhere else in the house. Hotter than outside.

"Nothing, ma'am." She turns back to the pump and begins working it until the water gurgles and sprays over the joint of meat in the sink.

"Emma, what's in your pocket?" I am not one to demand absolute obedience from servants, not like Mama, whose fits of temper were born of seemingly silly infractions, crumbs on the floor, a window left open, the sheets not ironed quite right. I see a flexion in Emma's shoulders, a tense shrug that immediately relaxes. Perhaps she hears Mama's voice in me. She turns and looks at me, reluctant yet obedient. She slips her hand in her pocket and keeps it there, fingering something small with mass to it.

"It's nothing, ma'am," she says without conviction. "It's really nothing at all. Just some silly idea Rachel has in her head."

I step closer, my eyes on her pocket. Perhaps it is something I would be happier not to see. "Show it to me."

She draws her hand out of her pocket slowly. It looks like a small piece of wadding, like the rough woven material used for cotton sacking. It is tied into a tiny bundle with a piece of twine. Emma closes her hand over it, and she gives a small frown. "It's just a thing Rachel made. A charm." She puts it back in her pocket.

"A charm? For what?"

"To ward off sickness," Emma says, and she exhales through her nose.

Rachel fancies herself a conjure woman. Rachel's mother was a famous midwife in Albion and attended the births of hundreds of babies before the war. While the doctors saw their patients die from childbed fever, old Sarah's mothers always seemed to survive the ordeal. Her reputation was so high that white women would ask for her specifically to wait on them at their lying-in. Rachel has that reputation, too, claiming she learned things from her mother and the wise women of the slave quarters. Emma and Rachel were in the room during Henry's delivery in spite of Dr. Greer's grumblings.

Emma slides the small burlap purse into her pocket. I want to grab it from her, touch it, open it up, and see what it is made of. I want to throw it away.

"I don't believe it none," she says quickly. "But you know how Rachel is."

"What sickness, Emma?" My fingers go cold and start to tingle.

"Any kind of sickness, Miss Gus. It's not meant for anything special." Emma rubs her hands against her skirts and looks away from me toward the sink. "I should get this roasting." The heat off the stove is intense. The air refuses to move through the open door and window.

"I don't believe that." The sound of buzzing cicadas comes through the garden door in a rhythmic, endless chant. "It's because of Eli."

"Rachel's just scared. That's all. She's got a little boy, and you know how she can be. She's worked up, and she's doing what she does to feel better about it."

"I have a boy, too."

"I know. I know." She speaks almost tenderly, as if she wants to reassure me.

"What is the charm?"

Emma shifts uncomfortably and breathes out through her nose again.

"Tell me, Emma," I say. "What's in it?"

"Ma'am," she says slowly. My hands make fists. "It's chicken blood. And some rattlesnake bones. And some dirt from the graveyard." Emma stops short. I must have cringed.

"From Eli's grave?" I ask.

"Yes," Emma answers.

"What else?"

"And some of Mr. Eli's hair Rachel clipped."

The sweet, ripe odor of blood and rot from Eli's deathbed rises in my throat.

"How did she get it?" I ask softly.

"She trimmed up his hair and whiskers. Before he was buried. I asked her to because Mr. Weems made such a mess of it. She held on to the clippings, I guess." I am too confused to be angry. Too confused and frightened. What is all this? What else are they keeping from me?

"Have there been other people sick like Eli?" I avoid her eyes.

"Not that I know about. Rachel thinks there is, but she doesn't know anything at all." Emma catches me with a sad glance.

"What has Rachel heard?"

"Rumors from the hands on Mr. Eli's place. John's cousin has a farm up toward Pennyton, past Three Forks. She says there are sick folks there, but she doesn't say how, and Rachel gets her mind all worked up." Emma's hand moves back into her pocket. "I'll talk to Rachel and tell her she has to give all the clippings to you. She was wrong to do that."

"No, don't say anything. I don't want you to say anything to her. I just wanted . . ." What did I come here for, after all? "I wanted you to see if Simon could take me out to Three Forks. Have John bring the carriage around. The gig. With the hood up."

Her hand stays in her pocket, playing with the charm, as I leave the kitchen.

Ten

THE RED CLAY BLUFFS rise in high banks along the river like a cup filled with muddy water. Everything is darkened by the thin net of my veil, so that even the sunlight seems gray. The river runs below us, sluggish and black. The hood is pulled as low as it will go. Simon sits on the horse in its harness, guiding her. He bounces in the saddle but handles the horse with ease. There is no box for him to sit on, so he must ride the horse. We are both more comfortable this way.

Simon slows us as we bounce from the dirt track onto the Chattanooga Pike. The iron-rimmed wheels clatter on the uneven boards, jostling me. The road is not much better than the half-timber corduroy the armies threw down as they moved across the county during the war. Simon salutes the passing Negroes, who jounce in the back of buckboards or stand idle at the edges of fields of parched red earth, half green with struggling cotton plants.

Simon has a charm from Rachel. I think it is, at least. A small burlap purse like Emma had. He carries it in his jacket pocket and reaches a hand in to touch it. Simon is coal black—pure, dark African. But he has a prominent nose, high-ridged. He must have Indian blood, too. Eli never said where he came from. Certainly not from Albion. I would have recognized him. Maybe from the county or somewhere downriver. He doesn't have the Gullah accent of Negroes from low-country South Carolina or speak the Geechee from Georgia. And he is too dark to come from the Mississippi Delta.

Many Negroes in the area, many of the freed slaves in the county, if they were not brought here overland from Georgia or South Carolina, came upriver from New Orleans. The steamboats would ply the Mississippi and the Ohio, then down the Tennessee as it curves backward and scoops into Alabama. In the spring, when the rains fill the rivers, a boat with a shallow draft could make it past Triana to the mouth of the Oosanatee and all the way to Albion.

Simon takes his hand out of his pocket to hold the reins. He pulls back and the buggy jolts to a stop. A wagonload of Negroes rolls toward us. There are a half dozen of them, dressed poorly in overalls and torn and dirty dungarees, in the back of the wagon driven by an old white mountaineer. The white man is grizzled, with red-rimmed eyes, and he spits his tobacco through a wide gap between his brown teeth.

One of the hands in the back of the cart calls out, "Howdy, Simon." He is dark, too.

Simon nods and smiles. "Howdy, Jesse. Where are you all headed?" His accent sings, not the laughing, bumptious accent of the local Negroes. It is more liquid, with a solemnity that makes him seem grave, as if he is singing a very sad psalm. He is so much more dignified than Eli was. Eli was like one of the dirt farmers who scratch out a living at the edge of the mountains. Simon must come from a different caste.

"We're going down to Judge Heppert's place over on the other side of Hayfork. We've got to give him his days." The other men in the wagon nod agreement, waving to Simon in recognition as they roll by.

"How many days does he take from you?" Simon calls to them.

"Forty days in the season. I barely have enough time to tend my own patch," Jesse calls back. "Shame Mr. Eli ain't around to make my contract!"

Simon nods, and another man calls to him. "When you heading off to Kansas? Any room in your wagon?" The man is dark. He slouches, his legs hanging off the back of the wagon.

"Not yet," Simon calls back. "Not yet."

Buzzing like cicadas vibrates in my ears. Did I hear that man right? The motion of the carriage makes me dizzy and sick. We are turning onto the cowpath that leads to the mill. The lane is covered with a thick blanket of pine needles. Simon clucks at the horse and we cross the roadway. The wheels don't clatter anymore. The woods are darker. These trails. I rode them with Buck a long time ago. The sunlight falls in shafts between the thick pines and dapples the brambles.

"Simon, are you going to Kansas?" I ask.

"Eventually, ma'am. Yes." He moves gently in time with the easy pace of the horse.

"Are you going with Rachel and John?"

He turns to look at me. "Did they tell you?"

"Yes, Rachel came to me and said they are leaving. Is everyone leaving? Is Emma going?"

He laughs and turns forward. His wide shoulders shrug. "No, ma'am. Emma has no plans to leave."

"Why are you going? To be a farmer?"

"I might. This time I'm going to help people get settled on homesteads. I'll come back and let folks here know how things stand up there, and then maybe there'll be another group of folks interested in going, too."

"Colored people?"

"Yes, ma'am. Colored people."

"Do they all want to leave so bad?"

"Some do. Most want to know there's a real chance for something better before they go. That is what I'm going to find out for them."

"Is that what you want the money for?"

He nods once without looking back. He only half turned his head to speak to me.

"Was Eli helping colored people go to Kansas?"

Simon turns his head to me again. His eyes are serious. "No, he was not. I am." He turns away.

My gloves make my hands itch. The pines stand tall and dense beside the road, cutting the sunlight into thin slices as we pass.

"You seem to know everyone. They must trust you."

The carriage rides easier without the constant racket of the plank road.

"Yes, ma'am." His hand is back in his pocket, toying with the charm. "I'm very lucky to have a broad acquaintance."

"How do you know so many people?"

"Through Mr. Eli's influence, ma'am. I worked with him to organize the freedmen back in '66 and '67. To organize the Union League through the whole county. And then I was a registrar of elections in '68. I met many people in our community that way."

"That's very fortunate for you." I remember, of course. Eli seemed to go out of his way to disgust my old friends and my family. Mama was scandalized when Eli made the Union League in Albion. Organizing the freed slaves to vote for the Radical Republicans. Organizing them as if they were some sort of secret army. I felt like I couldn't go out of the house.

My veil feels hot. Tall pines rise up on all sides. Their scent is spicy and earthy and sweet.

"Yes, ma'am," Simon replies. "There is good fortune in it."

"What does a registrar do?"

"A registrar? He stands there with another man on voting day to make sure all the men voting are who they say they are. To make sure nobody votes twice. And that no dead men vote, either." Simon turns his head halfway to me and smiles.

"Dead men vote?"

"It is a highly unusual occurrence, but it has been known to happen." He turns forward and adjusts the round derby he is wearing. They are a new thing, and all the Negro men in the county seem to have bought one.

"Do you still do that?"

"I only had the pleasure a few times. You understand, Miss Gus, there being some hostility to a Negro man serving in such a position."

"Weren't you going to run for office, Simon?"

He doesn't move and does not hesitate to reply. "No, ma'am."

"No?"

"No, ma'am," he says again.

He is lying. Was it three years ago? Maybe four?

The November elections were nearing. There had been talk, some kind of talk, from Eli, I guess, or something I overheard when he was downstairs with officers or his Republican friends. He said Simon was going to run for sheriff in the next election.

Then Eli had gone traveling. He did travel. Trips to Nashville and New Orleans and Montgomery and Mobile. The colored men would come in the morning, and Emma would tell them to scat, that Eli wasn't home and to tell their friends to stay home, too. They would linger for a few minutes, standing by the carriage house talking to John to make sure Emma was telling them the truth. Then they'd drift toward the square or back to their shacks in the North Ward. By noon, they'd be gone.

At night, I'd make Emma check all the doors to make sure they were locked. I was sleeping across the hall then, in the rose room with the ribboned wallpaper. What a relief it was to sleep there when Eli was away. It was autumn, I think, well into it, because my windows were closed and I had a fire that smoldered and gave the room the dry, coarse odor of burnt wood.

I heard men talking, shouting in the lane. It was late, past midnight. From my window, I could see a group of men on horses back by the carriage house. The Knights of the White Cross. I pulled my wrapper tighter. They were wearing dark clothes, like robes, with a cross on the chest and hoods. They shouted at Simon, but I couldn't understand the words. One of them hit Simon with a truncheon, and another pushed him down and tied his hands. They ripped back his shirt and took turns, one by one, each of them whipping him. They each gave him twenty lashes. They counted every strike out loud. Simon cried out again and again until he lay still, as if he was dead. Except at each stroke of the whip, his body would jerk like he was electric. They left him there in the dirt and the dark alone. He was still, his back shiny and wet in the moonlight, striped from the whipping. Like in slavery days. It was like any whipping from slavery days. For anything. Mama used to make a man on our place give out the whippings. They said he never did them hard. But this was hard, the way they whipped Simon, and he just lay there still, and Emma ran out to him with a blanket and covered him and helped him up to his room. She stayed with him, I think.

Eli was so angry when he came home. But Simon isn't lying. He didn't run for sheriff.

"I'm sorry," I say to Simon. "I thought you were going to run for office of some kind once. I made a mistake."

"No, ma'am," he says to me. "I never ran for any office here."

"Did you run for office someplace else?"

"I once ran for captain of my company during the war."

"During the war?" We saw black troops after the war. Drilling by the depot, following the orders of white Yankee officers. But Simon?

"Yes, ma'am," Simon says, and he looks back at me quickly. "I was in the army, like a lot of folks."

"You were a Confederate?"

Simon laughs out loud at that. "No, ma'am," he says through his laughter. "No. I was a volunteer with the twelfth United States Colored Infantry. At your service."

My face is hot. I wipe the perspiration at my temples. "Did you win your election?"

"No, but it wasn't a great loss. The captain was killed a few weeks later at Nashville." He looks back and smiles again.

"My brother was killed at Nashville."

Simon's smile vanishes. He looks ahead and then back, somber. "I'm very sorry for it," he says. The air is still and heavy. The horse has an effort pushing through it. Always back to Hill. I am half sick of these memories.

"Do you vote, Simon?"

He is surprised. He shrugs. "No, ma'am, I haven't voted in a while." The horse's feet thud into the dirt at a trot. "Would you like to vote, Miss Gus?" He turns back. Is he sincere or is he making fun of me?

"Me? Of course not. It's not my affair. Nor is it yours!"

Simon laughs again. I wipe at the moisture on my cheeks.

"No, ma'am, it is not," he says, and he gives a laugh with a hard edge to it.

There's the roar of the engines at the mill, faint but closer. We round a bend, and the mill is in view down a long alley of pines.

Three creeks tumble down the Cumberland foothills to form Three Forks Pond. The pond feeds Three Forks Creek as it meanders through the valley down to the Oosanatee. Fifty or more years ago, the water that flows through Three Forks was captured for a ginhouse and cotton press. When Eli took over the place, the old mill was a burnt wreck. The foundations bear black scars from the war. The rotting sluices were repaired. During the months when I carried Henry, Eli received letters of advice from millwrights in Lowell and Fall River. Yankee factories contributed the machines, great contraptions to spin thread and massive, roaring power looms that bang threaded shuttles back and forth through the warp, inching out miles of cotton cloth. The old shed that housed the cotton press was incorporated into the long brick building. No one in Albion had ever seen such a massive venture, standing lonesome in the woods by the creek.

The roads that meet at the mill come from the little market towns of the area. Cotton is carried, already baled, in wagons that creak down the lanes. Women and children ride on the bales, coming to work at the mill from the villages that bear silly townlike names, Pennyacre, Hayfork, Black's Cove.

Simon pulls back on the reins suddenly. He squeezes his legs against the horse's flanks and turns back to me, taking his hat in his hand. "I can't go into the mill with you, ma'am."

"No, of course not."

He looks at me in an earnest way. He holds the hat and reins in one hand and leans the other against the horse's rump. "I hope you'll look around for that package. For anything. Maybe you can collect Mr. Eli's personal effects. I'm sure you want them."

"I'm sure Judge collected Eli's things. He is in charge of the estate."

He nods to me and looks down.

"I will look for it, Simon. Of course I will. If it exists."

He looks at me, his lips pressed together, then turns and digs his heels into the horse. The carriage jerks forward. The trees fall away until we're in the clearing with the massive brick and frame pile of the mill before us. A thick column of black smoke climbs into the sky from the brick stack of the engine house. The machines roar.

The hairs prick up on the back of my neck. I feel that itch again. Near a doorway, leaning on a hitching post with his horse's reins in his hand, is Buck Heppert, looking thunderous. What is he doing here? The nerve he has to stand there looking at me like I've kept him waiting.

A group of women, all white, cluster together outside, snorting snuff from their fingernails and spitting in the dirt. They stare at me as Simon drives up to the single doorway by the hitching post. Down another path into the woods, there is a row of houses—small whitewashed shacks, each with a small wooden step at the front door. Children, babies yet, of the white families who work in the mill sit in the dooryards. One sits in a cotton shift but is otherwise naked, her face dirty and smeared, grasping at the straggling weeds that spring from the open space under the cabins. The houses are set up on bricks, and chickens cluck and flutter at the corners, chased under and out of their shelter by a lean dog that looks like he doesn't even have the strength to make a kill. Our hands had better cabins before the war.

I was here with Buck ten years ago. The ginhouse was a blackened shell, and the old shed and press stood broken and idle. It had a charm to it, as calm as a graveyard next to the pool fed by the whispering creeks. Tall trees waved lazily in the breeze. Buck wanted to show me the spot. He frightened me with stories of how the gin would eat a man's hand if you weren't careful. The place had been the Harrisons' back then. They had moved north to Illinois, leaving their land to the tax collector. Eli had gotten it cheap.

"Mrs. Branson," Buck says as he approaches the buggy. "How was your trip out?" Simon climbs off his horse, but Buck steps in front of him, offering me his hand. The eyes of the mill women are piercing.

"How do you happen to be here, Mr. Heppert?"

"I am here for you. Now, why are you here?" His tone is dark. His brows crease as he narrows his eyes at me. Dark eyes. I had forgotten how deep.

"I am here looking after the interests my late husband left to my son."

He raises his eyebrows and takes my arm. What presumption. He is so like his father.

"What do you mean you are here for me?" I ask.

"Pa asked me to meet you here. He's been occupied, as you might imagine, with Mr. Branson's affairs."

How long has it been since I stood next to him? He has stayed away from me. I am glad he has. His face is changed. Lines crease his mouth and eyes. His skin has lost its softness, has grown tough from too much sun and spirits. I have heard about his gambling and running around. The rumors I have listened to, sought out over the years. But it is the same face before me, with his black mustache and his noble nose.

"You followed me here," I say.

"No, I didn't, Gus. I took the trails through Pa's woods. You remember them?"

My face is hot, red, I'm sure, from blushing. "How did your pa know I was coming here?"

"Pa knows everything. You know that." He barely smiles. It looks more like a grimace. His attempt at humor.

"Have you spoken with the foreman?"

"I told him you'd be along. He didn't seem too happy about it, but he offered to show us around."

The door into the mill is a wooden panel with a bolt and lock hanging loose from a metal loop and seems to be one of the few ways in or out of the building.

Simon stays outside in the sunlight, holding the carriage reins. He nods at me as we leave him. Buck and I walk inside, and it is another world, swollen with noise and cotton dust. The roar of the machines pushes everything at a vertiginous rush. The jennies and power looms are arrayed in long rows of tentacled machinery, whirring at a wild pace like thousands of Simon's whirling lawn mowers. The chaos is dizzying. My veil is dusted with cotton fibers that float like snowflakes in the thick, humid air. The floor is peopled with white women and young boys and girls. A glassed-in office looks out on the mill floor. Two men in shirtsleeves and collars sit at desks piled with ledgers. A thick little man in a vest approaches us with red-faced irritation. He nods as he rubs his hands together.

"Mrs. Branson," he says with the nasal twang of New England. "Welcome, ma'am. Everyone here at the Three Forks Mill is very sorry for the death of Mr. Branson. If there is anything we can do to help, we're ready to do it."

I nod. The racket of the machines makes it difficult to hear, so the little Yankee has raised his voice, which makes his face darken a deeper shade of red.

Some of the children are so small, even Henry's age, that they stand on the fenders of the spinning jennies, delicately grasping at the bobbins when they are full and replacing them with thin wooden spools. They nimbly tie the thread into place as the new bobbin begins to coil, wrapping itself in the fine thread. The heat is oppressive.

Buck takes my elbow, and I look back to the two men. "Mrs. Branson," he says. "This is Mr. Hunslow. He is the mill foreman."

Mr. Hunslow shakes his head at me. "I apologize, Mrs. Branson," he says. "We met at your husband's funeral, but it was very quick." He shakes my hand in long, hearty strokes. "Mr. Heppert here advised me that you were on your way out. Did you want to see the place? It's yours now, so I'd be happy to show you around."

"Of course." I have to yell over the noise. "Thank you, Mr. Hunslow."

He waves us forward down the long aisles of throstles, spinning with thread and spindles. The women, gaunt-faced, stand back from us in their soiled cotton dresses. They pull their hair up off their necks. Some wear kerchiefs tied over their faces. Already on my black gloves I can see tiny strands of white lint. It floats in the air, almost imperceptible. The children move like sleepwalkers. Sweat beads above my lip and on my forehead. Hunslow's face has a sheen of moisture on it as he shouts.

"There are two thousand spindles operating here. We employ about fifty people, mostly women and children from the area. Some niggers, too. Back here, this is really where the process begins."

Through a pair of wide barn doors, we enter an open shed. Wagons are lined up along the outside, and Negro men with large hooks unload the bales, cut them open, and pull out the cotton. It billows like clouds, rushing from the burlap skin onto the brick floor. The cotton is blinding white in the sunlight. Black women gather around the mountain in groups and beat at it with long sticks. They pick over it, pulling out twigs and branches and the blackened dried husks of cotton bolls.

"The cotton is cleaned and batted here, then taken into the carding room," he continues. The black faces turn to us, impassive, but they keep at their work without pausing. Two white men, overseers, stand in the corner, talking and watching them as they work. They hold thick cudgels.

I pull in my breath, suppressing a cough from the dryness in my chest. Hunslow leads us through wide doors back into the mill, into a different room filled with more machines attended by women. They feed the clean cotton into wide metal mouths. The cotton is pulled in by rollers bristling with metal teeth that chew into it. The women gingerly push it into the metal maws, the tips of their fingers coming perilously close to the teeth of the carding rollers. We move close to them. Their nails are cracked and dirty. The cotton fibers feed out of the other end of the machine in thick braids, winding themselves into tall cans.

"The carded cotton is fed into the drawing cans and then goes into the spinning room, where it's spun into thread. The threads are rolled onto bobbins, and the bobbins are loaded onto our power looms. We have sixty of them, and when we're running at full speed, we can produce hundreds of yards of cotton cloth a day." Beyond the carders are the great power looms, where more women stand monitoring and managing the machines. The warp threads rise and fall in an alternating cadence, and the shuttles fly back and forth with a bang, merging the weft through the web of threads. Cloth inches its way from the mouth of the machine as it is rolled onto bolts.

"It's quite a system, don't you think, Mr. Heppert?" Hunslow turns to Buck. We walk between the dead-eyed women, who stand reaching their thin hands out to the threads on the machines. The relentless roar is deafening.

"Yes, Mr. Hunslow," Buck shouts back. "Very impressive."

"As fine as any factory we have back in Rhode Island, I can assure you of that. I made sure of it myself. That's why Mr. Branson brought me down here." He nods with obvious pride, and the tiny blood vessels across his nose and cheeks stand out.

"Very ingenious, Mr. Hunslow," I shout, looking back across the mill floor as we enter the glass-enclosed office. Mr. Hunslow shuts the door, and a hush surrounds us. The noise of the mill is muffled and we are in a silent paradise. The two men in the counting room stand up at their desks and nod solemnly to me as Hunslow introduces them. We stand awkwardly together, the three of us, with the accountants watching. Hunslow huffs and shrugs.

"Will there be anything else, Mr. Heppert?" he asks.

Buck extends his hand. "Thank you, Hunslow. That was very informative." They both turn to me. The bullet-headed Yankee offers me his hand. I will not reach out to him.

"There is something more, Mr. Hunslow." The accountants have beady, probing eyes. Buck stands over me.

"Yes, ma'am," Hunslow says, puffing out his cheeks so the red lines stand out like rivers on a map.

"I appreciate your survey of the operations here. But I also came to collect my husband's possessions. Whatever he may have here. And to see if there are any packages. I was expecting a parcel of books from Mobile. *Macaria* and *St. Elmo*."

"Of course, Mrs. Branson. I have left everything just as Mr. Branson left it. Come into his office. Everything is just as he left it."

Hunslow shrugs nervously and motions to a door behind the accountants' desks. Buck steps aside to let me pass. His eyes bore into me. I will not look at him. Hunslow opens the door. The air feels cooler inside. The light is dim and Hunslow throws back the heavy curtains, stirring the dust off them.

Eli's office. I can feel him in this room. I can see the curve of his back on the chair behind the wide pine desk. There are his footprints across the worn Persian rug. There are tiny blots of ink soaked into the wood of his desk. The desk is clear, but it is as if the papers were just swept from it. I can see them there by the metal inkstand, criss-crossed with his spidery hand.

Through the window, the sunlight flashes off the surface of the collecting pond of the mill creek, surrounded by trees that dip their branches down to touch the water. Three Forks Creek vanishes into a curve of their drooping leaves. Beyond, fields lay bare and open. The Cumberland foothills stand in the distance like painted scenery.

Eli was not a ripple of water that smooths itself but something more permanent. The things of my past will never meet the things of my present. Buck is here as if he has some right to a role as my guardian. Like Judge. Buck talks to me as he used to. How easy to slip back into the past, to pretend like we are here again at Three Forks on our horses and there is no Eli and no war and no mill. But the fit is rough on me. He makes me uneasy. He watches me. I think he is waiting for a sign that we could go back to that summer after the war, that we could somehow sew together that year and this and cut away all that has happened in between.

Hunslow steps behind the desk, rubbing his palms against his vest front. "Let's see," he says. "What sort of things were you looking for, ma'am?" Buck stands too close.

"Everything. I would like to take his things home. Are there any packages? I have been waiting for those books for so long."

"Papers, too? Some of them relate to our business here."

"The business papers can stay, of course. What you haven't felt a need for since his passing, I'd like to take with me."

"Gus," Buck interjects. "Do you need these things now?"

"If you are pressed, you can go anytime, Buck. There is no need for you to stay on my account."

Buck lets out a grim laugh. "No use arguing with ladies, is there, Hunslow? Especially when they're waiting for their novels."

Hunslow gives him a weak smile in return. He is opening drawers, pulling out ledgers and stacks of loose paper. A penknife and a larger one that still has wood shavings stuck on the blade. A gold watch that has stopped running.

"Will you be wanting the other things?" Hunslow asks, wagging a hand around the room, indicating the inkwell, a clock, and some pens.

There isn't much else. Some prints tacked on the wall—cutouts from a magazine. A stack of old newspapers in a corner by the fireplace. A pair of tin candlesticks.

"If you could box everything else and send it to my home, I'd appreciate it very much. And any packages?"

Hunslow surveys the room again and shrugs. "No, ma'am, just these things. I can take them out to your carriage now." He collects the papers in a large pile.

I slip the watch into the pocket of my dress. "Just one more thing," I say.

Buck shakes his head with exasperation.

"Dividends. When are the dividends paid?" I force a smile. My hands clasp. Is my voice shaking? My teeth clench.

"Well," Hunslow stumbles. Heat rises in my face. "Well, ma'am. We once paid dividends quarterly. But Mr. Branson suspended dividends since—well, over a year ago now."

"Suspended dividends?"

Buck is grim-faced and nodding in agreement as if aware of all this.

"Yes, ma'am," Hunslow says. "The mill has had some difficulties. We hope to turn things around soon."

"What sort of difficulties, Mr. Hunslow?"

"Well." Hunslow looks at the papers and back to me. "Maybe we ought to sit down." He coughs into his hand, looking at Buck with discomfort. He takes the chair behind the desk and motions Buck and me to sit. He looks around the room slowly and coughs into his hand again. "The mill has operated without interruption for almost four years. We have not fully recovered from the panic. We were building out a list of buyers, cloth merchants and the like, but with the panic, we saw our business fall off quite a bit. The operation was only two years old and given the amount of capital that was put in for the building and the machinery—well, you can imagine. We have recovered some clients and found some new ones. The cloth is, you know, of a coarser grade—osnaburgs and the like. It was always the intention of Mr. Branson to move into finer cloths. We've found merchants in Atlanta and Nashville who have been consistent buyers, and now some in Birmingham. It's been a difficult return to profitability. But things are getting better."

"The mill isn't making money." I blurt it out. What are these meaningless subtleties between profits and losses?

"Oh, yes, ma'am, it is," he insists quickly. "Oh, of course, it is. But we've had some reverses, you see, in the cloth market and so on. We've been unable to realize profits that the investors expected. And you are now the main investor."

"But Mr. Heppert said the mill was profitable. He said it was very profitable." Hunslow looks at Buck with raised eyebrows. "The senior Mr. Heppert," I say.

"Yes, ma'am, I see," Hunslow says. Buck shifts in his chair. "And Mr. Heppert, Mr. Everton Heppert, is correct, in a way. With careful management, the mill should be very profitable and very soon. I've guaranteed Mr. Heppert that I can do it. That I can turn it around and make the place a model for the whole South." Hunslow smiles with pride.

"How soon will that be, Mr. Hunslow?" My voice is sharp, like Rachel's. I am hot and tired and confused. Hunslow flushes.

"Now, Gus," Buck says and reaches for my arm.

"It's my mill, Buck," I say. "And it's my money. I don't even know why you're here."

"To keep you from exposing yourself," he says quickly. He rises from his chair.

"When will the next dividend be paid, Mr. Hunslow?" He squirms, looking to Buck to intervene. "It's a fair question," I insist.

"Yes, ma'am, of course it is," he answers, then turns to Buck. "As I said, Mr. Branson suspended dividend payments."

"Well I want them resumed."

"Gus, that's enough. Pa is handling all this," Buck interjects.

"I will see what we can do," Hunslow says. "The first of July, we can see how much of a dividend might be paid. But it's going to put us behind, Mrs. Branson. You don't want to cut off your nose to spite your face."

"Pay the dividend and then we can see about cutting off noses."

"Thank you, Mr. Hunslow," Buck says, interfering again. "We'll be on our way." I refuse to get up.

Hunslow gathers the papers and moves toward the door. "I'll let your coachman know you're ready, Mrs. Branson," he says, and he leaves us in the office.

My hands are shaking and my knees, too. These men, pushing me all the time. Eli never pushed. He didn't need to. Buck can rot.

"Do you think your pa will be pleased with how you've accomplished your errand for him?" I ask. He frowns as I walk past.

In the outer office, the machines roar. The office door is wide open. The accountants are out on the mill floor, working their way into a cluster of women. The spindles are unattended, spinning wildly with white threads like streamers flowing behind them. The great gears and flywheels rotate, and the leather belts that power the looms keep roaring. Shuttles bang back and forth, but there is no thread in them, and the machines put out unwoven warp.

I approach the women, my black hat and veil in my hand, moving between them in their drab grays and whites that are yellowed and stained with dirt. They are gathered around a woman. She is lying on the floor, sprawled out, semiconscious. Her dress is soaked through, and her hair is drenched with sweat. She is younger than me but worn and wasted. Her hair is coming loose from her kerchief in brown strands that stick to her temples. She is on her back, staring up at the ceiling, wide-eyed. Roving eyes like Eli's, looking for something. Her body begins to convulse, as if every muscle flexes in a single simultaneous contraction. A thin foam gathers at her mouth. The light is dim, but is it pink—red-tinted?

"Give her some air," the overseer shouts, and the women and children take a step back. "Give her some air," he shouts again.

"It's the heat. The heat got to her," a woman near me says to another. They wipe the sweat off their foreheads with bare hands and rub them on their aprons.

"It'll kill us all if it doesn't break soon," the other says back. "The third this week."

The dust around me spins like the threads spinning around the bobbins. Thousands of spindles turn wildly, whipping the powdered air. It is so hot in here.

Buck takes my arm. "Come on, Gus," he says to me carefully. "Let's go. Simon is ready."

Eleven

SIMON PRODS THE HORSE with his heels, and she picks up her gait, jerking the carriage forward. Buck is beside us. He rides a jet-colored gelding and heels into him to keep up. The battering noise of the carriage on the plank road pounds into my head like those looms. The face of the woman on the floor of the mill, her ghostly face, pink foam at her lips. So much like Eli.

Buck is too close. I do not want him here. The thick, ringing clip-clop of his horse's shoes against the boards maddens me.

"Did you find out what you wanted?" Buck calls to me.

I grit my teeth. Simon's head makes the slightest of turns. He is watching Buck. And Buck is watching him.

"Yes, Buck. Thank you."

Simon's back moves in time with the battering of the horse's hooves on the planks.

"Can you hurry, Simon? I need to get back home."

Simon nods without looking back and shakes the horse's reins. He brings his heels sharply into her flanks. The papers slide against my leg. My gloved hands can't grip them.

Buck hurries his horse, trying to stay close. "Is it about the money, then, Gus? You know Pa can tell you the same thing," he says. He is painfully serious.

"Thank you," I say. We ride along in silence, Buck keeping up as he can.

"I have missed you, Gus," he says suddenly. He lowers his voice, as if to keep Simon from hearing. Heat and blood rush to my face, draining the rest of me, turning my body to ice. I cannot answer him. Not with Simon here. Not even if we were alone.

"I have," he goes on. "These years away from you, they've been like a prison for me. I am happy to be near you again." His words are sweet, but his face remains hard. If I move or try to speak, I'm afraid I will shatter and be unable to find myself again. The horses trot in time, and we clatter along. The sun has moved lower on the horizon so that it burns my eyes. "I just want to help you. If you'll tell me what you want, I'll help you get it."

Buck's closeness is melting me, and I do not want to soften. I do not want to be kind to him.

"You don't need to tell me you've been climbing mountains for the past ten years. I've been unfortunately aware of your pastimes," I say. I taste metal in my mouth.

"You still remember that night," Buck says with a frown. "I remember it, too."

My hands itch in the soft kid gloves. I scratch at my palm, keeping my eyes on Simon's back. How humiliating to have this conversation within his hearing.

"Gus," Buck says softly, edging his horse too close to the carriage wheels. "I've thought about that night—of all the time we spent together back then."

"You should be ashamed, Buck," I whisper hoarsely. "Coming here to tell lies like that." Buck's horse loses its footing and stumbles to the side, but he recovers and rides close to the carriage again, looking wounded.

"They aren't lies. I can't help what happened between us. You're the one who married."

His gall is stunning. Like a blow to the stomach.

"Let's start again," he says. "What is past is past. I want to be your friend again, if nothing else."

"We were never friends."

"Is it so easy for you to say that? You know that's not true. I was always your friend. You promised yourself to someone else, and I stepped aside. I don't blame you for it. You did what you thought was right."

It isn't true. He left me alone. He left me alone to face Eli and Mama. He abandoned me. If he had said one word to me, I never would have married Eli. But he was gone. I could not get to him.

"You are right, Buck. It is past. Let's forget it. There is no need to discuss it."

"We had good times together, Gus. You can't forget them. Remember when we would walk down by the river? Or take rides out here when there was no one else around?"

My hand grips the arm of the seat. I struggle to hold myself still against the bouncing of the carriage and keep the papers in my lap. My throat closes. I must hold my breath.

"We're kin, too. That blood connects us. Let me help you."

"How can you help me?"

"However you want. You want to get a dividend from the mill? I can talk to Pa. I can make him see reason. I can help you." He looks honest. His eyes say that he is trying to be truthful. Maybe he does want to help me.

"What did you tell Mike?" I ask directly, watching his eyes.

"Mike?" he says blankly. He is pretending now. I notice Simon nod faintly. He does not turn or make any other motion. It could be the bounce of the horse. "Tell Mike what?"

"About the money. About Eli's estate. He came to me. He seemed to think there was a great deal of money—at the mill, he said. He said he had talked to you about it."

Buck considers for a moment. His gaze scrapes across the row of cedar trees that line the edge of a field. The stubble of last year's cotton crop has been plowed under, and new plants are starting to break through the orange-red earth.

"I talked to him, I guess. I never said anything about Eli's money. How could I know anything about it?" He looks at me without blinking.

"I just wondered, that's all," I say, meeting his eyes. "He seemed so agitated, and I thought maybe your father had told you something."

"He told me just what he told you. I thought the mill was doing very well, but according to Hunslow, that's not the case."

"No, not quite the case."

"I'll talk to Pa. I'll convince him to help you with the money. Hell, he can give you something, too, if you like. He's not busted up like the rest of these folks."

I smile at him through my veil. Should I lift it? I take an edge in my hand and pull it back from my face. He sits taller than me on his horse, so my eyes tilt up to him. What can he really do for me?

"I do appreciate your help, Buck. I'm sorry if I was rude. It's just that so much has changed since we were—since we were last together."

That sadness comes back into his eyes. "I know it has. We've all seen the change. You've had it better than most."

"I guess I never realized how bad things have been for people. For everyone else. We were all starting to get along, and then the panic—"

"The panic hit a lot of people. They're going off to Texas and Arizona. And these dirty Republicans running Alabama like it's a common trough for them to root in. Taking whatever they want. It's disgusted a lot of people. They won't stay here and let the niggers lord it over them. They'll pick up and leave rather than stay here." Simon is perfectly still, as if he is all alone.

"Not you and Judge, I hope. You wouldn't leave, would you?"

"No, ma'am," Buck says with a twisted smile. "We're here to stay. This is our country. Our home. It ain't theirs. We won't let them have it."

"Judge wasn't hurt by the panic, was he?"

"Sure he was. It hit just about everybody. Pa was nervous there for a while. But now the Democrats have taken back the state, and it looks like he'll be able to make things work out all right."

"Will he? I'm so glad."

The first houses from town come into view. They are old farmhouses, weather-beaten and quiet but not abandoned. Many of these homes seem abandoned—in town and out in the county—though there is life in them, desperate life. There is a thin difference between a place that has been abandoned and a place where the people have simply given up. It is all around us.

"Are you going to see your pa now?" I ask.

"No," Buck answers, looking surprised. "Why would I?"

"I only ask because I wonder if I should go see him. You're right. He's trying to help me, and I have been shameful. It's my nerves these past weeks."

"You should see him. I know he would want to know you want to be good, but let me talk to him first. I'll let you know what he says."

"Thank you," I say with only a little difficulty, and then add, "I have missed you, too, Buck. I would be happy for you to call on me."

"I will, Gus. Very soon." His face is calmer, less sad. The sun seems like a friend to him, shining on his glossy black hair and warming his tanned face. "I will." He tips his hat and pulls his horse's reins to the right, leaving us. The dust rises as he gallops up Chickasaw Street until he is out of sight.

"I'm sorry, Simon," I say. "I think that conversation might have upset you."

Simon turns back and looks at me with a curious face. "No, ma'am," he says. "There was nothing to be upset about for me."

"Really? I'm sorry. I—Well, I don't understand, perhaps."

Simon smiles. "I think you understand well enough. Well enough to handle Mr. Heppert."

"Do you think so?" I ask.

"Yes, ma'am. And anything you can't handle, I have the means to handle for you." He pats his side pocket, where there must be a gun. It bulges against his side like a gun. Most of the Negroes around Albion do not have weapons. The white men, the men of the Knights of the White Cross, disarmed most of them and intimidated the others with whippings so that some gave their guns up without a word. But Simon still carries his.

"Oh," I say, my eyes on his pocket. "That is good to know."

The papers are ungainly in my lap. It's a miracle they haven't spilled onto the carriage floor or out onto the street. "These are all the things in Eli's office. There wasn't any package. I asked several times, but nothing."

He turns back to look at the papers and nods. "Thank you for collecting them."

"Do you really think there ever was a package? Eli was sick. He might not have had the strength to put it together."

He shrugs. We are along the edge of the cemetery. The sun is burning down on the headstones. Eli's grave is unmarked but for the mound of earth. The dirt has dried from its fresh red color to the shade of brick.

"As far as I can tell, that only means the money is hidden away still," he says.

"You won't give up on it, will you?"

Simon laughs and turns his head back to me, showing large white teeth. "I guess not. And I do appreciate your directness." He turns the carriage up the lane behind the house. The iron wheels crunch on the gravel.

"You're as bad as Rachel, with her charms. Neither of you will give up on your wild ideas," I say.

He pulls at the horse's reins. We are already home. The stable doors are open. This heat is absolutely withering.

Simon dismounts at a jump and comes to hand me down. "We are both single-minded people." He grins at me, taking my hand like a dancing master.

I take the armful of papers. They shift against me as I step down, almost spilling out of my arm.

Emma is coming from the kitchen. She must have heard the carriage. She rushes to us, twice looking back at the house. Simon turns to her, breaking my gaze.

"Miss Gus, there are ladies to see you," she whispers. "They've been here a while. I told them you were indisposed. I didn't want to say you had gone out. But they won't leave."

"My Lord, Emma, who is it?" What a scandal that would be. What are they doing here? Buck knew we were at the mill. Maybe the whole town already knows.

"Miss Bama, and she brought a bunch of ladies with her." Emma's eyes are wide. She looks nervously back at the house. She wipes the sweat off her forehead with her apron.

Simon frowns at me and looks at the papers.

"Tell them I'll be down shortly. That I've—I've recovered. I'll go up the back stairs." Emma nods and rushes back to the house. Simon steps toward me as if he will follow me.

"I'll leave the papers in Eli's office for you. Don't be too conspicuous. You know how the servants are." I smile at him.

He stops short, watching me walk away.

Take a breath, Gus.

The doors glide into their pockets. Five women sit in the front parlor fanning themselves, all of them in black. My God, they can't all be in mourning. That's six of us dressed like crows. Next time they'll come wearing mourning masks, like Roman women, lined up bearing the faces of their dead husbands or fathers or brothers.

"Gus," Bama cries out. She stands, waving her fan and leaning on an umbrella. "You're feeling better? Normally, I wouldn't wait, but I've brought you a full delegation, as you see." She laughs hoarsely and slaps her fan shut, using it to point at the dour women around her.

"I'm so sorry to keep you waiting." Only Bama has risen. The others remain seated. Beth Mastin. Her mother. Jennie Heyney. Bama's niece Emily Whitcomb. And Bama. "I came down as quickly as I could. You know how slow maids can be. I didn't even know you were here until a little bit ago."

They exchange glances. Bama is still standing.

"Well, you came down in good time," she says. "We were all starting to talk about you in your own parlor. And you should always be present when ladies talk about you in your house." She laughs again and practically falls back into her seat, pleased with her joke.

"You've all had tea? I can call for some more?" The pitcher sits sweating but empty. Their glasses are scattered around the room.

"Enough, Gus. Sit down."

Bama is used to being obeyed. I take the seat she indicates.

"We didn't come here to be waited on. We came to see how you're getting on."

"Of course. It is very kind of you all to come."

"Nonsense," Bama shouts out. "We're all old friends here. Half of us are kin in one way or another."

"You look very fine, Gus. So rosy and healthy," Jennie says.

I touch my cheek. It is warm in here. They can't know I've been to the mill, but I feel as if it is on my face. Jennie looks so sad and thin. Her blond hair is pulled back from her face. Her bonnet sits in her lap. We were such good friends in Huntsville.

"We were just saying how the house is so changed," says Mrs. Mastin. Why isn't she in Chattanooga? "On the inside. It still looks like the old place from the street. But very changed inside."

"Yes, Mr. Branson insisted on the latest style. We both did."

"Mr. Branson insisted on a lot of things, I guess, but they can be undone," Emily says, smiling. Her face is a ragged canvas ravaged by smallpox.

"I don't know how you do it," Mrs. Mastin says. "Living in some-one else's house. I couldn't do it. Not someone I knew, anyway."

Bama hacks in derision. "Bah, Ida, you rent your house from some Yankees. You know them, don't you?"

Mrs. Mastin blushes crimson. "I didn't take their home from them, Bama."

"I know what you mean about servants, Gus," says Beth. "It's so hard to find just one good help anymore."

"They were bad enough before the war," her mother chimes in. "Now you have to pay them ridiculous wages, and if you so much as lay a finger on them, they go running to the Freedmen's Bureau. They used to, at least."

Beth blushes. "Don't mind her, Gus, she doesn't mean any offense."

"No need to dwell on all that," Bama interjects. "The world is being set right again. We won't see any more darky soldiers marching on the square. Our men are seeing to that."

"That's right," says Mrs. Mastin. "The Democrats are back. And we have your cousin to thank. He is our most valiant soldier. He always was."

"Old Judge does what he sees needs being done. Bless the Lord for him," Bama says, nodding, her eyes closed.

"Yes, Judge is a blessing," I say. "I didn't realize how important he has become."

"Listen to you, Gus. You'd think you were in different families. He has never lost his importance. He has led us through some dark times. I'm sure he'll tell you all about it someday."

"I'll be sure to ask him."

"You can't blame Gus, Auntie," Emily says, smiling sweetly. She's wearing powder that has settled into the scars, leaving strange patterns on her skin. "Shut away here for so long with no society. It must feel like you've come alive again, doesn't it?"

"Oh, hush, Emily." Bama is so gruff with her. "We're not out of the woods yet. You know there's word that the party will send him to the convention this fall. Your bloodlines go back far, Gus, and the men have always distinguished themselves."

Emily's face goes sour, and she makes a considered study of the mantelpiece.

"What convention?" asks Jennie.

"The state convention, you silly girl." Bama sighs. "Don't you listen? The Democrats have the state again, and they're going to throw out that nigger constitution and write a new one."

"Is the old one no good?"

Bama rolls her eyes. She flips her fan open with a crack and waves it vigorously in front of her. "You girls. In my youth, it was an embarrassment not to be *au courant* with the events of the day."

We sit looking at our hands. Jennie shakes her head as if throwing her thought away, then opens her mouth again. "Isn't the heat terrible? When will it end?"

The ladies all nod agreement.

"Ah, yes," Bama intones. "When in doubt, back to the weather."

"Did you hear Mary Perkerson died?" says Mrs. Mastin. "They say she sweated herself to death in her own bed."

That woman at the mill. My Lord. Is it just the heat?

"But Ma," Beth says, "she's been dying for years!"

"She wasn't a well woman. No, she was never well. The weak go first. We should be heading off to the mountains soon, Beth."

"You should come to Monte Sano," Bama says. She waves her fan at them. "I'm going to see my cousin Virginia Clay for a week, and then we're all going up to Viduta. She was a Tunstall, you know. Emily will be with me." Bama's mouth curls down. She doesn't look at her niece.

"We always go to Chattanooga," Mrs. Mastin replies. "With this heat and everyone sick, we're likely to go sooner rather than later. I never liked Viduta much. There's nothing there."

"Gus is coming up with me, too, aren't you, dear?"

Mrs. Mastin's look changes from dour to intrigued. Bama certainly is going all out for me.

"Yes, ma'am," I say. Emily frowns and returns to her consideration of the mantel. "I'm so looking forward to it."

Bama's charm is working. Mrs. Mastin sits higher in her chair and smiles down her nose at me approvingly.

"If you are looking to escape the heat, Jennie, you can join us, too." Bama gives Jennie a wide-open smile, showing her missing teeth again. "You won't be able to flirt with the young men like Emily and Gus, but there's as much fun in watching, isn't there?"

Emily's mouth goes hard, and she cuts her eyes at me quickly.

Jennie blushes and tugs at the ribbons on her bonnet. "Oh, Miss Bama." She sounds scandalized. "I couldn't, but thank you."

"Why on earth couldn't you? That man of yours keeping you at home?"

Jennie keeps her eyes in her lap. "Charlie does work so hard. And I haven't been able to find any good help." She turns a deeper shade of scarlet.

Charlie must not make very much at the railroad. Maids are the easiest thing to find. I don't think Jennie would have married Charlie if her pa hadn't died.

"You won't be missing a thing, Jennie," I say. "I doubt there will be so many men up at Viduta as Bama likes to think." What else can I say to her? Poor thing, blushing herself to tears.

"Easier prey here in Albion, isn't there, Gus?" Emily smiles sweetly again.

"Oh, ho!" Bama exclaims, pounding her umbrella against the floor. "Now we're on to something. Do you have a particular someone on your mind, Gus?"

The women are hushed, watching me. Emily looks as if she smells blood.

"Not at all, Bama. I have just lost my husband." I look at my hands. When will this ordeal be over?

"The choice is yours. You could have your pick of men. But enjoy your freedom while you can." Bama gives an exaggerated nod. "I've been waiting to see when Buck Heppert will come snooping around your door. He's sure to!"

"He's my cousin, Bama. I am sure he will call on me."

"Besides, Auntie, Buck Heppert is looking for an heiress." Emily smiles at me with narrow eyes.

"Money is money, however you get it, right, Gus?" Bama grins at me.

"As long as you really have it. People are so rarely what they appear to be." Emily's lips stretch wider, pulling back to reveal her teeth.

What has she heard? Word must be going around.

I look her in the eye. "I think you're right about that, Emily."

"We just came from Mrs. Stephens, Gus. You wouldn't believe the gossip we heard there." Emily smiles again. The banker's wife. Of course.

"Yes, Gus," Beth says. "We heard there's a whole group of Negroes heading off to Kansas."

"Kansas? Lot of good that will do them. They might as well emigrate to China!" Bama shouts.

So everyone knows about that, too. "Is it a big group, Beth?"

"Mrs. Stephens talked like it was, didn't she, Ma?" Beth nods at Mrs. Mastin, and the old woman shakes her head, looking at Bama.

"Big enough for people to talk about," Mrs. Mastin says. "Which is too big. Somebody's got to put a stop to this nonsense, or there won't be any darkies left!"

"Did she say when they are leaving?" I ask.

"You're very curious about all this," Mrs. Mastin snaps. "Are you planning a trip to Kansas? No, she didn't know when they were leaving. She said one of her servants brought home a broadsheet they found at the depot. She confiscated it at once. It said to contact a Simon. You have a man here named Simon, don't you? A rabble-rouser, isn't he?"

My face turns hot. They are all such painful gossips. "Mr. Branson used to have a man named Simon, but he's been gone years now. And we have so many servants, it's hard to keep their names straight. I'm sure you remember what it was like—I mean before the war for you, of course." Let her choke on that.

She scowls and turns to Bama, huffing in her chair. "There are certainly not that many servants in this house, and I'm sure that Simon is still here!" She sounds like she's cawing.

Bama almost grins at her anger. "That's enough, ladies," she says. "I think we should be moving on. We'll be back, Gus. Is this a good time for you to receive callers? We'll make it a regular stop."

"Yes, Gus, we'll come back," Jennie says. She rises and walks over to me, taking my hands and giving me a kiss on the cheek. "I'm so glad to see you again."

"Thank you, Jennie. I'm glad to see you, too."

"Don't smother the woman with kisses," Bama says, pushing Jennie aside and giving me a kiss of her own. Beth comes up next and hugs me while her mother and Emily stand behind her. They nod and turn to the door.

"You remember what I said about letting ladies talk about you in your parlor," Bama says. "We will be back!" She laughs again and shoos the other women with her fan until they have all filed outside.

I hope they don't come back. It would be far better if they stayed away. Spreading gossip. Poor Jennie. She didn't marry well.

Emma comes into the hall. "Are they gone?"

"Yes, thank the Lord."

"They sure are impatient ladies." She shrugs and shakes her head.

"More than that, I think. Next time I'll keep the headache."

Emma smiles. "Next time I'll get a headache, too."

We both laugh.

Twelve

SWEAT COVERS ME AND soaks my nightdress. The room is dark but for the moon. The only sound is the tick of the mantel clock. The windows are wide open. There is not a breath of air to rustle the leaves in the trees outside. Dreams keep me waking. They give me a panic that takes hold of my limbs, and I cannot fight it.

I dream that I am in the mill, the machines pounding and roaring around me. The noise is deafening, and I cry out, but I cannot hear myself over the mad chorus. People rush around me. I am lying down, stretched out on the mill floor, and I try to speak, but no sound comes out. I search the faces around me. I search the dark rafters that are dressed in cotton cobwebs. When I try to speak, the taste of blood fills my mouth.

Forget the dream. Forget that woman at the mill. Just like Eli. Those eyes were just like Eli's. But I cannot forget the money. Could Simon be right? Is there money hidden somewhere in this house? Or at the mill? Where has he searched? He said everywhere. He spent all afternoon in the carriage house with John.

I pull my wrap over my shoulders. The heat is too much. The straw mats on the floor feel hot under the soles of my feet. The bedroom door creaks as I open it. Down the stairs, there is only darkness and quiet. Across the hall at Eli's door, the handle is newly cleaned and polished with water and saleratus. The handle turns, but the door will not give. Locked still.

My feet scrape on the woven matting. Moonlight fills my room. On the side table, the dark blue bottle sits, almost black against the ghostly white marble, so that it seems like it is floating. I grasp it. The glass feels cool against my palm.

Three small drops fall into a glass of water. They seem to glow as they dissipate in ribbons. I take a breath and wipe the sweat off my mouth. My hands tremble. The water is warm, with a bitter taste. I gulp at it until the glass is empty.

The moon shines clear and full in Henry's room. He is washed in pale rays that make him look like marble, like the cool white marble of my bedside table. His breathing is soft and even. He lies on his back, his eyes shut tight. His small lips are pursed. They move slightly, not like a kiss, so much, but like he is talking without opening his mouth.

The numbness is taking hold. It creeps up on me. I reach my hands out and touch the wall to guide myself half blind back to my bed.

On top of the counterpane, still in my wrap, I feel like I am drifting away. The feeling is gentle. I lie wrapped in its folds. I abandon myself to it, not fighting the waves as they carry me off.

Buck standing there at the mill waiting for me. Did Judge send him to watch me? He must have. I don't know what I feel for him. I want to hate him. But that summer after the war. My God, that summer seemed like forever. I never wanted it to end. I wanted it to go on and on because of Buck. He was so handsome. You want to believe someone that handsome. And the sadness in him. You want to heal him, though you can't see his wounds. If only I could have felt them, like his bullet scars, then I could have fixed him. No, I don't think anyone could fix him or ever can.

Buck was nothing to me when he first came back to Albion in February—before the war had ended. He wasn't well. He had been wounded at Franklin and stayed at the hospital until he was moved to convalesce with a family. He was not at the Battle of Nashville. Hill had fought alone, without Buck. Maybe if Buck had been there, Hill would have come back to us.

After Buck had healed enough to walk, he said he went to Pond Spring, where the Union forces paroled him. They even let him keep his pistols. Then he returned to Albion. He told us of Hill's death on the battlefield south of Nashville. We hadn't had any word from Hill for weeks. Buck heard the story from another soldier in their company, a man from Marengo County. He gave Buck the small morocco-bound book of the Gospels that Hill carried with him, and Buck gave it to Mama. She kept asking why he didn't get a lock of Hill's hair. Mama asked for the soldier's name. Buck couldn't remember it for certain. Mama wanted to write him a letter to thank him, and to ask for the soldier's story of Hill's death. What were his last moments? Were they painful? Did he say anything? Did the soldier think Hill had been a good Christian—had he been saved?

Buck brought me an issue of *Godey's Lady's Book* from the November before. He said he hoped it wasn't too out of date. A girl in the home where he convalesced gave it to him. For me, he said. He had rolled it up and carried it inside his jacket, so the edges had started to fray and the pages refused to give up their curl.

He stayed in our house and slept in Hill's bed. Mama loved having him in the house. He eased the pain of Hill's absence. Mama asked him again and again to tell the story of my brother's death. Hill was at the forefront of the fighting, he said—as he always was, leading the men of the 26th. The ragged, tattered few who remained, who had survived the slaughter of Franklin and were more or less whole. The man said they were coming out of their earthworks and moving north up the Granny White Pike when the shelling started from Fort Negley. He said there was nothing he could do.

After the surrender, when Buck moved back to Judge's house, he found ways to meet me. He courted me. It was a true courtship. He waited for me on Allen Street, grinning, leaning against a mulberry tree, holding a bundle of peaches wrapped in cheesecloth. Or bread that Sally had made. The streets weren't safe, he said, for a lady alone, especially one as pretty as I was.

We went to Three Forks on long rides through the woods, where the forest was so dark and quiet that all you heard was the horse's breath and the drumbeats of the woodpeckers. That was before the mill was built. We went out alone together, and Mama let us. What could she do? She was so terrified herself with the way Albion had changed. Freedmen and poor whites flooding into town, loitering on the square. Soldiers likely to burst into your house to search it for God knows what. Mama was beside herself with fits. She barely paid attention to anything I did.

Buck brought me flowers. Bouquets of lilacs and cape jessamine clipped from a neighbor's yard. Nosegays of roses and mountain laurel. He told me how pretty I was. How deep and thoughtful my eyes were. He caressed my chin with his fingertips, ever so gentle, but I knew their strength. All those things he did. He reached for my hand more than once. And I let him take it. When I told Mama what I hoped, she laughed nervously, clucking and moving around the parlor to pick up whatever gewgaws we had left, looking at them to see if they might be worth something.

And that night of the barn dance. That terrible night of the barn dance. Judge decided out of nowhere to have a ball, and it sent Mama into paroxysms. She thought it was imprudent. He used the old barn east of town that had not been used for anything in years. He said though he had sworn off politics, he wanted to do something to welcome the boys home. We could not say openly what the dance was for—the Federals would not have allowed it. We were trying to pretend like things were as they used to be. That was what Judge was pretending, anyway.

The night was clear. The day's heat seemed to have been swept off the bluffs with the setting sun. My dress was of twice-turned sky-blue lawn, and I wore it with Mama's black cashmere shawl. I trimmed the dress with blue satin ribbons and flounces, like I saw in the *Godey's* Buck had given me. I stitched at it for days, tearing up an old silk dress of Mama's. It was the first time that I had not worn black since Hill's death. Six months had passed and Mama insisted I wear something gay. The dress was careworn, but I was beautiful. I could see it in everyone's eyes. My hair was combed up in curls gathered at the back and over my ear. I wore tea roses, and their perfume mixed with the spicy scent of the pine torches that lit up the old barn.

By some negotiation, Judge had guaranteed the men would not bring their weapons into the dance, and soldiers checked the boys' pockets and coats, taking away for the evening whatever small arms many of them carried. The barn was draped with garlands of honeysuckle and jasmine and wide swaths of blue and white bunting. All the young men in town who had come back from the war were there, such as they were. Some were on crutches or bandaged, nursing wounds that refused to heal. There were as many men missing an arm or a leg as there were men whole and complete. In between us danced the ghosts of the boys who never came back—like Hill. The eyes of the soldiers—paroled and pardoned or not—were not the careless, proud eyes of four years ago, but eyes stunned behind their forced gaiety. The Confederate insignia was forbidden, so they wore their old gray uniforms stripped of braid and with buttons covered in black cloth to hide the embossed CSA.

Mama sat in a corner with Bama Buchanan and the other matrons. She smiled at me as the men came by, asking for a dance. Buck had asked me that day for the opening reel, and we lined up, the sons and daughters of the defeated South, and danced to the music of the banjos and guitars. The fiddler of the little band sitting atop a pile of hay bales whipped up the dancers, and we clapped along.

We danced with a frenzy under the torches, knowing the dark blue uniforms were near. If I narrowed my eyes and blurred my vision, I could see the gray coat of my partner looking new, with epaulettes and bars glittering in the flickering light. The dresses were fresh, and hopes were high, like in '61. The world had not ended, and the promises that had been made four years ago could still be kept. We could all pretend that for a dance.

Judge beamed from the side, talking with Dr. Greer and Mr. Lilly and the other men. At the supper break, he spoke and brought so many of us to tears. I thought of Hill, buried somewhere in the lonely country around Nashville, lost to us. Mike was gone, too, we did not know where. Mama cried in her corner, and Bama gave her a handkerchief. Buck came over to me and put an arm around my waist and squeezed me so close that I blushed.

Punch glasses were raised and the men whooped and the fiddler jumped up and started playing a tune we all knew, although it was a new song. Someone began to sing it, and soon we were all singing, laughing against each other, laughing sidelong at the blue soldiers.

> *Oh, I'm a good old rebel*
> *Now that's just what I am,*
> *For the fair land of Freedom*
> *I do not care a damn.*
> *I'm glad I fought against it—*
> *I only wish we'd won,*
> *And I don't want no pardon*
> *For anything I done.*

Hats flew in the air, and men cheered from all sides as the blue soldiers began to step forward. Judge went to the colonel in charge and talked to him. He waved his hand at the fiddle player, who immediately swept up the crowd with "Sally Goodin."

Buck took my hand and pulled me into his arms, and I saw Ralph Jennings, his right sleeve rolled close to his shoulder and held with a gold pin. He stood alone against the wall, betrayed by me for the dance. Buck sang the words to me as we hopped around the room, swept along in the heat and swirl of the other dancers.

Had a piece of pie and I had a piece of puddin'
An' I gave it all away just to see my Sally Goodin.

Well, I looked down the road an' I see my Sally comin'
An' I thought to my soul that I'd kill myself a-runnin'

I laughed and sang, too. We skipped and turned, and the torches and bunting spun around blue and yellow, blue and yellow, until I was so dizzy the only thing holding me up was Buck.

I'm going up the mountain an' marry little Sally
Raise corn on the hillside and the devil in the valley

The music stopped. I couldn't catch my breath for laughing, my stays were so tight. Buck laughed, too, and his black eyes gleamed. It was so good to see him laugh, to see that sadness leave his eyes. I thought I could make his sadness go away. I didn't realize how much a part of him it was. He took me out a side door of the barn, pulling me into the quiet night. I looked back to see if anyone was watching. The wide barn doors were empty but for the music of the beautiful, sad waltz "Aura Lee." The light from the barn cast pale gold shadows on the unmown grass, and the stars glittered. The dew had settled in, and I pulled up my skirts to keep them from getting wet. The night air held a coolness that was like breathing after being underwater a long time. Like some intense desire relieved.

"Do you want me to climb a mountain for you, Gus?" Buck asked and his voice was sweet and low like the music. I blushed and turned from him, walking in the tall grass, but he tugged at my hand, pulling me back to him. "I would if you asked me to. I'll go climb Monte Sano all the way to the top if you ask it."

I didn't answer, just looked up into his face, knowing that as foolish as he sounded, he was trying to make love to me in his sad, romantic way. I laughed and turned my head away.

"Don't laugh at me, Gus. I mean it." I knew he did. He meant it then.

He took my waist in his hands, pulling me closer. I could feel the whalebone pressing into my skin, pinching my sides, but I didn't feel the pain, only breathlessness, like from our dancing. My arms went up around his neck, and he leaned his face to mine. We kissed and the stars seemed to spin and I felt myself fall against him. He was holding me and he kissed me again and I kissed him back for a moment that seemed like my entire life. All the fear of the war I exchanged for that moment. And it was all right. Everything was all right.

He pulled away from me, drawing his head back and looking into my eyes. I could see only a blur, shades of blue and gray shadow fractured by tears.

"I'll climb a mountain and build a house for us—away from all this," he said, and it was like a rushing in my ears. I rested my forehead on his chest, feeling his lips on my hair and his nose nestled in the tea roses.

Then there was a sound, someone near us, someone running. I pushed away from Buck for shame, fearing that Judge or Mama was coming outside to scold us. It wasn't them. A man was running toward the barn. He had a lamp or a light of some kind in his hands, and he threw it into the barn, smashing it through a window into the middle of the dancers. Even outside, we could see the flames leap up from the burning fluid as it spread across the dried old wood. Women shrieked as the wild blaze spread.

The man cried, "That's what you get, you dirty rebels! You can all burn in hell!" He raced back across the meadow and disappeared into the woods. Buck pushed me aside and went running across the grass and into the woods after him as soldiers followed, shouting.

The cries inside grew louder as people rushed out, chased by the flames. The fire climbed the walls and leapt across the rafters. Soon the roof was on fire, and the thick black smoke bellowed from the building as a hole opened and it began to collapse in on itself. Girls came outside with singed skirts, and the men beat at their feet with coats and blankets.

"Mama," I cried out, coming close to one of the doors. I was pushed aside by the terrified dancers. I saw the fiddler leap from a blazing bale with his coattails in flames. "Mama," I cried again, and heard her voice in response.

I ran to her. She was in front of the barn with Bama Buchanan. She was fanning herself and trying to catch her breath. "Augusta," she said, and put her arm over my shoulder, leaning on me as we moved away from the blaze. "I'm fine. I'm fine."

"Did everyone get out?" I looked at the crowd outside the burning barn. The heat was intense, almost singeing us. The soldiers moved us all back, further and further away. The orange light lit up the meadow like daylight, and all around us women cried, comforted by fathers or lovers. Some of the men ran off, chasing the soldiers into the woods. "Is everyone safe?" I asked, looking at Bama, who stood staring at the flames, great wicked tongues of it that leapt up to the stars. Her black dress shimmered in the white-hot glow of it.

Bama said something like "Yes, we all got out, but I would not say that any of us is safe."

We stood watching those wild flames, dancing and leaping from the barn like demons released from hell fleeing up into the sky.

Thirteen

RACHEL SWEEPS OPEN THE bedroom door and startles me. She carries a bundle of linens in her arms—my chemises and undergarments, bed linens and pillowcases. It is morning. She must be ironing today.

"Miss Gus," she says. She walks past the bed to the wardrobe and swings its doors open.

"Good morning, Rachel," I say to her. It is late and I am still in bed.

"Mr. Buck Heppert is in the parlor to see you. I told him you were feeling poorly, but he wanted me to send word up to you."

"Thank you, Rachel." I turn to get out of bed. "Where is Henry?"

"He's out back with Little John. My John is watching them." Rachel shoves the linens in between the narrow shelves. She never pays attention to where things go, rather, pushes them into the empty spaces. I long ago gave up asking her why she bothered ironing things only to crumple them in the wardrobe.

My feet are on the floor. I have to turn my head to see Rachel over my shoulder. "I should see Buck. Can you tell him I'll be right down? And come back to help me dress."

"Yes, ma'am." Rachel walks to the door. She won't look at me.

"Rachel."

She stops and turns, her hands on her hips. "Yes, ma'am?"

"It's the sickness, isn't it?"

She raises her eyebrows. "Ma'am?"

"That's why you are in such a rush to go to Kansas, isn't it? The fever."

Rachel narrows her eyes and shakes her head at me as if I am a schoolgirl. "The sickness that killed Mr. Eli, ma'am?" she says. "No, ma'am. We've wanted to get out of Albion long before this sickness came. I don't know what Mr. Eli died of, but I know I never saw anything like it. I know your white doctor never saw it, either. My mama was a mean old conjure woman, Miss Gus. She put a curse on Rooster Cobb after he whipped my daddy and put him in a box to die. She put a spell on him that burnt up his cotton and his house and gave him the croup that killed him. She knew everything there was to know about conjuring."

Rachel's eyes are wide and shining. She steps closer to me. I lean away, but I don't know where to retreat from her.

"She comes to me when I call her now. Her spirit is in me, and her mother's spirit that was in her. They are a part of me and they answer my questions, but they can't tell me what this sickness is. I know it isn't any sort of breakbone fever I've seen, but my mama told me once a long time ago about a sickness that eats at you from the inside until you sweat yourself away to nothing. An old sickness, ma'am. That blood that came out of Mr. Eli—when I saw it, ma'am, I thought, My God, that's this man's insides coming out. And it's got to come out for a reason. That blood is what's coming out of people all over, Miss Gus. Don't you touch it. Don't get near it or it'll kill you, too. I heard Emma lie to you. There are people out in the county—and yes, at the mill like you saw—whole families, black and white, bleeding all that pain out of them, and then they die. It's the truth, that blood that's coming out of them. It isn't the sickness that's making us go to Kansas. No, ma'am, it's the truth that's making us go."

She fixes her eye on me, and I am frozen. Emma is lying to me. They are all lying to me. The sickness is spreading, although no one will say it.

"You should keep a charm on you, Miss Gus. Keep a charm on you and Henry to keep you safe." She looks at the bedside table, where the bottle of laudanum stands. Beside it are two small burlap purses tied with twine. She nods to me and leaves the room.

That blue bottle. And those charms. Buck is downstairs. He must have talked to Judge. If I get the dividend, then I won't have to think about Simon or Rachel and their wild stories. My head feels thick and heavy. I must get up. I hold my breath as long as I can and then exhale in a burst. I breathe slowly, drawing the air deep into my lungs. I take one of the charms in my hand and squeeze it. I can feel the bones and earth wrapped in the coarse cloth.

Buck's hat is gripped in his hand. He turns from the window when he hears me enter.

"Good morning." He does not seem happy or sad. More sad, I guess. Still the same distance in his eyes. The same stiffness to his mouth. He looks at me so intensely. He makes me self-conscious. My hands move across my arms by themselves. I can feel where I've missed buttons on my sleeves. The white of my chemise is showing, though it should not be. I did not have the patience to cover it. Rachel never came into my room to help me dress. Loose tendrils of dark hair hang around my face, and I try to brush them back.

"You are as beautiful as ever," he says. He bows his head to me. He can be courtly, like his father.

"Did you talk to Judge?"

"Is that what you're interested in? I thought we might visit."

He is upset. I have been too brusque and thoughtless. Buck always needed a gentle hand. A hand willing to pet. Growing up without a mother makes him dislike forward women. Judge surely had something to do with that.

"Of course we can talk. But that is why you came to me, isn't it?" I make a very pretty smile for him.

"Yes, I talked to him." He turns his back on me and walks to the window. "He's fine to lend you a little money to spend the summer up at Monte Sano." He looks back at me. "Are you happy enough with that?"

I step toward him. The morning sun has settled in the room, and the air from the open windows does not move it.

"And the dividend?" I can't resist asking. He knows that is what I want to know.

"He said he'll think about the dividend." We stare at each other. His eyes challenge me to question what he has done for me.

"Thank you so much," I say. "Please sit down." I indicate a chair, but he waits for me to sit on the divan and pulls a chair forward to face me.

"Pa wants to talk to you." His eyes are steady and hard.

"He does? About what?"

"I don't know. He didn't seem happy that you were taking Eli's things from the mill."

"They're my things, aren't they?" I should not have said that. That is no way to win Buck.

"Pa says if he's in charge of the estate, they're his papers. He wants you to bring them to him."

"You heard Mr. Hunslow. He said he didn't need the papers." My wrists feel hot and damp.

"I don't remember hearing any such thing, and I'm not going to argue with you. That's what Pa says. I recommend you gather them up and take them to him today."

"To him? He won't come to me? I'm in mourning."

"You went to that mill without worrying about your mourning. That's what Pa thinks."

The clock ticking is so loud. It counts on and on each silent second that sits between us. Buck won't take his eyes off me.

"Yes, of course, I'll take them to him. Whatever he wishes. I didn't mean any harm by it."

"Really?" One corner of Buck's mouth curls up in mockery. "What did you mean by it?"

"Why, I didn't mean anything. It just occurred to me that I'd like to have Eli's things. His possessions. And then Hunslow gave me all those papers, and after making such a fuss over it, I could hardly say I didn't want the things. I mean, I can't say that I have the slightest idea what all Eli's scribbling meant anyway. I haven't even bothered to look at them. I'll take them to Judge today."

Buck looks at the floor between his knees and breathes out. He looks at me again. His eyes have darkened. "What have these years done to you?" he asks. "Did Eli turn you into a Yankee? Is it all about money?"

"What have they done to me? What have they done to you? How can you ask me that? I've been through the same thing you and everyone else in Albion has been through. Forgive me if I have borne it better than you." He knows what I have been through.

"You haven't been through the same thing. You've been in this house, safe and protected, with everything you want given to you. That's not anything like what the rest of us have been through. You didn't have the Yankees watching every move you made, listening in on everything you say, following you everywhere you go like you're a criminal. That's how they treated Pa. Like a criminal. And me, too. You were friends with them. You had them over for supper. Did Eli have the niggers sit at the table with you, too?"

"No, he did not."

"Well, that surprises me." His face is dead. Motionless. He watches me without expression, with that hardness underneath. "He did everything else for them. He used them to get back at us. He told them to vote and showed them how, right down to putting the ballots in the box himself."

"My Lord, can anyone talk about anything but the Negroes for longer than ten minutes at a time? You'd think we were fighting them during the war."

"They're not better than us, Gus."

His face is turning red. I can't help but look at his face. There is such ugliness under there. What I thought was sadness has turned into ugliness.

"I don't think it would be very hard to be better than us," I say.

He stands up, his voice rising. "That's Eli talking again. You really have taken up the mantle, haven't you? You should understand right now that we aren't going to be humiliated by them. We aren't going to be humiliated ever again."

"Buck, please sit down. You sound like your father."

He freezes. His fists clench. His eyes seem to bulge out at me.

"I'm sorry, Buck. I didn't mean it like that. I understand things have been harder for other people. I know Judge is right. Judge is right."

"Gus," he says, and it sounds like he's spitting at me. "I didn't watch men die for this. My friends. Hill didn't die for this."

"I know Hill didn't die for this."

What did Hill die for? What did any of them die for?

"Every battle could have been my last. Every one of them. Your first one is the only time you're not scared. You hear the bullets whizzing past your head so close you think they're hornets. A swarm of them all around you. You don't imagine you'll ever get hit the first time. But then after, you look around and see all the dead. Your friends. Men you've known your whole life, dead and staring in smoldering woods or in a pool of mud and blood. After that, you know that at any moment you could be the one staring at nothing. Cold and dead and left behind unburied like carrion. Every battle after that is like death staring at you in the face, waiting to take you. I didn't live through that for this. I don't know how or why I lived through it, but I know it wasn't for Eli and the Republicans and scalawags to do what they've done." He exhales. He seems calmer now. He unclenches his fists. He picks up his hat from the chair. He looks down at the rug.

"I'm sorry if I've upset you. I lost control of myself." He is sad Buck again. The rage is buried and he is ashamed.

"You didn't upset me. It's been nice visiting with you."

I won't get up. He can walk himself out.

"Yes. Thank you." He makes a small bow to me but will not look in my eyes.

"Please let your pa know I'll be by shortly." He cannot deny to me that he is going directly to Judge.

He scowls and doesn't answer. He stalks out of the parlor and into the hall, swinging the heavy door wide. His footsteps tap on the brick walk. He has left the door open. That is his last word. He'll go tell Judge I'm a Republican and a Negro lover and God knows what else. You can't see straight with that kind of anger inside you. Judge doesn't seem as angry as Buck. But Judge didn't fight in the war. He just talked about the fighting. Buck and Hill and all the rest of them actually did it. Only Buck came back. It doesn't seem fair. Buck can't see the fairness of it, either. Mama kept asking him for a lock of Hill's hair like it was the only thing that mattered.

The door latch clicks. It is Simon in the hall. He has closed the front door. "Miss Gus?" he asks.

"Hello, Simon. You move as quietly as Emma." He smiles a little. "Were you nearby?"

"Yes, ma'am. I was in the dining room, helping Emma with the silver."

"Did you hear?"

"No, ma'am. I just wanted to be nearby."

"Oh. Thank you for that." He is so calm and grave always. But he has a sense of humor. He likes irony. I can appreciate that. "Thank you, Simon."

"Do you need anything?"

"Yes, we have to go to Judge. He wants the papers I took from the mill. Buck sent him here to ask me. He asked specifically that I bring them to his office."

Simon's eyebrows lift. He doesn't smile. There is nothing to smile about. Quite the opposite. "Did Buck Heppert say why?" He rests a hand on the door frame.

"No, Buck pretends to be ignorant of his father's reasons, only the instrument of his will. Would Judge know about the packets Eli would prepare for his friends?"

"He might have been aware that Eli would be preparing something. He was aware that politics requires a lot of lubrication. He and Eli both knew that. If he knows of this package, it is because someone told him."

"Someone from the mill?"

"Perhaps."

"We should go. Judge will be angry enough without me keeping him waiting."

Simon nods and steps back. He will get the carriage ready, and I must rebutton my sleeves.

"Simon, you will stay nearby, won't you?"

He turns back to me, ever grave. Simon the snake killer. "I will stay as close as I can, ma'am."

"Thank you."

Fourteen

JUDGE WAS NEVER A real judge. Not one appointed by the governor or who rode a circuit. Mama said when he was young, his pa said he was as serious as a judge. So everyone calls him that.

Simon drives the buggy around the square. The courthouse sits across from Judge's office and dominates a space of lawn shaded by oaks and magnolias and bordered by a picket fence—the wrought iron was torn up in '63 and fed to the foundries in Selma. The fence frames the courthouse, lined on its front and rear with eight Doric columns and topped by a green copper dome. A weather vane with a brass rooster sits at the top of the dome. It is still, facing northeast, and glistens in the sun.

Judge read law in Huntsville when he was young, about the time Pa was courting Mama. He opened his practice right on Albion's town square before I was born. The three-story brick building sits on a lot his father had purchased well before Albion was anything but grid lines on parchment. His practice has been in that same office for almost forty years.

The streets around the courthouse are lined with brick buildings, two or three stories with simple facades, some more ornate with rusticated stonework. They line up like militiamen waiting for orders. The massive brick pile of the Maples Hotel sits in their midst like their captain, surveying the square, dressed with ironwork balconies over the wide entrance.

The square is so quiet. Before the war, the hotel and square bustled with activity. Teamsters and merchants moved back and forth along Alabama Avenue from the riverfront up to the railroad depot and the Cotton Exchange. On market days, there is a hint of the old activity. Bales of cotton piled onto wagons. Men, black and white, flocking the sidewalks and gathering outside the taverns, talking cotton and weather and politics. Today there is only an odd dray with a cursing teamster making his way from the river to the railroad with no sense of rush. The hot air slows the few men who walk between the bank and the courthouse or the remaining merchants and factors who bother keeping their offices here. They watch the man with his wagon from their second-floor windows, waving tired hands at lazy flies and listening to the echo of the horse's clip-clop bounce from building to building. There are so many empty storefronts. Broken windows gape at the street. Some are boarded over, with FOR RENT painted across the warped, weathered wood.

On the far side of the square is the burnt-out hulk of the old Union League. The building was put up for the Albion Agricultural and Mechanical Society, some long-dead organization Pa had been a part of. After the war, Eli used it for his Union League meetings. The league was not exactly a political party, not that I ever gathered, but it acted like one, organizing all the freedmen in the county to vote. Who else would they vote for but the Republicans? Back then Judge couldn't vote. Nor could Buck nor Mike, even. All the black men in the county did, and they had marches around the courthouse and up to the depot. Canvassers for state office would come and step off the trains, groups of men, white and black all mixed together, wearing suits and beaver hats, talking about the responsibilities of freedom. Eli took me to some of the speeches until I insisted on indispositions. It was almost enough to make you laugh, seeing master for slave and slave for master. That all went on until the Knights began harassing them, even in broad daylight. There were many Negro men dead from it. I don't know how many. Probably no one knows, except maybe the Negroes themselves. I wonder whether Rachel would know if I asked her.

The building caught fire a few years ago. They never found out the cause. No one really tried to find it out. People whispered that the Knights had set the fire. The blaze could have taken down the whole town. There were guns and gunpowder in there, secreted away, that blew up with a terrible noise, shattering windows along the square and rattling people out of their sleep as far north as Black's Cove. The whole block bears the charred scars of that night, piles of blackened rubble and rock.

Eli seemed tired after that. He stayed in his office more, and out at the mill. He seemed to have thrown up his hands and given up on voting and politics. The Union League didn't disband, it just blew away like smoke.

Simon pulls the buggy up to the curb and helps me down. "I'll be near," he says in a low voice.

I take the bundle of papers under one arm. Narrow stairs lead up to Judge's office. They are high risers. They make me dizzy even with a hand on the banister. On the second floor an antechamber is divided by a baluster that protects his office door. There is a colored boy asleep by the back windows, one arm hanging off the bench, his fingers nearly grazing the floor. I wait, holding my hat and veil in one hand and the papers against my hip. I bite my lip and knock lightly at the door.

Papers rustle, and Judge's gruff voice calls out, "Come in."

The heavy door creaks as it opens. "Judge, I'm so sorry to bother you," I begin. He sits at a wide desk of dark mahogany and glowers at me over the papers spread out before him, his blue eyes like ice freezing me.

"Come in, Augusta. I've been waiting for you." He waves me to one of the empty chairs in front of him, and I sit obediently. That is Judge. With a wave of his hand, you are rendered speechless. He scribbles on a sheet of paper, dipping his pen into a turtle-shell inkwell as he refers to other sheets scattered across his desk. The windows are open and catch a weak breeze that lifts the corners of the papers. The creak of a wagon passes near. It is coming up from the river, moving toward the depot. I can see the crumbling brick of the old Union League hall, like the engravings of Richmond after Grant burnt it.

Judge lays down his pen and looks at me with thinly disguised irritation. He crosses his white and wrinkled hands on the desk and clears his throat. "How was your visit to the mill?" he asks.

"It was fine," I say, smiling. "Very fine, thank you. It's quite an enterprise."

"I sent Buck to join you. I thought it would be best. No need for you to expose yourself traveling alone all over the county with a nigger coachman." His mouth curls down, and anger burns from his pale blue eyes. I open my mouth to speak, to defend myself, but there are no words. To argue such a vulgar suggestion would be to give merit to it. To suggest that Buck would somehow be a chaperone for me and Simon makes me shudder.

"No matter. It is all nothing. You spoke to Hunslow, didn't you? I guessed you would. And was he clear on the situation at the mill? Are those the papers you took?"

"Yes, Buck said you wanted them, so I brought them right away." I heft the papers from my lap and lay them on a bare corner of Judge's desk. "They aren't of any use to me, but Hunslow insisted."

He grunts and nods, looking at the papers. "So I gather. Is that all of them?"

"Yes, everything. I just wanted Eli's personal things, but there didn't seem to be much there. Only an engraving and some candlesticks."

Judge stares at me. He is digesting what I say, evaluating it coldly. He looks at the ledger in front of him and taps it with his pen. "I'm going through the books now. Just the past six months. To be honest, there are some very serious irregularities in them."

The office feels so hot. My palms are wet in my black gloves. I wait, seeing no purpose to further talking. Judge will have his say. He picks up his pen and leans forward, poking at the figures, talking more to himself than to me.

"Purchases of raw cotton. Dozens of bales of it each week. Thousands of pounds of it. It shouldn't be more than ten or twelve cents a pound, but the mill purchased it at fifteen cents a pound. How do you like that? Fifteen cents. Like it was Sea Island cotton! Some of it for as much as seventeen and eighteen cents."

His face turns pink. He is shaking his head at the paper, furiously stabbing at it. "I asked Hunslow about the purchase, and do you know what he told me? He told me Eli did all the purchasing and kept all the records. Kept pretty tight control of it. Now, what do you think of that, Augusta?"

I shake my head. "I'm sorry, Judge. I was never very interested in Eli's affairs. He was so busy all the time."

"I'll tell you what to think of it," Judge resumes impatiently. "The mill has been having trouble turning a profit because the cotton Eli was buying was so expensive. I'm going to go out to some of these farmers, and I'm going to ask them how much they were paid for their cotton, and I will wager you that they were paid no more than eight cents a pound!" Judge slams the pen down on the desk so hard it rattles the tortoise shell. "Eight cents a pound!" he shouts, and I lean against the back of the chair. "Eli has been robbing the mill!" His face is fiery red and his eyes are wide, bulging at me.

"Judge, that's impossible," I say. I must say something. "How could Eli rob the mill if he owned it? Why would he?"

Judge turns quickly back to ice. "Because," he says, staring down at me. "Those precious dividends you are so interested in did not go exclusively to Eli. There are other investors in the mill."

"I see. Are you an investor?"

His mouth creases in a disgusted frown. "That is neither here nor there," he hisses at me. He has the glassy gaze of a reptile.

"That is all over, isn't it? Eli is dead. Can't the mill become profitable quickly? That's what you said. That's what Mr. Hunslow said. So a dividend could be paid in July?"

"There will be no dividends paid from the mill. Not until it becomes clear how much Eli Branson stole and it is paid back to the other shareholders in full. If those are your future dividends, so be it. You won't see a penny from that mill until the money is repaid."

"That's not fair! I didn't steal the money!"

"You should thank me. If this wound up in court, you'd be lucky to end up with the clothes on your back. It is high time you fall back on your own resources." He sits rigidly, watching me.

"My own resources? I don't have anything. You said you would handle it all."

"That was before you began meddling in my business. What did you want with all these papers?"

"I didn't want anything. I don't know why Hunslow gave them to me."

He waits, his eyes on me. "Augusta, you are my blood kin. I had a great fondness for your mother, and the things I am doing for you, I know she would want me to do. But don't test me. You stay out of this business. And don't go meddling into anything on behalf of the Negroes, either. Do you understand?" He points the pen at me.

"No, I don't understand. What is all this about? I've just lost my husband, and you tell me I am destitute and I have to go begging to you for money? How can you be so hard-hearted?" The tears are working their way up. But I cannot cry now, not yet.

"You made your bed when you married Eli. There's nothing I can do about that."

"You let Mama force me into marrying him!" I feel almost as if I am choking. That I cannot get any words out. "I didn't want to! And now you want to punish me for his sins? I thought you were kin to me. I thought you were a friend." I stand up, trembling. I can barely hold myself upright. The tears come. Tears of hot rage from my eyes, not weakness, like Judge would think.

Judge stands and comes to me from behind the desk. "Now, now," he says in a calmer voice. He reaches a hand out to my shoulder. He feels guilty, that is clear, and I cannot let the advantage go.

"I don't think I'm asking for anything outrageous. Just a little money so that I can go away for the summer. And with the sickness," I say, a handkerchief to my face. Yes, the sickness, too. "I saw a woman collapse at the mill, covered in blood. And to be spoken to like this. To be followed—and by Buck! You act as if you hate me!"

Judge lays a cold hand on my arm and I shudder away from him.

"I'm sorry," he says. "I spoke too passionately. I thought you were—well, it doesn't matter what I thought. Here, take some money." He goes to his desk and pulls out some bills. "Here's fifty dollars. More than enough to get you and your family up to Monte Sano. Why don't you go up there with Bama? You'll feel better once you're away."

He looks at me as if he is truly concerned. "You're tired," he says. "You need to rest. Why don't you go home, and I'll have Greer come to see you."

"Ask Dr. Greer, Judge," I say. "Ask him what it was like with Eli."

"I know all that already. I don't need to ask Greer anything. You are beginning to get me worried. I'll send Buck over to keep you company. I want you to be good friends now. The past is the past."

"No, I don't want to see him. I need to get away from Albion. To get out of that house."

He walks me out of his office to the narrow stairs. The colored boy is sitting up on the bench, rubbing his eyes. He watches as Judge takes hold of me and walks me down each step. We are pressed together, shoulder to shoulder. I gather my skirts so I do not trip on them.

"There is nothing wrong with the house. Or you. Or Henry. Or the servants. You are all fine. We will get you up to Monte Sano if that will make you happy. As soon as things are worked out down here, Buck and I will join you. Would you like that?"

We reach the bottom step. He leads me outside into the heat and light.

"Yes. I think Monte Sano would be the right place for now."

"That's right," he says, keeping his hand on my arm. "Now go on home, and I'll send Greer over to you to give you something to calm your nerves."

The sunlight is almost blinding. Simon stands at the curb, waiting with the carriage reins in his hands. Judge gives a start when he sees Simon, then recovers himself. He hands me into the buggy without acknowledging Simon, even though Simon nods to him and says, "Sir." I lean back against the seat, fanning myself, watching Simon as he mounts the horse.

"Get some rest, Augusta," Judge says through the slats of the carriage bonnet. "You'll be up in Monte Sano before you know it." The horse starts and the carriage pulls away. We round the square. I don't need to look back. He will already be gone up to his office, scribbling notes for his Negro runner to take to the doctor and Bama. To go to Monte Sano. When we all know there is far more than fifty dollars somewhere.

Simon turns the buggy onto Greene Street, and trees reach their long arms over us.

"I'll take the carriage to the back, ma'am?" Simon has read my mind. After the ugly things Judge said, I should avoid exposing myself.

"Yes, Simon. Please." We turn up Elm Street and then onto the narrow lane that divides the homes facing Pulaski Street from the ones on Greene Street. The dirt path leads to outbuildings—carriage houses and stables and servants' quarters that mostly show neglect, with weatherworn clapboard where the paint has peeled, broken windows and shutters, or loose shingles. The gardens aren't so much gardens as weed beds, untended flowers and hedges choked out by loosestrife and chickweed. We turn in to the back of my house, and Simon stops the carriage before the open stable doors. Big John sits in the shadows of the stable, polishing harnesses. He salutes us as Simon climbs down from the horse.

"Simon?" I say. He holds my hand as I step down onto the grass.

"Yes, ma'am?" His voice is quiet.

"He knows. He suspected something. I don't think he suspects anymore, but he did." The harness John is polishing makes an irregular jingling noise that sounds like pennies in a can.

Simon's eyes dart to John and back. "What did he say?" Simon whispers. John can't possibly hear us.

"He said I should fall back on my own resources. He thinks—or he thought—I have money hidden away. Do you think he meant the package?"

Everything is quiet except for the jingle of the harness in John's hands. Simon's voice is grave, as it always is.

"Perhaps. I don't know. But we should assume he did and act accordingly."

"Act like what?"

"Act like we have no idea about the package. And that all you are interested in is going to Monte Sano."

John has not looked up at us once. He sits with the side of his face to us and works slowly and methodically, rubbing down the long leather straps with oil and polishing the metal fittings. He must know that we are here.

I lower my voice to a whisper, watching John. "I am interested in going much further than Monte Sano. But where could it be? You've searched everywhere, and it's not at the mill."

Simon looks into the barn at John with the same impassive expression. "Maybe I didn't look well enough," he whispers. "Emma and Rachel were always around. I didn't want to raise any questions. Ask me to pack up Eli's things upstairs. Sort through his clothes. Then I'll have a reason to spend more time in the house."

"Shh. Here comes Emma."

She rushes from the kitchen down the path by the carriage house. "Miss Gus," she calls. "The doctor's here to see you."

"How did he get here so quickly?" Judge must have runners with wings.

Simon shakes his head and looks back at Emma. The harness stops jingling, and John looks up.

Emma is breathing hard from hurrying. "He's in the front parlor. I didn't think you were home, but he said you would be soon. I don't know how he knew."

"He was informed. Like Buck said, Judge knows everything."

Emma looks at me curiously. Simon frowns. I'm being too cryptic.

"I'll go to him. Simon, can you look through Mr. Branson's things for me? It's time we got that sorted out."

"Yes, ma'am," Simon says. He follows me and Emma into the house. The faint jingle of the harness begins again.

Fifteen

GREER'S FAT HAND, PALE and dotted with red freckles, holds my wrist. A thick finger presses into my vein. He looks at his watch while he counts under his breath.

"How have you been feeling, Gus?" he asks as he drops my hand. "Judge seemed very concerned about you." Amber sunlight streams through the parlor windows.

"I've been fine. Very fine. It's so good of you both to be so concerned about me. Everything here is fine."

"No more attacks? No episodes of neuralgia? You can't be too careful, especially with your history." Greer sits in a chair near mine. His black kit sits openmouthed on the small table between us. The sunlight burnishes his hair and shines golden off his liver-spotted forehead.

"No, nothing at all."

"Even this afternoon? Judge said you seemed . . . not yourself. Agitated and frightened." Greer's eye is skeptical. Damn Judge and his notes.

"Yes, this afternoon. I suppose I was a little worried. But it's nothing for you to bother about. You must be so busy with people who are truly sick. Not just ladies with nervous disorders." I laugh dismissively. Greer keeps his eye on me.

"There is no lack of ladies in Albion subject to some sort of nervous disorder, that is certain. And I take their cases as seriously as every other ailment I see. You are far from alone, and you should take your condition seriously, too."

"Oh, I do, Doctor, honestly. And I have Emma here to help me. I can assure you I'm perfectly well. Surely you have more important cases to attend to than mine." The sun slants directly across me. Even in its weakness, it holds heat. I dab my handkerchief at the perspiration at my temples. Greer's gaze of concern annoys me. I wish he would go.

"I am very busy, Gus, but I was in the neighborhood when I got Judge's note and thought I'd drop in and see how you were."

"Is someone sick?"

"It's this heat. It seems to be affecting everyone."

"Like Eli?"

"No, Gus. Not at all. Nothing like Eli. Where did you get such an idea? Judge said you had some story about a fever." Greer almost glowers at me, as if I have been diagnosing cases and playing doctor across the county.

"There was a woman. At the mill at Three Forks. She seemed . . . she seemed to be sick like Eli was."

"That infernal mill. I'm sorry. I'm sick of hearing about it. Enough of it. I'm headed out there tomorrow with the mayor and aldermen for an inspection. This story of yours has caught on. You didn't hear it from anyone?"

"No, Doctor. Why do they want to do an inspection?" The hair bristles on my neck and a cold chill moves down my spine. The charm is in my pocket. I feel it through my dress.

"It's an absurdity, to be perfectly honest." Greer huffs and leans forward with his hands on his knees. He looks out the window, almost directly into the sunlight. "A complete absurdity. Whenever politicians are involved, things end by being mucked up. There is a lot of talk about sickness out at the mill."

"I saw it!" I lean forward, and Greer leans back, almost affronted.

"We're in the midst of some terribly hot weather, Gus. When it gets hot, people become ill. There's nothing unusual about that." He shakes his head. He is perspiring, too. It glistens in his long red whiskers.

"Of course," I say. "Of course." A puff of air stirs the thin curtains. The mantel clock ticks. Greer looks at the floor and then at his open kit. He pulls it toward him, looking inside as if he is looking for something he has forgotten.

"Did you—Dr. Greer, did you end up investing in the mill?" I ask the question as carelessly as I can.

Greer keeps his eyes on the case. "Yes, a little bit. Just to stick my toes in the water, you know." He snaps the case shut.

"Are there many other investors—besides you and Judge, I mean?"

"I'm not sure what it matters."

"I'm an investor, now, too. And these things are new to me—I don't understand them at all. Eli never explained them to me. I thought you might be able to help me." I fold my hands in my lap.

He is embarrassed or perhaps surprised. "Well, of course," he says, taking his eyes from his kit to look at me. "I'm sorry. I didn't mean to offend you."

"Please, you didn't offend me. It's only with Hill gone—and Mama and now Eli. I just don't know who will take care of these things. And Mike. What will become of him?"

"Augusta," he says, and he lays a thick, sweaty hand over mine. His whiskers wag at me. "Judge will handle it all. Don't you worry. He's going to take care of everything."

"I know he will. But he's not so young anymore, either. And if he . . ." I leave it hanging.

"He's got a lot more years in him, for sure. You're worrying yourself too much, is all, Gus. No wonder you have these nervous attacks. You worry yourself. Now, look, when Eli started the mill, both Judge and I took a piece. So there's nobody who cares more about that mill than me and Judge." He hesitates. He is waiting for me to agree. "Excepting yourself."

I smile gratefully. "I know. Thank you. I just wish that Hill were here."

Greer gives a heavy sigh and casts his eyes down. His hand rests on my arm. The heat makes it difficult to even speak. "Your pa was a fine man. You know that. Hill was, too. He was such a good soldier. A real Spartan. One of the finest I knew during the war."

I nod and smile. Those memories of Hill. Like my thoughts of Buck. Who were we then? Simon was at the Battle of Nashville. Imagine him being so close to Hill without even knowing it—but on different sides.

"What did they fight for, after all?" I say it aloud without thinking.

Greer puffs up, ready for a speech. He pulls his hand away. "They fought for us. For you. He made Albion proud. And would have made your pa proud. He did honor to the name of Sedlaw."

Would Pa have been proud? Or wanted the war the way Judge wanted it? They were so different. Sworn enemies. Would Pa have encouraged Hill to fight?

"At Murfreesboro he led the charge through those frozen fields again and again. It was the New Year and bitter, bitter cold. Right into the guns of the enemy, he charged. Right across those fields and into the woods, where the Yankees sat waiting. The lines were torn up. All those boys. But he never shrank back. He was brave, your brother. Like Buck. The both of them, wild and fearless."

Greer looks through the windows to Greene Street and beyond it to those battlefields that are scarred into his mind. The wound from the grapeshot throbs, a red slash across his pale face, almost pulsing with the blood from each beat of his heart. After a moment his cheeks sag, and his eyes become vacant. So odd, the way we find it so difficult to keep our minds in the present.

"Gus," he says, "I'm going to give you a mild dose to calm you, and then I'll have to be on my way." He opens his kit again and pulls out a small blue bottle like the one upstairs. The blue glass winks at me in the fading light. "I can leave this with you if you need it." He smiles.

"Thank you, Doctor." Maybe a small dose. Something to help me through. But I must talk to Simon. The money. A small dose I can manage. And another bottle. If we travel, laudanum might be hard to come by. "No, I shouldn't."

"Now, Gus, I insist. We can't have you wrecking your health with all this worry. And in this heat. You should think of going away for a while. Is Emma nearby?" He moves to the parlor door and calls for her. "Emma! A glass of water for Miss Gus."

He comes back to stand over me, holding the blue bottle. The sunlight flashes on it in his hand as he gestures in wide circles. A flash of white, then blue. Bright white, then blue.

"I don't have to tell you how to administer this, but you know you should be careful with it. It's perfectly safe in the right doses. And just the cure you need right now. Doctor's orders."

"Just a small dose, then. To calm me."

"That's better. That's a good girl."

Emma brings the glass to Greer, her eyes downcast. She doesn't look at me, but she sees the bottle in his hand. A drop. Two. Thin opalescent ribbons that spread through the clear water. Though the perfume is faint, it penetrates, bittersweet. Greer holds the glass to my lips. "That's right. Just a small dose to calm you."

I take it in my hands and drink. Yes, the bitterness. I can taste it. I wait a moment. The medicine does its job quickly.

"Can you help Miss Gus upstairs, Emma?" Greer asks. He snaps his case shut. "I'll check in on you tomorrow, my dear. And don't fret about the mill. I'll handle everything there."

"Oh, Miss Gus," Emma says. I want to laugh at her expression. I don't know why it strikes me as funny. I laugh softly. Under my breath. I think I am laughing.

"Goodbye, Doctor," I call after Greer. He is outside now. Isn't he? He's gone out the door, vanished. Away down the street to those sick people. All sick from this heat. Sweating themselves away. Sweating God knows what.

Emma takes me by the arm and helps me out of the chair. She has to gather my skirts up so I don't step on them as we go up the stairs. Like when Eli was sick and I ripped out my hem. Poor Eli.

"It's like Jesus in the garden, Emma," I say. "Jesus in Gethsemane." Emma nods and I laugh again. "He sweat out blood in Gethsemane. He knew something terrible was happening to him. That it was going to happen." Emma hushes me like a child. I can't help laughing again.

There's Simon at Eli's door, like some kind of specter.

"Is it like that for you, Simon? Like Jesus in Gethsemane—always knowing something terrible will happen?" I smile at him. "Did you find the money, Simon?"

Simon isn't laughing. He doesn't think it's funny. Emma looks at him and then at me, him and then me. With those sad eyes of hers. Poor Emma. She always has such sad eyes. Those babies of hers, lost. Like Hill was lost. Poor Hill, taken away in his prime, fighting like a wild man on those frozen fields of Nashville. Like my poor child.

The wallpaper is pretty. Pink ribbons and roses, climbing up the wall together.

I am in bed and I do not even know how I got here. Two of the little blue bottles are next to me. A richness of this medicine. Should I take more? My mind works. In spite of the draught. I cannot stop thinking of Hill. If he were here, I would not feel so alone. If he were here, none of this ever would have happened. Dying on that frozen field, alone like me. He would not have let this happen.

My fingers feel numb. And my feet. Is it working? Should I take more? If Hill were here. His face, so handsome. Fair, where Mike and I have dark hair and eyes. The winter was so cold when we saw him last. He must have been so cold out there in the camps, on the battlefields. But he would fight. It was his duty. The Cause. What cause?

The last time we saw Hill was February of '63. To think I would be married only three years later. The battle at Murfreesboro erupted around New Year's, and my cousins in Winchester said you could feel the guns booming for three solid days. We had no news then, only the rumors and rare newspapers from Nashville or Chattanooga that trickled in through the lines. We knew that Hill and Buck were with General Bragg at Tullahoma. We worried and begged for news from the neighbors, from the servants, from anyone who might know anything.

And then one night in early February, after the lamps had been put out and the fire banked, I heard something in the kitchen. Noises and whispers. I tiptoed into Mama's room and shook her awake. Neither of us wanted to wake Mike because we were afraid he would charge down the stairs and get us all killed. Raiders and sharpshooters had crisscrossed Riverbend County since the Tennessee River had fallen to the Federals. During Bragg's disastrous foray into Kentucky, the Union troops had deserted North Alabama, and their forces were concentrated south of Nashville.

I was barely fifteen. I was in my nightclothes, and Mama wrapped herself in a brocade dressing gown and grabbed a pistol from her chest of drawers. She kept it loaded and ready to fire with the constant hope that the powder was dry.

We crept down the stairs together, trying not to make a sound. She held the pistol in front of her with both hands. I was behind her, holding on to her waist. The noise seemed to be coming from the kitchen in the basement, and we crept down there, feet freezing against the cold brick floor. We could see a pale gleam of light under the kitchen door, and we heard hoarse voices whispering and laughing. Men in the kitchen, at least two. I heard Buck's voice.

"Damn it, Hill, you're putting it out!"

I gripped Mama tighter, and she looked at me in astonishment, letting the gun fall to her side.

"Hill?" she whispered, looking at me. And then louder: "Hill?" she called and raced into the kitchen with me at her heels.

Buck and Hill stood surprised, with smiles on their faces. They were in the dark, trying to light a fire from the last embers in the kitchen stove. Mama started crying, and I did, too, and pretty soon, with all the noise, Emma and Cora came from their basement rooms and started hugging everyone like a big reunion. Cora put on coffee made from parched corn and yams that smelled like earth. Emma made corncakes and fried thick slabs of cured ham. Buck and Hill looked as skinny as beanpoles and as shaggy as dogs. They were filthy with lice and fleas, infested with every type of vermin imaginable, but they just kept their smiles and their laughter as if there were no war and we weren't hiding in the dark in the kitchen.

We asked them about the battle, and Hill joked that Bragg had won a victory with a retreat. They were camped down the railroad around Tullahoma. Hill was sure they'd make a stand and retake Murfreesboro and Nashville, too. He promised they'd beat back the Yankees. The Yankees would never get past Tullahoma. They'd never take Albion again. Buck agreed, and they exchanged a look that showed more doubt than their words.

Since they were so close to home, Buck and Hill had left their company to come to us. A lot of boys did it, they said. Half the company had been killed or wounded at Murfreesboro, and the other half had run off home on what they joked was unofficial leave. Their captain had to turn a blind eye to it. If they didn't come back, that was a different story, but they would only stay the night and leave the following evening in the dark. They would rejoin their company in Tullahoma and pretend they had not been away at all.

Buck would stay with us that night, too. We listened to their stories until the early hours, laughing with them to keep from crying.

Listening to their portraits of Beauregard and Pat Cleburne. They talked about Bragg and his meanness and how all the soldiers disliked him. They told us about the strange religious blaze of Leonidas Polk's eyes and the prayer meetings he led every Sunday and how the whole army went to them.

When we were all exhausted and frayed from the talking and the coffee, we went to bed. Cora had run upstairs to lay a fire in Hill's room and put down fresh linens. Buck and Hill laughed about how it was the first bed they had seen since they left the university over a year and a half ago.

I kissed them both good night and went to my room, but I couldn't sleep. I was too thrilled to have Hill home, too excited from the coffee or love, and I tiptoed back across the hall and tapped on the door. Hill whispered for me to come in, and I entered as silently as I could.

The small fire gave out a faint yellow glow, and the room felt warm from it and their breathing. They gave out a musky, humid odor. They lay side by side in Hill's bed. He leaned up on his elbow and said, "What now, Gus? Can't you sleep?"

I knelt beside him and grabbed his hands, which were so warm they took the chill off mine. "Oh, Hill, I just can't believe you're really here!"

Buck leaned up on an elbow and laughed. "Hey, now, don't leave me out! I'm here, too."

I blushed and said I was so happy they were both here.

"Can't you stay, Hill?" I asked him, almost begging. "Do you have to go back to the army?"

Hill looked over at Buck with a wry smile and turned back to me. "Yes, Gus, I guess I do. We haven't finished up yet." He looked grim suddenly, and far away.

"When will it all be over?" I asked. I gripped his hands almost as if I were praying.

"I don't know when, dearest. But you don't need to worry about a thing. We're going to whip the Yankees right out of Tennessee, and then we'll all come home, and everything will be the way it used to be."

"That's right," Buck agreed. "You don't think my pa would let the Yankees stay down here for long, do you?" We laughed, low whispering laughs. "Have you heard the original gorilla has freed all our darkies?" Buck was smiling in the faint light, and his long mustache and whiskers curled up over his mouth in a shaggy smile.

"Who said that?" I said, honestly confused.

"Abe Lincoln! That's what they call him." He and Hill laughed.

I didn't understand.

"But what does Jeff Davis say?" I asked in perfect sincerity, which made Buck and Hill laugh even harder.

"Jeff Davis says it ain't so," Buck said, grinning at me. "So you should feel safe, 'cause that's who's in charge here. And we've got the guns to back him up." Hill nodded and squeezed my hand.

"But aren't you scared fighting?" I asked, and it seemed like the most important question I had ever asked. "Aren't you afraid at all?" Hill looked at Buck again, and they smiled at each other with the same look they'd given in the kitchen.

"Sure," Buck began. "We all start out scared. You never leave being scared, but—" He paused, thinking, and Hill picked up his thought.

"But you forget about it. You realize you're there to do a job, and that's what we do. We try to kill as many Yankees as we can, and you forget about being killed yourself. I tell you, at night when we sit across the field from them, sometimes it seems like a great big joke. You can hear them singing and see their campfires and the pickets calling to each other from across the river. But when the sun comes up—"

He paused, and Buck and I waited.

"It's so freezing cold, Gus," Hill continued. "Bitter freezing cold, so that you can't feel your fingers to load your rifle, and some of the men's shoes are so torn up they leave bloody footprints on the snow and ice. When it's that cold, I swear the ice can cut you like a razor. Everything you do hurts a hundred times worse when you're that cold. But we lay down in the woods that morning as the sun came up, and it was clear and bright through the trees, and we knew the Yankees were over there not making a sound. Everything was ghostly white, the fields and the ice in the trees. The tree branches would brush against each other and make a far-off sound like glass. Then all of a sudden a herd of white rabbits—white, Augusta, as white as snow—came running from the woods where the Yankees were. They came running across the field toward us and then shied away to the right and vanished back into the woods. And you feel at those moments—you feel when there are moments like that, you feel that God is speaking to you. You know that He's watching. He's there and He's with us and you forget yourself. You forget your fear and everything, and you just do what you have to do, 'cause God is with us. They're the enemy and God is with us."

Buck had turned his head toward the fire and nodded without looking away from it, staring so deep into it, his thick black whiskers moving up and down with his head and those dark eyes that I thought were so deep they were bottomless.

"If anything should happen," Hill said, looking into the fire with Buck. "And nothing will happen. Buck here's the one who likes to get shot up." He laughed, and Buck did, too, but I couldn't bring myself to find the humor in it. Buck had been wounded at Shiloh. A minié ball cut him against his ribs by his chest, missing the bone but leaving him stiff-armed in the cold and lucky to be alive. "If anything should happen to me, Buck here will take care of you. He'll make sure you are taken care of. He's promised me."

I nodded and felt myself crying again. I took a hand off of Hill's and wiped my eyes. Buck looked at me solemnly and nodded, those dark eyes just watching me.

Sixteen

SIMON CANNOT BE HAPPY with me. I should not have let Dr. Greer give me the laudanum. I don't know how long I slept. Drifted, really. And then lying in the dark for hours waiting for the sun to rise. I should not have taken the laudanum. Perhaps Simon does not trust me now. Perhaps he found the money and won't tell me. I hope he comes to me soon. How could Emma not know where he has gone?

I open Eli's desk drawers. They are cluttered with papers, old-fashioned quills, and the newest type of mechanical pens. Some of them have bled from their nibs and left spots of ink on papers and the base of the drawer. There is the pocket watch that stopped, the one from Eli's desk at the mill.

Other drawers are filled with ledgers that date back for years. Some of them are labeled with the years of the war. I thumb through the grid-lined pages covered in Eli's script. His penmanship is almost illegible, but I can read the names of families I knew then. Families who came to his funeral, too. In 1864 there are loans to the Sheffields and McQuinns, pledges on silver chargers and teapots and platters. There is my mother's name, with Emma in parentheses, an exchange of money and foodstuffs for a gold locket and chain. Was Pa's picture in that locket? Other families turned over carriages and paintings and furnishings. Glassware, guns and sabers from the Mexican War. All of it filtered through Eli's hands and gone to God knows where. The Yankee soldiers for greenbacks. Silk dresses that they brought home to their wives and sisters. He even had Confederate bonds received from families in town, a foolish venture, but his markings suggest he bought them for pennies of their stated worth.

In 1865 there are more notations, and the collateral is more important. Horses, cotton lands in the county. At first in small parcels and then larger ones associated with people who were once the wealthiest in the county. The Griffins. The Collinses and Cobbs. The Porters. And the Hepperts. Judge's name jumps out at me like a snake. Everton Heppert. Bonds. Land. His house on Elm Street. Everything, it seems, that he could muster, mortgaged to Eli—the only source of cash at the time.

I close the ledger, sick, and look up to see Simon at the garden door, holding newspapers in his hand.

"Are you feeling better, ma'am?" he asks as he enters. He takes a seat across from me and lays the papers on the desktop.

"Yes, Simon. Thank you. I have been waiting for you."

"Emma told me you were here." The open doors and windows make me nervous, and I lower my voice.

"Did you find anything in Eli's room?"

"No, ma'am. I looked through everything, although after you went to bed, I had to leave. Emma was suspicious of what I was doing."

"I'm sorry." My face feels hot. I hope I am not blushing. "Greer is going to the mill today with the mayor and the aldermen. There have been more people there sick."

He nods, digesting the information. "That's what I hear."

"You'll all be gone to Kansas soon, won't you? When we find the money."

"Yes, ma'am. I hope so."

"And to get away from the fever."

"That, yes. But our hope had already started to run out. Being afraid of a sickness is just being afraid of dying. And living here, I think all of us are already afraid of dying."

"Afraid of dying? Why?"

Simon looks at me with an ironic lift to his eyebrows. "Well," he says, "we believed—The freed people believed that there was an important change in the weather back at the end of the war. It seems the climate remains just as inhospitable for our well-being as it ever was."

"You're talking politics again," I say, irritated by this recurring conversation.

"Yes, ma'am, to a certain extent. And I am talking about the way we live."

"The way you live?"

"The way all of us live."

"I think you've done quite well with Eli, Simon," I say tersely. "It appears to me he always favored you—went out of his way for you. To hear you talk, someone would think you were ungrateful." I rest my hand on the ledger, resisting the urge to tap my fingers against it. I don't know why I am angry, except maybe for Simon's tone—so familiar. There is a condescension in it that I hear from all men, but I cannot accept it from Simon.

"I apologize, ma'am," he says quickly. "I am in no way ungrateful for the affection and care that Mr. Branson showed me. We are all indebted to him in one way or another, aren't we?"

My face goes hot again, and I pull my hand off the ledger and into my lap, lacing my fingers together tightly. "Are you afraid of dying, Simon?"

He looks at me with a sort of smile in his eyes and laughs a little. "Some of us are afraid, I guess. But I'm not."

The newspapers lie between us. The *Advocate* and the *Register*. They are several days old already.

"Rachel does not seem afraid. Not really. She seems like a very strong person," I say.

He does not respond, and the moment stretches out. Simon seems like a strong person, too. But all those years with Eli. It bothers me.

"How did you come to be with Eli?"

Simon nods and looks at the floor, taking a long breath. His face softens. His eyes lose their hardness, almost melting with melancholy. He looks at me and asks, "Do you really want to know how we met?"

I nod, but my brow knits together. I am not certain that I do want to know.

"I was born on a plantation down on the Cahaba River. I didn't know my daddy, and when my old ma died, I ran away. I was fourteen or so and decided to run away. I made a pretty good go of it. Got up around Florence, running through the woods and along the back roads at night, eating what corn I could steal or what I could scavenge from the woods, always feeling the urge to move, always listening for the dogs behind me. But the exhaustion got to me. I was too tired. I thought I might go ahead and lay myself down to die. And so I did. That was when Mr. Eli caught me."

"He caught you?" I ask.

"He was a slave trader, ma'am. He'd chase down runaways when he had the chance."

"Runaways? Eli was a slave catcher?"

"Yes, ma'am. That is what he did. He traded slaves from up along the coast of Georgia and South Carolina, and he'd march them here and south of here. Down deep into Alabama and Mississippi. And sell them."

Sitting in the sunny office with the hickory and magnolia trees on the lawn, with the irises and peonies and the bright white paint of the house, it doesn't seem possible. It doesn't seem real.

I grew up with slaves, we all did. I saw them sold away south more than once. Sold from my father's estate to pay off debts after he died. Sold by Mama when she wanted a new carriage or for money for a trip to White Sulphur Springs. It was a heinous act, to sell off your own people. An ugly, cruel act unless you were in the direst of straits. And the men who profited from that misery, the conniving dealers who would shackle them together, whole families chained one after another, marching off under the bloody eye of the slave trader, selling them downriver where the weather and the overseers were so punishing. It always made me shudder to think of those men. And Eli was one of them.

"But he didn't—he didn't sell you, Simon? Or take you back to your master?"

"No, ma'am. I never told him I was a runaway. Although he could see it well enough. I never said where I was running from. I told him I had lost my papers, that I was free and on my way to Nashville. That my father would reward him handsomely if he would return me. He didn't seem to believe me, but then I showed him I could read and do figures—"

"How could you read? It was against the law!"

Simon laughs at me again. "At my old place, I was about the same age as two of my master's children, and for some reason, the missus let me sit with their tutor, a Yankee man. My ma was a favorite of the missus and could convince her to do just about anything she wanted. So she got me a little reading and writing and numbers. And Mr. Eli thought—I guess he thought that I might come in handy for him."

"But you didn't belong to Eli! He might as well have stolen you!"

"Well, Mr. Eli wasn't one for the fine points of the law. I can't say I know too many white folks who paid attention to the law when it came to a colored person. And I was half dead from running and starving in the woods. I guess I gave myself up to him.

"After I realized he was going to keep me, I stopped talking altogether. But Mr. Eli waited. He kept me with him. Kept an eye on me that first trip to South Carolina. The rice country along by Beaufort. Swampy place. Diseased. I don't know how anyone who labored there could survive it. But they did. And Eli bought them up. Colored people. We marched them down south together, first here to Albion, then down to Montgomery and Demopolis, until we sold them all. Thirteen men, women, and children. Funny number to come up with on my first trip. They talked in ways I never heard before. A whole different language. And superstitions. Mysteries. Some of them cursed me, I believe, for dragging them west, bound together in a line. An old man pointed at me and spoke in his strange language, rolling his eyes back in his head."

Simon is looking out the window at the garden, with its neat boxwoods and well-tended beds, all carefully maintained by his hand. His eyes are far away. His voice is, too. He's not really speaking to me. He is back there, in those days, like Greer.

"That's what we did together. For years. He was almost my father, if you could say someone who keeps you captive can be a father. But he did do good for me. I didn't realize too much of it back then. Later, he did good for me. What would have become of me if Mr. Eli hadn't found me?" He pauses again, his mind wandering.

"I guess I didn't know any better. Better for them all to be slaves than for me to be back on that plantation without my ma. You know why I ran away?" He looks at me. "I had taken a book from the master's library. I got a good lashing then. The first one of my life, though I had seen it done many times. About the worst—maybe not the worst, but it was bad enough to make me run off. They bound my hands and tied me to a stake in the yard, and Master himself gave me the strokes." He looks into the garden, and we sit in the hot, still air. Is he thinking of when the Knights came for him?

"Something else you should know, ma'am," he says. "Something neither I nor Mr. Eli ever told anyone. We promised not to—well, Mr. Eli did. But he's gone now, and I'm here talking to you, and I think it's important that you know that back in those days, years before the war, Eli was in the employ of your cousin Mr. Everton Heppert."

I open my mouth to speak. I stumble over the words. "Eli worked for Judge? What did he do?"

"He worked as a slave dealer on Mr. Heppert's behalf, ma'am. Mr.

Heppert got Eli started in the business of dealing slaves. Eli was his agent. Mr. Heppert provided capital for Eli's business activities, and Eli split the profits with him. I've known Mr. Heppert since I was fifteen years old. Almost longer than you've been alive."

I feel that I have lost my ability to see, the shock comes over me so quickly. I put my hands on the desk and feel the ledger.

"My God." And after the war, Judge was borrowing money from him. "But Eli worked at Val Heyward's mercantile."

"Yes, ma'am, but that was only right before the war. Mr. Heppert helped him to get the position there. He had done with dealing in people at that point. We both had."

I take my time, not saying a word, trying to understand this story. Perhaps it is a lie. Too much to believe. Eli employed by Judge to trade in slaves?

"I don't see how any of this is possible. Why would Judge do such a thing? How could he ask Eli to keep such a secret for him?"

Simon is impassive. "Perhaps you can ask Mr. Heppert that when you have the chance. He might actually tell you the truth."

"What do you mean?"

"Mr. Heppert at the time did not want word getting out that he was in that line of business. He was concerned about his political career. He was running for the statehouse back then. But now he doesn't have a real political career to speak of, does he? Unless he gets sent to the state constitutional convention. By popular demand."

Simon smirks and pushes the newspapers toward me. "But there are other things that I am sure you wanted to discuss with me, aren't there, Miss Gus?"

I take the papers and unfold them in front of me. I look at Simon, gauging his honesty. "What do the papers say?" I ask him. He remains quiet. On the front page, a notice of deaths around Pennyacre and Whittle Cove is reported at the bottom of a long column of county news. Families. Poor whites. Women and children employed from the mill. The deaths, it reports, total fifteen. They do not mention Eli. They do not say how they died. They say that Dr. Epaphrase Greer has insisted there is as yet no cause for alarm. That it is a phenomenon of the great heat we have experienced recently. There is no need to suspend the operations of the mill. It is a paper owned by Mr. Lilly, *The Advocate*, a friend of Greer's.

Simon watches me. My head feels as if it is spinning. I breathe in slowly.

"It's spreading," I say.

"Just among the poorer classes, ma'am. That seems to be what the paper says. Although they don't bother mentioning the deaths among the colored population." Simon's voice is low and even.

"Eli wasn't a part of the poorer classes."

"He was once, ma'am. They don't seem to include Mr. Eli, either. Dr. Greer doesn't, at least."

"Greer is a part owner of the mill," I say.

"Yes, ma'am, I know."

"How do you know?"

"I was there when they signed the contracts. I delivered them."

"And he's taking the mayor and aldermen to the mill. Have more people died than the papers say? What else do you know, Simon?"

He looks out the open door toward the carriage house. John has the bay mare out of the stable and is brushing her down. Her name is Helen. That is what Eli called her. "There are other people getting sick and dying. They don't seem to count for much. I don't know how many. But people are nervous. If the mayor is going to the mill, people are nervous. Things seem normal. People are still doing business, but they're tense. You can see it in their faces."

He pauses as if thinking carefully, then begins again. "They stopped delivering the newspapers here. I checked with Mr. Lilly to see if they had stopped because of Mr. Eli's death, but he said he didn't realize the boy wasn't bringing them by."

"Why did the boy stop?"

"Because he was afraid of the house, he said."

"Afraid of the house? Why on earth?" The answer is obvious to me. Why did I bother asking the question?

"Because of the sickness, ma'am. I guess his mama up in the North Ward told him not to come near this house."

"What? That's ridiculous!" It's not ridiculous. How many people must be saying the same thing? Those women at Eli's funeral. My old friends. They already talked like that days after he died.

"It is an odd thing to say."

"Let's just find the money, and then we can go away. Not pay any attention to this." The mill will make more money. Judge will get his share back. Eli's estate will be settled. Everything will be fine by the time we come back.

Simon gives a grim smile. "I haven't had the chance to look in the stable. John said the saddlebags are all in order, but he is very dedicated to those horses. And I want to finish upstairs in the house."

"Where can I look?" I ask.

"Maybe you can search the attic. You're planning on going away. It wouldn't raise any suspicions for you to look through some old trunks in the attic. Miss Gus, if you find anything, please come to me first."

Simon jumps from his chair, turning toward the garden. His hand moves instantly to his hip, where there should probably be a gun.

Mike is outside on the gravel path, watching us. How long has he been there? His face is pale and his eyes are narrow. He stands watching us, his eyes on Simon, who is looking steadily back at him. Mike is armed, a gun on his belt. I step to the door in front of Simon and turn to him, my back to Mike.

"Please go upstairs. I will talk to my brother." Simon's eyes are still over my shoulder, trained on Mike. "I will talk to him. Please leave us."

Simon looks at me and then to Mike. "As you please, ma'am," he says. He goes into the house through the small office door, still keeping an eye on Mike.

"What's going on here, Gus?" Mike calls to me from the garden.

I smile at him through the open door. "Mike, what are you doing here?"

He saunters across the grass and up the porch steps. "I told you I'd be around. I heard you made a visit out to the mill."

"I don't have any money, Mike."

He stands in front of me, smirking. That knowing smile of his, the same one he gave Eli just before Eli gave him money. I never knew how much, but I am sure Eli was generous with him. Certainly more generous than he deserved.

"Aren't you going to ask me in, sister?"

I turn, and Mike eases past me. His breath is sour, as if his insides are rotten, half preserved in corn whiskey. Up close, his skin is sallow, almost yellow, and his eyes are bloodshot and drooping. My little brother.

He walks behind Eli's desk and kicks a leg of the chair, jarring it from its place with a mournful scrape. He looks at me again with narrowed eyes. "You taking Eli's place, Gus? Helping all the niggers in town? Are you going to be their savior now?"

"I don't know what you're talking about."

"Don't you? Or maybe you've just got one special nigger in mind?" Mike leers at me.

"You're disgusting. If you've come here to insult me, then you should leave right now."

"Who's going to make me leave? Your big nigger man? Are you going to sic him on me?" He kicks the chair again, sliding it back, and then he falls into the seat. "Nice chair," he says. "Feels good to sit here, doesn't it?" He coughs out a laugh. I won't answer him.

"Doesn't it," he goes on, a curl to his lip. "To sit in Eli's chair? To have everything he had. I bet you like how it feels."

"Why did you come here?"

"Just to check up on you. See how you're getting on. How did things go for you at the mill?" He opens Eli's drawers, rummaging through the papers. He takes out Eli's watch and opens the case with a click. His fingers are unsteady, and he has to grip the watch with both hands to open it. "Does this run?"

"No, it's broken. Unfixable." Mike clicks the watch shut and holds it in his hand. He must be gripping it tightly to keep his fingers from trembling. My God, what has he done to himself? If Hill had lived, would he be like Mike and Buck? Better that he died than to become this.

"Then you won't mind if I take it," he says, and smiles again, laughing at me.

"Fine, take it and go."

"I'll be expecting a little more than Eli's broken toys soon." He turns the watch in his hand awkwardly, as if he is afraid he will drop it. His hand trembles. He slips the watch into a vest pocket. "You're a smart girl, though, Gus. You probably already knew that."

"There isn't any money, Mike," I blurt out. The garden door is open behind me, and I lean on it until it touches the wall. My hands reach for the small oval knob, cool metal. My shoulder rests against a pane of glass.

"That's what Judge told you?" Mike sneers again. "Is that what they told you out at the mill?" Condescending and ugly.

"Yes, Mike, that's what they told me. Why would they make something like that up?"

"Buck was out there with you, wasn't he? You two are pretty chummy now, aren't you? Why do you think he went out there with you? Huh, you ever think of that?"

"I don't know, Mike. You know more about Buck than I do. Why don't you tell me?"

"I don't have to tell you anything. For being so smart, you sure do act stupid, don't you?"

"You're drunk. If you don't have anything to say, then get out." I twist the door handle. I can hear the faint squeak and click of the latch.

Mike stands, his hand on the desk. He smiles again, sly and superior. "Wouldn't you like to know what I know, sister? It's worth a lot more than this broken watch that probably works fine once it's wound up."

"What do you know, Mike? What is this about?"

"Just about Judge and the kind of fellow he is. I don't think you want to partner up with him, if you know what I mean. I think you need somebody who's going to tell you the real story. Somebody who knows the real story."

"I think I already know all I need to know about Judge. But thank you for your offer of help, if that's what this is. Or do you need a bribe? Is that what you're here for?"

"If I learned anything from old Eli, I learned you don't give away something for nothing. You need me, Gus. You may think you're smart, but you need me." Mike steps toward me, and there is something so strange in his face. There's anger, but there's hurt, too. Something desperate. I have never seen him like this. He always had meanness in him. Now he's a shadow of that person. His breath comes quickly, as if he has worn himself out from running.

"Are you ill, Mike?"

"What are you trying to say?" he growls and folds his arms tightly across his chest.

"You don't look well."

"Why in the hell do you want to say something like that?" He shudders and looks out at the garden. He wipes the sweat off his forehead with his hand. "There are people getting sick, aren't there? I hear people talking about it. Is that how Eli really died? Is that what's happening to everyone?" His eyes are suddenly fearful, darting to the windows and back to me. He wipes his hand on his pant leg.

"I don't know, Mike. I just mean you don't look well."

"Is that your joke? Don't you goddamn tell me what I look like." He folds his arms tightly again and looks through the windows.

"If you have something to say, Mike, say it and go." The handle turns, smooth and slippery under my hand. The money Judge gave me. It's in my pocket still. Fifty dollars. Too much for Mike. What does it matter? We will find Eli's money and this fifty dollars will be meaningless. And if it will keep Mike away from me for a little while . . . He needs it. He needs something. Why else would he be here, acting so crazy, so desperate? How has he been living since Eli died? "How much do you want?"

Mike looks up at me. His eyes glimmer faintly for a moment, then fade. They narrow. He is calculating. "How much can you afford?" he asks.

"I'll give you fifty dollars, Mike. But go away. Just leave me in peace."

He licks his lips. He can almost taste the whiskey, I am sure of it. Or whatever else he might be poisoning himself with.

"You got yourself a deal. But fifty dollars doesn't last forever. You know that, I bet." I reach into my pocket and feel the crumpled banknotes. They rustle as I pull them out, and my hand goes out to him, holding the edges of the bills with my fingertips. He grasps it, and his hands are trembling worse than before. But he is smiling. Relieved. Almost ecstatic. "It's not a lot, you know, Gus, but I'll give you a piece of information to give you an idea of who you're dealing with."

"No, Mike," I say, and turn to the door, looking through the two layers of glass at the porch, warped through the uneven glazing. Do I want to know it? I know I do. "Just go. I don't need to hear it."

"I think you should know some things. Back after the war, it wasn't too long after, the Knights of the White Cross started running around here. Running after Yankees and some of them smart-ass niggers. And do you know who started it all up? Do you know who it was? I'll give you one guess."

His eyes don't blink. They are sunken and hungry.

"It was Judge. It all started out to get the free niggers running scared and make them Yankees mind themselves. But now it's all over Alabama. All over everywhere. They rule the roost down here, Gus. And Judge is the Grand Cyclops. How do you like that?"

Of course. Why not? Judge's ruthlessness. His own secret army. He always talks as if the war isn't over.

"You know," Mike continues.

"Please, that's enough."

"They say the Knights killed Eli. Poisoned him to make him die like that, all bloody. Was it all bloody like that? You saw him."

I try to move away into the office, but Mike has me pinned against the door. His hand is on my arm. The grip is weaker. Not like before.

"No, Mike. Just go."

"Huh. You know Judge won't stop at anything. That's why you need to mind yourself. That's why you need this piece of information. Buck told me back after the war, Judge got the Knights started up by setting fire at a barn dance."

I look at Mike. My mouth is open. The blood drains from my face.

"That's right, sister. You don't have to make those wide eyes at me. He paid some fellow to run up and fling a lamp in there and scream something about the crazy rebels!" Mike laughs, and it is almost a cough that shakes his shoulders. He pulls his arm in and coughs hard into his hand and laughs again, looking at me. "Then Judge went around to all the old Confederates and said, 'Lookee here! We's got to do somethin' 'bout this!'"

"Who told you that?"

"Buck did. Buck was there that night. He said he was outside watching for the fellow. Dumb Buck. He'll do whatever his daddy says."

I cannot look at him. He moves past me to the door, and his breath is hot and briny. Poisonous. He passes outside.

"Just so you know who you're dealing with, Gus," he says almost in a whisper, as if he can't bear to say it. As if he is afraid to say it aloud.

He treads across the soft grass. I can see him through the double panes, hunched over, thumbing the bills, fractured and disfigured by the glass. He is a liar. He always has been. And all that is ten years ago. Ancient history. It can't be true. There were people from Washington down here. An investigating committee. Eli spoke to them, although I never knew what he said. Was it three years ago? They were at the courthouse, and all sorts of people went to testify, to tell them stories of the outrages committed by the Knights of the White Cross. If that were true, then surely they would have arrested Judge, done something to him. Word would have gotten out. Unless they were all lying, too.

What does it matter? All that matters is finding the money and getting out of Albion. I have the attic to search. Simon told me to search the attic. Maybe they are all liars. Buck is a liar. Just like Mike. They are all after Eli's money. They'll say anything to get it. But I must get away from here. I have to get away from Albion. From this madness. From all these lies.

Seventeen

ENTERING THE ATTIC IS like walking into a fire. Sweat trickles behind my ears onto my neck, soaking the collar of my dress. I unbutton my cuffs and roll up the sleeves. Heat comes off my wrists. I open the top buttons of my bodice and take a handkerchief from my pocket, soaking up the perspiration as it runs off of me. I can hardly believe the things Mike says. He's so desperate, he'll say anything. He must be lying. What does he expect from me?

The light from the doorway is diffused and dusty. There's another thin shaft of light from a small dormer that faces the garden. The ceiling vanishes into the dark rafters over my head, and I can make out the beams where swallows have abandoned their nests. Large objects clutter the uneven floors, trunks and valises filled with I don't know what. The detritus of my marriage. The cumulative effects of the union are strewn across the room, long forgotten. I find it hard to believe Eli would have come home ill, climbed these stairs, and hidden a fortune in this dusty cave.

But there are interruptions in the pattern of filth on the warped planks. The footprints of Big John and Simon when they came for my traveling trunks. Perhaps Eli's as well. I follow them, mostly clustered near the door, where the trunks Eli and I used were normally left. There are faint trails of footsteps that lead into different corners of the room. They could just as well be Simon's as Eli's—or mine or John's. What would prevent Simon from coming up here and searching? What am I doing here? Being kept busy so that he can search Eli's room without my interference?

The dust runs before my feet and chokes my throat, making me cough. Like that horrible dust at the cotton mill.

My head is bent to avoid the rafters. I keep a hand on them as I move, feeling the heat off the wood beams. The cobwebs reach down and cling to me. I sweep at them with my handkerchief. My sweat mixes with them, and the muck smears itself on the back of my hands and forearms. The air tastes like hot coals.

What has been happening here for ten years? Judge setting fire to that barn. He would have to be mad to do that. But Judge said there is still a war going on. He said as much to Eli more than once. And it was a threat. It must have been. Like when they whipped Simon. If what Mike says is true, that was Judge, too. Eli must have known. The Union League hall and the terror that the Knights of the White Cross spread. All Judge. A man who will stop at nothing, Mike said. For what? To keep colored men from voting? To undo what the war did to us? There is no undoing it. We cannot go back. We cannot reverse that loss. The horrible loss. Hill's death. If only he had not died. He was a good man—a man of honor. True honor, like Pa. But they're all gone. If only they had not died, I would not be here.

The objects loom at me in the darkness. A large basket with a wicker top is filled with Mama's old dresses, moth-eaten for having been stored so carelessly. All the colored dresses that she put away after Hill died. Permanent mourning. Not that they were cheerful colors, grays and browns and lavenders. Threadbare, with torn trimmings hanging loose from the fabric.

There is the trunk, the small one that holds the spools of ribbon and mementos from Mama's funeral. The dust is marked where I knelt two weeks ago, now covered in a fine layer of new dust. Footprints lead to a larger trunk, an old-fashioned cabin trunk from thirty years ago. I lift the lid and peer into the darkness. Slowly, the objects reveal themselves to me. There are old pattern books and piles of magazines. *Godey's* and *Peterson's* and some old *Mrs. Stephens' Illustrated* from before the war. I brought them with me when Eli and I were married. The piles have grown since then. Emma has conscientiously stored them here. The *Godey's Lady's Book* that Buck brought me is in here, too, buried somewhere.

I sift through the yellowing papers, pulling them out and piling them on the floor. There are so many. Years of them. They were something to occupy me. Tatting lace and making tobacco pouches and antimacassars and silly macramé lamp tassels. I would look back to the issue Buck brought me every now and then. To read the poems and stories and to think about that summer after the war.

There it is, edges still curled and frayed. November 1864. He said he had gotten it from a woman in Franklin sometime after he was wounded. Who was that woman? He said he carried it with him to make a present of it to me. The pages are worn. A color plate folds out like an accordion and shows a group of women dressed in the latest fashions. One woman is in lavender half mourning. The fashions of the war. I close the magazine and put it in my pocket. The trunk lid drops with a dull thud.

Buck is his father's son, isn't he? Following me to the mill. Trying to take charge of me. Trying to take my hand again. I won't do it. It is convenient for him to pursue me. It is convenient for Judge. Buck is a boy who does what his father tells him. To pretend with me that he has some influence over Judge. He's as tragic as Mike, and as ruined.

Mike's hands. He could not keep them from shaking. He could barely hold Eli's watch.

The corners and crevices where the floor meets the roofline are dark. Perhaps there is a concealed place in these nooks. But only cobwebs and dirt are here. The heat is almost unbearable. My dress sticks to my back as if it has melted onto my skin.

There are other trunks, smaller ones, banded with wood and leather. And a leather frame valise with buckles and a key lock under the handle. The dust on it has been disturbed. I brush away the clusters of dirt. Faded initials, gold-embossed, are above the tarnished brass lock. H.S. They are my father's initials. Henry Sedlaw. Mama presented the case to him when he was running for the statehouse almost twenty years ago.

I sweep away more of the dust. The leather is worn and puckered. Pa never traveled with it, but it seems used, exposed to the weather. It never went anywhere. Pa left it in the basement of the house on Allen Street. After he died, when did I last see it? Not since then, I think. It must have been there when Mama died. Did Eli bring it over then and put it in the attic for me? One of the few items of my father's that was left to me after Mike had sold the house, the books, everything. The novels and mineral guides and atlases. Whatever he didn't take or destroy—only the bench in the hall and now my father's valise. I rub the leather and grab the handle, as Pa would have done.

The trunk is heavy. The leather buckles are stiff from years of heat. They are hard to loosen, but I twist them, watching the dried tongues crack, almost splitting and crumbling in my hands. My fingers are damp with sweat. The latch has a small metal button that I press, but the lock does not respond. Maybe I need a key. The ring of household keys is in my pocket. There is a small key that is for a case in the pantry. I insert it, playing at the lock, twisting until there is a snap. The mechanism must be rusted, and I have broken the spring.

I withdraw the key and press the button again. My fingers leave wet prints on the lock. Sweat falls in thick drops from my forehead and makes dark spots on the leather. They soak into the skin of the case almost immediately.

The latch will not move. I pull on the handle, jerking at it. My arms strain. Beads of sweat fall off my nose, spraying the floor around me.

The latch gives suddenly and the case flies open. Papers flutter out and settle over the floor. I gather them up. The valise is full of them. This is no five thousand dollars. This is a fortune beyond that. Hundreds of thousands of dollars. My heart is in my throat. They are denominated in fifties, hundreds, five hundreds.

But they are worthless. Bonds pledged by the Confederate States of America. On cotton. All in Confederate dollars. They are paper covered in worthless words. Many have the coupons attached, unredeemed for interest payments, due in to the Confederate Treasury Department every six months. Two-dollar coupons. Three dollars. Some for fifteen dollars payable to the bearer. Others have coupons missing, neatly clipped with a pair of scissors and a steady hand. This is a grand joke. I gather the papers and pile them back into the case.

My name. Out of the corner of my eye, I see my name. It is written on the back of one of the bonds—my own handwriting. A scrawling fancy penmanship, printed over and over again. Augusta Belier Blackwood Sedlaw. And letters. Rows of S and T. Curves and flourishes that march down the page. On several of them. My handwriting is so even, so studied. The handwriting of a schoolgirl. These must be Mama's bonds. Mama's hand clipped them. Some of them, at least. And she caught me writing on their reverse. I can still feel the sharp sting of her hand across my face. She hit me hard and with anger. It was a foolish prank. Silly. Her slap wiped the smug smile off my face.

It had to be in '65. Mike had been gone for a long time already. What a girl I was. A silly foolish girl. As resentful and rebellious as Mike. We had no writing paper, and I took the bonds, since Mama had said they were good only for letter paper. Her friends who braved the streets to visit us had said it, too. I had written on them. Mama caught me and flew into a rage. She slapped me hard so that tears came into my eyes from the pain. I stood looking at her, sullen and stunned. How dare she hit me, I thought. Pa never would have let her hit me.

"Gather them up, you fool," she said. "Gather them up. These are going to Judge to sell if he can make any money out of them."

These are going to Judge. Mama must have put them in the case and delivered them over to him. And now the case is in my attic. Judge must not have sold them.

How long ago? Over ten years? My handwriting is so different now. My name is different. This was written by another person, not me. A person in another life. But it wasn't, really. Judge was the same person then, wasn't he? He was someone people looked up to and respected. A man of honor. But he isn't, is he? Buck, too. Can it be true? Can he really have done what Mike said? Was it all a part of his father's plan? Like the barn dance.

"Miss Gus." Emma's voice comes to me from the open doorway. "Come out of there, Miss Gus. You look a fright."

I turn and look at her, scowling. The anger is full in me, and the sting of Mama's slap on my cheek feels as if it just happened.

"What is it, Emma?" I mean no friendliness with my voice.

Emma doesn't answer me. I close the case and stand up, catching the handle and pulling at my skirts. The weight bears on me, tilting me lopsided. Emma's face is open in surprise as I walk past her, the case under my arm. The air on the landing feels fresh after the confines of the attic.

The case bumps against the banister as I struggle with it down the narrow stairs. Emma stands above me, outside the open door of her room, her mouth agape. My hair is coming undone, unraveling in loose strands around my face. Dirt spots my hands and wrists, sweaty smears of dust and cobwebs that are hot and wet. Long strands stream off my dress like so much mourning crape.

Eli's door is open. Simon is in there. The light in the hall seems washed out, it is so bright. The walls seem gray, and the rugs and pictures are monochrome, like a tintype. The hickory bench that was my father's is dark and hard.

The case slips and slides fast off the railing. It tumbles to the floor with a bang. The broken clasp slips loose, and the lid flies back, dumping sheaves of promissory notes across the hall.

Simon appears. Our eyes meet. He must sense my anger. Voices come from my room, and Henry rushes into the hall with Rachel behind him.

"Mama," he says when he sees me. "What is it?" Rachel looks at all the papers and then looks at Simon. She can't know what they are, but she knows there is something wrong. One look at me tells her that things are not right.

"Henry," she says and puts her hand on his shoulder. "Henry, come away from that." She holds him back as he grasps at the papers. Little John is behind them.

"It's nothing, Henry," I say, trying to control my voice. "It's nothing. Mama just had an accident, and now she's got a big mess to clean up."

"You had an accident?" Henry asks, his blond hair lustrous in the light, his blue eyes clear and sharp. "Can I help, Mama?"

"No, Henry," I say, still catching my breath. "Mama and Uncle Simon will take care of it. Go back to the nursery with Rachel and Little John." Rachel's eyes rest on me. She doesn't make a face but nods, holding Henry gently and leading him back to the nursery, leaving us in the hall.

"You seem to have a lot of knowledge, Simon," I say. My voice is shaking, and my hands hurt from the struggle with the case. "Maybe you can tell me what these are doing in the attic."

"What are they, ma'am?" he asks me cautiously. He leans down and picks up several of the bonds, considering them.

"Don't lie to me, Simon, or pretend like I'm an idiot." My voice rises. "You knew the case was up there. You knew that finding it would upset me. You know there's no money hidden in the attic. Why did you send me up there to find this?"

Simon's face becomes serious. He stops looking at the bonds in his hand, letting it fall to his side.

"Didn't you?" I insist. "Answer me." He stands in front of Eli's bedroom door, but I can see around him. The wardrobe is open, and Eli's clothes are piled neatly on the floor. The drawers of the chest are open, too, and papers are piled on top of it. "What was this? Some ruse for you to hunt Eli's room alone? Did you find it?" I rush against him, trying to get into the room, but he takes my wrists and holds them. I struggle, but he is too strong.

"Shhh," he says. "Quiet now. Do you want them to hear you?"

Emma's feet are on the top step. Her skirts shift, and she steps up, out of sight.

"Come in here," he says. He pulls me into Eli's room and shuts the door.

"How dare you put your hands on me," I hiss. "If my brother saw you, he'd string you up for daring to touch me!"

"Shhh," he says again. "I'm sorry. I apologize, but you are losing control of yourself."

I suck air into my mouth, my hands on my knees, trying to breathe, glaring at him. "Tell me. Tell me why those bonds from my mother's house are in the attic."

"Because they belonged to Mr. Eli."

"That's a lie. That case is my father's. Eli Branson never had that case."

"Yes, ma'am, he did," Simon says. He walks away from me, across the room, then turns and begins again. "Your mother gave these bonds to Mr. Heppert, your cousin. He put them together with his own, and he sold them to Eli. Didn't you know that?"

"That's a lie. Why would Eli buy something he knew was worthless?" The notations in Eli's ledger. Those bonds from Judge. And what was I? Did Eli have a special Greek character for me? Loans advanced for goods pledged. No, a purchase. Funds paid for goods received.

"Some people think the state of Alabama may yet have to honor these bonds. And Eli was getting something else he valued."

His face is quiet, neither angry nor ironic nor condescending. He looks at me in a simple, factual way. My body is something apart from me. As if I can watch myself and listen to myself. As if I am locked outside of my body. A valuable body. Something that I would gladly be rid of. Yes, like the carriages and the silver and the farmlands in the county. Eli collected things of value, and he wanted me. Mama was excited by the prospect of our marriage, almost frenzied about it. And Judge was so adamant. Sympathetic but firm. Of course he was firm. Of course marriage to Buck was unsuitable. He arranged the entire transaction. And pretended that it was all Mama.

"What did Judge get in return?" I don't want to know. Don't tell me.

"An income for your mother. Cash and other considerations for Mr. Heppert."

"The mill?"

"No, the mill came later. I believe what Mr. Heppert sought was relief and a pardon. Eli got the taxes on what remained of his property forgiven, and he intervened with Governor Parsons and President Johnson to secure a pardon for Judge."

"I see." I feel so far from sight. I am blind, feeling my way along with my hands. "I see," I say again automatically. "Of course." I was traded to Eli like the Meissen figurines. I was the only thing of value left in my mother's house. I have the Blackwood name. Did I prove as valuable to Eli as he thought?

I turn against the closed door. I do not want Simon to look at me, nor do I want to look at him. I put my hands over my eyes. I can see it all.

"Miss Gus," he says. His footsteps approach me.

"Keep away from me," I say. I push my hand out at him. "Keep away from me." Quieter now. My hand out for the doorknob, wiping my tears, not wanting him to see. Not wanting anyone to see.

"Miss Gus, please," he says behind me.

"You keep away from me." I shout it.

Emma is on the stairs, coming toward me. She follows me into my room, pushing her way past the door. "What's the matter?" she says, and I fall against the bed, my head buried in my arms. Emma is near me. She kneels next to me, taking me in her arms and holding me against her breast. We sit on the floor together. She knows how this feels. Of course she knows. They all know much better than I do. It's supposed to be fine for them. But not for me. It cannot be like this for me.

The laudanum takes effect so slowly. Not like it used to. That's what they say. The more you take, the more you need. I've heard women complain of it. I've heard of women who have taken too much and slowly fade away, cold as stone by morning. Mama used to take it. Never often. Sparingly. Mama always knew herself. She didn't need to take it. Maybe I need it because I don't know myself. I need it to forget myself. If I could just get away from Albion. This sickness is creeping in around us. It started here. With Eli and Greer. It was Greer who first gave me laudanum. Years ago. I had been married to Eli for two years. Our anniversary. I have not been able to get far away from it since. They keep giving it to me. I must stop this. I must think clearly.

The current is taking me. I want it to take me. I am letting go of the room. The bed and the roses and ribbons seem far away. I feel like I am floating in a river, being carried in its coolness. I drift in nighttime darkness, and I can hear the cicadas with their droning refrain down the whole long, lazy river. Just drifting. They buzz and hum in the high boughs of the live oaks and hickory trees, and I drift away down the river.

It's like swimming. My hands feel so cold on my forehead. I feel as if I am swimming against the current. If I just let go, it will take me away. Like Hill and Buck, when they would sneak down to the riverbank to swim in the Oosanatee. I followed them sometimes. A child spying on children. I would go by myself and put my feet in the water, too scared to jump in. Too nervous that there might be someone watching me. Buck and Hill would strip down to nothing, naked and pale. They would climb out on a tree branch, hairless bodies flying out as far as they could over the water. Splashing into it. The waves would ripple out from them with their laughter and shouts. Daring each other to climb farther on the tree, to leap farther. They weren't afraid of the river or the snakes.

Hill is dead. The river took him. No, the war did. Judge fired his rifle fourteen times from his front yard. It wasn't patriotic. It was a warning to men like Weems. To everyone. Judge and his guns and fires and whippings. He said the war wasn't over. The words stick in my head. It was an anniversary—my second wedding anniversary—and they fought across the table about the Republicans and Negro voting and Johnson's impeachment. Eli made awful jokes about setting the Richmond pudding on fire. Judge said the war wasn't over. It's not over, is it? No, it ended, but badly. It ended in such a way that it will never be over. "The field of battle has changed," Judge said. He's still fighting. Buck is still fighting, too, though he doesn't know why. And Simon fought. Wasn't the war enough for them?

Buck has scars from it. Bullet wounds from Shiloh and Kennesaw Mountain and Franklin. He showed them to me that summer after the war. In the house on Allen Street. In my room, sitting on my bed with his shirt off. The sun lit up the dust that floated in the air, holding it suspended as if time were standing still. I traced the scars with my fingers. Two fingers delicately tracing those purple patches of lacerated skin. On his back, under his shoulder, a small ring from a bullet at Franklin. On his belly, under the wiry black hair, a large scar, dark, from a shell at Kennesaw Mountain. Just under his chest, the minié ball that gouged him in the burning pines at Shiloh. He didn't know he'd been hit until he saw the blood. Mama burst into the room, scandalized. She shamed us, but Buck just laughed and put his shirt on. I had so much need for him then. That was a lie, too. That first time in the woods by the mill with the soft blanket of pine needles under me. The strength in his hands. A soldier's strength. It all faded away. The itch I got from those scars. Who doesn't have scars? Greer does, across his face. Eli had scars on his arms from a knife fight. He would sell and buy people. He bought me. Judge sold me to him for a bunch of worthless bonds and a pardon. Who would really pardon Judge? I don't. I should have listened more to Eli. He never told me where or why he had a knife fight. From the slaves he dragged south? From rough men in highway taverns? Simon must have scars. What does a scar look like on black skin? I've seen them, dark ribbons on arms or a back. What must they look like on Simon? Could I touch his scars if he showed them to me? Could I bring myself to touch a colored man's scars?

If Hill hadn't died. Or Pa. What if Pa had lived? Would I still be in the house on Allen Street? Pa on the bench with his newspapers. The sun setting over the Oosanatee, slow and black, winding its way through the trees. The thick clover under me and the warm sun on my back. School in Huntsville with all the girls, giggling, straining for a look at Albert Sidney Johnston. Little flashes like fireworks. All stitched together.

The room is so hot and my hands are so cold.

I wonder, would Simon let me touch his scars?

Eighteen

THE HEAT IS SO intense, and the smothering humidity, but it may break. Monstrous dark clouds obscure the sun, and shivering breezes sweep across the garden. The trees shudder against them. My head feels so thick. I took too much of the laudanum last night.

I don't know why we haven't found the money yet. Simon is still searching. I don't know where he is searching, but I feel it like a second sight. Henry leans against me, his head on my knee, and I pat his blond hair. He raises his head when the breeze wakes the curtains. He cranes his neck to peer out the window into the garden. He lays his head back down as I stroke him.

I don't know how long this waiting can go on. Waiting to find the money. Waiting for the sickness, this blood fever. Waiting for Buck to come again, or Judge or Mike, to take what little I have. I feel like I am in some sort of nightmare. And yet I move so slowly. I am stultified by this heat. And the laudanum. I do want to get away, but to where? To beg off of Bama for a room at the back of her house until the sickness fades or my fortunes turn?

There is no sound from anywhere in the house. I am alone with Henry, as if there is no one else in Albion.

"Let's go see Emma," I say. I rise from my chair and take his hand.

"Where's Aunt Rachel?" he asks, but he really wants to see Little John. I do not know where they are.

The door into the kitchen is open. It is not so hot in here. Emma has not lit a fire in the stove. She sits at the table drinking coffee.

"Emma, can you watch Henry? Where is Rachel?"

"She said she had to go home for a while. She didn't say when she'd be back." Emma peers into the bottom of her cup.

"Have you seen Simon this morning?"

"He's out in the barn." She looks at me, nothing strange in her look, except for the fact that she is looking at me. "John's off seeing if he can get some wood for the stove. We've run out."

"How do you have coffee?" I ask. The pot sits on the stove.

"It's from yesterday. Ain't no reason to start a fire if you can't keep it going."

"They haven't stopped delivering wood? What do they still deliver?"

"Nothing."

I let go of Henry and head to the garden door.

"Come here, baby," Emma says, and Henry walks over to her, mounting her leg to climb into her lap.

The horse chestnut in the garden is in full bloom, cones of snow-white flowers covering it, shivering in the odd gust of wind. There is the catalpa, trembling with white flowers dotted red as if they have been sprinkled with blood. Blood, too, in the orange-red flowers of the trumpet vine along the carriage house, climbing lush and wide almost to the window of Simon's room. The garden has not stopped growing. It will grow on long after us, perhaps wild and abandoned without Simon's hand to keep it in check. It will look like the other gardens after we have gone. I do not know what we can do but leave here, money or not.

"Simon," I call into the half-light of the carriage house.

"Ma'am?" he says. I step into the shadows. Simon stands before a wall of pegs and tack. His shirt is off. He is black and shiny with sweat. Fatigue is in his eyes. When he turns, I can see the wide scars crisscrossing his back, glistening ink black against his dark skin. A shiver courses over me. I should stay away from the laudanum.

"What are you doing in here?" I ask.

"Still searching. John's gone to gather firewood where he can. I wanted to look here before he came back."

"Have you found anything?"

"No." We look at each other. Sweat drips down my forehead and from my nose. I feel for my handkerchief, but I don't have it. I wipe the sweat off with my hand.

The air is thick with the rich pungent odor of hay and manure, and you can almost feel the heat rising to the rafters as if it's coming out of the hard-packed earth. The space is wide and high with stalls for four horses, though we have only two, the bay, Helen, and the thoroughbred, Paris, whose glossy black coat is shiny with sweat. There is the gig, and a phaeton that Eli bought for me, but that I never drove, and the old rockaway that we took on our wedding day. There are pegs and broad shelves over a work space where the harnesses and gear are stored.

"Ma'am, yesterday—" he says.

"No, Simon." I want to speak first. I look him in the eyes. They are brown, deep chestnut brown, like mine. "We will not speak about what happened yesterday."

"I just want to say, I didn't mean—"

"No," I insist. "We will never speak of it again." I can't look at him. Not in his eyes. Nowhere near his face. I don't want him to look at me. I walk to a stall and lean against a post.

He looks at his feet, then back to me. His face has turned to stone again. "All right," he says. "All right."

He turns back to the shelves and saddlebags. Jagged scars course across his muscles, smooth purple-black ribbons. Sweat beads on their raised surface. It is like Braille. I could read his life if I touched those scars. He takes his shirt made of stiff, cheap cotton and pulls it on, wet still with sweat. He doesn't mind that I watch him as he goes through all the drawers and cubbyholes. He is meticulous in his work, an orderly process from an orderly mind. But he bangs tack against the walls and kicks at the saddles. He pauses, looking at the wall of pegs lined with reins and leads and leather pouches.

"What will you do when we find the money, ma'am?" he asks, not looking at me.

"I don't know." I scratch at the dirt with my boot. The heat seems to have turned liquid, like a warm bath. "I guess I just want to go away. I don't want to go to Monte Sano. It's too near here. But the money won't last forever. I'll have to come back eventually. I wish there were enough to go away forever. Maybe to White Sulphur Springs. Or Philadelphia. Have you ever been to Philadelphia, Simon?"

"No, ma'am, I have not. Not at this point in my life." He pulls down saddlebags from a long row and searches them. The silence stretches out. I watch his shoulders move.

"What do you plan to do?" I ask.

He turns to me. He answers thoughtfully. "We can't live here. Colored people, that is. Most are too poor or too crazy to move. Pap Singleton has the right idea. Going out west to land of our own—land that we can own. That's the only way for us to get ahead. That's what I'll keep doing until it's done."

I can't help smiling a little. He is a new Moses. "You brought them from the Carolinas to here, and now you're going to take them to Kansas?"

Simon's eyes lose their thoughtfulness. At first he is incredulous. Then he becomes hard. He doesn't smile, but turns back to the saddlebags. "Something like that, I guess," he says.

How stupid of me. What an ugly thing to say. I should not have said it.

"There is a saddlebag missing," he says. He looks at me.

"How can you be sure?"

"I am sure," he replies simply.

I cannot doubt him. "What does that mean?"

He is desperate. Looking for meaning in the most meaningless evidence of nothing. "I don't know what it means. Maybe nothing."

"So we should be looking for a saddlebag?" My hands are on the post behind me. I lean my head back and look at the rafters of the barn. Hay dust fills the filtered light, and swallows flutter back and forth. That tingle in my stomach. That itch. It is because Simon is so near.

"Have you taken your medicine, ma'am?" His face is sideways to me, and he watches me out of the corner of his eye.

I feel jolted from sleep. "What do you mean? What medicine?"

"The medicine you take, ma'am. I'm asking if you've taken any today."

"No. Of course not."

He turns back to the shelves and squats to look in the drawers under the worktable.

"A small amount. Insignificant," I say. "To calm me. It is necessary."

"Yes, ma'am," he answers without turning. "I had word that the mill has been closed."

"What?" I step away from the post as Simon rises and turns to me again.

"Yes, the aldermen determined that it was unsafe. It has been closed and boarded."

There is something in his eye as he looks at me. I don't know what it is. I feel paralyzed. The mill is closed. Now what? I turn my head away. I am blushing, I think. "We can't stay here. We have to go. The mill is closed."

Simon takes a step toward me. "Just a little more time. All I need is one more day. I know we're close." His eyes are pleading. I want to do what he asks.

John is there at the wide-open doors. He is pushing a wooden wheelbarrow piled with firewood. He is sweating, laboring with the balance of the wheelbarrow, which he sets to rest just inside the doors. He looks up, seeing us, seeing Simon first and then looking where Simon is looking to me. John's face relaxes from a grimace into nothingness, but wide-eyed, comprehending. Our eyes meet.

"Ma'am," John says.

Simon turns away from me and walks back to the wall of harnesses and leather thongs and drawers and cubbyholes. He is purposeless. His hands move over the table without being directed to anything. John's eyes move away from me, scattering glances across the barn, up high to the hayloft, to the drawers and pegs and tables and finally to Simon. My face goes hot.

"I'll see if I can find that saddlebag for you, Miss Gus," Simon says, mumbling under his breath.

"Thank you, Simon," I say. My limbs feel numb and unresponsive, but I force them to move. I walk past John quickly out into the light. "I'll tell Emma there is wood for the stove." I call it back into the barn carelessly, as if it is the most normal thing in the world for me to do. But this is madness. What was I doing there at all? I've lost my mind. Everything is madness. The mill and the sickness and me.

Henry has his wooden blocks spread out across the brick floor of the kitchen. He watches me when I come in, pausing, his little hand in midair. He doesn't say a word, just watches me.

There is a rapping at the front door. Emma and Henry both stiffen, sitting upright and looking toward the front of the house.

"Stay here," I say. "I'll see who it is."

Bama's coachman is in the hall, looking right and left, the door open behind him.

"Miss Gus, Miss Bama's outside. She wants you to come with us," he says. He is an old man and moves with visible discomfort. "Come outside." He turns, waving his hand for me to follow.

Bama is in her carriage, her umbrella open, covering her in shade. Emily sits beside her with her two children on the bench across from them. Emily's bonnet is tight around her face. Sweat streams down her cheeks, cutting through her face powder in dark streaks. Her face is pinched closed, and her eyes are slits.

"Augusta." Bama begins talking before I am out of the gate. Homer struggles to climb back on the box. "Don't dawdle! We're going to Huntsville, and you're coming away with us. Get your boy and let's go. Tell your servants to pack your things and come right away. But you must come with us now. There is no time to waste."

"You're running away?"

"Yes, we are fleeing. No sane soul is staying. It's an epidemic. They've shut the mill. We must go!" The umbrella trembles in Bama's hand. Her sense of humor is gone, and under her command is a plea.

"I can't go now. The servants—I couldn't leave them here."

"They will follow you," Bama insists. Emily shakes her head at me. "This is no time for discussion. Get Henry and come with us."

"We'll pack our things. We'll follow you. I can't just take Henry and run." My hands are before me, empty. I should go. We should all go. Bama is here to take me away.

"You can't reason with her, Auntie," Emily says. Her voice is bitter. "Listen to her. She'd rather stay here with her Negroes. She's as bad as her husband was."

"Would you leave Homer behind, Emily? How can you say that?"

Homer looks back at me. He does not like me bringing him into this. He turns his back, black broadcloth spotted with sweat. The sun is unbearable. How can they sit in the carriage without the top up?

"You're one of them, aren't you, Gus?" Emily leans forward, her eyes violent. Her hands are gripped in tight fists in her lap. Her children, a boy and a girl, shrink into their bench. "I always knew it. The way you threw your head at Buck Heppert and then married Eli Branson. You should be ashamed."

"You don't know anything about it." I am trembling, too. My hands are shaking. I feel the vibration in my knees and shoulders. "How dare you spread lies. You're a vicious woman."

"I know why she's staying, Auntie. I've heard the stories." Emily leans back against her seat, a look of gluttonous triumph on her face. "She loves all the Negroes. Yes, she does. And one Negro man in particular. She lied about him the last time we were here. That Simon. It's disgusting, Gus. You're disgusting."

Bama's face is blanched whiter than paper. She looks at Emily with horror and then turns back to me.

"Let's go, Auntie. There is no saving her. She's not worth it."

"You shut your mouth up, Emily." Bama has erupted. She looks as if she will strike her niece. She turns back to me, her lips trembling. "Gus, this is not about Negroes or politics or the war. This is about your life and the life of your boy. Get him and get in the carriage."

Emily's face turns red under her ruined powder. She presses her lips together and sinks into her seat like her children.

"I can't, Bama. I appreciate your kindness. I do." I look back at the house, shining bright white in the sunlight. I can't leave here. Not yet. "I won't leave here. Not without the servants." I look at Emily. "And not with you all. We are too different now."

"Don't be a fool, Gus. We will forget what's been said here. Just pack your things. Bring your servants if you like, but you must come with us." Bama slams her hand on the carriage door, fiddling with the latch to open it.

"No, Bama. You all should go. I am staying."

Emily looks across the street, away from me. Bama's mouth gapes and her eyes are fearful.

"Goodbye, Bama." I turn away from them and walk up the path.

"You'll regret this, Gus! Think of your boy!" Bama calls after me, but I don't turn back. "Drive on, Homer!" she finally shouts. "You're making a terrible mistake, Gus!"

I turn back at the door, watching the carriage roll swiftly down the hill toward the cemetery. The dust is kicked up by the horses and hangs in the air in a red cloud. It just hangs there in the heat.

My travel trunks are standing in the hall, lining one wall, empty and waiting. I should pack them and go. But the money. Simon says he will find the money. Then we can go. We should go from here. I know that I should do something, though I do not know what.

What has possessed me? Some wildness or fear. It's the laudanum. It has made me lose my mind. It is all cloudy from the medicine. I can't see black or white. My skin crawls on me and makes me shiver. This is madness. Should I have taken Henry and gone with Bama? I want to cry again, alone, not with Emma. Even Emma would not understand. I must stop this. We must leave. I will pack a trunk. We will leave tomorrow no matter what. With Simon or without.

A voice is calling from downstairs. "Gus? Emma?"

Is it Jennie Heyney?

Emma's voice. "She's upstairs, ma'am. I'll let her know you're here."

"I'm coming, Emma." The sound of my voice echoes off the walls of the stairs.

Jennie is standing in her faded black dress, twisting her hands together. She rushes to me, grasping at me. Her bonnet is on a table, and her blond hair flies loose around her face. Her eyes are wild.

"Gus, thank God, you haven't gone. Everyone is running away.

Bama's gone already to Monte Sano. She didn't even let me know, and I was counting on going with her." She swallows hard. Her eyes are pleading.

"What's wrong, Jennie? Come into the parlor." She resists my hand on her arm, pulling back from me. Rivulets of sweat trickle down her temples.

"Oh, no, Gus. There isn't time. Please tell me you're refugeeing, too. Please tell me you're taking me with you."

"We're not. Not yet." Of course, I want to go, but the money. Simon wants one more day. My Lord, what will that day cost us?

"Haven't you heard? The whole town has gone wild. Anyone who can is leaving. They closed the mill, and they're talking about a quarantine because of the fever. Bama left without a word to me! And just now at church, Reverend Easton collapsed in his pulpit. In front of the whole congregation."

"What?"

"He looked terrible, Gus. There were whispers everywhere. The church was packed to the rafters. I've never seen such a crush. People are terrified. They don't know what to do. So everyone came to church, but Charlie couldn't. He's been called away by the railroad. He said if things go on like this, the trains won't stop in Albion anymore."

"They're stopping the trains, too?"

"Yes, and then Reverend Easton got up, and he was covered in sweat, head to toe. This heat. It's made everyone crazy. I feel so out of my senses, Gus. I don't know what to do. It's this heat. I've never felt such a heat, and it isn't even July. My God, we have to go away, Gus."

"Reverend Easton?"

"He stood up to the pulpit and began to preach, but I couldn't understand a word he said, and he seemed to falter. He held himself against the pulpit and leaned on it and there was such a rush of talking and whispering and fans and then he fell right back. In a pile, moaning by the altar, his eyes wide open and covered in sweat. Women started screaming and running. Everyone did. It was a stampede."

"Is he that sick? What did he look like?"

"I don't know. He was just lying there. No one would go near him. Only Mrs. Easton, and she held his head and wailed, but everyone ran away. He was soaked through. My God, I feel like I'm soaked through. This heat. We all must go. My father rescued you from Huntsville, Gus. You must take me away with you."

Her eyes seem feverish. The charm is in my pocket. I squeeze the burlap and bone in my fingers. "Oh, Jennie." Is she sick, too? Simon wants one more day.

"Please, Gus. Don't look at me like that. Just grab anything and have your man harness the horses, and let's go to Bama."

"I can't, Jennie. I need one more day."

"What do you mean? Have you lost your mind?"

"I know I should go. We should all go. But we are leaving tomorrow. We will go tomorrow, and you can come with us. We'll take a carriage if the trains aren't running. I can't go until tomorrow."

"Tomorrow is too late." Jennie steps back. Her face is flushed and her eyes are hard. "My father saved you from the Yankees. You owe me."

"Jennie, I'm sorry. I know that your father helped me. I've always been grateful. But tomorrow. Surely one more day can't make a difference."

"You're a madwoman to stay here. At least give me a little money to get away. That's the least you can do." She is shivering with anger. That fifty dollars I gave to Mike. If only I had it back.

"I haven't any money at all, Jennie. I wish I could give you something, but everything is tied up with the estate. Tomorrow. I might have something for you tomorrow."

"Enough with tomorrow. Everyone knows that you are the richest woman in town. They were right. You've turned scalawag, just like your husband. He brought this on us. This is all his doing. I've heard the stories about him. You can't even give your friend something to get away from here?"

"But Charlie—can't he get you on a train?"

Jennie's face is stained with tears and sweat. She glares at me. "You'll have the truth, then. Charlie's dead. He died last night, and I've got to get away from here." Jennie rears her head back and spits at me. I turn away, and it spots my sleeve and shoulder. "That's what you deserve, Gus. Dirty turncoat. You'll get yours."

Jennie spits again at my feet. She rushes out the door, her bonnet in her hand. Out into the intense sun. This heat. She's gone mad, too. And sick. Maybe I'm sick and I don't even know it. The whole town has gone mad and Simon wants one more day.

Simon closed and latched all the shutters on the front of the house and bolted the door. He feels guilty for asking for another day. He knows it is a mistake. We all know it. But the money must be found. It is too much money to run away from. It will make all the difference.

Rachel came back. She is making a bath in my room. She thinks it's best after Jennie. I step into the tin tub. Though the water does not need to be hot, the weather is too warm, Rachel has made sure it is not cold. She enters from the back stairs, carrying a kettle of hot water, and closes the door behind her. I shield myself, hiding my nakedness from the open door. But not from Rachel. After years of her bathing me, I have lost my modesty with her. She slowly pours the water in, looking at my face without a word, wanting to know from me when the proper temperature has been reached. The stream of water flows into the tub, blending with the cooler water. The swirl of warmth caresses my calves and ankles. I wait, attuned to it. The water will warm slightly even after Rachel stops pouring, so I must stop her just before it feels comfortable. Rachel steadies the stream and slows it gradually.

"Yes, that's fine," I say under my breath. My hand is on Rachel's shoulder. All my weight is on one foot, and the other moves in a small circle, rippling the surface. Rachel waits for me, watching. "Yes, Rachel, that's fine."

She nods, rising, and places the kettle on the empty hearth. She takes a thick-cut cake of milk soap and a cloth from the mantel and places them on the floor beside the tub. She said she made the soap herself.

"Come down, ma'am," she says. I lower myself, almost kneeling into the tepid water. A small seat is built into an angle of the tub. Rachel takes a tin cup and pours the water over my shoulders and arms and across the back of my neck. It runs over my breasts and down my back. She gathers my hair behind me and pours the water over until it is soaked through. I close my eyes as the water runs down my face. It runs along the edge of my nostrils, and I taste it on my lips. It warms my cheek and chin. The pump water is sweet with the faint taste of the cedar logs that deliver it to the house.

"Up, ma'am," Rachel says, and I rise out of the water, which runs off of me, from my fingertips and elbows, from my hair down my back to my buttocks. Rachel takes the cloth and soap and dips them into the bathwater, then rubs them together between her hands until the lather drips from the cloth back into the tub. She stands next to me and begins washing my neck and shoulders and my back. "Miss Gus," she says.

"Mm-hmm." My eyes are closed. The soap is taking the sweat and dirt away.

"I'm sorry to say, ma'am, but John and I and Little John are leaving tomorrow."

I turn to Rachel, and she steps back, holding the sudsy cloth in her hand. The soap bubbles drip onto the straw mats. "You're going now, too? The whole town is running away."

"Yes, ma'am. John's brother, Garson, got some extra money, and he wants us to go now. Things are bad. You should be going, too. Why are you still here?" She steps forward and takes my shoulder, gently turning me back around.

"Is Simon going with you?"

She lifts my right arm for me and runs the cloth along its underside from the wrist to the shoulder. She runs it along the top of my arm before letting it fall back to my side.

"No, ma'am, he's staying. He says he's taking you and Henry and Emma out of here, and then he'll find us."

I have stayed away from Simon all afternoon. I can't look at him. Thank God he is staying.

Rachel gives me a sharp look. John must have said something to her. "Yes, he's very good to help us. We will leave tomorrow, too. I know he'll catch up with you very quickly."

She says, "Mm-hmm." She scrubs across my shoulder blades. "You just keep that charm on you, ma'am, and don't stop for nobody on the pike."

"You don't have any idea what you'll find in Kansas, Rachel. Aren't you worried?"

Rachel washes me down to the small of my back, then moves to the other arm. "No, ma'am. John has cousins who have gone out west already. Garson sent us a letter about it. They got a bunch of land cheap from the government, and they're farming for themselves and doing fine. They've got plows and mules and everything you need. They'll lease it to us, they say, just come. It ain't going to be easy, but it's honest living. I'm not afraid. It would be easier if we had that money from Mr. Eli, but we're going anyway."

I turn and look at her over my shoulder. "I'm sorry, Rachel. I'd give you something, but the estate . . . it's—"

"I'm not asking you for anything, ma'am. I'm just telling you. You asked me and I'm telling."

Rachel kneels down to the water again. She feels on the bottom of the tub for the cake of soap and scoops it up like a slick white fish, gathering it into the cloth and working up fresh lather.

"Why is John's brother so eager to go?" I ask.

"We're all eager to go. We're all ready to be our own masters rather than slaves to someone else. This isn't freedom here, whatever they say."

She rubs the cloth down my leg, dipping it into the water, reaching to my ankles with her arm submerged as if she's reaching to the bottom of the tub for something.

"Was Mr. Cobb—was he a bad master, Rachel?" I don't look at her, but I know she has turned her face up toward me.

She pauses for a moment, then stands. "Well, ma'am, if you ask me, there weren't any good masters under slavery. Some were better than others. So I hear. I can't imagine any of them were good. I can't imagine they could have been much worse than Rooster Cobb, either."

"My father was a good master." I steal a glance at Rachel, looking for her reaction. Her skin is like very pale molasses, a little lighter than caramel. She has freckles across her cheeks and the flat bridge of her nose. She doesn't meet my eye, but I see her mouth curve slightly at the corners. She kneels again, and her hands look brown against my skin as she washes me. She rubs the cloth down my thigh to my knee. My skin against her hand is so white, like alabaster with a hint of pink underneath.

"He was, Rachel," I insist. "You didn't know him. He was one of the finest men who ever lived."

"I'll take your word for it, ma'am." She gives her head a quick shake.

"He was, Rachel," I say again, interrupting the long strokes of her hand. "Not all masters were bad. There were good masters. Men who cared about their people like their own family. Like their own children."

Rachel leans back on her heels and looks up at me. "I reckon there were a lot of slaves who really were their master's children, ma'am. Why do you think Mr. Cobb killed my daddy other than he was trying to make children with my mama?"

I turn away toward the wall in front of me. I will not hear it. I will not think about it. Rachel dips her hand back into the water and pulls it out. The water drips from the cloth, making a tinkling sound that is like music. She rubs my leg from the hip down to my ankle, dipping into the water and then rising again. The drips fall back into the tub with the same music.

"Miss Gus," she begins suddenly, "I know there were white folks who tried to be good to their people under slavery, but there ain't a way you can be good to someone when you're taking things away from them. And that's what slavery was, people taking things that weren't theirs. Their work. Their bodies. Their love for themselves. And we're free now, all of us. God has given us our freedom. But He says it's up to us to do something with our freedom. 'Cause there are always going to be people who want to take things from you. Some of them are white folks, and some of them are colored folks, even. It's the way God made the world. There are always going to be people trying to take your freedom away. John and me, we know that we've got to fight to keep free and to keep our boy free, and if we have other children, them, too, if God gives them to us."

Rachel has paused her hand while she speaks, but now she moves it against the back of my knee.

"Or maybe none of us are free. It's just a word they give us to keep us quiet. But I'll find it out," she says, then looks up at me. "Do you feel free, ma'am?"

Her hand rests on the back of my leg. I look down at her.

"I don't know, Rachel," I say. "Maybe I've never been free."

I feel my nakedness in front of her, and I sit in the tub, pulling my arms over my breasts. "That's all, Rachel. I can finish on my own." I take the cloth out of her hand and lay it across my knees.

"I guess this'll be the last time we see each other, ma'am." She stands near the tub with her hands folded in front of her.

My arms are pulled around my chest. "Yes, I guess it is," I answer. "I hope you find your freedom, Rachel."

She nods and looks at the door, then back at me. "I hope you find yours, too."

I wait for her to leave. She moves quietly and looks back at me as she closes the door to the back stairs. The two little blue bottles stand on my bedside table like a pair of eyes constantly watching me.

Nineteen

MY FEET ARE RESTLESS. I walk the floor in my nightdress. The walls are warm to the touch. Even before my hand is close, I can feel the heat coming off the brick and plaster.

The laudanum whispers to me. Two small blue bottles side by side on the little table. In the dark they cast no shadow. They are twin black sentinels at my bedside. They have fooled me before. I cannot let them fool me again.

I walk room by room, feeling my way. Henry sleeps with a small snore, shifting under the thin sheet. The heat is going to kill us all. Or drive us to madness.

The narrow stairs of the back hall are bare, and the wood feels smooth and warm as it creaks under my feet. The back parlor is so dark, I can barely make out the furniture. The front parlor. The hall. The music room. The dining room. They are all shadowy, shapeless spaces that I navigate by memory, touching the objects that are familiar to me. The carved wood sofa with its heavy brocaded upholstery. A horsehair settee. Figurines in glassy porcelain of a shepherd and shepherdess. The delicate wood reeding on the mantelpiece that bumps my fingers as I run them over it. I feel my way like a blind person, touching the cool glass of the Argand lamps in the dining room and the sheer summer drapes that line the tall windows.

In Eli's office, I sit again in his chair. Simon offered it to me as a matter of course, as the most natural thing in the world. There is no sense to be made of his stories. Eli working for Judge all those years. Eli protecting Judge's secrets? That must have been the only thing that ended up protecting Eli from Judge and from the Knights of the White Cross. But it could not protect Simon—or at least it protected him to a different degree. So many Negro men have been killed for less. Like Rachel's brother-in-law.

Rachel must not be sleeping now, either. How could she, with their departure set for tomorrow? She deserves more than what I did for her tonight. I swear she saved my life when Henry was born. She surely deserves better. Eli would have done better by her. I am ashamed of myself. Ashamed of listening to Bama about Henry and Little John. Ashamed of being so lost to myself that I did not see these other things, of accepting it all as the way things are. As the way they should be. That is what Judge would have me do—accept his ordering of the world as he dictates it.

Eli sat in this chair across from men and women, more black than white, but certainly his share of white men seeking help or favors. Did he do it without a thought? Did he think that he was doing right? What was it all for? Judge would say Eli did it for power and gain. Eli did make money. He did get power. Was there more in it than that? Even if he didn't intend it? But he was a slave trader. He hunted people down. And Simon helped him. He hunted Simon down and kept him. Who was Eli really? Who are we, any of us?

All of these secret panels. What was this room to him? This house? My hand gropes in the drawer for the spring that reveals the false bottom, but I can't find it. The walls are smooth under the windows. There are wooden panels under the bookshelves on the inside wall. Eli's gun closet. Small panels that don't even appear to be doors, yet with slight pressure, they swing open to reveal a dozen guns mounted on pegs. Tiny derringers and larger guns from the war, Colts and

Remingtons. The handle of a pistol is made of mottled horn colored black and white. The barrel and cylinder are shiny even in the shadows. It feels heavy in my hand. The thin crescent moon casts pale light over the garden, making it appear as if it is under dark water.

Simon has a gun. Unlike most of the colored people. Their weapons were all taken from them. All those colored men who went away to the war. Who died in the fighting. And the rest who came home thinking they had won freedom. They're not really free, like Rachel said. They have to leave here to be free. Like me. Do I have to leave here? If only we could find that money.

The sliver of moon shines off the barrel with a dull glimmer. I raise the gun and aim as if I am going to fire it. Does Rachel have a gun? Or Big John? How could they? The roads can't be safe for a group of colored people emigrating west. She could use a gun. She doesn't seem like a person who would be afraid of firing it. I want to see her once more before she goes. She saved my life when Henry was born, I am sure of it. I should go to her. I cannot leave things as they are. Eli would have been better to her than I have been. I can at least try.

I almost wish I were going with them. Going away from Judge and Greer and Buck. If only I had that money. We could get away for a while—and if the mill weren't closed, I might never have to come back. But where else could the money be? We should go to the mill again. There must be a way to get into Eli's office alone.

In my room, the blue bottles look at me like a pair of eyes. Perhaps I should take the gun and shoot them out. I can't, that would be like shooting myself. No, I could shoot them, and my body would still be whole. If only I could sleep. Just a drop of it in a glass of water. Just one drop to help me sleep. That would not be too much. Just to ease me out of this anxiety.

I won't. Rachel would not succumb like this. I must be up early to see her. I owe her that. I almost died the day Henry was born. Five years ago. Less—he was born in August, the hottest month of the year. He was early, the doctor said. I was here in this room with the pink-ribboned wallpaper, confined away, and yet there seemed to be so many people around me.

I labored for hours in this bed. Rachel and Emma tied a rope between the posts of the headboard for me to grip when the pains came, and Rachel gave me a slat of smooth wood marked by teeth from other women who had used it. The spasms came hard and went on for hours. A blur of sweat and blood and agony. The bedclothes were soaked, and my nightdress, too, that was pushed up over my knees so that I lay shamelessly exposed before Mama and the servants and Dr. Greer. More than once, he asked Emma and Rachel to leave, but I shook my head in panic, wild with pain and exhaustion and, more than anything else, fear. I was sure that I was dying.

The room was hot. The windows were shut tight, and candles guttered in the steamy atmosphere, thick with the stench of sweat and excrement. Mama sat by the bed, worrying herself and me with a handkerchief always at her eyes or under her nose. I could smell the choking, putrid scent of the cologne water she had soaked it in. Lemon verbena, an odor that I cannot abide to this day. Mama looked disapprovingly at Rachel and Emma. She clucked her tongue and shook her head and called it silliness. I was afraid. I could not listen to her. I could not allow her to take charge. After I cursed at her to leave Emma alone, she and the doctor resigned themselves to Emma and Rachel's presence. Emma took cool rags and washed my face down, murmuring to me to keep breathing, that it would be over soon.

I heard Rachel arguing with Dr. Greer. She wanted to give me a cold tea she had made from roots, but he refused and dosed me with tiny grains of calomel that gave me convulsions between the contractions. I began vomiting.

"To hurry the child on," he said, his red whiskers wagging over my face. I felt hot and suffocated and sick. The light of the room was a blur. It seemed to move against the walls like a magic lantern. I felt dizzy and would have cried if there were tears left in me after the sweating and sickness.

The waves of pain came crashing over me. My muscles flexed. I had no strength to reach for the rope. Emma and Rachel each took a hand and told me to squeeze as hard and as tight as I could. Dr. Greer knelt at the end of the bed, looking between my legs, and I whimpered in shame and suffering. God, the horrible indignity, the shame and awfulness of it. That shame seems so ridiculous now. But the pain, as if each muscle were stretched taut to snapping. I cried out but could not hear myself or feel the sound come out of my throat. The pressure in my belly, the hard flexing pressure, like red-hot hammers beating down on me all at once. Dr. Greer said, "I see the head. He's coming." And I thought, My God, it's a boy. It's a baby boy. But Greer could not have known then, he could not have seen until minutes later or hours. I could not tell the passage of time, only the screaming pain and those hands over mine. That was all I could tell, just the grip of the black hands in mine as I pushed harder and harder. Not pushing really at all, squeezing, pulsing, and panting out my breath, the desperate desire to expel this thing from my body and to survive. To outlive this moment. To try to forget it like everything else. And then there was quiet. That live stabbing pain was dead, and instead I felt a raw throbbing in its place. I was alive. I looked down at the blood-soaked nightdress and sheets, and Dr. Greer held this small purple animal in his bare hands. He dangled him by one leg.

It was a boy, my God, it was a little boy, and the pale and purple cord ran from his belly back inside of me. Dr. Greer slapped his rump and the baby boy—Henry, named Henry like my father—he let out a wail like a rebel yell. A wild holler that filled the room. I could hear Eli's feet pacing outside, just outside, excited. I didn't want to see him. I wanted Henry. To hold him. To see if he was real, if he was truly alive, this screaming red and purple thing, slick and wet and alive. Dr. Greer cut the cord and Henry wailed. Rachel bundled him quickly in cotton blankets and brought him to me. I could have cried again but for my weariness and shock.

Mama leaned in and looked at him. "He's a screaming thing," she said. "He'll get bigger, I suppose. When Hill was born, he was a little giant. He nearly killed me, but what a cry he had." We both looked up because Rachel and the doctor were arguing again. It was a surprise to me to hear a servant girl argue with a doctor.

Emma sat at my other side and smiled at me and the baby. She held out a finger to him, played with his tiny hand. He grasped her finger, and she looked at me and said, "Don't worry, Miss Gus, Rachel knows what she's saying. Her mama birthed more babies than Dr. Greer."

Dr. Greer didn't hear, though. He was red-faced like the baby, and Rachel stood in front of him, her arms crossed and her face set hard and determined.

"You ain't cutting her with that thing," she said, and she pointed at a scarificator in his hand.

"You nigger fool," he said furiously. "Get out of the way. If she doesn't get bled immediately, she could die." The doctor held a small wooden box in his hand. It had a spring lever that activated a row of tiny razors. When the lever was tripped, the little blades popped up, cutting a row of incisions about an inch long, freeing the blood from an engorged area. Dr. Greer is a committed bleeder, and bleeding the fresh wounds of a new mother after childbirth is a common practice for him. He wanted to place the scarificator between my legs and cut me. He insisted that the birthing forced blood down there, and now it was concentrated and needed to be relieved. Rachel was adamant.

"You stupid girl, get out of here," Mama said, standing up. "This is none of your affair." But I shook my head and Emma held my hand.

"No, sir," Rachel said to Greer, nearly shouting. "Her flux should be packed onto her wounds to make it heal. How many women have you killed with your cutting machine?"

I shook my head again but could not speak. I knew only that I did not want to bleed anymore.

Greer's face was thunderous. He went to the hall and got Eli. They stood over me, and Eli beamed with pride. He had a son.

Mama stood up and said to him as he approached the bed, "Mr. Branson, my daughter has borne you a little king." She was smiling and so was Eli, but Greer frowned. He pointed his finger at Rachel and said ugly things. She stood solid and unmoved.

Rachel said, "Ask Miss Gus what she wants." Greer scoffed at the idea. I could barely think myself.

Eli looked at me and I shook my head at him, looking into his blue eyes rimmed with pale lashes. Milky eyes, washed out and blurred from that horrible night. I shook my head again and said, "Rachel." I couldn't say more, but he understood. He took Greer out into the hall, and they raised their voices at each other until Greer finally left.

Mama stayed with me while Rachel and Emma banded the flux between my legs. Then they left, touching Henry first, playing with his little hands. Rachel whispered over Henry a chant that was like some sort of blessing. And then I was alone with Mama and the baby.

"You two should sleep," she said after the servants had left the room. "You've been through enough." Mama picked up her knitting that she had in a sewing bag, and she began work on a cap and jacket for the baby in gray yarn. "You're a mother now, Augusta," she said, her needles clicking together. "So I feel obligated to tell you, mother to mother, that you should be careful of Emma." I looked at her weakly, not sure I understood what she was saying.

"Yes. You love Emma. She is a part of our family, but she's not our blood. Don't forget that. Ever since she lost her own children, she has been unnaturally fixated on mine."

I must have looked confused, unsure, because Mama put down her knitting.

"Yes, Augusta, it's true," she said. "It was just before you were born.

Emma had two babies. Two boys. Twins. I wasn't going to have some screaming babies in the house upsetting us both, so I had your father send her down to Point Place. They got whooping cough or something and died. Both of them. It was a bad winter for sickness. She came back, and God knows she had enough milk for you and her others, too, if they had lived. Anyway, it's all in the past. But you should be mindful of it."

I nodded and turned back to Henry, sleeping quietly, still coated in a slick red wash, so tiny and delicate. The breath came out through his tiny nose. His nostrils flared open with each tiny exhale. I wrapped the blanket tighter around him and pulled him close on my chest, hugging him to me, watching him sleep until I, too, lost consciousness.

Twenty

LIGHT HAS SLOWLY CREPT into my room, thin and gray, so that I can see enough to dress myself. Emma will be up soon and so will Henry. Emma will tend to him while I am gone. The gun and a gold chain are in my pocket. Now Simon must take me to Rachel. I have been so impatient for the sun to rise that I have barely slept these past few hours. I think of nothing but Rachel. I only hope we get there in time.

They will be gathering up in the North Ward, piling their belongings into wagons for the trip to Nashville, where they will join other Negroes who are leaving the South. They will travel by wagon to St. Louis and then across Missouri to Kansas. There have been many colored families who have passed through Albion on their way west. Sometimes riverboats will not accept them, or they will be barred passage at river crossings. There are men like Judge who are nervous about these emigrants. They see the men and women who plow and pick cotton leaving. Without them, who will labor on the land?

Rachel will make her way. She is strong and tough, like my Blackwood grandmother. She will make a better farmer's wife than she did a servant. I will make up for what I should have said last night.

The air outside is damp and warm. The sun is beginning to crest

above the trees. No rain after all. No respite, either. The heat has settled in with the same oppressive force. The traces of mist that hang
around the trees have been singed away by the sunlight.

I knock lightly at the outside door of the carriage house.

Emma's attic window is open. There is no movement inside.

"Simon," I whisper, loud enough so he will hear. "Simon." I knock
again, and his head emerges from the window, looking down at me.
He does not say a word, though his expression is clearly confused,
almost stern. He holds his hand out in a sign for me to wait. I hear
his feet on the stairs and the door opens. He is still pulling on his
suspenders.

"I have to see Rachel," I whisper. "You must take me to her."

"Miss Gus, the whole town's sleeping. What's so urgent?"

"She's leaving, Simon. I have to give her something before they go."

He grimaces and shakes his head but walks to the back of the carriage house and opens the wide doors. He is not happy, but he will
take me.

Simon harnessed the horse quickly. We head down the lane toward
Tulip Street, where it borders the cemetery. Eli's grave is beyond the
stone wall to the right, by a young oak. There is still no marker. Mr.
Weems asked me to order one, but I couldn't. Perhaps I will leave it
unmarked and no one will find it. Only I will know. Only Simon and
I will remember Eli. Simon is sitting beside me. He went to mount the
horse, but I told him to climb into the gig. What is the purpose? It is
absurd to worry about exposing myself now.

"Ma'am, look." Simon points the whip to the center of the graveyard, where there are a number of new graves. It is too far away to
make out. Simon whips the horse. He turns us up Tulip Street. The
carriage runs close along the cemetery's edge. In between the trees and
the few marble monuments, there are rows of graves, fifteen, maybe

twenty. Some of them are mounded high with fresh red earth and others gape, openmouthed, waiting for the dead. Bodies sewn into sheets lay nearby. Four of them. They do not even bother with coffins or ceremonies now. Is it Mr. Weems's hand that sewed those shrouds? Who will keep the memory of these dead alive?

Two colored men, their shirtsleeves rolled up, dig another new grave. The early-morning light is golden and slanted, shining off the sweat from the grave diggers' heads.

The Collins family plot has two new graves. The Sheffields have three. The Yankee officer McCoy bought a plot for his family, and there is a small new grave there.

"My Lord, Simon."

He touches the horse with the whip and she picks up to a trot. We head quickly through the quiet streets. The homes seem so still, shuttered under trees bursting with leaves. Their doors and windows are shut, and they remind me of those homes along the pike from Three Forks—vacant, abandoned, given up. We turn onto Jefferson Street and head toward the depot. The houses are smaller, modest shotgun shacks of two and three rooms that face the railroad tracks on our right. They are quiet, too, but some windows are open. Some doors. Smoke pours from a few chimneys as if they have a great blaze in their stoves. Others are quiet, with weathered clapboard coated in peeling paint. There is an X in whitewash on several of the front doors.

"What is that?"

"Order of the mayor. All sick houses get marked with an X."

"What good will that do?"

Simon shrugs. We shouldn't be here. I know it and he knows it. We should be long gone from Albion.

The depot looms ahead, a massive brick pile three stories high, painted yellow with green shutters. In tall letters along one gable end, the word ALBION is painted in black.

At the ticket window there is a large crowd. A group of men—

and some women—jostle each other on the sidewalk. The doors to the waiting rooms are closed, and there are two men in rough, dirty clothes struggling to pull them open. There is shouting. There is no order here. These people are not ticket buyers but a mob that is becoming agitated.

Simon turns the carriage to cross the tracks to the North Ward, but he pulls back on the reins hard. A loud whistle blast, high and shrill, comes from the west. The blasts are long, longer than I've heard them before. Down the tracks, a train is pulling in fast. Black and menacing, the engine charges down the rails with a thick plume of smoke trailing behind, widening fanlike into a great tail. The train has no intention of stopping. That is clear. The men and women race toward it. They stampede after the cars, charging up to the rail bed. Some are ahead of it and climb on the tracks, waving their hands and screaming for the train to stop. Only the whistle shrieks back, warning them to clear the tracks. By some miracle, the men jump clear, brushed by the cowcatcher to tumble down the gravel slope.

The cars roar by us, the windows closed and the blinds down. It is twelve cars long and going at breakneck speed. The men on the ground shake their fists, shouting profanities as the train barrels into the distance.

"My God, Simon. What's going on?"

"I don't know, but I don't think we should go to see Rachel. I think we'd better get back to the house."

"No, I must see Rachel. Do you have your pistol?" Simon smiles wryly at that. "Then we will be fine."

He whips the horse to hurry across the tracks, and from the rise we have a view of the shantytown that houses most of the colored people of Albion.

Some of the houses are little cabins, split log with mud and daub in the chinks to keep the wind out. Smoke from kitchen fires hangs in the air as if to half hide their squalor. They look little better than old slave cabins. Others are even more primitive, lean-to huts with a hole in the roof for a chimney. An old railroad car without wheels sits crossways to the street with a white X on its side. There are white X's everywhere. How many of those doors hide the abandoned dead?

Simon turns the carriage up a dusty street, sunbaked and lined with shacks and old army tents. These fields in '65 were filled with tents then, too, but of the U.S. Army. It was here that Eli would come to oversee the arrival of the trains loaded with cornmeal, hardtack, and green bacon. Judge would claim he kept the best to resell to soldiers or whoever could afford it. Has Judge refugeed away, too, without a word to me?

Down Moore Street stands a row of wagons harnessed to mules. Simon stops the buggy at the side of the street. I step down without waiting. The odor of smoldering refuse lingers in the still air. A knot of Negro men stand whispering by one of the wagons. They watch me as I walk toward them. Their conversation stops, and they turn curious eyes on me, a brazen white woman alone in their part of town. They step back from me nervously. One man stands with his mouth open, looking at me as if I am death coming for him.

"Where is the home of Rachel Simmons?" They look at one another and then back at me. One of them nods in the direction of a small wood-frame house and tips his cap to me.

A pile of bricks serves as a step up to the open door of what is hardly more than a shanty. In the half-light, I can make out a few pieces of rude furniture on a gap-planked floor, a small hearth, and a rope bed in one corner. Rachel is on her knees, working to untie the ropes, with Little John standing beside her watching. The walls are lined with bundles of dried herbs and jars of powder like an apothecary.

"Rachel, I'm so glad you're still here."

"Miss Gus, ma'am," she says as she stands up, brushing the dirt off her apron. "What are you doing here?" Little John looks at me, blinking and smiling.

"I'm sorry to bother you like this. I just—I wanted to give you something before you go. It's not much. But maybe you can trade it for something." I take the gold chain from my pocket and hold it out to her. She looks at it.

"Ma'am?" she says.

"Please, Rachel. Take it."

She holds out her hand, and the chain pools into her pale yellow palm. The gold shines brightly in the dusky room. "You don't need to give me this—"

"Yes, I do. I should have paid you something. Eli never would have let you leave empty-handed. And I want you to have this as well." I pull the gun from my other pocket. The shiny Remington with inlaid horn of black and white on the grip.

Rachel takes it by the barrel and turns it to grasp it by the butt with her other hand. She looks at it. She smiles. Her eyes are gold-colored, with flecks of pale green and brown. They shimmer like the chain in her hand.

"I wish you the best of luck, Rachel. I know you'll make your way out there."

"Thank you, ma'am," she says. "Thank you." She steps forward in a rush and takes hold of me, hugging me so tight that I can feel her strength.

"Miss Gus, you have got to leave town, too. Right away," she whispers into my ear, then leans back and looks me in the eye.

"I know."

Rachel shakes her head. She puts the chain and gun in a small bundle tied with a bandanna. "Just take you and your boy and go. Emma, too. The sickness here is bad. You can't see it, but it's here. You shouldn't even be in this part of town."

"Eli died from it. I was with him. We were all with him. Maybe we can't get it?"

"None of us touched it, ma'am. His blood. You didn't, either. But don't be fooled. It's a slow creeper, this sickness. And it respects no-body. It ain't going to stop until its work is done. This is God's work, ma'am."

"God's work? How can you say such a thing?"

Rachel's face loses all expression, but her eyes scintillate. "God's work. That's what I said. Just like in Pharaoh's time, God sent ten plagues to punish Pharaoh for holding people in bondage. It's our time now. God's people know enough to run ahead of the plague. You should, too. The first plague was blood, ma'am. You know enough of your Bible to remember that. This is a sin that's being paid."

"Rachel, that's all in the past."

"Ain't nothing in the past, Miss Gus. You look at Emma. You look at her hard and close, and you tell me slavery ain't still a sin that has to be paid. You look at her."

My tongue feels thick and dry in my mouth. The rivers and seas turned to blood. That's what happened in the Bible.

"Don't wait for nothing, ma'am. Just go."

"Thank you, Rachel. I will." Outside, I turn back to look at her once more. "Thank you, Rachel," I say again.

She follows me into the light with the bundle under one arm, holding Little John's hand. The men are staring at us. One of them calls across the street to Rachel. "You done already? Where's your man at? We've got to get going." They shift on their feet anxiously, looking around at the quiet shanties. They are eager to be gone.

She walks toward them. "He'll be along directly. Don't worry. He had one last thing to do," she says.

Simon waves at Rachel, and she waves back as she stuffs the bundle into a half-empty wagon. He helps me into the carriage and leads the horse around. He keeps the horse moving slowly, then mounts the step with one foot as the other leg swings away. He climbs in beside me, takes the whip and touches the horse's back, but pulls on the reins suddenly. Rachel is calling out to us.

"Miss Gus, wait!" She rushes up to the side of the carriage, waving a fist that has tiny strands of gold leaking from it. "I can't take this, ma'am. I want you to take it back." She is beside the carriage and takes my hand, forcing the chain into my gloved palm.

"Rachel, I insist."

"No, ma'am. You need it as much as I do. I'm keeping the gun, though." She smiles, though it fades quickly. "And ma'am. I'm sorry to say this. You can't imagine how it hurts me, but John, my husband John, he's been working for Mr. Heppert, too. I don't know what he's been doing for him, he won't tell me, but I don't think that you should trust him, ma'am. Mr. Heppert, that is. I don't think you should trust him at all."

My eyes meet Simon's. We both look at Rachel.

"That's all I know," she says. "Honest, Simon. That's all I know."

"Thank you, Rachel," I say as a chill comes over me. "Goodbye. And Godspeed."

"Thank you, Rachel," Simon says. "I'll see you in Nashville." He clucks to the horse. Rachel steps back from the carriage, and we ride away.

Simon urges the horse into a fast trot. His jaw is set and his lips are a grim line. We cross back over the tracks. The people have gone, mostly. Just a few are gathered outside the depot, but now the doors are wide open, and many of the windows are smashed in. Papers litter the street, tickets and blank forms trailing where the rioters must have tossed them as they ransacked the depot.

Simon's face is tired. His jaw seems to sag and his eyes are haggard.

"John has been working for Judge. That is how Judge knew everything. He betrayed us," I say.

"I don't know. It may not have been a choice for him," Simon responds. He doesn't look at me.

"What else could he have been doing for Judge?"

Simon almost snorts. He gives his head a faint shake.

"You don't think he was watching me?" I ask.

"Oh, he was watching you, and probably more than you."

"Watching all of us? He was watching Eli."

Simon's hands clench and unclench on the reins. "Yes, ma'am. I suspect."

"He's looking for the money. He thinks I know where the money is."

"I suspect. Yes."

"Then they can't have found the money if they're still looking for it."

"I think they've found it. So John is free to leave. He probably made some good money, too, to help them get on to Kansas."

The streets are so quiet. Simon and I are the only ones foolish enough to be out. My skin tingles along my arms down to my fingertips. This dread I feel.

"How can you be sure they've found it?"

"Because we haven't found it. It's not in the house, and I don't know where it could be. Judge must have it by now."

We turn down Tulip Street. The cemetery is before us again. So many graves. The grave diggers are gone now. They've thrown the dead into a shallow hole and barely covered it before running away, too. Simon looks at the cemetery and at the row of houses on our right, their shoulders turned to us as if they don't want to look at the cemetery, either. There is no one around. We must leave, like Rachel says. We should gather what we can and go. There is no hope. Not if Judge already has the money.

Simon sighs and shakes the reins. "The only place we haven't searched is the mill," he says. "Maybe Eli hid the money there. Maybe it's still there."

"Then we should go to the mill."

"I'll go tonight after it gets dark. With the mill shut down, it should be easy. That's the only thing I can figure."

"I'm going with you, Simon," I say, and I reach for his arm. "I want to go."

He looks at me and shakes his head but doesn't answer me. The money must be at the mill. If it's not in the house and not at the mill, then Judge must have it. We will know tonight and then we will leave.

"How could John do such a thing?" I ask. "And for Judge? Rachel hates Judge."

Simon snorts again and looks at me out of the corner of his eye. We are behind the carriage house, and he pulls back on the horse and puts on the brake. He turns to me, the reins clenched in a tight fist.

"Miss Gus, who do you think John's loyalties are to? To you? To any white folks? No, ma'am. He's got a boy and a wife, and he's going to do whatever he needs to do to protect them. Even if that means doing Judge's dirty work. He's going to do what he needs to do."

"Yes, of course. John must look out for his family. I'm sorry."

"No, I'm sorry. I suspected it. I thought something strange was going on—even that day Judge came and told you about Eli's will. I should have known then."

He lets go of the reins, and they slip over the dashboard and trail in the dirt behind the horse.

"I should have known then. I didn't think it was possible, either. I should have known in this world we're in, anything is possible. We all act from fear and hate, Judge included. This place has been whipped and kicked to pieces, with all the people in it."

He steps down from the carriage and heads into the barn, leaving me in my seat. He is frustrated and scared. We have waited too long to leave.

We will go to the mill tonight. I will go with Simon whether he likes it or not. We will find the money, and then we will leave. We must leave either way.

Twenty-one

CARPETBAGS ARE PACKED, AND Emma is making corncakes and boiling the last of the eggs. I know we will find the money. Simon agrees it will be better to travel in darkness as long as we can. We will go to my cousin Mary Lee in Winchester and from there we will see. Simon will go to Nashville. If we have the money, we will see where I go.

Dresses are everywhere. I can only take a few. Henry's things do not take up much room. We will be back someday. I will miss this room. This house. There does not seem to be much order in the streets. The police have fled with no one to take their place. The house may be empty when we come back. The stories we heard about Athens during the war. We were all terrified. Women were violated and their homes set on fire right over their heads, everything stolen. But we will get out. Simon and I will get us out.

The door opens suddenly. Emma comes in with wide eyes. My God, she made me nearly jump out of my skin.

"It's Mr. Judge and Mr. Buck, ma'am. They seem awfully excited."

They have come.

Emma leaves without closing the door. My reflection in the washstand mirror is disheveled. My face is beaded with sweat and my hands are dirty. The water from the ewer is warm. What could they want here? Are they here for the money?

The case of bonds is on the floor near the door. I grab a fistful and fold them, putting them in my pocket. They are so large that the edges and half-cut coupons spill out of the pocket and rustle against my dress. Walking down the stairs makes them even louder.

Father and son. They are standing side by side near the front door, watching me. The light floods in behind them. Judge is huffing, looking into the parlor to see who else is around. He doubtless has something to say, but I am not in a mood to listen to his twisted truth. The bonds feel coarse and cheap between my fingers. They bulge from my pocket. My dowry, these were. My price.

"Leave it to Augusta to check her dress when the world collapses," Judge snarls. He steps forward, and I look at him evenly without any welcome. Buck remains back, as if he is a spectator. "What's the meaning of all this? Why are you still here?"

"The trains aren't running, Judge. We are preparing to leave with the carriage to meet Bama."

"I know the trains aren't running! You could have left before now! Bama Buchanan is already in Huntsville. The army is moving in. The governor has declared a military quarantine. You won't be able to go anywhere in your carriage. My God, Gus, what a simpleton you can be." His face is red and his voice is high. He holds his cane in his hand and shakes it at me as he speaks. Buck has not moved. He watches with dark, nervous eyes.

"Did your informer tell you that?" I look steadily into Judge's ice-blue eyes. He blanches and takes a step back. I am not afraid of him. I know who he is.

"What do you mean? Jeff Sprague told me before he took his family to Stevenson. You should be in Huntsville with Bama. Don't you know there are people dying in this town? Jesus Christ, we're all three of us lucky we're not dead." His face starts to color again.

"But we're not. We're here. And if what you say is true, we can't go anywhere."

The stiff paper rustles in my pocket, and Judge's eyes follow the sound and then move swiftly back to my face. He knows about the money. His glance says that he is looking for it. And the list. The list of men Eli was bribing. That would be more important to Judge than the money. Simon said they had the money, but maybe they don't have it. Judge's accusations and the high pitch of his voice. He is looking for that list. Perhaps he thinks the paper in my pocket is the money. He must wonder what it is.

"There are still ways out," he says. He wants me to leave Albion. "I can cable the governor. I will see what we can do." His voice is hard. He looks back at Buck, who nods agreement. His eyes dart to the papers in my pocket.

"How can they put the whole town under quarantine?" I ask. "After Dr. Greer said we were all safe. Was that another lie?"

"Greer is dead, Augusta," Judge says. "So anything he might have said can at this point be ignored."

My God, Greer is dead. Dead like Jennie's husband.

"Yes." Judge's voice is like a brass bell. "In the early-morning hours, he died. His wife died a few hours before him. Now do you take me seriously?"

"And for what?" I say to myself.

"What? What do you mean for what?"

"All those lies just to keep the mill open. We should all have been gone from here long ago."

"May I remind you that you were particularly interested in the continued operation of the mill. If he did it for anyone, he did it for you. The blood is on your hands." He is venomous, like a white snake.

"No, that's not true," I say. "You wanted this. You made this happen."

"It is on your hands," he hisses again. His eyes move back to my pocket. "What is that?" He points with his cane. "Where did you get that money? What did you do with the money I gave you?"

The bonds. They crackle as I pull them slowly out of my pocket. "These?" I ask. "These are old bonds. Don't you recognize them?"

"Confederate bonds?" He steps forward, his hand out.

"Yes, I found a case of them. In Pa's old trunk. There are thousands of dollars. All in that trunk in the attic."

Judge's eyes narrow, and his cheeks go red. "In this house?" he asks. He is lying. His voice has a forced edge. He insists on playing this pantomime.

"Yes, upstairs. They were Mama's bonds, but I didn't bring them into the house. Mama gave them to *you*, didn't she? To sell to Eli. Did you sell them to him?"

Judge takes another step forward and tears the bonds from my hands. He shuffles through them, his eyes roving over the faded text printed on cheap paper with cheap ink. He looks at the denominations and the dates. He shakes his head. "Filth. Wasted filth." He throws them on the floor at my feet, and they scatter like leaves across the carpet.

"You didn't always think they were filth, did you?"

His eyes are blazing blue fire. His face turns dark red.

"I think Eli must have compensated you quite well for them. More than they were worth. I always wondered how you held on to your land while we lost ours. What else did you give him, Judge, to save your fortune? What else did you bribe him with to save yourself?"

I hear a snap, like someone breaking a piece of wood. Or was it the sound of Judge's cane as he passed it from his right hand to his left? His eyes are raging, and he snorts from his nose in disgust. I look at him steadily as he takes a step toward me. I cannot think what he intends. He couldn't mean to strike me. But his right hand goes up in the air, and I watch it as if everything has slowed and the hand must be moving swiftly. I can count the seconds as it falls down upon me, against my face. He hits me so hard against my cheek that I am thrown off my feet and back against the stairs.

Everything is black except for the feel of that slap, that hand on me. My head bangs against the carpeted steps, and it is dark. Just a brief second of darkness, and then my senses come back and there is an ache on my head and my face is throbbing. The outline of his hand stings on my cheek. He is over me, threatening me with his cane. Spittle flies from his mouth.

"Enough of this, girl. Enough of this attitude from you. You'd better learn your place. Now tell me where your servants are." He is glowering at me, and I am afraid he will hit me again. I shake my head and he growls. He reaches out with his right hand and takes my face with it, holding me tightly under the chin and forcing me to look at him. His eyes are ice blue and so full of hate that I cannot speak. He is so close that his poisonous breath fills my nostrils.

"Answer me, girl," he hisses, shaking my head with his hand. "Where are your servants?"

"Emma—" I begin, but he shakes me again.

"Not Emma or that nigger manservant. The others."

"They're—they're gone," I choke. "They're gone to Kansas." He lets me go, and I gasp in air, turning on my side, trying to turn away, to pull myself up the stairs away from him.

Judge looks back at Buck and he almost heaves. He seems to choke, but he doesn't cough, just shudders in a series of spasms. The breath comes out of him in hacking convulsions.

"Pa, are you all right?" Buck rushes forward to him, taking him by the arm.

"I'm fine," Judge says in a croak. "Take your hands off me." He swings his arm up, pushing Buck back, and he teeters to the door, holding his cane. "You best leave Albion, Augusta," he calls back as he stalks out the door. "It's not safe for you and your boy here."

Buck watches him go. He turns to me with his mouth open. He

shakes his head at me. "God damn it, Gus. What in the hell is wrong with you?" He takes long steps toward me. His fists are tight against his thighs.

I hold the spindles of the stair rail, pulling myself up on the bottom step. The crumpled bonds litter the floor in front of me. My jaw throbs with each beat of my heart. Buck squats in front of me.

"What's gotten into you?" His brows knit together as if he is my father, admonishing me for my behavior.

All I can do is draw in my breath. My hand grazes my cheek to feel the pressure from Judge's fist.

"Pa wants to help you, but everything he does, you just throw it back in his face. You should have left town days ago." He reaches for my hand and takes it in his. He squeezes it, but I pull it away from him. He looks at me hard. "You'd better do what Pa says."

My whole body feels like stone. There is no pain, just the weight of this awareness. It bears down on me like something I've always been afraid of but could never see. He was always there, but he was never who I believed him to be. None of them is. I am not who I was ten years ago.

"Neither you nor Judge can make me leave this house against my will. I'll go when I want."

"Trust me, Gus," he says. "You should go."

He stands and walks out, leaving the front door wide open. A large whitewashed X is coarsely painted across it.

My knees are trembling. I pull myself up by the railing. My head is spinning.

Simon comes from the dining room.

"What a coward Buck is," I say.

"I'm sorry," Simon says. "I'm sorry I couldn't stop that."

I shake my head. "That was not the time. They would have killed you if you'd tried."

"Are you hurt?" He steps toward me, his eyes looking hard into mine. He is so worried.

"They haven't found the money, Simon. I know they haven't found it."

Twenty-two

THE HOUSE IS DARK and deadly quiet, like the town. The silence is interrupted by distant gunshots or breaking glass, as if we are under siege. Yet there are no shells, no people on the streets. The army is posted at all the roadways, keeping people in at bayonet point. We have locked ourselves in the house until full darkness, when we will go to the mill—as long as the back trails are not guarded as tightly as the main roads.

We are hidden away in the rear parlor. The lamps are out for fear of attracting attention. Simon believes the marauders avoid houses with a white X. He said the burials have stopped and there is a trench at the edge of town. He saw it on his nighttime search of the neighborhood. He said he is telling me everything, but I think there is much he is not telling me.

Emma's fire is roaring. She said it must be as hot as we can stand it to keep the fever off, so we sit around the blaze, sweating in the stuffy heat of the closed room. Henry is sleeping in fits. His head is on Emma's lap, his damp blond hair clinging to his forehead and temples.

The firelight flickers across the four of us. How are Rachel and John and their boy? Where are they now? Did they make it to Nashville? Or perhaps they're in Murfreesboro or Shelbyville, pushing their way north to Kansas and their freedom. Where should we be if we had left this morning?

The blue bottles are upstairs. I hold my knees and rock gently, watching the fire. I will not take any, not with Simon and Emma watching—not ever again. We sit together on the floor. Our breathing combines into a long sighing whisper punctuated by the crackling fire and the ticking of the wall clock. We are listening so closely for sounds from outside. Simon says the army will come in eventually, after the worst is past, but for now we are left as if we are in the middle of a desert.

"I think Emma is asleep," I whisper to Simon. Her heavy-lidded eyes are closed, and her breathing is slow and even.

Simon nods at me. The firelight flickers, throwing flashes of white and yellow off his dark skin. His eyes are unblinking. He looks at my cheek. "How is your face?"

I put my hand up to the tender bruise. I don't know if it has colored, but I guess that it has. "I'm fine. But I'm worried. That won't be the last from Judge."

"No," he says and looks back into the fire.

Whatever I have suffered from Judge's hand, Simon has borne worse. And if Judge comes back, it may well be worse for all of us.

"He is not an uninformed man," Simon goes on. "I think he knew Mr. Eli's habits. I think that's why he wants you to get out of the house, so that he can tear it apart for that money—and that list."

"But we know it's not here. So it must be at the mill." His irises are so dark, they seem black in the firelight, with just the faint reflection of the flames deep in their centers that give them some spark.

"Yes."

"Do you think John told Judge we were looking for something?"

"It's hard to say. If John was working for Eli and for Judge, I don't know that he would be a trustworthy source of information. I don't know anything for certain except that I am worried, too."

"But you worked for Judge and Eli both," I say. He is a wonder to me—this Simon whom I know and the Simon who used to be. Like the Eli who used to be.

"Yes, ma'am, I did. Back in the old days."

"Are they that far behind you?"

"They may not be far for everybody, but they are far for me. I left a lot of myself back there. A lot of myself that I don't need to go back and get."

Simon shifts on the floor and moves on all fours to the fire. He takes a fresh log, shifting the red coals with it to make a bed, and then lays it across. His face basks in the glow as he watches the flames burst out from under the new log, bright yellow flames with blue edges.

"What did you leave back there?"

"Too much to tell," he says as he crawls back to his place near the sofa.

"Why did you stop working for Judge?"

Simon gazes at the fire, at the new log now wrapped in fingers of golden flame. The room is thick with heat and the rank odor of sweat. "Did something happen between you? Is that why he won't speak to you?"

"Something happened. But it wasn't between me and your cousin. More so between me and Eli." Simon draws his knees up under his chin and wraps his arms around them, his eyes fixed on the flames. "I was a child back then. A young man but a child in my mind. And working with Mr. Eli—doing what we did to people—it seemed like nothing to me. I had been a slave, was a slave still, like almost all the colored folks I had ever known. Freedom didn't seem like something real. It was a sort of lie we told each other to keep going. Freedom up north. Freedom in Mexico or Canada. Freedom in heaven."

Simon rests his chin on his knees and closes his eyes for a moment.

He is squinting them shut hard, not as if he is trying to remember but as if he is trying to block something out. He opens his eyes and blinks at the fire, trying to adjust to the light.

"We'd walk those gangs of people down the old Indian trails through the mountain passes. Walking them steady through the mountains and woods toward Albion and Huntsville and down to Tuscaloosa and Demopolis and those Black Belt towns. Sometimes as far as Meridian, Mississippi, if Eli thought he could get a good price on them. It was what we did. We didn't make a lot of money at it. Mr. Eli didn't. But he made enough, and he always planned on buying his own place around here. He had some attachment to the town. That's what he always intended. For me, I didn't see much life outside of slavery. I had taken my chance once. And that taught me enough not to risk it twice. I don't think Eli would have hunted me down. He was never mean to me. That's what you think. In this world, you always risk finding something worse when you go for freedom."

Simon nods at the fire, agreeing with himself, as if he needs to show himself that what he is saying is true. I watch him, still and waiting.

"It was springtime, and we were about to Albion. A clear day, good weather. The sun was warm, even though a breeze ran through the woods and carried a chill on it. The trees were just putting out their leaves, soft and tiny and green. New green that's almost yellow. We were at the ford for Three Forks Creek, lower down from where the mill is now. Closer to the river, where there are some sandbars that let you cross in the shallows. The rains had been hard that spring, and the water coming down from the mountains was heavy and fast. The creek was deeper than we'd seen it before. And these people, seven of them—did I even see them as people? They were slaves, like me. Merchandise with nothing human about them.

"Eli pushed through the ford, and I could see his horse tripping through the water, having a hard time with the footing. Eli looked back at me and waved like he wanted me to bring them through. But they didn't want to. I could tell they were nervous. Scared like the horse was. There were two women, two children about eight or ten years old, and three men, one an older man with grizzled hair and beard and he was in front. He looked at me and shook his head, and I had to get the whip out. After I cracked it a few times, they were more willing to give it a try. They entered the ford, and the water rushed around the old man's ankles and then his knees, and the others were tied to him all in a line, inching out into the water. They were like a dam wall, lined up across the creek, which was plenty wide then, and the water was rushing against them up to their thighs and then their waists. Eli watched from the far bank and shouted, 'Come on, then,' and they moved. The two boys looked back at me. They were afraid and didn't know what to be more afraid of, the rushing creek full of water or me. But they kept moving, creeping on out into the middle of the creek."

Simon pauses and rests his forehead on his knees.

"I don't know who fell first. Maybe one of those children or one of the women. But once one was down, it was too much for the rest. They fought it at first, grabbing on to the ropes, trying to pull each other back. But they were swept into the current, knocked against the rocks. I jumped off my horse and tried to toss the whip end to the old man, but he couldn't grasp it. There was nothing to hang on to. Eli and I followed them down to the river. He was on one side and I was on the other. We shouted at them to grab hold of something, a branch or a log stuck on the bank. First one stopped struggling and then another. And soon they vanished under the water. We stood on the riverbank, the two of us separated by the mouth of the creek as it gushed into the muddy river. We watched as a head bobbed up or a limb. Dead-eyed faces. Dead. All of them drowned in that creek for nothing. For what? For money? Because they were nobody to nobody? Maybe to each other somehow, but not to anybody else. Not to me.

"I told Mr. Eli after that, I told him, 'You can do what you want with me. You can sell me south, beat me until I'm dead, do what you want, but I won't ever go selling misery again.' I wouldn't do it. It was like I had come awake all of a sudden. And Mr. Eli, he was moved by it. I could see that. I could see that he knew what we were doing was wrong. Though he pretended not to. But that was it. He went to Judge, who was hopping mad over the whole thing. Eli had to pay Judge out of his money for the loss on those people. The *loss* of them. Paid to Judge. And Judge was running for the statehouse at the time. He wanted the whole thing hushed up. Eli took the blame. He testified at the inquiry. And then Judge got him a job at the mercantile. And we never spoke of it again."

Simon's head is still on his knees. Perhaps he is crying. I turn my head from him and look at Emma and Henry. I should be crying, too.

"This terrible sin," I say. "We're all bound to each other in it. And we can't get out of it, no matter what we do."

The fire crackles and spits out sparks. Simon's head is on his knees, and he does not move. The clock strikes the time for us to go to the mill, for us and all the dead who follow us.

Simon holds the reins of both horses as I climb onto the mare. He leads us away from the house. The whole town is unearthly quiet, as if the looters, too, are hiding. The night is moonless and the streetlamps are not lit, but the sky is clear and the stars overhead are like a sparkling veil against an ink-black screen. Once we are on the trail, I will lead, since I know the way by heart. I have traveled those trails in my mind as often as I have ridden them.

Simon walks us past the cemetery, dark and still with its graves abandoned, half dug. He walks between the horses, his hand high on the reins on either side. We turn left at the Patterson farm, its door open and the windows smashed out, then down a cow path lined with trees, and finally, to the large oak where the trail splits.

"Take the path to the left," I whisper. We vanish into the black woods, and now we are safe. Simon hands me the reins and mounts his horse. He keeps an eye down the trail behind us, his gun in his hand.

I feel for my pistol. It is so small, it gets lost in the folds of my skirts. Leaves and sticks crunch under the horses' hooves while the branches reach out, scraping at my face, hidden by the deep shadows until they are against me. The path is almost invisible. I must trust the horse to lead us. She stops short, confronted by a wall of bramble. We have gone off the trail.

"I have to lead her, Simon," I say. I leap down and push the horse back gently, my gloved hand on her nose. "That's right, girl," I whisper to her. She is skittish in the dark, too.

We move slowly, but I can see the trail, feel it with each step. The pine needles are cut by two narrow ruts, sand-colored by day but, in this darkness, only shades of black and blue. The branches catch at me and I brush them away. My skirt hem is caked with dirt and dead leaves. The white of the petticoat, pale blue in the dark, is like a shock next to the somber shadows.

"Here," I whisper to myself. "Right here." There is a narrower trail that has crossed our path in the close woods. Tall hickory trees tower over us, and their canopy blocks the stars. Thorned vines scratch at the horse's legs, making her jump. I tighten my grip on the reins, close to the bit, as Simon did. Her hot breath wets my glove. The night is humid, and the sticky wetness clings at my armpits and under my breasts.

I check behind, making sure Simon is there. I hear a rushing, a sign that we are in the right place, Three Forks Creek, but far downstream from the mill. There is a small bridge, mossy and decayed, that we must cross. When Buck and I rode here during the summer after the war, there was no bridge at all. We crossed the creek here, though, in the shallows at its narrowest, where the ridges fall down to a sandy bed.

What must Simon be thinking? Was this the crossing he and Eli used? His face is obscured by darkness, but I wonder if his mind is back there with those people.

I push the mare's head up so she does not look down into the creek. She snorts, and her hot breath washes over my face. The planks of the bridge feel soft and mossy under my boots. They creak as I lead her forward a step at a time. The trusses are half broken, rough-cut from raw timber. I hold my breath and Simon watches nervously.

I take another step, walking backward with my eyes focused on the mare. She shivers and her foot slips. She whinnies and I can hear it echo through the trees. An owl calls a mournful warning.

My foot feels for the earth. The horse's front hooves move forward. The boards groan louder. I step more lively, tripping back, pulling the horse with me. We move off the bridge and I nod at Simon, though in the darkness he cannot see me.

He does not waste time in worry but clears the groaning bridge in a few steps, his horse close behind. The lane to the mill is just ahead. We remount and turn in to it, riding slowly. The rushing grows louder. We are closer. I can almost feel the money between my fingers.

The trees part, and we are in the clearing, with the open sky overhead and the blazing stars. Simon dismounts. I am on the ground beside him, and he takes my reins and ties the horses together.

The mill is gaunt and massive in the darkness. The woods seem to swallow it up as it extends into the trees. Down the dirt path I can see the small workers' cottages, forlorn and empty, each of the doors marked with a roughly painted X. The high windows of the mill are all shut, and the doors and the few windows close to the ground are boarded. The mill pond shimmers faintly with starlight, and far off across the fields in the deep woods behind them is the flicker of yellow light, like fairies in a grove.

"Campfires," Simon says. "The army is close. We must be careful." He nods to the mill door, frowning. It was boarded over, but the boards have been pried loose and lay scattered. Some of them are split in two. The door itself is stove in and its window broken. The shards of glass on the ground sparkle like the mill pond.

"They've been here already. They've beaten us to it," I say.

"Judge," Simon says.

"Yes, of course." I untie the small lantern from the horse's pommel.

Simon follows me, and we walk through the door into the darkness. He lights a match and places it in the lantern, lighting the wick, which burns with a weak light, fading, then growing, casting long shadows around us. The light fades into darkness above us. The great silent machinery sits abandoned, tangled in webs of cotton threads. Is there a mark on the floor where that woman collapsed?

I lift up the lantern and move to the glassed-in office. The door is ajar, and glass litters the floor. The lamp casts a ring of light, revealing hints of what is here, then darkness hides them. Torn papers coat the floor and hang off the edges of the desks. Ledgers have been ripped off the shelves and torn in two. There was a rampage, like a wild animal let loose to destroy for the pleasure of destruction.

In Eli's office, the same chaos is pulled from the shadows, chairs overturned, his desk on its side, papers—contracts, ledgers, manuals—shredded and torn, scattered across every surface. Behind the desk, a small well of blackness gapes in the floor. Two floorboards lie next to it that must have once covered it—Eli and his secret compartments. The lantern light is reflected golden from deep inside the hole, throwing watery amber shadows around us. Simon peers down into it. He smiles and looks at me. It is Eli's secret stash of whiskey. Three rows of bottles sit under the floor where his chair was. There is no money here and no missing saddlebag.

We search the office, but halfheartedly. They have beaten us to it. Did John tell them to come here? They were at the house today, hoping I had gone, so they could search there. They must have come here tonight.

Anger pulses through my veins, seeping out of my pores with my sweat. Judge has won and by a few hours, no more. The old goat has the money and the list of names and the havoc he will wreak with them—when they should have been mine. By rights, I own them, and he has stolen them from me like he has stolen everything else—all of it—from me.

Is this defeat? Is this what Hill and Buck felt at Shiloh? Or later at Atlanta or Nashville? To be beaten and pushed back again and again, only to rally, haggard and wasted, for one more hopeless charge?

"Ma'am," Simon says, his hand on my arm.

"They won, Simon. They must have just been here."

"I don't know. This seems like it didn't just happen."

"How can you tell?" The room is so devastated.

Simon kneels down and wipes a finger across the bottles in the floor, showing a fine layer of cotton dust. "I think this hatch was pried open a day or two ago." He looks at me, but I cannot read his face. "You should go back to the house."

"What?" I ask. "If they were already here—if they didn't find the money here . . ." My feet are unsteady on the litter of torn pages.

"I don't think they have the money. John must have it. He must have taken it. I have to go to them."

"How is that possible?"

"I should have known all along. I should have thought of it." Simon's fists are clenched tight, and his jaw flexes. "John has the saddlebag. He must. I don't know why they stayed here. Maybe to avoid raising suspicion. I don't know. But they are in danger now."

"I told Judge they were headed to Kansas. He can't have gone after them."

Simon doesn't answer. He walks out of the office. "Put out that lantern," he says.

I snuff it out quickly with my fingers. He rushes across the mill floor and outside.

"I'm going with you," I say.

"No, ma'am," he says, climbing on his horse. "Get back to the house. Who knows what might be happening there. I'm going to try to catch up with them. They can't be that far up the road to Tullahoma."

"No, Simon, I'm going with you." I pull myself up onto my saddle.

"It's too dangerous. You should get home and wait there for me."

"It's too dangerous for me to go with you but not too dangerous for me to ride through the woods back to town alone?"

There is doubt in his eyes but little time to argue.

"All right, then. Stay behind me and keep quiet."

I mount the horse and kick into her sides, slapping the reins against her neck. We follow a trail that skirts a branch of the mill creek, a worn wagon trail to Hayfork. Simon crosses over the creek at a small bridge, looping back west into the woods—Judge's woods. His land starts out here somewhere. Simon keeps the campfires on our left, far in the distance. To ride hard through here might attract attention, so we trot, easing our way under the trees and through the open spaces bordered by corn and cotton fields.

I no longer know where we are. We are farther out than I have gone, beyond the old trails of years ago into an unknown land, but Simon leads us with certainty. How old are these trails? Are these the trails he took, leading slaves? Or did he ride them between the farming villages on his canvass for Negro votes—when the Negroes still voted?

I see the Tullahoma Pike. We are riding parallel to it, hidden in the pines. Simon picks up to a canter and I follow him, hurrying the horse to keep pace. The horses pound against the dry earth, kicking up dust. I pull Helen to the side to avoid it. The stars have shifted above the black heads of the trees. It is late, sometime in the morning. Does he know where we are going or what we are looking for?

The army camp is miles behind us. We cannot be far from the Tennessee line, but Simon keeps moving, weaving east, then west, sometimes approaching the pike and then veering sharply back into the woods, crossing other trails that vanish in unlikely directions, up into the black depths of the forested hills, around a narrow bend, or down toward a shallow cut by a creek. The forest is quiet but for the horses' drumbeat, a steady rhythm moving ever faster. Simon leans forward, all alertness, looking ahead and left and right all at once.

He stops, and I pull hard on the reins, nearly tumbling over the horse's mane.

"What is it?" I whisper.

He shakes his head, looking into the depths of the woods where nothing is visible. He inhales deep through his nose, looking left, then right. He inhales again. I smell it, too. The faint, acrid odor of smoke from a fire that could be anything, a kitchen fire or a campfire. He looks at me and jerks his head forward. I follow him with the reins and bit rattling. The horses snort, nervous and unsteady in the darkness.

Simon rides through a bramble, and I urge Helen forward into it. We emerge onto the wide and rutted pike, staying close to the road's edge in the shadow of the trees' canopy. We see the glimmer of fire-light ahead, several fires. Simon kicks his horse, leaping into a gallop, running far ahead of me.

He is already off his horse and in the middle of a roadside clearing. It was a campsite before and is a battlefield now. Through the smoky haze are the wagons, lined up in a phalanx and tethered to their mules, as they were this morning, though the mules are dead. The five of them lie one before each wagon, still harnessed but dead, as if someone walked to each one of them and shot them through the head. Their fat tongues protrude from their open mouths. Their skulls are shattered and blood-covered to blackness where their brains were blown out. Two campfires smolder with dying embers and savaged tents are burning, cut to pieces. The cargo of the wagons is thrown aside, littering the ground, clothing, bedding, kitchen utensils, pots and pans, furniture, chairs and tables, hoes and farm tools cluttering the field, some of them smashed to pieces.

And several bodies, Negroes, black heaps lying facedown, dead like the mules, as if they were nothing more than that. In the smoke and darkness, it is like a mirage, too horrible to be real. What happened here? Simon was right. They were in danger, and it is all over now. Could they have known the danger?

"Who is that? What's she doing here?" a Negro man is shouting at Simon. He came from the edge of the woods. I slide off the horse and hold her by the reins as I walk toward them. Simon is trying to calm him.

"She did this," the man shouts and points at me, his eyes wild and filled with hate. He lunges as if he is going to attack me, but Simon grabs him by the shoulders and talks to him in a low voice.

"She loves Rachel," I hear Simon say. The horse bumps against me and shies away, whinnying and shaking her head.

The Negro man glowers as Simon holds him. The hate in his face is raw, a hate that blocks everything else out, as much hate as Judge. And he is crying, in a mad rage, like a wild dog.

What is Simon saying? Where is Rachel? The bodies are scattered across the field, their arms cast wide, motionless. There is a woman in a plain dark dress, crumpled behind a wagon, her turban loosened and her shiny black hair undone and falling from the bright cloth. I must see her.

"You keep your hands off of her, you white bitch. You keep away from her."

The gun is in her hand, a pistol with a black and white horn handle. Her hand has clawed into the earth, and I take it, bending the fingers out straight to hold it between my hands. It is so cold.

Oh, Rachel. I am sorry for this. They should not have done this to you. You should be on your way to Kansas. You should have your farm and your children and live long. But not this. I am sorry they did this to you, Rachel. What can I do to right this? These wrongs that we have done to each other will never be right. If only you could speak to me again and tell me what I can do to change it all for you and your poor boy.

Simon is beside me. He rests a hand on my shoulder and takes my arm, pulling me up. The other man stands back from us with clenched fists. He looks as if he will leap forward at me. What did Simon do to stay him?

"Gus, are you okay?" Simon asks.

"He's right, Simon. This would not have happened but for me."

"That's not true." He takes me by the shoulder and looks into my face. "None of this is your doing. You helped Rachel. You can't stop Judge."

"Is John dead, too?"

"Yes, John and Rachel and two others."

"What about Little John?"

"Little John is safe. Back in the woods with the other women and children."

"That poor boy. Can I see him?"

"Don't you tell her anything, Simon." The man is shouting, stepping toward us. "Don't you tell any white person anything about us."

"Garson, it's not her fault," Simon says. "She isn't like the others. She gave Rachel that gun to protect herself."

That is John's brother, Garson. I can see him now, his pale eyes, like John and their boy. He has a right to his anger.

"She used it, too. Two of those Knights are dead. One rode off into the woods, but Rachel shot him right in the heart. Those crosses make a fine target. If I had my choice, all of you would be dead. Every single one of you run off the earth like dogs. Rachel was right. God is punishing you all with this sickness, and I hope it kills every one of you." Garson spits at my feet.

"Garson, stop," Simon says. "John stole that money from the old man. That's why they came after you. It isn't her fault. She had nothing to do with it."

I told Buck and Judge. If I hadn't told them, would this have happened?

"Garson, let me help you," Simon says. Garson scowls at him. "We can hitch up a wagon and get people back to Albion."

"You can go to hell," Garson shouts at him, "and take your white woman with you. You'll be next, Simon. Those Knights will come after you, running around with a white woman."

Garson stalks away and then turns, coming back to us. I draw my arms close around myself.

"We aren't going back to Albion," he says to Simon in a hoarse voice. "We're going to bury our dead—we're going to do it by ourselves. We've got two of their horses, and we'll hitch our wagons to them and take what we can and get out of here. We're never going back to Albion." Garson points at a Negro man standing at the edge of the woods, holding two saddled horses. One a gray and the other a bay and white skewbald that looks just like Mike's horse.

"Garson, you should come back to Albion with me. Listen," Simon says. He pauses to look over at me. "Gus?"

The horse is not tall, fourteen hands, maybe, and Mike is not tall. I do not need to see the saddle or the initials embossed on the leather. MBS. It is Mike's horse. He was a part of this.

"Where is the man—the man they killed?" I ask. Simon does not answer. Garson looks by the last wagon and then stalks back toward the trees. Simon follows, taking his arm. They stand at the edge of the clearing, whispering fiercely to each other.

My feet carry me without my thinking. The contents of the wagon have been torn apart, strewn across the raw boards and on the ground around the wheels. There is a body in a blood-colored cassock, the face covered with a dark mask. I take his shoulder; it is too thick, but I must be sure. His body is heavy, the immovable weight of the dead. His mask is half off, and I pull it back to see his bloodied face with a yellow beard and glassy dead eyes. Not Mike. But where is he?

Simon is beside me again. "The horse that came from the woods," I say. "The pinto. Did Garson say which way it came from?"

Garson emerges from the forest with several other Negro men.

"We should go. You can't stay here," Simon says in an urgent whisper. The men are watching us. They carry shovels and some of them axes.

"Mike is in the woods, Simon. That is his horse. I know he did this terrible thing. I know it. But we must find him. I can't leave his body in the woods for animals." I will not let him be like those two men on the road from Huntsville when I was a girl. Those two men, black and bloated, abandoned in the woods to rot.

The men stand in a row, leaning on their shovels, glaring at us. They do not want me here. Simon tugs on my arm, and I follow him into the shadows of the trees.

He scans along the edge of the woods. I don't know what he can see in this darkness. He takes his horse's reins and plunges into the brush. I take mine, too, and creep behind Simon as he follows some invisible trail.

I listen for Simon as much as see him while he pushes his way deeper, nothing more than a shadow ahead of me, pulling his horse along with the instincts of a slave catcher. My horse pulls back on the reins and I jerk at her, dragging her with me, demanding her obedience.

"There," Simon says, and in the darkness under a tall pine is a black mass. I rush up to it and grasp the coarse cloth, pulling the body over to reveal a white cross that glows in the darkness. It is Mike. His face is still warm, and I feel the faint brush of breath against my hand.

"Simon, he's not dead." Simon stands over me, just behind me, his face emotionless, like Cicero when he watched Pa dying. Or is it disgust? "I know, Simon. He should be dead. But I won't leave him here. I can't."

I tear at the cassock, which is warm and wet, tacky with blood. His shirt is soaked through from the wound by his shoulder just above the chest. I pull up my skirt and tear at my petticoat, ripping off strips of cloth to bind it.

"Simon, I can't leave him here. I am asking for your help. I will not ask any more from you."

"I understand," he says. "He's your blood. I understand. I will give him mercy for you. But this is all. There is no mercy left in me after this."

Twenty-three

THE BANDAGES HAVE DONE little to stop the bleeding. Even the new ones I tore from the linen sheets have turned, spotting red at first and then growing until the entire dressing is crimson. There is no stopping the blood, regardless of how we bind him. It will keep flowing. Simon's coat was soaked red where Mike was tied to him for the long ride back. I thought he would die on horseback, so much seemed to come from him, but he only whimpered and never once cried out.

Emma was so terrified. She rushed up to the nursery with Henry, both of them dripping with sweat from the long night before the fire. How she cried over Rachel, whispering to herself some sort of prayer, as if she could speak to God or the dead. She looked at Mike's wasted body and shook her head. I have been praying, too, while I've been beside him, alternating between pleas for Mike's soul and salvation for John and Rachel while I wipe at the sweat and blood on my brother's skin.

These things I should have done for Eli. I should have felt this sadness for him and for the waste of all this. Mike's was another life consumed in this terrible fire that we have set ourselves and that none of us knows how to stanch. Even running away from it does no good, for the fire comes after you.

Mike murmurs in some restless fever, his lips barely moving, a faint incomprehensible whisper. The laudanum helped him. I put a few small drops on his tongue, enough to keep him sleeping, to ease him through without any pain, although Simon is right to wonder if mercy is wasted on him.

The daylight streams through the shutters in thin rows, harsh and white, on the rug and across the counterpane. It is not so late, I think, still morning. Emma slips in and sits on the other side of the bed from me, her hands folded in her lap, so patient.

"Miss Gus, you should rest," she says. "And Henry's asking for you."

Yes, I should go see Henry. I wonder why it should surprise me that he would ask for me. And I am tired, with a deep ache in my bones that I must resist until this long day is over.

"Do you mind, Emma? Watching over Mike?"

She shakes her head, looking at Mike's pale face and my clumsy bandaging, soaked with the blood that we cannot stop.

"No, ma'am," she says. "He is a disturbed soul. So much hate in him. He always had it. A troubled boy and a troubled man. If Christ can forgive him, who am I to question his plan? He's going to meet his reward and it will be terrible. But I've known him since he was a tiny baby, like he was one of my own children."

She pours fresh water into a bowl and takes a cloth, wetting it and squeezing it out between her hands. She wipes his forehead tenderly and along his nose, down his cheek to his jaw, like a caress. I should go and leave her alone with him.

"You had—" I trip on the words that I shouldn't be saying. "You had your own children once, didn't you, Emma?" She must know that I know.

"Yes, ma'am," she says, wiping at Mike's cheeks. "Two little boys. Twin boys. They're long gone from this world. God rest their souls." She shakes her head.

"I'm so sorry, Emma. You were down on the farm?"

"Yes, ma'am. Your mama didn't care too much for having the boys in the house, so she sent me with them down to Point Place. To the quarters there. I left the babies with Old Mammy Circe and worked in the fields like the other hands. Chopping trees and hauling them in. Clearing new fields. It was winter yet and it was wet and cold. The wind cut right through that old shack, not enough mud in the chinks to keep it out. Enough holes in the roof for the rain to come through." Emma sighs, her lips tight, and she looks at Mike, but not as if she is seeing him. "It wasn't too long before my babies got sick and died, one right after the other. Then your mama said I could come back to the house."

I look away, ashamed for Mama.

"Did their—" I ask, stopping myself. "Their father—did he know? Couldn't he have helped you?"

Emma gives me a level stare that is so full of knowing, my nerves tense like I am about to be cut. "I don't know, ma'am," she says. "I guess he didn't think he could do anything to stop it. Or didn't want to. I learned how to keep from having babies after that. But he's long dead, too. No use talking about all that. No use talking about things nobody wants to hear."

"Was he someone on the plantation? One of Pa's people?" I should not ask, but I can't resist.

"No, ma'am. He was here in town. You don't really want me to answer you, now, do you, Miss Gus?"

Her eyes stay on me until I have to turn away. She wipes Mike's forehead and hums to herself, then starts to sing in a whisper.

Dark was the night,
Cold was the ground
On which my Saviour lay
Blood in drops and sweat run down,
In agony he pray.

Lord move this bitter cup,
If such Thy sacred will

If not, content I'll drink it up
Whose pleasure I'll fulfill.

"Like you said," Emma says. "Jesus in the garden."

"Yes. Like Gethsemane." On the walls are the oval-framed daguerreotypes of Pa and Mama that I hung in this room. They look at me with cold, impenetrable eyes. "Was their father one of Pa's people? In the house?"

Emma looks at me. "He was in the house, yes."

I get up slowly from the chair. My feet don't want me to leave. I hold on to the door frame and turn back. Emma wipes Mike's face with the cloth. She shakes her head, humming to herself, lost in the past, like Rachel said. Those days aren't gone. Emancipation didn't end any of it.

"Why did you stay with us, Emma?"

Her hand is still against Mike's head. Maybe she will not answer me. Mike mumbles, his eyes closed.

"Where would I have gone?" she asks me. "What could I have done? I'm not like Rachel. I don't have her spirit. I may have had it once, but I lost it. I lost the chance to be Rachel. Maybe I was born too soon for freedom." She dips the cloth in the bowl of water at her elbow. She twists it until the water stops dripping from the cloth and wipes Mike's cheeks with it. "We all want a home, Miss Gus. Maybe I would have gone if you hadn't married Mr. Eli. But when you did, I knew I could find a home with the both of you."

Emma watches Mike slowly breathing with so much sadness, so much tenderness in her face.

I close the bedroom door behind me. The hall is bright. Pa's bench is before me, the one thing I took from the house on Allen Street to remember him by. It is a solid piece of furniture, hand-carved of hickory, a hard, hard wood. I sit and lean my back against it, feeling the turned slats press into me. The arms are smooth, and I run a hand across the polished surface of the wood. I close my hand over the arm and curl my fingers around it, moving slowly up its length and back. This was my father's bench and I loved him very much, whoever he was. The bench is smooth and solid and has a coolness to it that feels good in the heat. I could sit here all day, like when Pa used to sit here with me and show me the newspapers. That's how I learned to read, from Pa reading from the newspapers while I sat in his lap. The hours he used to spend with me reading. That was real. That is something that I know for certain. His name was Henry, like my boy. What were Emma's boys' names? Was one named Henry?

I must go see him. Henry has been asking for me.

Mike is dead. It has happened, and he is dead, too, after a spluttering moment of semi-lucidity. He seemed to recognize me and Emma, and he talked as though the war were still on. He threatened to join the army and kill all the Yankees. And then he died.

Did Hill die like that? Alone, with nothing to ease his pain? That is what I wish I had been able to do for Hill. I wish I had been there to wash him, to read the psalms over him, to wrap him in a winding sheet and carefully stitch it. But he never made it home. The deaths come so fast, one upon the other, just like during the war. We will bury him, Emma and I. Even that she has agreed to do. Simon rode away while it was still dark and he has not been back.

The two carpetbags are packed and ready, but what will running away do? All the things I am running from will follow me wherever I go. I do not want to leave this house. All those things that were real to me are false. And the things we denied are true. Eli and Rachel knew it. Simon does, too, wherever he is. I must stay and do what needs to be done. I knew what it was last night in the woods.

Twenty-four

EMMA STANDS OVER THE pot of simmering water, stirring it slowly. It steams earthy and bitter, and the water has turned dark from the oak bark, but there is willow in there, too, and arrowroot and the white dried vetch roots from the garden. She takes a towel and wraps it around the pot to move it to the sink.

"We should let it cool before we mix it," she says. "That oak bark and sour vetch are sharp." She nods and smiles to herself. Henry sits at the table, his chin on his hands, watching us. These past days have made him even more quiet than he usually is.

I swing the stove door open and shovel out the hot coals, tossing them in the cold hearth of the old kitchen fireplace behind the stove. I shatter the coals with the shovel, and Emma pours on dirt from the garden.

"There can't be smoke from the chimneys," I say. "No more fires tonight."

She nods. She doesn't seem to be worried. I am not, either. My body feels cold and hard, bitter from all these losses. How fearless Rachel was. She never doubted herself.

"You have the pistol, Emma? I wish Simon hadn't taken all the guns." The coals are buried. There's not a trace of smoke.

"What do you think they're doing?" she asks.

"I don't know. It's better not to know."

"I've prayed for them." She looks at Henry and gives him a warm smile.

"Yes, I've prayed for them, too."

The sun has set, and a rich twilight has descended over the garden. It is almost time. "Do you think it's cool enough?"

Emma dips a finger into the water and draws it out. She tastes it and shakes her head, frowning in disgust. "Yes, ma'am."

She empties the pot into a bowl. I add a jigger of whiskey and sugar. I take the stoppers off the two small blue bottles and pour them in together. The laudanum floats on the surface and has a bright sheen. My nerves jump at the sight of it, and I can feel the odor settle deep in my lungs. My body seems to scream at me for it, like the throbbing in my head. The kitchen has grown dark, and outside, the garden is purple fading to black.

Emma mixes the liquid carefully with a wooden spoon. I take the glass flagon and slip the funnel into its mouth. Emma pours the tonic through the funnel in a steady stream. The laudanum swirls in the murky fluid with a swimming paisley pattern. There is enough to put a horse to sleep. Emma takes out the funnel. I press the cork firmly into the bottle.

"Thank you," I say.

"Rachel would be proud to see me making one of her tonics." She smiles with that old sadness, and I want to reach for her to give her back some of the comfort she has given to me.

"I know she would."

"She'd be proud of you, too, Miss Gus." She puts her hand on my shoulder and squeezes.

"Thank you, Emma."

I take her hand and hold it. She has small, rough calluses on her fingers, but they are full, soft hands and warm to the touch. My hands feel cold against hers.

"Henry, honey," I say, and he looks at me anxiously. "Come here to Mama."

He slides down from his chair and walks to me. I kneel in front of him and take him in my arms. "Mama is going to go out for a little bit. But I'll be back very soon. You're going to stay here with Emma, and you'll be very good and quiet for her, won't you?"

Henry whispers, "Yes, Mama." His breath touches my ear. He smells sweet, like fresh-mowed clover.

"That's a good boy. It is important that you both keep very quiet. Emma will stay with you in your room until I get back." My hands are on his shoulders. I look into his eyes that are like Eli's. He studies me with so much caution. I kiss his fine hair. "You're going to be very safe. Emma will protect you. You do whatever Emma tells you, yes?"

"Yes," he says, nodding. He looks up at Emma.

"That's right, little man. Your mama and I are going to keep you safe." Emma's hand is on her skirt pocket, pressing against the derringer.

I stand. "Make sure you bolt the nursery door behind you, Emma. And no light or noise."

She nods at me. She knows all this already, but I must say it.

"I will go now."

Emma wraps her arms around me, and my arms find their way around her. She feels so warm and safe. She pulls away and hands me the bottle of tonic. I slip it into my dress pocket. Emma takes Henry's hand and gives me one more glance before leading him upstairs.

I slip out of the kitchen and lock the door. Full darkness has settled in. They will be safe locked in the nursery, and I will not be gone long, I hope.

The night is moonless, but the stars blaze. The gravel paths and trimmed hedges are dark blocks, even black lines running parallel to each other leading to the street. Fistfuls of blossoms blare bright white against the dark horse chestnut in the unnatural glow of the stars. The broad leaves undulate in the breeze. A gust sweeps through the garden, shaking the trees and making the leaves whip wildly.

The wind is picking up from a front that is coming in. A rumbling line of clouds sits in the west like a black sheet being pulled across the stars by an armada of thunderheads. The forgotten gardens line the lane, hiding the large homes behind them like a weedy bulwark. The soldiers dug trenches and cut down thorny osage-orange trees as defenses at Franklin. The wind blows hard, snapping at me with a bone-cold chill and carrying a fine mist—the first assault of the storm. The wind twists the leaves on the towering trees, turning them around so that they seem silverbacked in the starlight. The roaring wind comes from all directions, strong currents battling each other amid the wild overgrowth. The tree branches whip their leaves up as if pulled by the magnetic force of the clouds. The trees blaze silver and black, all consumed in a horrible, roaring white fire. They flame up toward the clouds, and the tree roots strain to keep themselves set in the ground. The leaves are torn from the branches like balls of flame and are tossed against the houses, threatening to consume them with the same cold fire.

The houses are decrepit in the darkness. Rather than hide the damage, the lurid light makes them crumble before me with fractured cornices and brick dissolving into powder. I push through the weeds of the Sheffields' garden. The vetch and thistle pluck at my skirts and sleeves, grasping at me on the wind so that they almost pull me down. They have grown so tall, it is a wild living forest of these weeds, standing in rank rows around the path like a silent army. Vines climb up the brick walls, eating the houses. These houses, the homes of my friends from years ago, are all abandoned, left back to the earth that is sending up its armies to swallow them back whole.

I rush across Pulaski Street, the wind whipping dust and leaves against me. The storm is moving so fast, it may break soon. I am sweating, though the wind is chilling. It howls, and the great black clouds cover the sky. Judge's house is across the street. I crouch in the Jamesons' yard behind the hedges and the black iron fence. There are men behind Judge's house, three men on horseback in wine-colored cassocks. They ride up Elm Street, kicking up dust that is spun into whirling devils by the battling gusts. Branches scrape against each other, groaning to the point of breaking, like limbs torn from a body.

There must be eyes everywhere—Judge's eyes, watching everything. Does he know I'm coming to him? The handle of the front door gives with little resistance. I close the door and shut out the frenzy of the wind, but it shudders over the house with a low moan.

There is someone here, I feel it. The inky darkness fades to gray. I can hear breathing, soft but labored.

"Miss Gus?" There is a form in front of me, a shape. She seems to materialize from the air.

"Sally? Is that you?" The words float from my lips, barely audible.

"Are you here to see Mr. Judge?" She wheezes the words. I can see her face. Her eyes are wide and black, like dark, empty holes. She leans on a chair.

"Are you ill, Sally?" My hand reaches out to her, but I pull it back. She seems to be dripping. Dark drops fall from her face and mark the floor around her with small black spots. Sweat or blood. The fever has her.

"I've been with Mr. Judge over thirty years and never been sick. I ain't sick now." The rhythm of her breathing is uneven and loud. She does not look at me but straight ahead, like a sleepwalker. "Go on up, ma'am. He'll see you."

"Sally," I whisper. She turns and shuffles into the darkness. She isn't in her right mind. She stumbles against the wall and struggles through the back of the house.

I cannot run away. I must see Judge. I hold the thick carved banister and climb the stairs. The bottle is in my pocket. I grasp it through my skirts. The house does not make any noise of its own, no creaking from the force of the wind. The stairs are noiseless, no sighing groans under my feet. The beams do not shift or crack. The house is perfectly still, as if built of solid stone, like a giant mausoleum. There is only the noise of the keening wind outside.

"Judge?" My voice is a hoarse whisper. "Judge, are you home?" There is a light from under the door of his study.

"Who's there?" Judge swings open the door. He is a silhouette against the lamplight. A gun is poised in his hand.

"Judge, it's Augusta." His face is too dark to see, but he is looking at me. I come around the top of the stairs. His arms relax.

"Augusta, what are you doing here? What do you want?"

"I wanted to tell you that Mike is dead. He died today from gun-shot wounds." He is close to me, and his skin is sallow and sagging, but his blue eyes blaze like sapphires. The bones of his cheeks bulge out from the shadows, giving his face the appearance of a fleshless skull. He looks down at the gun in his hand and slips it back into his belt.

"I am sorry, Augusta. I heard there was a skirmish. Come in." He walks into the study. A lamp flickers on a small writing table, and pen and paper are beside it. The wick makes a faint hissing sound as it burns. Judge notices me looking at the lamp. "All I have left is burning fluid. The whale oil has run out. Sit down." He takes his seat and picks up his pen.

"Judge, I think Sally is ill. She doesn't seem well."

He looks at me sharply. "Nonsense. Sally is as solid as Gibraltar. There's no sickness in this house."

The double doors to his bedroom are wide open, and a single candle flickers by his bedside. Judge's bed is massive, carved wood with a high headboard, and floats in the shadows like a great black barge. A worn saddlebag sits on his bedside table by the candle. It is a match to the saddlebags in the carriage house. Eli's saddlebag.

"You shouldn't be on the streets tonight," he says. "There's a Negro insurrection. They've used the weakness the fever has caused to rise up and attack us. They killed Mike and who knows how many others. I'm writing a telegram to the governor to ask that he invest me with military authority to quell the uprising. Since the governor is a friend, I am sure he will do it."

Judge picks up the pen and dips it in a small inkwell. He scratches the paper. His bright blue eyes steal a glance at me.

"A Negro uprising?" I ask. He's a liar. He killed Mike. He killed those other men, and he killed Rachel. He is why Hill is dead, too. The blood is on his hands.

"Buck and some of my men caught them organizing on the Tullahoma Pike. We gave them a pretty good thrashing, but I understand they are planning on making a stand tonight. Cowards. They won't even fight in the daylight, like men."

He's the one who attacks at night, wearing masks and disguises and terrorizing people. My heart feels like it is bursting out of my chest. "What will you do if the governor agrees? Isn't the army moving in?"

"They're outside town for now. They're afraid of the fever, but so are we all. The governor will agree we need support in town. This can't be allowed to continue. We'll mop them up fairly quickly. My men are already at work. The telegram to the governor is a practical formality. When he sees the names of the men who are involved, he'll be stunned. Politicians in government who support this nigger revolution."

The list. He's using the list from Eli's saddlebag.

Desperate tears well in my eyes. I must cry. He must believe me. "I am afraid of the fever, too, Judge. You were right about everything. I'm so sorry. I'm terrified. The whole town has gone away, and now an insurrection? Emma and Henry and I are all alone in the house. Everyone else has run off." My voice is pleading.

"That nigger Simon is gone, is he? He's their leader, Augusta. Or didn't you know that? He's the first one we'll flay and string up alive. We won't have any rabble-rousing niggers in Albion."

They'll kill Simon if they catch him.

"I heard, Judge, but I couldn't believe it. It makes sense now. He was Eli's man. You were right about everything. Please forgive me. Tell me you forgive me."

I kneel before him. He is surprised and embarrassed. I reach out for his hand and pull it to my breast. "Please, Judge, you must forgive me." I kiss his hand, my Judas kiss. His hand is wet from my tears.

"Get up, Augusta. Enough. You are forgiven." He pulls his hand from me. "There's real work that needs to be done tonight. You should leave me in peace. Go back to your home."

"But Judge, we're all alone in the house. Can't you send someone to protect us?" My hands are on my face. The sobs come lurching up my throat.

"My men are all in the field, Augusta. Good Lord, get ahold of yourself."

"I'm sorry. I can't help it." The wind is roaring outside like a wild beast.

"Let me get you a brandy." Judge rises from his seat.

"I'm so sorry, Judge."

He walks to a chest of drawers in the corner and pours a small brandy into a glass. He holds it out to me and I take it. I push myself off the floor and move back to my seat. The bottle taps against my leg. I pull it out. The bottle feels cold between my fingers.

Judge's eyes are on me. I remove the cork. The acrid odor is intense. My head jerks away, but underneath, I can smell the laudanum. The liquid is darker than the brandy, and they swirl together in gold and brown as I pour in a little tonic. I can smell the bark and liquor, too. I tilt the glass back, feeling the heat of the laudanum against my lips. I open slightly, taking a small taste into my mouth. My mouth reflexes into a grimace in spite of myself.

"What is that?" Judge asks sharply.

I look at the bottle and place it on the table. It shines in the lamplight. "A tonic that Emma made to ward off the fever. I swear it's the only thing that has kept us safe." I lift the glass again. The liquid touches my lips, but I cannot drink.

Judge frowns at me and looks at the bottle. "It works, you say?" he asks. "What fear will do to people. You believe these darky superstitions?"

"I know it seems foolish, but Eli died from it, Judge, and we were all with him. But none of us have gotten sick. I worry myself all day about it. The only thing I can reason is because of Emma's tonic."

Judge picks up the bottle. His hand holds it tightly so that bones and veins bulge through his waxy skin. He lifts it to his nose and inhales in a huff. He pulls back quickly, his eyes wide and his mouth creased in a deep frown. He brings it back to his mouth and tilts the bottle back, taking a sip. "Awful stuff," he says, wiping it from his mouth with the back of his hand. "It's bitter."

"Yes, it is." Drink it. I tilt my glass back again. One tiny sip. My skin buzzes from the taste of the laudanum. I cannot have more. This much I can tolerate, but no more. "Emma insists we drink it all at a gulp, but I just can't. I have to sip it."

His eyes are on the bottle, analyzing the muddy liquid inside. "It keeps the fever off, does it?"

"Yes, I'm sure it does. I'll have Emma send you over more tomorrow."

He sniffs at the bottle. "All at once?"

"Yes, sir."

He gives a grim smile and tilts the bottle back, drawing it into his mouth. His throat contracts as he swallows. Once. Twice. His Adam's apple bobs with each draught. Three times. Four. The bottle is empty. He gives a coughing groan, almost a belch, and sets the empty bottle on the table. "Terrible stuff. But if it keeps the fever at bay." He walks evenly over to a chest of drawers and pours himself a brandy, which he throws back quickly. He leaves the glass on the chest and sits at the table, picking up his pen. He dips it into the ink and scratches at the paper. "Buck should be by soon to give me his report. They've been combing the North Ward, looking for these insurrectionists." He coughs against his sleeve and resumes writing.

"Have they been out long? Hunting these men?" His face is mesmerizing. Is he reacting? His eyes squint. Will it work? The saddlebag is so close. How long before Buck comes?

Judge looks up at me and squints again. "Since sundown. With the storm now, I don't know how much more work they can do. At least it seems to have broken the heat." He holds his pen in midair, scanning the papers up and down. "Where was I?" He puts the pen against the paper and holds it there. He squints at the page. He lifts his left hand and rubs his eyes with his thumb and fingers. He squints at the page again. He looks at me.

His eyes are shocking blue. Though they blaze at me, they do not focus. They rove around me, trying to find my face. His mouth is open. His breath comes quickly. He has blanched pure white, the purple of his veins showing under the skin. He looks down at his hand. His hand is limp and the pen falls loose onto the table. He holds his hands before him, watching them as they tremble ever so gently. The wind is screaming through the trees. Rain has started to fall. It beats against the windows in waves.

Judge lifts his eyes to me, shaking his head. "My God, Augusta, what have you done?"

I stand and step back to the wall. "Nothing more than you deserve," I whisper.

He looks around the room, at the lamp with its hissing wick, at his papers. He tries to grab the pen, but it rolls off the table and clatters on the floor. The papers flutter down over it. He looks up at me again and places his hands on the arms of the chair. He tries to push himself up. "I swear to God, I'll kill you myself," he says. His voice is weak and slurred. He glares at me. He means to come after me, but he can't grip the chair. He pushes himself, but he has grown too weak. He wrenches forward in a convulsion. His body contracts as if he will vomit. He falls from the chair to his knees, hitting the small table, knocking it forward and crashing to the floor with it.

The lamp explodes into a million pieces of glittering glass, and a pool of flame jumps from the floorboards. Judge is curled up next to it, retching, his body rejecting the tonic and the poison. It floods out of his mouth in a river of mud. He is too weak already. The flames dance across the floor. They reach his legs and his dark pants flare up in bursts.

"Help me, Augusta. Dear God, help me." He twists his body in agony, his face contorted and ghastly, like a demon's from the depths of hell. He feels the fire. My God, the flames are everywhere. They leap from the floor to the drapes and climb until they are smoking garlands of flame that touch the ceiling.

I hold my skirts against me and race into his bedroom. I take up the leather satchel and pull it open to reveal a mass of banknotes.

The fire has swallowed the study. Judge is writhing on the floor, blanketed in flame, howling like a mad animal, like the wind outside.

I run down the stairs. I must hold tight to the saddlebag. I hug it against my stomach as I burst out the door into the torrents of rain. It is falling in pounding sheets, and the wind blows it against me. I am soaked before I reach the street. I don't care. My God, Judge is dead. He must be dead.

This rain. The heat has broken. I have broken its back, and it is all cold, driving rain against my skin, in my hair, soaked through my dress. The streets are black. I cannot see through the rain that surrounds me. If only it is not too late for Simon. The gravel lane is so long, lined with wild gardens heaving in the wind and rain. The houses seem to melt from the relentless drive of it. They twist and bend in the wind that is pulling them apart, cracking them open, and flooding them with rain as they melt back into the earth. I have won. I have killed the dragon. He will not hunt and kill anymore. It is all like laughter and tears and this cold rain. I have killed him.

The keys are awkward in my fumbling hands. Finally, it slips into the lock, and the kitchen door opens. I must lock it again behind me. Emma and Henry. I race through the dining room and up the stairs, through my bedroom, and back to the nursery.

"Emma," I whisper, tapping on the door. "Emma, it's Gus."

The door opens, and I fall into Emma's arms. She holds me tight. Henry is sitting up in bed in the dark, frightened. My hair is hanging in thick wet strands over me, dripping water from my sleeves on the floor.

"Henry, you're safe. We're going to be safe. Mama is back." I kneel beside his bed. He is in my arms. He is crying and doesn't know why but that he wants to cry. Through the window, even through the heavy rain and wild wind, there is an orange glow over the trees, rising up against the storm.

Emma steps behind me. "Whose house is that?" she asks, keeping her eyes on the orange light.

"Judge's house," I whisper, holding Henry close to me. "Judge's house."

Emma puts a hand on my shoulder. I feel as if my blood has suddenly reawakened, as if my heart is pumping again after being still for a long time. I am alive again. It is my father's blood in me. Hill had the same blood. And Mike. It is their blood, too, pushing through me.

There is a pounding like cannon fire, close. Is it thunder? It sounds again. I let go of Henry and look at Emma. Her eyes are wide with terror. There is another loud crack. It is not thunder, even though the wind roars and lashes rain against the windowpanes. It is coming from the house. From downstairs.

"Gus!" A shout. A howl louder than the wind. The howl of a wild animal, caught in a trap. "Gus!"

"Buck," I say. My mouth is dry. Emma is frozen, and Henry starts crying again. "Give me the gun. Take Henry to the barn. Quietly. Through Eli's office." Emma digs the pistol out of her pocket and hands it to me. She gathers Henry up in her arms.

I am already through the door. "Quietly," I say. Emma holds Henry against her and steps slowly down the back stairs. I close my bedroom door and bolt it. My skirts are soaked and drag at my feet. My hands tremble. There is another pounding and then a crash. He has kicked the door in. I am at the top of the stairs. I shove the gun in the pocket of my soaked dress and hold tightly to the banister. The shaking seems to overwhelm me.

"Gus, where are you." Buck is screaming.

"I'm here, Buck," I call out. One step at a time down the stairs. He is a silhouette standing in the dark hall, the front door open behind him. The rain surges in, lashed by the wind.

"Pa is dead," he says, and he looks up at the ceiling, bringing his hands to the sides of his head. His voice is thick, as if he has been drinking. "The house is on fire."

My hand twists in my pocket, feeling for the gun, for the loop and trigger.

"I saw you running from the house. What did you do, Gus?" He lurches forward. Water drips off his black hair and chin. He is possessed by a senseless rage. He must have done that damage at the mill. "Did those niggers do it? Why were you at Pa's house? Are you helping them?"

"I did it, Buck. They had nothing to do with it." I slip the gun out of my pocket and point it at him. I brace myself against the banister.

His mouth opens, but he doesn't speak. He shakes his head. "You've lost your mind." The words come heaving out of him. "You don't know your own mind anymore. Is this what Eli did to you? After everything we've all suffered. I can still hear the cannons, Gus. I hear them every day. And you go and join up with the people we are protecting you from." He steps toward me. I raise the gun.

"I can see with my own eyes, Buck. Eli didn't do anything to me. I know who you and Judge are. I can see the poison in all of you."

"Poison? We're getting the poison out, Gus. We're fighting to save us all from chaos, from madness! God is on our side!" His voice rises to a shriek.

"God should strike you dead. Like the night of the barn dance? You coward, that's how you fight?" My hand is shaking. Water drips from my sleeve.

He shakes his head, and the rainwater scatters. The force of the wind throws the front door back on its hinges. It slams into the wall and swings back. "We were attacked that night, Gus. I *was* protecting you."

"You're a liar. Why would you be so stupid as to tell Mike something that awful? It was planned. You and Judge did it. And now Mike is dead because of you and Judge."

"Those niggers killed Mike. They stole something that wasn't theirs, and they got what they deserved. You should be pointing that gun at them."

"It's all gone now, Buck, burned to ashes—the list and the money. You'll never have any of it in spite of the killing you've done."

"Why are you doing this, Gus? Why are you doing this to me? You had everything you needed. Why couldn't you listen to Pa?"

"You all act like you are so honorable, but you aren't. Not like Hill was. Or Pa. You tragic coward. You really do whatever your pa tells you."

"I don't want to have to do this, Gus." He steps closer to me. "You know that I've always loved you, even when you were with Eli. I won't take this from you. You're the one full of poison. And I'll rip it right out of you." He takes another step.

I hold the pistol out from me. My hand grips the banister so tight it will break. "I will shoot you, Buck. I'm just afraid the bullet won't kill you."

He takes another step toward me. Another. The shadows hide his face. He is a black figure moving closer. I have to shoot him. I aim and pull the trigger. There is only a click. A misfire. The powder is wet.

He leaps at me and wrests the gun from my hand, flinging it aside. "I'll rip the nigger lover out of you, Gus," he says.

I fall back on the stairs. He is on top of me. His face is wild with rage. He presses his mouth against my face, hard. The taste of metal is on my tongue. He holds my wrists, pressing them into the sharp edge of the steps. His legs are over me, pinning me down. The bones will snap. I am screaming, but there is nobody to hear. He tears at my bodice, pulling and ripping at my skirts. The thunder cracks over us as if the house has been hit by a shell. Buck rears up and his body loosens. The pressure is gone. He looks into my eyes, and a small ribbon of blood comes from the corner of his mouth. He sighs, and his eyes roll back in his head. He falls backward off the stairs into a pile on the floor.

Simon is standing at the open doorway. A thread of smoke twines from the muzzle of the gun he is holding.

"Oh, Simon," I whisper. "Thank God you're alive."

Twenty-five

IT IS JUST AN hour before sunrise and Simon must go. He must find that sad caravan and join them on their way to Kansas. He insists on going and he cannot stay in Albion. It is his duty, he says. And it is mine to stay here. The army will move in now. The sickness will abate. After last night, it is hard to worry about the sickness.

Simon was in the barn even before I got back from Judge's. He brought Little John with him. Emma must have thought a miracle had happened when she found them there. It must have been some sort of miracle. I stood with Simon while he dug a common grave for Mike and Buck in the soft earth under the grape arbor. The rain dripped through the leaves onto us. He told me Garson had too much to bear already with what had happened. He couldn't worry about an orphan boy, too. He laughed as he said it as if he were laughing at himself. Then he held the shovel and looked at me, both of us shivering dark shadows under the dripping leaves.

"I took him for me. And for Rachel. He will be my son."

"You are good, Simon," I said.

"I have a lot to make up for." He forced the blade of the shovel into the earth and continued digging. The graves are flat now. Simon cut the turf over them and carefully replaced it. In a week or so, they will not be visible. And if they are, what can anyone say when there are so many new graves everywhere?

I don't know how we slept last night.

Emma and I shared my bed with Little John and Henry tucked in between us. They curled up tight together and slept so soundly. Emma and I looked at each other for a long while. It has been so long since we shared a bed like that. Not since I was a girl. She took my hand and smiled. Her hands feel so good.

Simon slept in the nursery, but the doors were open, and I could hear his even, full breathing. It pulled at me. What will we do without him? We will go on. We have money and the house and whatever is left to us from Eli and from Judge after this chaos. But Simon will be missing. He will be an empty place, always waiting to be filled. I will wait for him. I know Emma will, too. He will come back to us.

Simon walks onto the back porch with Little John. Emma and Henry are close beside me. We are in our wraps and nightclothes. The morning mist is heavy, and the dark gray silhouettes of dawn rise up before a rose-edged sky. They must go before the light.

"Say goodbye to Simon, Henry. Shake his hand." Simon smiles at me. Henry steps toward him and holds out his hand.

"You be a good boy, Mr. Branson, and listen to your mama," Simon says. Little John reaches out to shake Henry's hand, too. Henry reaches for him, and they give each other a hug and cautious kisses on the cheek.

"Good, Henry," I say. "Tell Little John that you will write to him." He nods and holds on to my skirts.

Simon hugs Emma and whispers something in her ear.

Then he is before me. I do not know what to say to him.

"Thank you, Gus," he says.

"Thank you, Simon." I step off the porch and put my arms around him. He holds me for a moment, the two of us pressed against each other. He will come back. I am certain he will. "And I have this for you." I pull the bundle of newspaper from my pocket and put it in his hands.

"What is it?" he asks, and unfolds the paper and looks inside. "I can't take this from you. Not now."

"Yes, you can. It is yours. We had an agreement. That is your half." I feel as if my whole body is smiling at him. "I do not want to be someone who dishonors an agreement. Take it. I want to see the good you will do with it."

He smiles back. "As you say." He winks at Emma. "We should be on our way. Right, Little John?" He takes Little John's hand. "But you can't be little anymore. You're going to have to be a man to help me. You've got to be big now."

"Yes, sir," Little John says in his small voice. They turn and walk away down the gravel path to where the horse waits, tethered by the trough. Simon lifts Little John up and sets him in the saddle, then climbs on himself.

Emma puts her arm through mine, and we lean against each other. Henry stands between us, nestled in our skirts.

"What did he say to you, Emma?" I ask.

Emma smiles but keeps her eyes on Simon. "He just said he's putting me in charge until he comes back. He wants me to watch over you, but he knows well enough you don't need watching over." She laughs and I pull her closer to me.

Simon and Little John ride down the lane in the half-darkness toward the wooded trails that lead to the mill. The air is still but cool. The leaves droop off the trees, exhausted from the storm. He will come back.

There will be more like Buck and Judge, but I know what they look like now. I will be ready for them. I feel that there will always be something lurking in the darkness of the trees—whether it is the sickness or the Knights or blind hate. I know what it looks like. I will keep a gun with me, and I will be ready for it. I will make sure the powder is dry and Henry is close to me. I will take him to Eli's grave. He should know who his father was—everything about him. And Simon will come back. I know he will.

Acknowledgments

THIS IDEA WAS BORN many years ago, and I have spent much time since then in research to try to recapture a sense of place and time. All those hours reading and poring over period documents can be a lonely process, but producing this work was not at all one of monastic isolation. I want to thank the good friends and family who were with me throughout this process. I owe a huge debt to my great and wonderful mentor in the master of fine arts program at Wilkes University who guided and goaded me to complete this manuscript, the very talented teacher and writer Kaylie Jones. Through Kaylie, I had the great good fortune to meet my agent, Trena Keating. Trena worked tirelessly and generously with me for many months, helping sculpt this novel into its final form. Without her, this book would have been very different. Through Trena, I had another stroke of good fortune in working with Trish Todd of Simon & Schuster. She connected with the book immediately and has remained a devoted believer. Other readers who gave critical feedback include Dr. Nancy McKinley, another faculty member of the Wilkes University creative writing program, whose knowledge of the period and insights into human behavior were indispensable, and the late Norris Church Mailer. I was privileged to receive a scholarship in her honor during my study at Wilkes. She immediately asked to see my book and generously read through a draft, including two different endings. She gave me honest and important criticism. Hers is a voice that is greatly missed.

David E. Lazaro, collections manager at Historic Deerfield, generously gave his time to the manuscript. Stephen Borkowski provided much guidance and his incomparable artistic acumen. I would also like to thank Beth Thomas for her detailed and thorough copyediting. And thanks to the city of Huntsville, Alabama, the model for Albion. The Heritage Room at the Huntsville Public Library is a researcher's dream come true. The antebellum historic district is a place in which you can easily find yourself a time traveler. And I have had some truly transcendent experiences at the Weeden House Museum, thanks to its director, Barbara Scott.

Author's Note

MASSIVE SOCIAL AND ECONOMIC upheavals altered the physical and human landscape of the Deep South after the Civil War. For many whites, it was the end of the world; for many blacks, it was the beginning of a new one. From the time of emancipation in 1863 through the end of congressional Reconstruction in the mid-1870s, the recently freed people saw a dizzying amount of legislation pass Congress that guaranteed their rights and provided the means to protect those rights. In practice, however, enforcement was often difficult or impossible because of the open hostility of many white Southerners and the terrorist activities of secret paramilitary organizations like the Ku Klux Klan and the Knights of the White Camellia.

The Civil Rights Act of 1875, the crowning (albeit posthumous) achievement of Massachusetts Senator and radical Republican Charles Sumner's career, typifies the strange paradox of Reconstruction in the South. Congressman Robert Elliott from South Carolina, a freed man, delivered an important and acclaimed speech on the House floor in support of the act, which guaranteed equal access for African-Americans in hotels, public transportation, theaters, and other "public accommodations." The same year, the Red Shirts of Mississippi, a white paramilitary group, successfully intimidated black voters, keeping them from the polls and enabling the Southern white Old Guard to take back political control of the state. With the presidential election of 1876, a compromise was struck whereby federal troops, the only authority that could guarantee access to the voting booth for African-Americans, would be withdrawn from all states formerly in "rebellion." By 1883 the Supreme Court had deemed the Civil Rights Act unconstitutional. Many of the same guarantees included in the 1875 act were again passed by Congress as part of the 1964 Civil Rights Act signed by President Lyndon Johnson. But by that time, disfranchisement and segregation had been the law of the land for almost a century.

For women, black and white, the latter half of the nineteenth century also left many promises unfulfilled. The woman's movement and its one-time ally, the abolitionist movement, became estranged. Movement leaders like Elizabeth Cady Stanton were often hostile to the guarantee of civil rights for uneducated freedmen when educated women were denied the vote. White male legislators were not interested in guaranteeing voting rights for women; most insisted that women's voices were heard through their male protectors in the "traditional" way. But regressive politics did nothing to stem the realities of economic and social oppression faced by women, particularly in the South, where they endured the hardships brought on by four years of destructive, bloody war. The plucky Scarlett O'Hara of Margaret Mitchell's *Gone with the Wind* is a jazz age creation projected against an Old South screen. The real voices of women who lived in the period, however, became a literary phenomenon long before Scarlett was imagined. Journals, diaries, memoirs, and books of letters flooded the literary market of the late nineteenth century, bringing to a hungry reading audience the real-life heroines of the Civil War along with their disappointments, humiliations, fears, and bravery.

Alongside the true-life accounts of the Civil War, fiction writers from the South added their voices to the great chorus that declaimed what the war had been about and what had been lost. These voices, as much as legislation and jurisprudence, influenced public opinion. The literature of the South achieved a national profile through the regionalist movements of the late nineteenth century. Writers like the Virginian Thomas Nelson Page and the Georgian Joel Chandler Harris wrote prolifically on the "Old South" and the "War of Northern Aggression." In spite of other perspectives, the charm of the "lost cause" captivated a national audience. *Gone with the Wind*, a great book in many ways, was the high point of a literature that emphasized white Southern culture and lampooned African-Americans.

Since the 1920s, at least, a growing chorus of contrary voices in literature has changed the landscape. Writers of the Harlem Renaissance and white writers like Julia Peterkin took a closer look at the myths constructed around African-American life in the South. Writers of the Southern Renaissance dealt with the legacy of slavery, deploying themes of race and injustice, innocence and depravity, the macabre and the grotesque, as they developed the Southern Gothic tradition. William Faulkner, Flannery O'Connor, Carson McCullers, and Harper Lee among many others could simply look in their backyards to find the strange dichotomies of Southern life on full display.

Today many novelists have continued to deconstruct those myths, like Alice Randall in *The Wind Done Gone*. But many of those traditions persist. My hope is that my novel serves as another perspective in the reconception of the aftermath of the Civil War and the Reconstruction era. In the development of this story, I have used as broad a variety of resources as possible. My youth in Huntsville, Alabama, amid the beautifully preserved vestiges of the antebellum era, was a starting point. Since then, I have used works of fiction and nonfiction to tap into the spirit of the time as well as historical monographs detailing many different aspects of Southern life. Newspapers, journals, and lifestyle magazines played a critical part in my research. And most of all, the voices—through diaries, letters, and memoirs—of the women of the time were fundamental to the creation of Augusta. A sampling of these works can be found in the Bibliography on page 289.

Selected Bibliography

The research for this book spanned many years, in some ways my entire life. I relied on primary sources, such as newspapers, fashion and news magazines, and books from the period. I also relied on a large variety of secondary sources, both fiction and nonfiction. Below is a list I have compiled for those who have a further interest in reading the period.

The People Who Were There

The most well-known and worthwhile diary of the period is probably Mary Chesnut's, edited by C. Vann Woodward. Chesnut was not the only person to record her thoughts and feelings. Add to that the letters, memoirs, and oral histories that we have left from that time, and you could spend many years delving into the lives of the women and men who fought and lived through the tremendous upheavals of the nineteenth century.

Boney, F. N. *A Union Soldier in the Land of the Vanquished.* Tuscaloosa: University of Alabama Press, 1969.

Chappell, Frank Anderson. *Dear Sister: Civil War Letters to a Sister in Alabama.* Huntsville, Alabama: Branch Springs Publishing, 2002.

Clay-Clopton, Virginia. *A Belle of the Fifties: Memoirs of Mrs. Clay of Alabama.* Tuscaloosa: University of Alabama Press, 1999.

Cumming, Kate. *The Journal of a Confederate Nurse.* Baton Rouge: Louisiana State University Press, 1998.

Douglass, Frederick. *Narrative of the Life of Frederick Douglass.* New York: Tribeca Books, 2011.

East, Charles, ed. *Sarah Morgan: The Civil War Diary of a Southern Woman*. New York: Touchstone Books, 1992.

Jacobs, Harriet. *Incidents in the Life of a Slave Girl*. Mineola, New York: Dover Publications, Inc., 2001.

Kemble, Frances. *Journal of a Residence on a Georgian Plantation in 1838–1839*. Athens, Georgia: University of Georgia Press, 1984.

Myers, Robert Manson, ed. *The Children of Pride: A True Story of Georgia and the Civil War*. New Haven, Connecticut: Yale University Press, 1972.

Rosengarten, Theodore. *Tombee: Portrait of a Cotton Planter with the Plantation Journal of Thomas B. Chaplin (1822–1890)*. New York: McGraw Hill, 1987.

Ryan, Patricia H., ed. *Cease Not to Think of Me: The Steele Family Letters*. Huntsville, Alabama: Huntsville Planning Department, 1979.

Smedes, Susan Dabney. *Memorials of a Southern Planter*. New York: Alfred A. Knopf, 1965.

Sutcliffe, Andrea, ed. *Mighty Rough Times, I Tell You*. Winston-Salem, North Carolina: John F. Blair, 2000.

Tourgée, Albion W. *The Invisible Empire: A Concise Review of the Epoch*. Ridgewood, New Jersey: Gregg Press, 1968.

Watkins, Sam R. Co. *Aytch: A Confederate Memoir of the Civil War*. New York: Touchstone, 1997.

Woodward, C. Vann, ed. *Mary Chesnut's Civil War*. New Haven, Connecticut: Yale University Press, 1981.

Woodward, C. Vann, and Muhlenfeld, Elisabeth, eds. *The Private Mary Chesnut: The Unpublished Civil War Diaries*. New York: Oxford University Press, 1984.

Fiction and Poetry

Modern Reading

These works of more recent vintage provide diverse and changing perspectives on the Civil War, slavery, and the legacy of the nineteenth century.

Bradley, David. *The Chaneysville Incident*. New York: Harper & Row, 1990.

Faulkner, William. *Absalom, Absalom!* New York: Vintage International, 1990.

———. *Go Down, Moses*. New York: Vintage Books, 1973.

Frazier, Charles. *Cold Mountain*. New York: Grove Press, 1997.

Jones, Edward P. *The Known World*. New York: Amistad, 2003.

Mitchell, Margaret. *Gone with the Wind*. New York: Macmillan, 1936.

Peterkin, Julia. *Black April*. Indianapolis: Bobbs-Merrill, 1927.

———. *Green Thursday*. Athens, Georgia: University of Georgia Press, 1998.

———. *Scarlet Sister Mary*. Indianapolis: Bobbs-Merrill, 1928.

Randall, Alice. *The Wind Done Gone*. New York: Houghton Mifflin, 2001.
Styron, William. *The Confessions of Nat Turner*. New York: Vintage International, 1993.

Period Fiction and Poetry

The short list below proves that even in the immediate aftermath of the Civil War, there was disagreement on what the war was about and what its legacy should be.

Cable, George Washington. *Old Creole Days*. New York: New American Library, 1964.
Chesnutt, Charles W. *The Marrow of Tradition*. Ann Arbor: University of Michigan Press, 1969.
Evans, Augusta Jane. *Macaria; or, Altars of Sacrifice*. Baton Rouge: Louisiana State University Press, 1992.
Perkerson, Medora Field. *White Columns in Georgia*. New York: Rinehart & Co., Inc., 1952.
Preston, Margaret J. *Beechenbrook: A Rhyme of the War*. Baltimore: Kelly & Piet, 1866.
Weeden, Howard, and Harris, Joel Chandler. *Bandanna Ballads Including Shadows on the Wall*. New York: Doubleday and McClure, 1899.

Historical Monographs by Subject

Battles of the Western Theater

Castel, Albert. *Decision in the West: The Atlanta Campaign of 1864*. Lawrence: University Press of Kansas, 1992.
Cozzens, Peter. *The Battles for Chattanooga: The Shipwreck of Their Hopes*. Urbana: University of Illinois Press, 1994.
———. *The Battle of Stones River: No Better Place to Die*. Urbana: University of Illinois Press, 1991.
Daniel, Larry J. *Shiloh: The Battle That Changed the Civil War*. New York: Touchstone, 1997.
Foote, Shelby. *The Beleaguered City: The Vicksburg Campaign*. New York: Modern Library, 1995.
Sword, Wiley. *The Confederacy's Last Hurrah: Spring Hill, Franklin & Nashville*. Lawrence: University Press of Kansas, 1992.

Political History

Bailey, Hugh C. *John Williams Walker: A Study in the Political, Social and Cultural Life of the Old Southwest*. Tuscaloosa: University of Alabama Press, 1964.

Budiansky, Stephen. *The Bloody Shirt: Terror After Appomattox.* New York: Viking, 2008.

Craven, Avery O. *The Growth of Southern Nationalism, 1848–1861.* Baton Rouge: Louisiana State University Press, 1953.

Current, Richard Nelson. *Lincoln's Loyalists: Union Soldiers from the Confederacy.* New York: Oxford University Press, 1992.

Dorman, Lewy. *Party Politics in Alabama from 1850 Through 1860.* Tuscaloosa: University of Alabama Press, 1995.

Fisher, Noel C. *War at Every Door: Partisan Politics and Guerilla Violence in East Tennessee, 1860–1869.* Chapel Hill: University of North Carolina Press, 1997.

Foner, Eric. *Reconstruction: America's Unfinished Revolution, 1863–1877.* New York: Harper & Row, 1988.

Foote, Shelby. *The Civil War: A Narrative.* New York: Vintage Books, 1986.

Gallagher, Gary W. *The Confederate War: How Popular Will, Nationalism and Military Strategy Could Not Stave Off Defeat.* Cambridge, Massachusetts: Harvard University Press, 1997.

Gillette, William. *Retreat from Reconstruction, 1869–1879.* Baton Rouge: Louisiana State University Press, 1982.

Going, Allen Johnston. *Bourbon Democracy in Alabama, 1874–1890.* Tuscaloosa: University of Alabama Press, 1951.

Freehling, William W. *The Road to Disunion: Secessionists at Bay, 1776–1854.* New York: Oxford University Press, 1990.

———. *The South vs. the South: How Anti-Confederate Southerners Shaped the Course of the Civil War.* New York: Oxford University Press, 2002.

Groce, W. Todd. *Mountain Rebels: East Tennessee Confederates and the Civil War, 1860–1870.* Knoxville: University of Tennessee Press, 1999.

Hahn, Steven. *The Roots of Southern Populism: Yeoman Farmers and the Transformation of the Georgia Upcountry, 1850–1890.* New York: Oxford University Press, 1983.

Holt, Michael F. *The Political Crisis of the 1850s.* New York: Wiley, 1978.

McPherson, James M. *Battle Cry of Freedom: The Civil War Era.* New York: Oxford University Press, 1988.

Oakes, James. *The Ruling Race: A History of American Slaveholders.* New York: Alfred A. Knopf, 1982.

Potter, David M. *The Impending Crisis, 1848–1861.* New York: Harper & Row, 1976.

Sydnor, Charles S. *The Development of Southern Sectionalism, 1819–1848.* Baton Rouge: Louisiana State University Press, 1948.

Thornton, J. Mills, III. *Politics and Power in a Slave Society.* Baton Rouge: Louisiana State University Press, 1978.

Wiggins, Sarah Woolfolk. *The Scalawag in Alabama Politics, 1865–1881.* Tuscaloosa: University of Alabama Press, 1991

Woodward, C. Vann. *The Burden of Southern History*. Baton Rouge: Louisiana State University Press, 1968.

————. *Origins of the New South, 1877–1913*. Baton Rouge: Louisiana State University Press, 1971.

Slavery and Race

Bay, Mia. *The White Image in the Black Mind: African-American Ideas About White People, 1830–1925*. New York: Oxford University Press, 2000.

Dray, Philip. *Capitol Men: The Epic Story of Reconstruction Through the Lives of the First Black Congressmen*. New York: Houghton Mifflin, 2008.

Frederickson, George M. *The Black Image in the White Mind: The Debate on Afro-American Character and Destiny, 1817–1914*. New York: Harper & Row, 1971.

Genovese, Eugene D. *The Political Economy of Slavery*. New York: Pantheon Books, 1965.

————. *Roll, Jordan, Roll: The World the Slaves Made*. New York: Vintage Books, 1976.

Hahn, Steven. *A Nation Under Our Feet: Black Political Struggles in the Rural South from Slavery to the Great Migration*. Cambridge, Massachusetts: Belknap Press of the Harvard University Press, 2003.

Haws, Robert, ed. *The Age of Segregation: Race Relations in the South, 1890–1945*. Jackson: University of Mississippi Press, 1978.

Penningroth, Dylan C. *The Claims of Kinfolk: African American Property and Community in the Nineteenth-Century South*. Chapel Hill: University of North Carolina Press, 2003.

Schweninger, Loren. *James T. Rapier and Reconstruction*. Chicago: University of Chicago Press, 1978.

Stampp, Kenneth M.. *The Peculiar Institution: Slavery in the Ante-Bellum South*. New York: Vintage Books, 1989.

Stanley, Amy Dru. *From Bondage to Contract: Wage Labor, Marriage, and the Market in the Age of Slave Emancipation*. Cambridge, England: Cambridge University Press, 1998.

White, Deborah Gray. *Ar'n't I a Woman? Female Slaves in the Plantation South*. New York: W. W. Norton & Company, 1999.

Woodward, C. Vann. *The Strange Career of Jim Crow*. New York: Oxford University Press, 1947.

Women's History

Baym, Nina. *Woman's Fiction: A Guide to Novels by and About Women in America, 1820–1870*. Chicago: University of Illinois Press, 1993.

Faust, Drew Gilpin. *Mothers of Invention: Women of the Slaveholding South in the American Civil War*. New York: Vintage Books, 1997.

Fox-Genovese, Elizabeth. *Within the Plantation Household: Black and White Women of the Old South*. Chapel Hill: University of North Carolina Press, 1988.

Jones, Anne Goodwyn. *Tomorrow Is Another Day: The Woman Writer in the South, 1859–1936*. Baton Rouge: Louisiana State University Press, 1981.

Social History and Daily Life

Fahs, Alice. *The Imagined Civil War: Popular Literature of the North and South, 1861–1865*. Chapel Hill: University of North Carolina Press, 2001.

Faust, Drew Gilpin. *This Republic of Suffering: Death and the American Civil War*. New York: Alfred A. Knopf, 2008.

Foster, Gaines M. *Ghosts of the Confederacy: Defeat, the Lost Cause, and the Emergence of the New South*. New York: Oxford University Press, 1987.

Grimsley, Mark. *The Hard Hand of War: Union Military Policy Toward Southern Civilians 1861–1865*. Cambridge, England: Cambridge University Press, 1995.

Haller, John S. *American Medicine in Transition, 1840–1910*. Chicago: University of Illinois Press, 1981.

Massey, Mary Elizabeth. *Ersatz in the Confederacy: Shortages and Substitutes on the Southern Homefront*. Columbia: University of South Carolina Press, 1993.

———. *Refugee Life in the Confederacy*. Baton Rouge: Louisiana State University Press, 2001.

McPherson, James M. *For Cause and Comrades: Why Men Fought in the Civil War*. New York: Oxford University Press, 1997.

Wyatt-Brown, Bertram. *Honor and Violence in the Old South*. New York: Oxford University Press, 1986.